Molly Reid is a pseudonym used by Poppy Kuroki. Poppy was born in Scotland and has been living in Japan since 2014. Her Ancestor Memories series was bought at auction by Oneworld in the UK. *Gate to Kagoshima* (Book 1), a sweeping historical fantasy set in samurai-era Japan, published in summer 2024. It was published in the US with Harper Collins in early 2025. Poppy loves video games, cooking, history, and reading books of any genre. She lives in a beautiful town near the sea with her son.

THE
LIBRARY OF SECOND CHANCES

Molly Reid

WILDFIRE

First published in Paperback in 2025 by Wildfire
An imprint of Headline Publishing Group Limited

2

Cataloguing in Publication Data is available from the British Library

Paperback ISBN 978 1 0354 1944 9

Map © Tim Peters

Typeset in 9.98/13.3 pt New Caledonia LT Std
by Six Red Marbles UK, Thetford, Norfolk

Printed and bound in Great Britain by Clays Ltd, Elcograf S.p.A.

MIX
Paper | Supporting
responsible forestry
FSC® C104740

Headline's policy is to use papers that are natural, renewable and recyclable
products and made from wood grown in well-managed forests and other
controlled sources. The logging and manufacturing processes are expected
to conform to the environmental regulations of the country of origin.

Headline Publishing Group Limited
An Hachette UK Company
Carmelite House
50 Victoria Embankment
London EC4Y 0DZ

The authorised representative in the EEA is Hachette Ireland, 8 Castlecourt
Centre, Dublin 15, D15 XTP3, Ireland (email: info@hbgi.ie)

www.headline.co.uk
www.hachette.co.uk

*For my children, who I love more than anything,
and for Declan, my real-life book boyfriend.*

A reader lives a thousand lives before he dies.
The man who never reads lives only one.
— George R. R. Martin, *A Dance with Dragons*

Map of Wellbridge Library

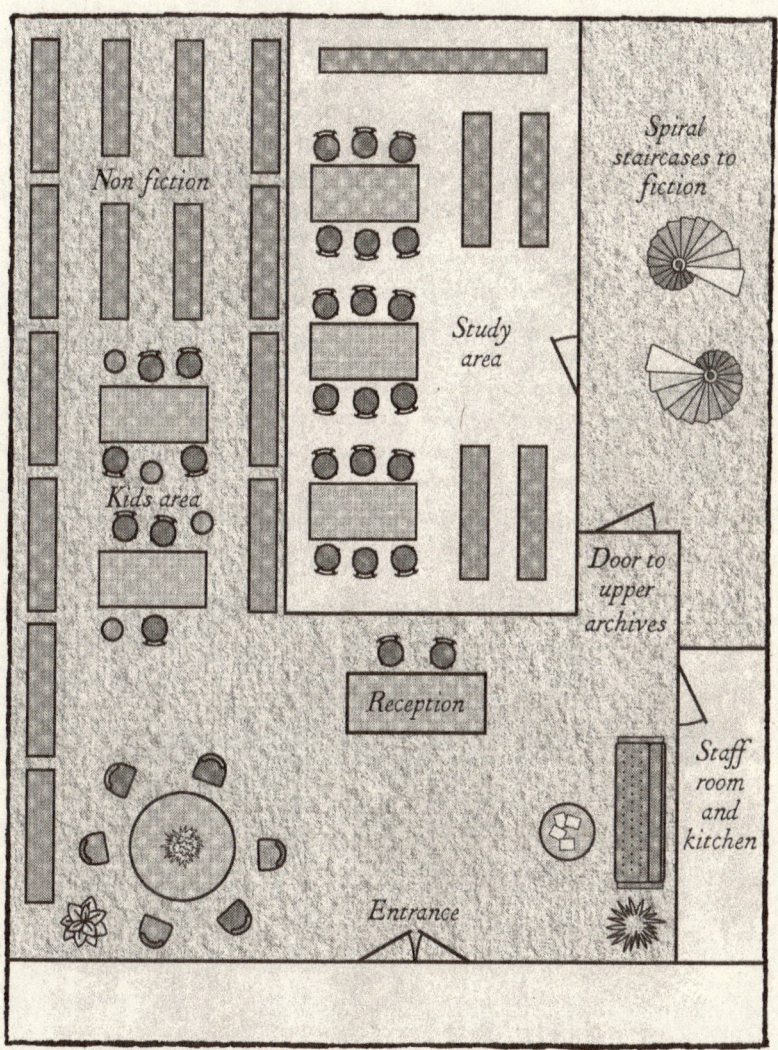

CHAPTER ONE

THERE WERE A lot of things Chloe had never thought would happen to her. One was ending up back in her hometown of Wellbridge, after years of living in the city. The other thing that she hadn't expected was to find herself marching alone down a wet cobblestone street on a dark and rainy autumn evening, frustrated, thirty quid down and soaked to the bone.

'Leave your umbrella at home, they said. It won't rain, they said,' she grumbled to herself, her heels clacking on the uneven street, threatening a twisted ankle. No one had actually said that, of course. It had been her own naïve assumption. Her wet hair stuck to her scalp, and it was another mile before she'd reach her house. Even in the rain, there were no taxis around.

Besides, she didn't want to go home right now. The thought of stepping into a cold, empty house was depressing. But that was the problem with small, quaint towns like these. Even at nine o'clock on a Friday evening, barely anything was open. Except pubs. Pubs were always open.

She slowed as she reached the Pride & Pint, glancing through the window. Raucous laughter came from inside along with the clinking of glasses, shouts and cheers at what was probably a football match. It looked warm, but she didn't much fancy stepping inside by herself, looking like a drowned rat.

Instead, Chloe walked up the hill towards her neighbourhood. She didn't want to climb the hill in these ridiculous heels. She hesitated, then turned left instead, grimacing as more icy rain fell on her head and tightly crossed arms. Her teeth chattered. This wasn't her idea of a fun night.

She could think of only one thing that comforted her at times like these. Books. There was one place of refuge for her troubled mind. The Wellbridge Library, which happened to be Chloe's new workplace.

She had the keys in her bag because the library manager, Mrs Cook, had asked her to open the library in the morning. Though she wasn't entirely sure she was allowed to use said keys outside the library opening times, Chloe didn't much care at the moment. She wanted to escape the rain and find somewhere warm, to seek solace in a quiet, calm space among books and paper. Somewhere that wasn't going to give her frostbite.

The streetlamps glowed yellow through the haze of the falling rain as Chloe strode across the empty car park, shivering now. After rummaging in her bag with icy hands for the keys, she finally pushed open the heavy doors of the Wellbridge Library.

She stepped into the dark silence and closed the door with a dull thud behind her, muffling the steady patter of rain. The lights were all off, the dim grey of the October night sky visible through the arched gothic windows. When Chloe had stepped into the grand library four weeks ago for her job interview, the rows and rows of shelves, the medieval windows, the enormous, stitched rug in front of the reception desk, and the wooden balconies that promised secrets had stolen her breath away. They had done a marvellous job of maintaining the old, sentimental charm of the place. It felt like stepping into Hogwarts library or the one in the castle in *Beauty and the Beast*. She'd never say it aloud, but there was something . . . otherworldly about this place. Like it was too good to belong here.

She didn't know how long she stood there, the dripping rain from her dress and hair likely making a puddle on the floor, when a soft meow startled her. It was only Clementine, the library cat. He was fluffy and orange, the little bell on his collar jangling as he stalked along the lobby desk, regarding her with a curious, haughty look. Feeling a little silly, Chloe flicked on the lights. She petted the library cat as the reception area flooded with comforting light. Clementine's amber eyes looked up at her, his tail swishing. The first time she had tried to pet him, he had scurried away and disappeared between the book cases. He must be in a good mood tonight.

The library's lights were electric, but they were designed to look like lanterns, bright enough to light the way, but dim and comforting, a soft glow rather than the stark, artificial white of most public spaces. Chloe loved the scent of this place: paper, ink, and mahogany. It made her think of hidden knowledge, of limitless imagination. She shrugged off her jacket, then changed her mind with a shiver and kept it on.

She shouldn't have been in the library so late, but ending such a terrible date by going back to her empty house to sit and ponder everything that had gone wrong was the last thing she wanted to do. Chloe kicked off her heels and strode through the reception area, the muffled sound of her feet on the carpeted floor familiar and comforting. She wished she could peel off her sodden tights, too. Maybe she shouldn't be doing any of this at all, but it wasn't like anybody was around. The only thing the library needed to make this moment even better was some fresh towels. Maybe a hairdryer.

According to Mrs Cook, this library had been here for over two hundred years; after going through various purposes – a courthouse, a hospital – it was finally made into a library in the fifties. The west wing was home to the non-fiction and the children's books, but this . . . this was Chloe's favourite section. Beyond the oak doors of the east wing were the archives, a large room on two levels separated by a spiral staircase of polished wood. Shelves stood on either side, the ground floor hosting educational texts, while the upper floor housed fiction books organised by genre and author name.

Simply being here made her feel better – who didn't enjoy being in the presence of books? But Chloe still burned with humiliation at the thought of her date earlier tonight. Dean had seemed pleasant enough when they had chatted on the app. Their messages hadn't made her heart skip a beat, exactly, but the red-headed, freckled mechanic from the next town over had seemed nice. And maybe that was enough for now. Chloe hadn't had more than two consecutive dates with anyone in over a year, not since she had broken up with her boyfriend in Sheffield, and she thought a meal with someone who might be interested in her would be a good way to spend her free time.

The date, however, had not been nice.

Dean, who looked at least a decade older than his Bumble photo, had arrived twenty minutes late without so much as an apology. He had looked her up and down, shoved his way into the pub first, then when it was time to pay for their food, he had conveniently 'forgotten' his wallet. Who casually mentions this without even saying sorry? Who brought up their ex-girlfriend twice during their conversation? And who rang their mum in the middle of the date to boast that he was out with a 'fit bird'?

Who the hell even does *that?*

Chloe stomped up the spiral staircase a little harder than necessary, the thumps echoing off the high-ceilinged room. Clementine followed her, his long tail brushing her calf before he scurried ahead, the little bell Mrs Cook had attached to his collar jangling as he went. He disappeared behind a bookshelf, maybe to find somewhere comfortable to snooze.

Up here, Chloe breathed in the scent of paper. This was what she craved. Shelves and shelves of various fiction genres. Contemporary romance, fantasy, science-fiction, historical, thrillers, literary, classics. Even just being in the books' presence made her calmer. She rubbed her hands together, blowing into her freezing fingers. She would have to talk to Mrs Cook about investing in some blankets to match the armchairs that sat below each window. She loved those. Cosy little reading nooks. Why was she mad again?

Oh yeah. Dean. She scowled, thinking of all the witty comebacks she should have come up with instead of awkwardly sipping her gin and tonic, desperately trying to find a reason to escape.

She'd finally paid the tab and muttered some weak excuse about needing to get home before leaving him alone in the street. She hadn't even wanted to share a taxi with Dean. She'd blocked him as soon as he was out of sight. Maybe that was mean, but she didn't think she'd be able to face an awkward post-date exchange.

Cold rain ran down the window in rivulets, the outside world bleak and grey. It was a terrible evening to be wandering around and a perfect evening to be inside with books. It beat sitting at home and worrying about being single for ever, anyway.

Wandering about the library at night was a welcome distraction, and not only from worrying about her current lack of boyfriend. Chloe was going to sink onto one of the armchairs, then decided against it; she was still drenched. Instead, she leaned against the banister overlooking the lower floor, relishing the silence and at the same time hating the thoughts that crept into her mind when there wasn't anything to distract her.

It had been just over a year since Mum and Dad had died in the car accident. Chloe had spent the one-year anniversary a few weeks ago getting drunk, watching her favourite comfort films, the box of tissues beside her, gradually emptying a bottle of wine. She had been too upset to even read, and had instead fallen asleep to *Titanic*, waking up to a disintegrated tissue clenched in her palm. Chloe's younger sister, Gwen, had been on holiday that day, according to posts on her social media, which Chloe was definitely *not* stalking under a fake name. Gwen had been somewhere in the Caribbean, sunglasses on her face and looking stunning in a white bikini.

Chloe supposed people dealt with grief differently. Gwen hadn't even come to their parents' funeral. She had been in Fiji.

The hurt was still there, and she doubted it would ever fade. A year had brought her out of her cloud of grief where all she wanted to do was sleep, but it hadn't been easy to come back to Wellbridge, to move into what used to be her parents' home, and to try and piece her life back together. Already, she was regretting coming here.

She had decided, upon moving in and dealing with the legality of things, that this would only be temporary. She would save up some money and then move back to the city. Maybe back to her flat in Sheffield, where she had worked until recently. Back to chaos and strangers and bright lights and unfamiliar settings, where it was wonderfully loud and busy. It distracted from thoughts that got too deep or depressing.

It was almost a relief to fret over her non-existent love life instead. It was a much smaller problem, one she could focus on without wanting to cry until she threw up. Chloe had had a boyfriend or two in her time, though never anything serious. Not for a long time. She was twenty-six now, and it was hardly too late, but her failures at finding love had led her down a slippery slope of believing all the good ones were already taken. Or worse, that *she* was the problem.

She closed her eyes and let loose a slow, steady breath. No, Dean had definitely been the problem tonight.

'Clementine, what even are men?' she asked. A low meow answered her.

She wandered along a shelf of classics. There was nothing like strolling among shelves of books to calm the mind. Her love for literature wasn't shared by her sister, who had declared, rather too proudly for Chloe's taste, that she hadn't read a book since her English Literature GCSE. It wasn't only in their love for books, or lack of, where they differed. Gwen never struggled to find a date. As far as Chloe could tell from her social media, Gwen had been flitting from rich boyfriend to rich boyfriend since she'd moved out at eighteen, travelling to various sunny countries and going on spending sprees at their expense.

Good for her, Chloe supposed. But she didn't want to think about her sister now. She caught up to the library cat, who looked up at her with his big, amber eyes. With the rain still drumming outside, it somehow felt like there was nobody left in the world except herself and this cute little feline before her.

'Do you think I'll ever find a boyfriend, Clem?'

He made a soft purring noise that sounded suspiciously like a 'no'. Chloe couldn't help laughing.

She wanted to grab a book, perhaps several, and find an armchair where she could bury her nose in a good story and forget her problems for a while, if only her dress would dry off first. Her house was within walking distance, but the drum of rain on the windows made her want to stay here a bit longer. And why not? Her shift didn't start until ten o'clock the next morning, and nobody knew she was here. Mrs Cook hadn't explicitly said she *couldn't* come here outside her work hours. Chloe would leave everything as she had found it and switch off all the lights before leaving. No one would know, except Clementine.

It was peaceful here, alone with the books and the cat, and Chloe found herself wide awake. The rest of this boring town was asleep or holed up in their pubs. Chloe couldn't wait to leave Wellbridge. She preferred cities. The noise, the distractions, the new faces every day. Here there wasn't enough to do, and whenever she wasn't in another world, either a new place or a new story, her thoughts liked to wander.

As she browsed the shelves of classics, Chloe's heart ached. These mahogany shelves were home to some of the world's greatest literary treasures, donated or sold over the decades and generations, all to find a place in this library. Chloe ran a finger along the spines, some bound in leather, others with gold embossing. A few were old and peeling, showing the many hands that had loved and thumbed through them. Dickens, Fitzgerald, Hardy, even a collection of Shakespeare's plays, thick as a Bible, graced the shelf of classics. Chloe wandered the shelves, scanning the alphabetised authors until her eyes found her favourites: some of J. R. R. Tolkien, Terry Pratchett, collections of C. S. Lewis and a healthy number of Enid Blyton's old adventure stories. Nostalgia and joy washed through Chloe. So many characters, adventures and lessons were hidden between the pages at her fingertips. How could anyone *not* love books? She felt sorry for people who couldn't live through fictional characters, joining them in their adventures, their heartaches and triumphs. There was so much to learn and love, even from the simplest of stories.

She stopped at one shelf. Was it her imagination, or was there a faint glow around one of the books? Perhaps the gold lettering caught the light overhead, although it didn't seem that way.

Curious, she slowly slid it out.

A noise at the end of the shelves made her jump like a child caught with their hand in the biscuit tin. But it was only Clementine, slinking around with his tail in the air. She was so jumpy tonight.

Chloe opened the book, pinching the corner of the page with her fingertips as though afraid rougher handling might damage it. Dad had given her a copy of this classic romance as a congratulatory present before she went to university. She flicked through the pages, lost in reminiscence. She had read it all in her first semester and eagerly discussed the novel with her parents as they'd carved the Christmas turkey. Gwen, who had actually shown up for Christmas that year, had rolled her eyes and loudly declared the classics were boring, much to Chloe's chagrin. When Chloe had pointed out that she couldn't know they were boring if she had never read them, Gwen had just gone back to filing her nails.

Chloe swallowed at the memory. That had been an awkward Christmas. Gwen had left first thing on Boxing Day morning, declaring she had 'better stuff to do'. Gwen hadn't come back the year after that. Or the next.

Stop thinking about her, Chloe silently chastised herself. In this edition of the book, the edges were sprayed gold. What an excellent find. Mrs Cook's diligent cleaning showed here; there wasn't a speck of dust on the shelves, and this tome was almost like new. Chloe wondered how many people had read this story, had gotten lost in the pages of this charming tale that had kept her enraptured through the toughest of times. She leaned against the opposite shelf, turning to the final page. A happy ending. Enemies to lovers was one of Chloe's favourite tropes in literature. Funny to think it existed even in the nineteenth century.

'I bet it was easier to date back then,' she said to Clementine, who was licking his paws. 'I should've been born in that era, with flowing dresses and gentlemen and horse-drawn carriages.' She grinned at her own musings. Were men easier to bag back then, or would she still have been hopelessly single even in a dress and corset? She supposed people were married off two hundred years ago, but it was still fun to imagine being swept away by a handsome nobleman.

She read out some of her favourite lines to Clementine, comforted by the words that filled the space around them. To his credit, the cat stuck around, cocking his head as Chloe's voice echoed around the upper archives.

A shuffle in the next aisle made her head jerk up. Was Mrs Cook here, working late? Had she forgotten something and come to retrieve it? It would be mortifying to be caught like this late at night, her wet hair still clinging to her neck, reading out loud to a cat. Chloe didn't want to have to explain to her new boss that her first date in ages had been so terrible she had found solace by breaking into her new workplace.

She slowly slid the book back onto its shelf, ignoring the way she thought it glowed. Maybe she could sneak out of here before she was caught. Chloe made her way towards the spiral staircase.

And crashed straight into someone.

CHAPTER TWO

'SORRY!' SHE GASPED as she stepped away from the person she had just collided with. He was a young man wearing a regency tail-coat of deep blue, his white collar high and ruffled. Her gaze travelled up to a curious look on the clean-shaven face of a man who held a look haughty enough to rival Clementine's. She blinked in shock. She could have sworn she was alone up here. She hadn't heard him climb the stairs.

The newcomer gave a stiff bow. 'Good evening, madam.' He did not smile as he stared up and down her sodden clothes, giving Chloe the urge to cover herself.

She took in his polished shoes, his curly dark hair, the slightly arrogant look he gave her as he stood among the library shelves. He looked like he had just stepped out of the nineteenth century.

'Madam,' he said, sounding affronted. 'What *are* you wearing? And what are you doing in my library?'

Chloe was lost for words, her mind struggling to grasp why he was here. Halloween was in a couple of weeks. Was he wearing a costume, perhaps? If it was, a costume that is, she had to admit he seemed really committed to the part. He had even grown out some sideburns. But what was he doing so late in the library when it was clearly closed? Had she forgotten to lock the front door? She couldn't remember.

'Erm,' was all she could say. 'Are you all right? Can I help you with something?' Then his words caught up to her. 'Wait. What's wrong with my dress? And what do you mean, *your* library?'

'Perhaps I have had too much to drink. Forgive me. I'm afraid I am rather lost. I am not sure how I got here.' The man held a certain sadness in his eyes, and for a moment, it was like Chloe could see her grief reflected in them. She quickly shook away the strange thought.

'Lost?' she repeated. How lost could you get in a library in the middle of the night?

'Yes, although, it is refreshingly quiet in here.' He glanced at her, taking her presence in as much as she had his, his eyes roaming over her damp chestnut hair to her black dress and stockinged feet. 'I am wondering how to get back. I was at a party, you see. Frightful things, with far too many people I'm forced to entertain. I'm told I have the charm of a shoe.'

Chloe's senses were catching up with her. She was alone with a stranger in the middle of the night. She took a step back, swallowing, unsure whether to try to point him towards the exit. Clementine saved her from the awkward silence by appearing behind her with a soft purr. The man started slightly, then favoured the feline with a small smile.

'What a charming creature. Though I really must be getting back. This doesn't look like my library, after all.' He didn't meet Chloe's gaze, but glanced somewhere over her shoulder, as though someone from his party would be hiding in a shadowy corner. He gave a soft sigh. 'Though as I was just so vehemently rejected, there doesn't seem to be much point.'

Was he playing a character? If he had come from outside, how was he not wet from the rain? Perhaps he had brought an umbrella with him.

'You must help me,' said the stranger.

Chloe didn't think she *must* do anything, but she didn't want someone making a complaint about her when she hadn't even been working here a week. She didn't think the man was here to steal anything. A tailcoat wasn't the typical outfit for a break-in. He didn't look particularly surprised to see Chloe; it seemed like he had simply wandered inside by accident.

'Neither of us should be in here,' Chloe pointed out as she headed for the spiral staircase. 'We need to leave. Where is this party of yours?'

Maybe they were celebrating Halloween early and he'd somehow accidentally wandered into the library, seeing the light on upstairs.

'At my estate, of course,' said the man, sounding surprised. 'I had thought at first that this was *my* library, but that seems to be a mistake.'

How drunk was he?

The man was becoming stranger by the second. The best thing would be to get them both out of here, and hopefully this guy wouldn't think to come back tomorrow and mention she was here.

'I'm sure you'll find your way back to your party in no time,' she called behind her.

The man had stopped at the top of the spiral staircase that would lead them to the lower floor. 'Where are you going?'

'To the exit.' She pointed towards the door that led to the reception area.

'No, I am quite sure it's this way.' He turned on his heel and headed back in the direction from which they'd come, his shoes clopping on the floorboards. 'That is how I got here.'

Irritated now, Chloe scooped up Clementine to avoid him getting trampled. The cat stayed quiet in her arms, then looked up at her. It may have been her imagination, but he held the same annoyed look as she felt.

'Sir?' She followed the man back to the shelves, wondering what on earth was happening. He half-trotted ahead of her, the ends of his tailcoat disappearing around the corner of an enormous shelf of Young Adult fiction.

'I need to get back.' He sounded upset now, moving aside books on shelves as though hoping to somehow find a door among the tomes. He straightened near a light, his height casting a shadow on Chloe. He was a marvellous actor, she thought. If she was being pranked, he was doing a decent job of convincing her he was really worried.

The man swallowed. He pulled on his ruffled collar as if he were trying to get more air. 'Madam.'

'Chloe.' She patted her chest with her free hand.

The man shifted for a moment as though trying to find the right words. 'Do you think first impressions are important?'

The question took her aback. 'I'm sorry?'

'First impressions, Miss Chloe.' He took a step towards her. 'Me, I am frightfully unskilled at socialising. I recently met a marvellous woman, and did I behave like a gentleman? I did not!' He threw an arm into the air. 'I was rude, uncouth, arrogant. She hated me for a long time. Perhaps she still does.' The corners of his mouth turned down like he was fighting to swallow his emotions. 'She has to know how I feel!'

Chloe couldn't imagine this strange man would get to confessing his feelings anytime soon, not when he was still standing around talking to her. Then something occurred to her. The glowing book she had picked from the shelf just a moment ago . . .

'Is it salvageable, Miss Chloe?' said the man again. His hand was frozen on a bookshelf now, almost as if his next action depended on her answer. 'Do you think she can forgive me? See past the terrible first impression?'

Chloe thought back to her disastrous dates, her seemingly eternal status of singledom, her failure to find anyone she could truly connect with. Even the guy she had been seeing in Sheffield hadn't felt like a true connection. 'Well, I just had a terrible date myself. That was a bad first impression, and I don't think he'll be getting a second chance. Online dating is a minefield.' She forced a chuckle. 'But you could say sorry and make it up to this girl. First impressions aren't everything, especially if you try harder next time.'

'Hmm.' The man rubbed his chin. 'I don't know this line date you speak of, but it can't be worse than the pomp and ceremony of a party. Not to mention the expense.' He gave another dramatic sigh.

'Right,' said Chloe quickly. Her experience with parties hadn't included much 'pomp.' Mainly beer pong and tequila shots. 'Well, when it comes to love, I'm not sure I'm the right person to ask.'

'No,' he said. 'I suppose not. At any rate, it's time for me to be getting back to my estate. I think I understand this well enough. You appear to have brought me here somehow, so send me back. Now, if you please. There's lots to do.'

Chloe stared at him. Clementine wriggled from her arms and landed softly on the floor. He shot them both a disapproving look before slinking into the shadows.

'How do you propose I send you back?' Chloe asked, resisting the urge to fold her arms.

'The same way you brought me here,' he affirmed as though it were obvious. 'Come now, there must have been something you did to get me here in the first place. I need to—'

'Get back to your party, yeah.'

The glowing book.

Throwing the man a glance, Chloe sidled back to the shelf where she had seen the classics. There was the book she'd flicked through earlier, and the faint glow she thought she'd seen before was more conspicuous now. A burnt-orangey hue emanated from its pages, as if a faint light were beckoning her closer.

She pulled out the book, letting out a small breath. This couldn't be real. Maybe Mrs Cook was playing some elaborate prank on her. Any moment now, the older lady would appear among the shelves, giggling at Chloe's expense. But when she glanced up, the stranger was watching her, worry and expectation on his face.

She opened the book anyway. She would humour them both, give this guy in costume and Mrs Cook a true laugh.

She thought it felt warmer in her hands than it should. She held it and looked at the cover, unsure what to do. The rain drummed on the roof above her head, lighter now, and Clementine appeared once again at her feet. He looked expectantly up at her as he sat, his tail curling around him as he watched. The light of the fake lanterns made his orange fur burn gold.

Go on, he seemed to say.

Chloe flicked through the pages, once again remembering reading this in her first year living away from home. She scanned the familiar lines, taking in the ink on paper, seeing a grand mansion and manicured lawns, gossiping girls in frilly dresses and well-dressed noblemen watching them from afar.

She continued reading from where she had left off. Nothing happened. The man waited.

'Try the back,' he suggested.

She flicked to the end, to the ending she loved so much. She could remember closing the book in her university dorm, giggling with pleasure as she hugged the book to her chest. She found the character's line and read it aloud, feeling a bit foolish.

She felt something this time: an ineffable energy washing over her, gentler than a breeze. Then silence.

'Sir?' She looked up, but the man was gone. Maybe he was in the next aisle. 'Did it work?'

Nothing answered her except the rain and her own breath.

'Hello?' She peered round the next shelf, expecting to see the man waiting there, perhaps brushing away imaginary dust from his jacket. But nothing greeted her save the bookcases, as quiet as when she'd found them.

Agitated, Chloe checked aisle after aisle, calling out for the mysterious man who now appeared eerily similar to the main love interest in the book she was holding. If she didn't know any better, she would say that *was* him.

The glow around the book had now disappeared.

Chloe put the book back where it belonged, thoroughly freaked out. She glanced around her again, then at the book, which definitely wasn't glowing any more. Had she just imagined that burnt-orange hue around it?

Her mind raced with explanations, each less plausible than the last. Then she allowed herself a small laugh, shaking her head. 'Nah.'

It was a trick or a coincidence. People liked to dress in all kinds of ways these days. Maybe he had seen her reading the book and decided to tease her a bit. He could easily have slipped off while she was reading.

Still, the way the man had looked so worried when talking about getting back, and how he'd suddenly disappeared . . . and what were the odds of him wandering the library, looking like he had just stepped out of the exact book she'd decided to pick up? The spiral staircase, which led to one of the library's two exits, was within Chloe's sight. If he had descended to the archives, she wouldn't have missed him. His shoes would have echoed on the wooden staircase at least.

'He's really not here?' she said to Clementine when the cat re-appeared around a corner, watching her with interest. She checked the rest of the shelves, half expecting to see the man hiding in a dark corner. But she was alone up here. She could feel it.

'Hmm.' She picked up the book one more time. She took a breath and read a random page, focusing on the scene. An image of the man she had just spoken to materialised in her mind.

She waited. She didn't feel a presence, that strange breeze-like sensation. She didn't hear a footstep or a cough or a breath. There was no one here except her and the cat.

Chloe grabbed another book at random and read out a passage. Nothing. She tried another, and still nothing happened. She slid a heavy collection of short stories back into its place, feeling silly.

The logical explanation held no logic at all.

Her phone told her it was already past ten o'clock. She had to be here in twelve hours to start her shift. Chloe quickly made sure she had left the library as she'd found it and did a final sweep of the upper floor. The man was nowhere to be seen, not hiding in a dark corner or sitting on one of the armchairs placed beside the rain-strewn gothic windows. She was alone up here, except for Clementine, who was now having a case of the zoomies, sprinting up and down the spiral staircases, the gentle jingle of his bell following him. The sound was comforting.

'See you tomorrow, Clemmy,' she said, catching him long enough to stroke his orange fur. She gave him a cat biscuit, then gave him one final pat before sliding on her heels and braving the cold drizzle outside.

I was tipsy, she firmly told herself as she wrapped her jacket tighter around her body, squinting through the rain as it fell on her head. *I imagined the whole thing.* As frightening as that thought was, that she had invented a whole scenario about a fictional book boyfriend to cope with the misery of her life, it was the only plausible explanation she could come up with.

That's what she told herself as she entered her house in the Moorhall neighbourhood, wet and shivering. At least this event had helped her almost forget the terrible date, but now, standing in her dark hallway, it all came roaring back, and she let out an embarrassed groan. At least it could be an amusing story sometime in the future if she ever had the guts to tell it.

After a long, hot shower and bed, Chloe could almost believe she had made up the encounter in the library. It made more sense than the alternative. Before she dozed off, she recalled what she had told the man about first impressions and second chances, and wondered if she believed it herself.

Clementine watched the new human leave through the heavy double doors, and the familiar sound of the door locking clicked through the lobby. Chloe, her name was. Well, it seemed she had a lot to learn about working in this library.

He finished his biscuit and lapped up some water from his bowl, listening to the rain, then curled up on his favourite cushion in the non-fiction section. The sound of the drumming rain comforted him and slowly lulled him to sleep.

CHAPTER THREE

'GOOD MORNING, MR Richardson.' Chloe waved to her elderly neighbour the next day. His house was opposite hers, and he had lived there for as long as Chloe could remember. When she and Gwen were children, he and his wife had sometimes looked after them and always gave them biscuits. Mrs Richardson had died when Chloe was a teenager, but she was glad the old man still seemed well.

She always waved to him whenever they crossed paths, but so far Chloe had been in too much of a hurry to stop and chat. This morning, however, she decided to say hello to him properly.

'Chloe, I keep telling you. You're not a little kid any more, so please call me Joe.' He shuffled over, using his cane. She couldn't help grinning back at him as he regarded her with a cheerful smile from beneath his flat cap. 'How are you?' The sympathy in his words let her know he meant about her parents.

'Oh, you know.' She gave a half-shrug, not wanting to talk about Mum and Dad right before work. 'Thank you for coming to the funeral. It meant a lot. How's the gardening?'

She couldn't see the back garden from the street, but she recalled Mr Richardson loved looking after plants and flowers. He had even grown some of his own vegetables the last time Chloe was in town.

'I've got a little greenhouse now. You should come along and have a look sometime. The leeks are coming on fantastic.' He looked pleased. Chloe happily let him chatter about his chrysanthemums until he added, 'I suppose I'm keeping you from going to work?' He gave an understanding nod. 'If you ever need anything.' He tapped his nose with a wink, then shuffled off. Chloe watched him, feeling fond of the old man and hoping he wasn't too lonely in his house by himself. They were both on their own, now.

She made her way into town. Autumn was Chloe's favourite time of year. The scent of coffee and baking floated on the wind as she walked down towards the library, making her think of cosy romances as she put her hands into her fur-lined pockets. She had found the coat at a charity shop a few months ago, almost like new, and it would probably get her through the cold winter. At least today it wasn't raining, and she had swapped her impractical heels for a comfortable pair of loafers.

Chloe shrugged off her coat at five to ten. With the lights on and daylight streaming through the windows, it was almost laughable that she had been here late last night, lamenting a bad date and talking to phantoms. Even so, she couldn't help glancing in the direction of the upper floors that held the fiction books. It was through another set of doors, separate from the reception area in which they now stood.

The librarian arrived at half past ten. 'Good morning, Mrs Cook,' Chloe greeted her. 'I've already given Clementine his breakfast.'

'Hello, love.' Mrs Cook was small and old, a delightful stereotype of a kindly librarian, from her gold-rimmed glasses to the way she always spoke softly, as though talking any louder would scare away the books. 'When you've got a minute, there's a new box of books that came in last week and I haven't gotten around to sorting them out. They're all in a jumble, so could you organise them and put them on the shelves for me?'

'Sure.' Chloe secretly loved tasks like these. The pleasing rush of dopamine she got from organising and tidying was partly what had prompted her to apply for a job at the library in the first place. Not to mention the perk of working with books all day long.

She found the cardboard box Mrs Cook was talking about behind the reception counter. It was indeed a jumble, a donation of random novels. At least they were in good condition and would find many new readers.

Chloe hoped the day ahead would prove to be busy. She had to finish organising some paperwork, refill the cat's automatic feeder in the afternoon, and firmly resist the temptation to keep an eye out for books that might sport an orange hue.

She had told herself it was a hallucination, her drink at the pub being perhaps stronger than she'd thought. But it had been so vivid, and Chloe wasn't the type to dream up scenarios so intense and detailed. She still remembered the worry in the stranger's soft brown eyes, the slight floral scent of his tailcoat. Chloe had a good imagination, but surely not that good. And Clementine had responded to the stranger's presence as strongly as she had.

She rubbed the bridge of her nose, wondering if she had been pranked after all. At least Mrs Cook didn't seem to be in on it, and she simply smiled at her when their gazes met.

'I'll sort these out now.' Chloe headed upstairs to the thriller section with the donated books heavy in her arms. Whoever had owned them before had been a huge fan of Dean Koontz and James Patterson, and she wondered why they had donated them. She couldn't resist glancing at the shelf of classics on her way, but they were all normal. No faint glow to be seen.

She took her time, finding a new home for each donated novel, organising each volume by the author's surname. She glanced out of the window. There were patches of clouds today, and the streets were still damp from the night's rain. Was the man from last night out there somewhere, maybe nursing a hangover, his costume draped over a chair? Had he told the girl he was talking about, the one from his party, that he was sorry about his poor social skills? Had she forgiven him?

Or was he really back at his estate, safely in the pages of his book?

'Chloe?' called Mrs Cook from downstairs. For a soft-spoken woman, her voice carried well.

'Yes?'

'Have you nearly finished putting away the donations? We've got a young man here looking for a book.'

Chloe half ran down the spiral staircase, flushed with embarrassment at sitting around daydreaming when she was at work. Mrs Cook was waiting for her at the doorway of the lower floor archives, her facial expression serene. Chloe hoped she wasn't annoyed. However, the older woman's eyes glinted with amusement. 'Did you find something interesting up there?'

'What? No. I mean, I've finished putting away the books. Sorry, I'll get to the visitor now,' she babbled.

An alarming thought came to her. Could this 'young man' be the guy from last night? She wondered what Mrs Cook would make of the man's outfit, from his polished pumps to his sideburns. She hoped he wouldn't mention meeting her here in the middle of the night. Her palms sweated as she followed the librarian to reception.

But the man waiting in the lobby wasn't the dark-haired noble. Even though his back was to her, she could tell by his broad shoulders and fair hair it was someone else. He appeared to be admiring the architecture of the library, and although Chloe hadn't been here long, she felt a surge of pride in its beauty.

'Good morning,' she said.

The man turned to face her. He looked to be in his thirties, with a strong, square jaw and a chin dimple. Definitely not the same man who had spoken of pompous parties at his estate on the upper floor last night. This man, when he saw her, didn't smile, but acknowledged her with a small nod.

'What was it you were looking for, again?' Mrs Cook asked the man. She added to Chloe, 'You'll have to help me use the computer, love.'

The reception PC, the only one in the library, was an archaic thing that still used Windows XP. Chloe fumbled through the search function, half her mind still upstairs with the mysterious stranger. She had to push the thought away for now and shelve it in her mind with all the other inexplicable clutter.

'I'm looking for a book.' The man's voice was deep and rich, with a Geordie accent.

Both women stared at him. Was he being pedantic? This was a library, of course he was looking for a *book*. 'What kind of book? We have lots,' said Chloe pleasantly.

He raised an eyebrow. 'Fantasy. Swords and heroes. Things like that.'

Mrs Cook clicked her tongue as the PC refused to load. The man turned from them, examining the beams and the gothic windows. Chloe wondered if Clementine was around, maybe watching from a beam. Mrs Cook abandoned the PC and instead grabbed a file from the back shelf. She started rifling through it while Chloe watched on in dismay. The file was as thick as her forearm. It would take ages to find what they wanted.

'There's a fantasy section on the upper floor,' she suggested after the silence stretched between them.

'Would you take him there?' asked the librarian.

Chloe guided the man through the archives, half nervous she'd meet the stranger from the night before, that he would have somehow snuck back inside to torment her. But the library was still empty. Even Clementine wasn't slinking around.

Chloe let the man go first. He climbed the spiral staircase with a confident stride, like he had been here before. Halfway up the stairs, Chloe thought she felt something. A flutter of . . . eagerness. Not from herself, though. It was like the room's mood had shifted. It felt like anticipation, like lying in wait at a surprise party.

Then it was gone.

She stopped halfway up the stairs, feeling strange.

'You coming?' asked the man, having reached the top. He glanced back at her.

'Yes. The fantasy section's just up here,' she said, shaking off the odd feeling. She sprinted up the last few steps and turned to the rows of bookcases. Up here, the sunlight from outside shone through the gothic windows, casting golden beams on the shelves.

'Here it is. There's a decent collection here,' said Chloe, showing the newcomer a few titles. Their collection of fantasy took up two bookcases, organised in Young Adult and Adult fiction.

'I've read that one.' He pointed at one she had pulled out. 'The writing style's too juvenile for me.'

Chloe was indignant; he'd just insulted one of her favourites. 'I see.' She slid the book back, hiding what she was sure was an annoyed look on her face. 'How about the *Wheel of Time* series? We have a couple of copies of the first one here . . . Yes, here it is.'

The man took the book in his hands and opened it, cracking the spine. The awful sound was a physical pain to Chloe, and she couldn't conceal her wince.

'What?' he asked, seeing her flinch.

'That's a first edition.'

He huffed. 'I didn't realise we weren't allowed to *open* them.'

Chloe felt herself puffing up like an angry bird, but she swallowed her anger. This man was a visitor to the library. Where she worked. She rearranged books on a nearby shelf, hoping he would go away soon.

When she glanced up, the man's eyes were roaming the first page again. Then he closed the book and said, 'Yeah, this'll do,' without smiling or looking at her.

'There's some Terry Pratchett too,' she said. 'You might—'

'No, this one's fine.' He turned and stomped off. His heavy steps descended the spiral staircase.

What a bum. Chloe was aware that working with the public meant the occasional rude interaction, but she had hoped people who visited libraries would be nicer. The more the minutes ticked by, the more annoyed she became. It was like being in the shower days after an argument and coming up with the perfect response.

'Yeah, you're welcome!' she called over the banister, even though the impolite stranger had long since left.

'What's that, love?' Mrs Cook's voice rang from downstairs.

'Nothing.' Her face on fire, Chloe hurried to her next task.

Clementine was alone up here now, and that was just the way he liked it.

He trotted along the tops of the bookshelves among the comforting scent of the books, his paws not making a sound on the wood, though his bell rang if he moved too quickly. He roamed each aisle, acknowledging the space as his own. Humans came here sometimes, yes, but how many of them could say they had climbed the beams and walked across them all, watching the others move around below? How many of them had explored every inch of the library garden? Slept here at night, listening to the building creak?

Clementine reached a section close to the spiral staircase and stopped.

He had spotted something. A cardboard box, sitting between the shelves. Oh, it was beautiful. Clementine meowed his approval, slinking his way around the box, taking in each exquisite detail: the scratches, the marks and imperfections only added to its appeal. The lid was open, tape still stuck to one part, and when he glanced inside, he was delighted to see it was empty.

The humans had done well, leaving this offering here for him.

Clementine hopped into the box, comforted by the four walls around him. He turned around and settled there, relaxed in this tiny space. What a great find. He would be safe and happy here.

He rolled over, playing inside the box. Then he rolled again.

The box rolled, too.

Clementine gave an annoyed yelp as the box fell onto its side, pinning him against the bookshelf. He meowed ruefully, stuck in the dark. What a silly, silly box. Why would the humans do this to him?

'Clem! Oh, poor baby.' With a rustling noise, the box was turned over. Light flooded onto Clementine. He lay on his back, his paws up, highly embarrassed. He quickly rose and leaped out of the nasty box, sitting down to lick his paw with dignity.

'Are you all right?' Chloe picked him up, her hands gentle. Her cardigan held a soft, floral scent.

He meowed to her, telling her of his horrible adventure with the box trapping him. She made a sympathetic noise and scratched him between his ears, exactly where he liked it. He couldn't help purring.

He decided he rather liked Chloe.

CHAPTER FOUR

CHLOE DECIDED TO buy a couple of croissants from a little independent café she had spotted the other day, the Brew House. It looked to be partly a patisserie and partly a café, and she found herself inhaling deeply as the bell jangled above her head and a smiling red-headed woman told her she'd be with her in a minute.

The woman did a double take. 'Oh my God. Chloe? Is that you?'

Chloe was confused for a second. But then it came to her. Hannah, her friend from school, was working at this café. They both squealed like teenagers and Hannah ran to her, wrapping her arms around Chloe. Chloe squeezed her back, a bit embarrassed but pleased.

'It's so great to see you!' Hannah gushed. 'How long has it been?'

Since Chloe didn't much use social media, only her sad fake Instagram where she occasionally stalked Gwen, Chloe and Hannah hadn't really stayed in touch over the years. That was something she regretted now, and Chloe felt a pang of guilt that she hadn't made an effort to reconnect with anyone after moving back to Wellbridge. Since then, most of her time had been spent either in the library or at home, with the occasional supermarket trip.

'It's been about seven years, I think,' said Chloe. 'How are you?'

'Give me just a sec.' Hannah scurried back behind the counter, breathless and pink-cheeked. An elderly lady was waiting for her order, though she didn't look like she minded the hold-up. 'I am so sorry. Thank you for waiting. What can I get for you?'

Chloe's mind spun. Hannah. They had hardly talked since Chloe had moved away from Wellbridge. Hannah had stayed here while Chloe had gone off to university after . . . well, after everything. Their daily chats had become the occasional message, then naturally petered out as they had both moved on. A quick look at her phone confirmed to Chloe that it had been five years since they'd spoken at all, their last message being 'Happy New Year' all those years ago. She had to fix that.

Chloe couldn't deny the charm of a small, family-owned business like this. The till was decorated with countryside-esque ornaments. A gnome grinned up at her beside a stone squirrel with a chipped tail. The piece on the far end was a mouse sipping a cup of tea atop a pile of books. Chloe could almost imagine its little nose twitching.

The elderly woman ordered her drink, and then it was Chloe's turn. Hannah gave another excited squeal, muffled behind her hands. 'I didn't know you were visiting!'

'I know, I'm sorry. I'm rubbish at staying in touch.' Chloe glanced behind her when the bell above the door jangled and a man walked inside. She couldn't stay and chat or she'd hold up the line. She was almost late for her shift anyway. 'Three lattes to go, please. And three of those chocolate croissants.' It was still wild to her that the girl she'd had sleepovers with was working at a café now. She looked older but the same, somehow.

'Three lattes and three croissants, got it,' said Hannah, professional now. 'Would you like any syrups today? Hazelnut? Caramel?' She grinned. 'Twenty pence extra for one shot.'

'I'm allergic to nuts,' Chloe reminded her. 'There's none in the croissants, right?'

'No nuts in those,' Hannah confirmed. 'For syrup, we have caramel and vanilla.'

Chloe grinned at Hannah's forwardness. 'Oh, go on, then. Caramel in one.'

When Hannah handed her the drinks, Chloe said, 'Let's catch up at a less busy time, okay? I'll message you.'

'I can't wait.'

Chloe wasn't staying in Wellbridge for very long, a couple of months at the most, but there was no harm in catching up with her childhood friend. Her steps had a spring in them as she headed for the library. She admittedly hadn't spared much thought for the people she had gone to school with; it all felt like such a long time ago. She had assumed they had moved on and moved to different cities, like she had. Not everybody, though. She would have to message Hannah when she got the chance.

She shouldered the library door open five minutes later, her hands full. Eric, a young A-Level student who worked there part-time, hurried to open it the rest of the way for her.

'There you go, Chloe,' he said eagerly.

'Thanks, Eric.' Chloe was a bit breathless, holding the bag of pastries in one hand and the coffees in the other. She planned to drink hers in the break room; she wouldn't dare risk damaging the books with a clumsily handled beverage.

'No problem.' Eric returned her smile with a friendly one of his own. He was a skinny boy, and his big brown eyes and floppy hair reminded Chloe of an excitable puppy. Sometimes she forgot he was already eighteen.

There were still a few minutes left before her shift began, so Chloe sipped her caramel latte in the break room. Hannah had been right to recommend it; it was terrific. Clementine the cat was there, staring at her as though she had let slip a terrible swear word. She didn't know if he was really regarding her with disdain or if he had resting-grumpy-face syndrome.

'I'm allowed to drink coffee in here. Good morning to you too, fluffy.' Chloe made to pet the cat, but he slinked past her and into the reception area with a haughty flick of his tail. A bad mood today, then. Chloe chuckled at the cat's indecisiveness. He certainly hadn't minded her touching him when she'd saved him from the cardboard box.

When the clock struck ten, Chloe got started with her tasks for the day. Mrs Cook had arrived and was looking at her computer, an exasperated expression on her face.

'Look at this silly contraption,' she said. 'Do you young ones know how to use this?'

'It's a computer, Mrs Cook,' piped up Eric.

'I know what it is, love. I just don't know how to use it. I thought it would make it easier to store library records, but I just don't know where to begin. Chloe, dear, could you . . .?'

Chloe and Eric got together in front of the screen. 'I suppose it will be easier in the long run to have all the records together,' she called after the elderly woman, who was carrying some books to the non-fiction section on the ground floor. 'It just might take some time to archive everything.'

'How long? I might be dead before I understand how it all works,' she called over her shoulder, and chuckled.

Chloe swallowed, not laughing.

'I think she means to get the books into a database so it's easier to search for them in the future,' said Eric. 'Then when customers ask, we don't have to check the big paper files back there, like we usually do.' He jerked his head towards the filing cabinets that lived behind the reception desk. 'We might have to start inputting them manually.'

'Why not just copy from the files?' Chloe jerked her head towards the disorganised piles of files on the back shelf.

'They're older than I am, and probably haven't been updated in a while.' Eric winced. 'We'll have to do it book by book, so the records are up to date.'

'That sounds fun,' said Chloe blandly, and Eric gave a high-pitched laugh.

'We can take turns,' he said.

It would be a long job but would definitely be easier in the long run. Besides, busy days meant quicker shifts and a hectic mind.

They started with non-fiction, Eric typing up the name, author, year of publication and other information that might help them locate the book in the future. The program he was using sorted the authors into alphabetical order automatically, which was helpful. After twenty minutes they switched places, Chloe typing up the information on the keyboard while Eric fetched piles of books from the shelves, returning them when she was done.

Chloe couldn't help noticing that Eric tried to carry far many more books than he could handle, often red-faced and panting by the time he placed them on the desk beside her. At one point, he carried so many he couldn't see where he was going, and she heard a mighty crash and the thunderous cascade of books thudding on the carpet, followed by a whispered curse. She tried to rearrange her face into what she hoped was neutral obliviousness by the time Eric came back with more books, his cheeks maroon.

When it was Chloe's turn to get books, she made her way through the empty children's area in the ground floor's west wing. She turned a corner then stopped, spotting a man in an armchair in the corner, an open book in his lap. His fair hair shone almost gold in the light, and his broad shoulders took up most of the armchair, like he'd had to squeeze himself into it.

She didn't remember seeing him come in. Maybe it was when she had been to the bathroom, or before she had even arrived this morning. She stood half hidden in the shadows, not sure whether to greet him or ask if he needed anything. He already had a book. He was the man who had been short with her the other day when she had recommended him a fantasy book.

He looked strangely lonely, sitting there by himself, though he looked to be so absorbed in the book he hadn't noticed her presence. This was certainly a good place to sit and read, without the distractions of home or the noise of a café. Chloe examined the man's profile, noting the straight nose, the serious furrow of his eyebrows. There was something charming about seeing a man read.

He dog-eared the page, glancing up. Chloe backed into the next aisle, feeling strangely nervous, like she was doing something wrong. She shook herself and went to get more books, being as quiet as she could until she had rejoined Eric. When she was safely back in the brighter lobby, she concealed a shudder.

She had caught the man dog-earing a page. How horrific.

On her way back to Eric, something caught her eye on a nearby shelf. It was a piece of paper, torn from a notebook. Chloe picked it up, wondering if it was some rubbish someone had left behind. She unfolded it and stared.

Inked in the centre of the page was a little black heart.

Chloe's brow furrowed, a small chuckle escaping her. She scrunched up the paper and tossed it into the lobby's waste-paper basket.

She threw herself into the tedious work of inputting the books with Eric, listening to him chatter about a video game he was playing.

'Did you know some games have stories that are just as good as books?' Eric asked, somehow able to talk and put the book information in at the same time. 'And games can even come from books, too. Like *The Witcher.*'

'I remember playing one on the PlayStation 2 years ago. It made me cry,' said Chloe, and Eric gasped in shock. 'The story was just so good. One of the characters died and I was inconsolable. My sister said I was being stupid.'

'You play games?' he asked. He looked so surprised that Chloe giggled.

'I even know who Super Mario is. Crazy, I know.'

'Sorry, just most girls fall asleep or walk away when I mention games. Hey, maybe we can play one together sometime.'

'Uh, yeah. Maybe.' Chloe changed the subject, asking Eric to pass her a huge encyclopaedia he had brought over earlier. It was so heavy she had to hold it in both hands. They worked through the morning, and paused only to help two customers check out books. Chloe was pleased the younger of the two, a girl who looked around eighteen, joining the library in order to check out some romances. 'That one is really good,' said Chloe, nodding to the one on the top of the pile.

'Yeah, I've seen it on TikTok a lot,' said the girl. 'Thanks.'

'Let's do some of the fiction books next, okay?' said Chloe when it was nearing lunchtime. Her bottom was numb from sitting on the reception stool, and going up and down the staircase to the fiction section would be good exercise. Eric nodded and took her place, frowning at the screen. 'We're making good progress.'

It would take months to get down the information of every single book, and poor Eric would be battling through the archives long after Chloe had moved away, though she didn't say so. The least she could do was help him out with as much as she could before she left. She ascended the spiral staircase to the fiction section above, inhaling the scent of paper and ink that she loved so much. Clementine purred at her from behind his favourite curtain, and this time, he let her run a hand down his soft back.

'What to start with?' Chloe wondered aloud, wandering through the rows of shelves. She supposed she could start with horror, since there were fewer of those. There were so many books in the fantasy and romance sections that it looked intimidating. She was about to pass the shelf when she spotted a faint glow emanating from one of the bookcases, stopping her in her tracks.

Her heart thumped. There it was again, the same glow she had seen that evening after her disastrous date. It couldn't be what she thought, could it?

A warm wind rustled behind her, like a gentle breath from a steam room. She glanced behind her. Clementine was watching her, his eyes reflecting the lamps.

'Did you feel that?' she asked, as though expecting the cat to respond. She rolled her shoulders and passed the shelf, ignoring what may or may not have been a beckoning in the shelves.

She thought she felt something in the air shift, almost like the library itself was sighing in disappointment. The thought made her feel daft, and she chuckled to herself as she grabbed some books for Eric. All of them were, determinedly, *not* glowing.

She left the bookshelves behind, deciding she was too busy to be looking at glowing books again.

CHAPTER FIVE

'HERE ARE SOME more,' she said brightly, setting down a pile of books for Eric to input. He was sitting on the stool, bent over and almost cross-eyed with concentration as he tapped in the book information.

'I'm just cleaning the feeder, dears,' Mrs Cook called to them.

With Eric and the librarian both busy, Chloe checked around the library for customers. Some loitered, too shy to ask for help. Others needed to see that she wasn't too busy before they could approach her and ask about recommendations. Chloe had worked in retail shops during her time at university, and every now and then people would regard her with faint loathing if she dared to greet them, as though suspicious she was going to try and force them to buy something. It was one thing Chloe loved about working in the Wellbridge Library. She could offer help without people assuming she was trying to pitch a sale.

She smiled to herself. Libraries really were a blessing.

Her thoughts strayed to the man she'd met the other day, the grumpy one who had borrowed the fantasy book. He wasn't sitting on the armchair where he was earlier. He must have left. She found herself relieved; he hadn't openly begrudged her help but her first impression of him hadn't been all that great.

First impressions . . .

The library turned out to be empty on this quiet morning, so Chloe arranged the shelves, making sure the books were in the correct places and in the right order. She thought of the book she had passed earlier, recalling the way it had glowed, how she had ignored it. The strange sense of warm air washing over her.

Would the book still be there, waiting for her to open it? Before she could stop herself, Chloe went over to check.

The glowing tome this time was in the historical romance section, a thick paperback with that strange orange hue around it. She wasn't imagining it, then, and there was no way she could blame the lighting. No other books around it were glowing. It was like the pages themselves emitted their own light, separate from the electric lanterns above her head. Chloe glanced around, making sure there was no one else lurking around the shelves. Then anticipation rose in her as she snatched it from the shelf. The book felt warm in her hands. Almost alive.

She thought of the man in the old-fashioned garb she'd met that rainy night, how oddly like a certain book character he had seemed. Maybe she should test this, see if what had happened was real. She had almost convinced herself it had been a joke or a prank, but somehow that didn't make any sense. And now she held a different book in her hands, one that almost shivered with hope.

Swallowing, Chloe opened the book. She knew this story. It was a series about time travel in Scotland, with battles and strong men in kilts and heartbreaking romance. Chloe read a random line aloud, then listened closely.

At first, nothing happened, and she stood there holding the book. The air was silent except for the sound of her own breathing.

Then a floorboard creaked.

Eric, perhaps, or Clementine returning to find a spot to relax behind the curtain?

A whisk of cloth and the sound of a man clearing his throat. She thought about calling out, but instead she stepped out from between the shelves, looking left then right.

A man was leaning against the far-off shelf. He was enormously tall and wore a kilt and a grubby jacket. He looked like he had been wandering hills and roads for a long time, old dirt clinging to his clothes and dark leaves in his curly red hair.

Chloe hadn't really expected it to work again. But she knew this man wasn't a regular visitor. He hadn't rocked up to the library with his sporran and mud on his bare knees and scars on his arms, looking around in confusion and suspicion as he half-crouched, as though sheltering from gunfire.

Her throat felt tight, but she managed to croak, 'Hello.'

The man glanced up, eyes narrowed. 'Who are ye? Where am I?'

As she had expected, his voice was rich and deep with a strong Scottish accent. The hairs on the back of her neck stood on end, especially when she spotted the dagger at the man's hip. This was real. It was actually happening.

'Um, Wellbridge,' she said. 'In a library. It's safe,' she added quickly, recalling that in most of his book, he was decidedly *unsafe*. 'You'll be back in Scotland very soon, I promise.'

He looked her up and down, as though assessing whether she was a threat. Then he straightened to his full height. He was immensely tall, his shock of red hair fiery in the lantern light. A crooked smile appeared on his face. 'Don't know if I trust ye on that, but I don't hear or *smell* any more sassenachs about.'

Chloe raised her hands, sweat springing up on her back. 'I just want to talk.' She gestured to a nearby set of armchairs, trying hard not to glance at his dagger. 'You're safe here,' she repeated.

'Despite ye bein' a sassenach, too?' The man still sounded suspicious, but there was also a tone of amusement in there.

'Despite that, yes.' She managed a smile.

She stared at him for a long time, marvelling at how this had indeed happened. He didn't glow or emit any kind of otherworldly vibe. He just looked like a normal guy in the flesh and blood. He smelled a bit of dirt and sweat, but that was hardly surprising.

'Do ye suppose I've moved through time?' he wondered aloud.

'You could say that. But you won't be here for long, you'll see.'

'Fine. What did ye want to talk about, lass?'

'I won't keep you.' Chloe had to treat this as an experiment. The last time this had happened, the character had been wanting to get back to his party. She wondered if reading a line from the book made the character emerge from that exact scene. It made as much sense as everything else so far. 'I'm Chloe. I was wondering if you could tell me where you came from.'

'The last thing I remember, I was sleepin' in the stables. I closed my eyes, and I must have drifted off. And next thing I knew, I was standing here.' He glanced around. 'I wonder if this is a dream. I've never seen so many books in one place before.'

Chloe marvelled at this. She was actually somehow pulling out characters from their books. Though it seemed it was the stories themselves that decided, not the characters. Clearly, they didn't know how or why they came here, either.

Clementine appeared, looking from Chloe to the newcomer. She picked him up and petted him, and her new friend smiled down at him.

'Och, a cat. Good for getting rid of rats. Do ye get a lot of rats here?'

'I shouldn't think so.' Chloe wrinkled her nose at the thought. 'They'd chew on the books.'

'All the better to have one of these little beasties around.' He petted Clementine, and the cat leaned into his large hand, purring. So Clementine had no problem with the library's magical visitors, either.

Magical. An improbable word, not one that she'd say aloud, but there wasn't any better way to describe it.

The red-headed Scot didn't seem worried about being here, or maybe that was because he was used to much more frightening dangers than finding himself in a library with one woman. 'Aren't you concerned?' she asked anyway.

'Naw, not really.' He leaned back in the armchair, shifting as though appreciating how comfortable it was. 'There are a lot of things I don't fully understand, but there's no harm in having some faith in them.'

'Yes,' said Chloe, thinking on those words. 'I think you're right.' She hesitated. 'Thank you for talking to me. I just wanted to check something.' She showed him the book in her hands. 'This is how I'll send you back. Are you ready to go back to the stable?'

His crooked smile made her heart flip over. 'Aye, if I have to.'

Chloe opened the book, making sure to go near the back of it. She didn't want to repeat his own words back to him, words he had said before in his life, and freak him out. She read aloud a random line, expecting him to disappear from in front of her eyes. Instead, he gave her a questioning look. He was indeed handsome, and she felt her cheeks warm.

'Bear with me.' She flicked closer to the end. When she had sent back the nineteenth-century noble that rainy evening, had she done something different? Finally, she flicked to the last few pages of the book, an idea striking her. 'All right, let me try this.'

She found the last line uttered by the character in front of her, then whispered it, loud enough for him to hear. Clementine leaped to the floor beside her feet, meowing softly. He stood on his back legs, gently laying his ginger paw on the page.

A gentle wind rippled over her. Chloe looked up.

The Scot had disappeared.

A shiver ran across her skin. There was no doubt about it now. Somehow, she had managed to pull out a character from their story. When books were ready to let their characters emerge, the tomes glowed and waited to be picked up. Then she spoke a line aloud from the book and the character would come out. That was how much she had gleaned from what had happened so far. And if she wanted them to return, she only had to read aloud their final line.

It sounded simple enough.

Nope, no, it didn't.

The book tumbled from her hands, landing with a loud thump on the floorboards. She buried her face in her hands as Clementine gave a soft mew, jumping onto her lap. This was all utterly impossible. Or so she would have believed if it hadn't happened to her twice now.

Chloe released a long, shaky breath, aware she had stayed up here talking for at least ten minutes. Eric was probably wondering where she had got to, or Mrs Cook may be looking for her. Chloe petted Clementine between his ears until she had calmed her racing heart, then rose to her feet and picked the book up, noting that the glow had gone. The same as last time. She quietly apologised to it for dropping it and slid the novel in question back onto the shelf. It sat in silence, innocently dim. It was as though . . . the character's job was done here. The Scottish warrior had been here, clearly from a story, and she had successfully sent him home.

He had told her to have faith in the unknown, even if she didn't fully understand it. Was that what she should be doing now? Embracing this newly found power instead of trying in vain to deny it? As the fear faded, excitement jolted through her. Seeing was believing, and she was ready to put faith into this.

Whether it would be wise to share it with someone else, well, that remained to be seen. She looked down at her hands in awe. How long had this power been dormant in her?

She thought back to the man she had met that rainy night after her date. He had asked her if first impressions mattered, had prompted her to think on it. And now the red-headed Scotsman had made her think about things, too.

She had no doubt she could do it again, pull another character from a story and have a conversation with them. Did Mrs Cook know about this? Did Eric? Or was it something Chloe had discovered herself?

She couldn't tell them, not without learning more and maybe prodding them for clues. If she told them outright, they might think she was hallucinating or lying. Yes, it would be better to keep this to herself for now, at least until she learned more about it.

She knelt to pet Clementine, feeling his bushy tail straighten beneath her fingers. She was sure the cat felt her disquiet and had come to comfort her. 'Thank you, Clem. I'm feeling a bit better.'

This was all so crazy if it was true, but she had to keep it under wraps for now. Characters emerging from their stories wasn't something that occurred often, especially in quiet little English towns where nothing ever happened.

Clementine was always the most energetic in the mornings and evenings, and the purple of the clouds through the gothic windows told him it was already twilight. His tail twitched, eager for a run around the library garden.

He watched Mrs Cook as she finished her work, then she opened the back door for him and he streaked out. The cold air rippled across his fur. He preferred staying indoors most of the time, but now and then he wanted to feel the cool grass against his paws, smell the flowers and soil – this place that was full of such heavenly scents, floral and grassy – and maybe even catch something. His noble ancestors were wild hunters, after all.

There was definitely something lurking in the bush there.

Clementine leaped with grace, his silent pounce marred only by the light tinkling of his collar bell. He caught his prey between two soft paws. A frog croaked beneath him in protest. Clementine picked it up in his mouth as the amphibian wriggled, trying to jump away. Rather proud of his marvellous catch, Clementine trotted over to where Mrs Cook was waiting for him.

'What have you got there, little boy?' The human lady crouched before him, then gasped, her wrinkled hands clamping over her cheeks. 'Oh, no! Poor little thing. Oh, you naughty boy, Clem.'

Clementine meowed, which wasn't easy around a mouthful of frog. The creature wriggled miserably in his jaws. Wasn't Mrs Cook happy with his present?

She didn't eat much, he could see. And she was very small. She needed feeding. Maybe she didn't like to eat frogs? Clementine didn't know much about human diets, though he had seen them use milk.

He didn't think he could hunt milk.

Clementine tried to explain, but Mrs Cook crouched before him, looking stern as she stretched out her hand. 'I know you need to hunt, but that little froggy hasn't done anything wrong. Give him to me, Clementine. There's plenty of nice food in there for you. You don't need to be out chasing little animals.'

Clementine sat down, indignant. This was no way to accept a gift.

'Clementine,' sang Mrs Cook.

The cat deposited the little frog onto the librarian's hand. It leaped off at once, jumping into the bushes and out of sight.

Clementine meowed at the librarian and passed her, going back into the warmth of the kitchen with his tail in the air. She didn't like his present. In fact, she had let the little thing escape. He wasn't sure whether it would have tasted good, but she should have appreciated the thought.

He leaped on top of the fridge and turned his back to her. It wasn't the most comfortable place to rest, but he wanted her to know he was annoyed. When she said his name, Clementine refused to look at her, studying the wallpaper instead, as his tail wrapped around his feet. The cheek, the *nerve* . . .

The sound of food hitting the bowl made his head turn. Mrs Cook was pouring his favourite mix into a plastic feed plate, right next to a fresh bowl of water. The automatic feeder gave him the same thing every day, but this was wet food, smelling deliciously meaty. Clementine watched, his whiskers twitching as the enticing aroma surrounded him.

'See you tomorrow, my boy.' Mrs Cook was halfway out the door when Clementine leaped down and rubbed himself across her leg. He meowed at her, not wanting her to go.

She chuckled, reaching down to pet him. 'I love you, too.'

CHAPTER SIX

As promised, Chloe sent Hannah a message, saying how glad she was that they had run into each other and that they should spend some time together soon. That was how she found herself in Wellbridge's town centre on a breezy Tuesday morning, waiting in front of the post office.

Hannah bounded over not long after, her hair in a high ponytail. How was it that she could look the same even though seven years had passed? When they were teenagers, twenty-six-year-olds had seemed so mature and put-together. But nothing had really changed.

Chloe smiled as she returned her hug. 'Right, now I don't have to make coffee all day, I can actually catch up with you properly,' said Hannah. 'Shall we go do some shopping?'

'Sure.'

There were a few high street shops in the little town centre, and Chloe and Hannah browsed clothes as they caught up with each other and the seven years they had missed. Chloe told her about moving to Sheffield and working in marketing after she had finished university.

'Do you miss it?' Hannah asked, moving along shirts on racks.

'The city, yes. Marketing, not so much.' The job had had little to do with her degree in linguistics and more with the rising rent prices. 'I moved here after . . .' She trailed off, realising with dismay that she hadn't told Hannah about her parents.

Hannah must have noticed the look on her face because she abandoned the rack of clothes, giving her a look of sympathy. 'I heard about what happened,' she said softly.

'You did?' Tears burned in Chloe's eyes and she quickly blinked them away. 'How?'

Hannah hesitated. 'Well, Gwen posted about it. On Facebook.'

Right. Chloe turned away, pretending to be interested in some skirts. She didn't know why it bothered her so much that Gwen posted about Mum and Dad on her Facebook page. She had every right to do so. Maybe it was because on her Instagram, she was painting herself as a fabulously wealthy and happy sugar baby, with no mention of them at all. She hadn't even made it to the funeral. She had asked Chloe to move the event a few days later to give her time to come back from Fiji, but Chloe had reminded her that the world didn't revolve around her. They hadn't spoken since then.

'Should I have unfriended her?' asked Hannah, sounding alarmed.

'No, no.' Chloe wiped her eyes, glad she wasn't wearing mascara. 'It's nothing like that. I'm glad you know, actually.' It would skip the painful process of telling Hannah herself, anyway.

Hannah hugged her. 'I'm so sorry about what happened. It's awful. I can't imagine.'

Chloe held her until Hannah pulled away. She forced a smile, not wanting to get lost in memories of Mum and Dad in this bright clothing store. 'Thanks. Tell me about you. What have you been up to?'

Hannah hesitated. 'Well, I have a daughter now. She's almost four.'

Chloe tried not to show her surprise, though she supposed they were at the age now when they were starting to have kids. Even if it did still feel like a far-off possibility for Chloe.

'Wow, that's great,' she said. Hannah had always been the one who said she didn't want kids and would never have kids, though she supposed people changed their minds. 'What's her name?'

Hannah gave a fond smile. 'Lily.'

She glanced at Hannah's left hand. 'I didn't know you were . . .' She trailed off as Hannah shook her head, looking like she had just swallowed something sour. There was no ring on her finger, and Chloe cringed at herself inwardly.

'He's an idiot. Sees her on weekends, but . . . it just didn't work out.' She scoffed. 'I wouldn't trade her for the world, though. I can't wait for you to meet her.'

'That'll be nice,' said Chloe. 'Though, um, you should know I'm not really planning to stay long.' She told her about moving into her parents' house after the funeral.

'Oh, Chloe. It must be so tough living in your house where they . . . That's . . . I'm so sorry.'

She let Hannah hug her again, her empathy bringing fresh tears to her eyes. 'It's all right,' she reassured her. 'I mean, it's not, but it is what it is. I came here temporarily, but I'll move on as soon as I've saved up some money. There are too many bad memories here, you know.'

'Not all bad, I hope.' Hannah sniffled.

Chloe nudged her. 'You were my best friend in school. I promise we'll stay in touch more.'

'Well, come and meet Lily before you leave. We could even visit this library of yours. Where are you going to go after this? Back to Sheffield?'

Chloe thought about it, barely seeing the clothes she was half-heartedly rifling through. 'Maybe back there again, yeah. It's a nice city, and I could probably get my old job back.' She didn't add that nothing would ever beat working in the library. Especially now. Standing here in the store, pop music playing in the background, her encounters with book characters seemed far-off, almost fictional.

'I don't think I could ever leave Wellbridge,' Hannah remarked. She had picked up a T-shirt for her daughter, and Chloe joined her at the till. 'Visiting other places is nice, but this will always be home.'

'Really?' said Chloe, amused. She herself hadn't lived in that many places – Manchester for university, then Sheffield afterwards.

She always chose big cities with lots of people, opportunities for anonymity. If things went south with someone, you could move on without risking bumping into them at every turn. 'What about gossip? In small towns like these, everyone seems to be in each other's business all the time.'

Hannah shrugged. 'All my neighbours helped out when I had Lily. You don't get that in a city.'

'No,' said Chloe as Hannah paid for her daughter's shirt. 'I suppose you don't.'

It was a week later when the man who had insulted one of her favourite books and dog-eared the page turned up at the library again. When Chloe heard the door open, she straightened, glad for a chance to be away from the computer. The stool always made her back ache after a while. The smile slipped off her face, however, when she saw who it was. His sarcastic '*I didn't realise we weren't allowed to open them*' still hadn't left her mind.

Still, she was a professional. 'Hello.'

'Hi.' He shrugged off his jacket. 'It's cold out there today.'

Chloe turned to the shelf behind her so he wouldn't see her rolling her eyes. She was well aware that October in Derbyshire could be frigid. She had walked here from her house this morning.

'I finished that book.' The man brought out the paperback from his satchel, holding it up. 'It was good, actually. I was wondering if you have the second one.'

Don't sound so surprised, she thought. Aloud, she said, 'Let me check for you.'

She ascended the spiral staircase to the fantasy section. None of the books had glowed for the past several days, and today was the same. Her eyes scanned the shelves, searching for the series she was sure she had re-organised here just a week or two ago.

'The second one is here somewhere,' she said. She hadn't read them herself, but her mother had had the first few on her bookshelves.

The man had followed her, and he placed the book he was return-ing on a random shelf beside him. It made her jaw clench. Didn't he know there was a return bin? Was he an idiot, or being annoying on purpose?

'Can you hurry up?' he called after her. 'I've got work to do.'

She turned from him back to the shelf, wondering whether it would be worth getting sacked to just throw the nearest book at his head. But as she glanced up, the book she was looking for – the second in the series he was reading – was right in front of her, sev-eral inches from her hand.

Strange. She could have sworn she'd just looked in that spot. Per-haps she simply hadn't looked properly before.

She took it off its shelf and passed it to the visitor. She couldn't keep the sarcasm from her tone when she snapped, 'There. So sorry to keep you waiting.'

At her tone, his lips moved as though he wanted to smirk, but he didn't. 'Cheers.' When he made for the spiral staircase, Chloe discreetly took the book he had set down and tucked it under her arm. She would have to smooth out the dog-ear creases once he was gone.

'Do you have the whole series?' he turned around and asked when he was at the top of the stairs, glancing back at her.

'I thought you were in a hurry?' she said, folding her arms.

He arched an eyebrow. 'Well, do you?'

'I can check,' she said. 'If not, we can always order them in. Can't tell you when they'll arrive, though.' She bit back a remark about checking at a bookshop or online. The library needed all the visitors it could get, even the rude ones.

'Okay.' He looked down at the book. 'Sometimes it feels like books are the only escape, you know?'

His words took her aback. Chloe did know. More than he could ever understand. 'Yeah, I know what you mean.'

It didn't seem like he had even heard her. He grunted and trudged down the spiral staircase, his heavy boot steps echoing around the floor.

'I'll sign it out.' With his broad back to her, Chloe glared at the back of his head. Who knew a book lover could be so . . . ugh?

Down at reception, Chloe scanned his library card. She wondered if he had moved from Newcastle as a child or as an adult, whether they went to the same school when they were teenagers, but she didn't ask. She probably would have remembered such a grump, and besides, why did it matter? Hopefully he'd find the series in a book sale or something and this was the last they'd see of each other.

While she was stamping the book, the man's phone rang. 'Harry here.'

When Chloe held the book to him, he took it and left without another word. 'Yeah. I'm on my way. Aye, that's canny. Tell them . . .'

The large doors closed behind him and his voice faded. 'See you, then,' Chloe muttered beneath her breath. She hoped someone else would be manning the desk next time this Harry walked in.

She supposed she would have to check if they had the rest of the books in stock, but right now she couldn't be bothered.

Later, when she was coming back from using the bathroom, a piece of paper caught Chloe's eye. Frowning, she opened it to see a heart drawn in black ink. Beside it was a smiley face.

Who left this here? she thought, a bit annoyed, and threw it in the bin.

It was nearing noon when she was doing some paperwork and felt something tickle her nose. Dust, maybe. The familiar sensation rose, and as she was about to sneeze, she spotted something on the desk right by her hand. A box of tissues, one peeking out and ready to grab.

Chloe ripped it from the box and sneezed into it.

'Bless you,' said Eric, a new pile of books in his arms as he approached. 'I just came in for my shift, if you'd like to take your lunch break.'

He must have grabbed the tissues while she was upstairs. She could have sworn they weren't there a moment ago, though.

Shaking herself, Chloe thanked Eric and went out for her lunch, wondering whether Hannah was working today at the café. She wasn't, but as Chloe waited in line, she looked at all the cakes and pastries they had available. They all looked delicious, and she loved the cosy warmth of this little place. Acoustic music filled the space and customers sat in couples or alone at tables, talking and sipping coffee. One man frowned at his laptop, a steaming black coffee beside him. A woman and her small son ate French toast together.

Outside, a man was parked, leaning out of his window to banter with a man he'd been driving past. A small smile reached Chloe's face as she passed them, catching snippets of what must have been private jokes. They laughed like old friends, then waved cheerfully to each other as they parted ways.

You don't get that in a city.

CHAPTER SEVEN

WHEN CHLOE ARRIVED back at the library, she worked at the computer a bit more, inputting several more books with Eric's help. The hours slipped by, and as the mid-afternoon slump hit, she decided to make everyone a cup of tea. She was heading for the fridge when she almost bumped into Mrs Cook.

'Hi, Mrs Cook. I was about to make a cuppa,' she said. 'Would you like one?'

'Great minds certainly think alike. I was about to do the same.' Mrs Cook beamed at her. The kettle was an old-fashioned metal one that clucked on the hob, the sound of the water heating strangely cosy.

'We've got some new books coming in,' said the librarian as she put teabags in the mugs. As with any good workplace, the library kitchen was always well stocked with coffee, tea, sugar and milk. 'A few new releases from last year. They'll be a great addition.'

'Great,' said Chloe, hoping to be able to borrow them herself. Buying books was all well and good until you had to fit them into a suitcase. She only owned one paperback at the moment, and she had almost finished reading it.

'Would you like to have a chat, Chloe? There aren't any customers here now, and if there are, Eric can sort them. Or would you rather be alone?'

'Hm? Oh, no, I don't mind.' Chloe found herself a little flustered as she sat at the kitchen's plastic dining table opposite the librarian, the mug warming her hands. She wondered whether to bring up what had happened since she had started working here: the night she had escaped here after her bad date, her conversation with the young man with the kilt. Would she sound insane by giving voice to what had happened? She took a sip of tea. Mrs Cook mirrored her, then let out a satisfied 'aah' that made Chloe giggle.

Chloe had mentioned her parents' accident during her job interview, not wanting the subject of her family to pop up down the line and make anyone uncomfortable. But she realised she didn't know much about Mrs Cook at all.

'How long have you been a library manager?' she asked her.

'Oh, my. Almost forty years now.' Mrs Cook smiled in reminiscence. 'From long before we had computers, when we had to keep track of everything manually, with pen and paper. I've worked at libraries all over the place, but I've been at this one for nearly ten years. I've seen people work here, coming and going. Some just worked for the wage. Others, like you and Eric, really love books. It's wonderful to see.'

'Wow,' said Chloe, trying to remember her time visiting this place as a child with her mother. The memories were hazy; in the past year, anything related to Mum and Dad had been shelved in a dark, cobwebby corner of her mind and were now difficult to grasp. She thought she had vague memories of this place, but she couldn't be sure. 'You must enjoy it a lot.'

'Being surrounded by books all day.' Mrs Cook's eyes crinkled as she smiled. 'What's not to love?'

Chloe agreed. There was no denying she liked this job far more than her last one. As a matter of fact, more than any job she had ever had.

'My husband never really understood it.' Mrs Cook held her mug in her wrinkled hands, gazing at the wall as though lost in memories. 'He did read sometimes, but he preferred sports.'

Chloe noted she used the past tense when she referred to her husband, and she felt a flicker of sadness for the elderly woman. 'You're alone, too?' she said before she could stop herself.

'Oh, he's not dead, love,' the librarian reassured her. 'We divorced when we were in our forties. Rest assured, he's living his best life somewhere in southeast Asia.' She rolled her eyes.

'Oh.' Chloe vaguely wondered whether he was rich and if he'd crossed paths with Gwen. *That* would be weird. 'So you're *Ms* Cook?'

'I like the ring of "Mrs" better.' The librarian shrugged. 'My ex-husband and I are still on good terms, on the rare occasions we do meet. And that's more than a lot of people get,' she added gently. 'And we were blessed with plenty of healthy children. They're off gallivanting all over the world, too. Do you like to travel, Chloe?'

Chloe thought of her friend, Hannah, who was happy with staying in Wellbridge. 'Kind of,' she said. 'My sister travels a lot.' She hadn't checked up on Gwen's social media for a while, hardly using it herself. Things were so tense between them, especially since the funeral, that it felt like a sting every time she saw Gwen beaming at her from a yacht or on a beach, hiding any grief she may be experiencing for the death of their parents, behind a raised cocktail glass and an oversized pair of sunglasses. The bitterness must have shown on her face, because Mrs Cook said, 'Perk up, lovely. You're still young. And if you would ever like time off to take a trip, you just need to let me know.' She patted Chloe's hand. 'Same for if you would ever like to borrow any books from the library. Just check them out as a normal customer would.'

'Thanks. That reminds me,' said Chloe, remembering. She told the librarian about Harry and him asking about the rest of the fantasy series he had started. He may have been annoying, but visitors requesting books was never a bad thing for the library. 'Do you think we can order them in?'

Mrs Cook set down her cup. 'How nice we have a returning

customer. We don't get enough of those these days.' She suddenly looked so sad that Chloe couldn't bear it.

'What do you mean?' she asked.

'Every year, we get fewer visitors. The children's section hasn't had much attention these past few years, and even our events fall flat a bit. The library misses having people around. People prefer television, I think.'

'What do you mean, the library misses people?' Chloe asked, curious.

'Nothing, love. It's a figure of speech.' Mrs Cook washed her mug and gave Chloe a fond, motherly look. 'Let me see if I can get those books ordered in. I'll take Eric his tea, too.'

Chloe thought about what Mrs Cook had said. It was true that, even on weekends, the library didn't see many visitors. She had been here for a few weeks now, and it was rare for them to see more than two or three people over the entire day. She didn't know if television was the reason or whether people simply preferred to get their books elsewhere, like in shops or online, but either way, it was a problem.

Chloe loved this place. Even if she wasn't going to be here for very long, she wanted to do what she could to help.

An hour before closing time, she made a suggestion. 'Maybe we could host a public event,' she suggested to Mrs Cook. 'Something to help reignite interest in this place.'

Mrs Cook turned to her from the shelves. 'What do you have in mind?'

'Well . . .' They walked together into the non-fiction section. The library's west wing was divided into non-fiction and reference books, from encyclopaedias to history to language learning, and the children's area. There was a large soft play area for toddlers, bright and happy animals and cartoon characters stuck to the walls, and bookshelves of kids' books, full and unused. 'Maybe we could ask the local school to bring over a class. And we could have a bake sale. People could bring their own things, or I could ask the café down the road. Children love challenges, don't they? We could work with

their teachers to have a challenge to read so many books in a month.'
She trailed off, not sure whether her idea sounded silly.

But Mrs Cook looked pleased. 'That sounds like it just might
work. You went to the local school when you were a child, didn't you,
Chloe? Maybe you could go there and ask them.'

'Me?' she asked in surprise. She had assumed Mrs Cook would
just get them on the phone.

'I think it would make an impact to go there in person. I can book
an appointment with the headteacher there.' She glanced back.
'Unless you'd rather I did it?'

'No, no, I can.' Chloe had wanted to help, hadn't she? 'You're right,
I did go to school there.' The thought of going back to her childhood
school sounded fun. She had so many great memories in Wellbridge.

Painful ones, too.

She had avoided a lot of the town since coming back. Being in her
parents' old house had been difficult enough, seeing their ghosts
whenever she entered a room, occasionally waking up in her childhood bedroom confused, thinking in the blurry moments between
sleep and awake that she was a kid again and her parents were alive,
only for reality to crash into her. There were places all over town she
had avoided, not wanting to unpack the memories that she might
conjure. 'It's just . . . there are a lot of bad memories, you know.'

Mrs Cook *didn't* know. Chloe had told her about her parents, but
not about everything else.

The librarian's voice was kind. 'Maybe you should give yourself
more time.'

But Chloe's thoughts flitted to the conversation with the Scottish
man upstairs, about putting faith in something even if you didn't
fully understand it. What was she achieving by putting it off? She
couldn't run for ever. 'I can do it,' she said, resolve filling her.

'I think this will be great for the library,' said Mrs Cook, her
steps more buoyant as they headed back to the reception desk.
Clementine had deposited himself on the computer keyboard,
slowly closing and opening his eyes as the librarian petted his
furry head.

CHAPTER EIGHT

CHLOE KNEW SHE couldn't spend her life only at the library, her house, and the streets in between. Things took time, yes, but she had been here for weeks already. She couldn't continue to avoid going around town and reliving her memories. There were good memories there, too. Sidestepping them only made it worse.

Mrs Cook had made an appointment with the headteacher of the local primary school for the following Tuesday. Today was Sunday, and since the library was closed, it was everyone's day off. Chloe couldn't help procrastinating leaving the house, and instead thoroughly cleaned every room.

That was a task in itself. Her old bedroom didn't look much different from when she had moved out at nineteen, though she had taken down the posters of rock bands she had thought were awesome back then. There was the room where her sister Gwen had slept, which Chloe didn't touch besides doing some dusting. She didn't like to think about her sister, either.

Chloe set her jaw and closed Gwen's bedroom door.

Her parents' bedroom . . . she had come here shortly after the funeral, when aunts and uncles and distant relatives had helped her put away her parents' things. Photo albums and ornaments and books were packed into boxes and put away in the attic, and Chloe didn't have the heart to take them out and look at them. As a result, the room was pretty much empty. A bedside table stood either side of the bed, which was now just a mattress. There was an en-suite bathroom with a large bath. If Chloe hadn't missed them so much, if wandering through this room to clean the dust and check for cobwebs hadn't made her want to break down and sob, she might have gotten some use out of this room.

Maybe one day. Moving in here had already been a huge step.

Releasing a breath after scrubbing the kitchen, Chloe decided there was little point in putting it off further. Her stomach rumbled and there was nothing to eat in the house except cereal. She had to go grocery shopping before the small-town supermarket closed at five.

She climbed into her car and switched on the radio to the classical channel. Another thing Gwen would tease her for when they were younger.

'You're like an old woman,' she said once when Gwen had caught her listening to Mozart while she studied for her A-Level exams. 'What's next? Darjeeling tea and crocheting?'

'Leave me alone, Gwen.'

'Can I use your vanity?' Gwen had already barged in without waiting for an answer. She had a mirror of her own in her room, but she'd always loved Chloe's three-piece vanity. 'I want to get my eyeliner right.'

'No,' Chloe snapped. She was trying to memorise history dates.

'Don't be so selfish.' Gwen tried to slide in next to Chloe, which wasn't easy as there was only one chair and it couldn't hold them both. She jostled Chloe's arm, and her pen streaked across the paper, leaving a smear of ink on her revision notes.

'Get out of my room!' Chloe roared, shoving her off her seat. 'You're such a pain.'

Gwen had thrown some lipstick at her and then slammed the door.

The memory faded. Chloe switched off the radio.

Her little car hummed through the town, past stone buildings with chimneys and a church and cafés with signs hanging above the doors. She passed Hannah's little indie café and made up her mind to go there next and ask about catering the event at the library. She drove until she found her old primary school. It looked the same but . . . smaller, somehow.

She didn't have any bad memories here in particular, not really. Chloe had grown up quite normally, doing best at English and spending rainy breaktimes reading Jacqueline Wilson and Enid Blyton books. She hadn't been bullied, nor had she particularly struggled in school.

No, it wasn't until later that *things* had happened to make her want to leave Wellbridge and never come back. Going to university had opened many doors for her, had allowed her to move to the city and get lost in the chaos of it all. She had settled in the noise and rush, so different from her quiet hometown in the Peak District, making new friends and experiencing new things. When she was a student, she hadn't ever wanted to come back.

She still didn't want to stay. What? Was she supposed to stay in her parents' house, trying to suppress the memories and the grief? No, as soon as she'd saved some money, she would be out of here.

On Tuesday, she had to visit Wellbridge Primary School for the meeting with the headteacher.

For now, though, she just wanted to head home and order a pizza. She'd probably regret not getting groceries today, but right now she just couldn't be bothered.

When Tuesday came, it was a clear, crisp day, and Chloe decided to walk to her meeting with the headteacher. The school was less than a mile away from the library, and Mrs Cook said she could return home straight after the meeting. Her scarf was wrapped around her neck and her hands were deep in her pockets. In her bag she'd brought several children's books from the library, should she need them.

The meeting was at one o'clock, and she was early, so she stepped into the Brew House, hoping Hannah would be working today.

'Hi, Chloe!' said Hannah, returning Chloe's wave. At midday on a Tuesday, the place was nearly empty. 'Are you eating in or taking out?'

She decided to eat in, and took off her scarf as she slid into a booth. This place was adorable. Chloe could imagine settling here with a book.

'Is this place new?' she asked Hannah when she brought her the menu. 'I don't remember it.'

'It's been here for three years,' said Hannah, looking proud. 'My uncle runs it.'

'It's really cute.' As well as bookshops and libraries, Chloe held a certain fondness for coffee shops. And the white brick walls and potted plants and ornaments of this little place ticked the boxes for the cosy aesthetic she liked so much.

They chatted and she ordered a drink and a cake and pulled out the book she was reading. This was the only physical book she owned currently and she made a mental note to take up Mrs Cook on her offer to borrow more from the library. She checked it wasn't glowing before opening it, allowing herself a small smile and wondering whether her new-found powers would work on all books, or just on those in the library. She had not encountered another book character for a while, and though it was a relief not to experience it again, there was a part of her that was wistful. She imagined summoning the villain from this book into this little café. No, best to make sure that wouldn't happen.

Hannah brought her a slice of chocolate fudge cake and her latte, glancing around before sliding into the chair opposite her. 'What a gorgeous cover,' Hannah said. 'I'd love to read more often. I just don't have the time. No nuts in the cake, I checked,' she confirmed, and Chloe gave a grateful nod.

She took a sip of her latte. It was creamy and utterly delicious. She found that people said they didn't have time to read when they would rather be doing other things, like watching TV or browsing social media. There was nothing wrong with doing that, of course, but Chloe thought it was more about how you chose to spend your days. Still, Hannah was a mother. That probably took up a lot of her time.

'You should see the library. More books than I could ever hope to read,' said Chloe. 'It sometimes makes me sad that I won't be able to read them all, even if I read one every week. It's amazing. You should bring Lily.'

The tinkling bell above the door announced more customers, and Chloe busied herself eating her cake, which was delicious, and reading her book. She would leave fifteen minutes before her meeting with the headteacher at the school. Despite her nerves, or perhaps because of them, she had left the library far too early.

'This cake is phenomenal, Hannah,' said Chloe, setting down her fork when they had a quiet moment. 'Do you make them yourself? Do you remember when you came to my house for a sleepover and we tried to make a cake, but we forgot the flour?'

They giggled. 'And we wondered why it was just sloppy brown goo? My baking skills have improved since then, I swear.' Hannah gestured to Chloe's empty plate. 'Hey, you should try the millionaire's shortbread next time. That's my favourite. And we make lemon Bakewells.'

'Well, I won't be staying for much longer,' Chloe reminded her.

'Right.' Hannah looked crestfallen, and Chloe felt a pang of guilt.

'I'll just have to try them all before I go,' she said. She rose and paid the bill, leaving a tip in the basket.

'You're the best, Chloe. I'll try and swing by the library with Lily, okay?'

Hannah might have just been being polite, but Chloe said, 'We have an event coming up for children. You can bring her along, if you like. Oh!' She smacked her forehead. She had almost forgotten. 'I actually could use your help with the bake sale.' She checked her phone. 'I've got to go, but remind me, okay?'

Her belly full of delicious cake and coffee, Chloe's mood buoyed her as she headed for the school. It was one minute to one when she knocked on the headteacher's door. The sounds of children laughing and playing echoed up and down corridors decorated with colourful drawings. It occurred to Chloe that Hannah's daughter would probably attend this school when she was old enough.

'Come in,' said a woman's voice.

The office was crowded in a cosy sort of way, one wall bright yellow, the one beside it filled with papers and notes pinned to a cork board. A Black lady wearing a bright blue blazer looked up from her desk, a smile spreading on her face, which was kind-looking and put Chloe at ease.

Chloe introduced herself. 'I'm here on behalf of the Wellbridge Library. I was hoping we could discuss an event of some kind. I believe you talked to Alice Cook on the phone?'

'Yes! I'm Mandy Jordan. It's so nice to meet you, Chloe. Would you sit down?'

Soon they were eagerly swapping ideas for an upcoming event, including arts and crafts and book readings. 'I was thinking a bake sale too, if we can,' Chloe said, thinking of Hannah's cakes and making a mental note to text her the details later. 'I might be able to get a local place to help with that. We're thinking of doing a bunch of activities, and maybe a reading. We could get library cards for all the children who don't have one yet, maybe get them to decorate them themselves.'

'World Book Day isn't until March, but I'd love to have something like this before Christmas.' Miss Jordan tapped her chin in thought. 'I'll admit, even I haven't visited the library in a while.'

Chloe thought it would be difficult to organise, but she left the office with promises of settling on a concrete date soon, once letters went out to parents and a suitable day could be decided. Chloe was in a great mood when she stepped out of the school. A cold breeze washed over her, carrying the earthy, sweet scent of autumn leaves. Winter wasn't far off.

She'd buy herself another latte and have a walk before taking the good news to Mrs Cook.

'Back so soon?' Hannah joked when Chloe walked in. 'Can't get enough of me?'

'I just couldn't help myself.' Chloe smiled at her. 'I need to talk to you about the bake sale I mentioned. Do you have a minute?'

Hannah was delighted that they wanted to hire the café for their bake sale. 'I'll have to talk to the manager about the finances of it, since we're hoping the proceeds can go towards the library,' said Chloe. Maybe they could buy some of the cakes in bulk.

'I'll talk to my uncle, too. He's working tomorrow.' Hannah was practically bouncing around. 'This is amazing, Chloe. Thank you so much. You've no idea how much this will help us.'

'Er – help?'

'Well, the café isn't making a huge profit.' Hannah had lowered her voice, and Chloe found herself conspiratorially leaning in. 'You know, people tend to prefer the big chains.' She swallowed, her friendly expression gone. 'Sorry, Chloe. It's not your problem.'

'Don't worry about it.' Chloe mimed zipping up her mouth and smiled. 'The library will benefit from this event too, I'm sure.'

She got a cinnamon latte to go. It felt fitting for this cold late autumn day. She waved goodbye to Hannah, hoping that this event would indeed do something to help the café as well, if it was struggling that much. It was such a lovely little place, and it matched the small town much better than a big chain coffee shop you could find anywhere. Sipping the hot drink, Chloe wandered around town. It wasn't a big town, and she mostly passed shoppers and dogwalkers. Some of them smiled or said hello as she wandered past. She wasn't used to it, but she found herself smiling and nodding back.

She could go home after the meeting with the headteacher, so Chloe took her time. She was about to turn towards home when she spotted the street that led to the local chapel. Chloe had almost forgotten it was here: the little stone building with its majestic steeple and brick walls, although now it seemed to have been lost to time, the garden overgrown. Though she hadn't been inside for years, she knew the polished wooden benches and stained-glass windows lent the interior a romantic look.

It hit her in the chest like a punch.

The memories. The nostalgia. The heartbreak.

This was the place where she and Liam were supposed to get married. Eight years ago, they had visited this chapel, admired the interior artwork, planned where the flowers would go, where the guests would sit. They had talked about their hopes and their plans for the future. They had wanted three kids. To buy a house near a lake somewhere. Have one room as Chloe's personal reading space, filled floor to ceiling with books. That was all before it had come crashing down, leaving her heartbroken and alone.

She turned from the chapel grounds, tears welling up so suddenly she could barely keep them down. She pressed her lips tightly together, hoping no one would see her as a ragged gasp burst from her. She turned a corner and leaned against the cold brick of a wall, sighing as tears slipped down her cheeks. The memories assaulted her without warning.

The dress she had abandoned in a closet.

The tear-filled phone call.

Mum helping her to cancel the wedding invitations.

Chloe crushed the empty coffee cup in her hand. There were no bins nearby, so she stuffed it into her coat pocket, sniffling, not caring right now that there'd be dregs of coffee inside. Whenever her mind wandered, she saw Liam's face in her mind: handsome, wavy brown hair, strong shoulders, forget-me-not blue eyes. The face she thought she would be waking up to every morning for the rest of her life.

She needed to get out of here.

At least Mrs Cook had said she could go home. She would buy herself some food from the supermarket, then go home and curl up on the couch with her book and a glass of wine.

She trailed to Aldi, feeling almost like the chapel was watching her go, silently laughing at her despair. She felt so stupid for crying like this; it had been years since Liam had broken her heart and her dreams of marriage and babies had been left in the dirt. Maybe she wasn't yet ready to be walking around Wellbridge after all. Mrs Cook had said once that it might be healing, but it sure didn't feel that way. More like ripping open a wound that had only just started to heal.

CHAPTER NINE

THE NORMALCY OF the artificial lights and rows of packaged goods in the large Aldi supermarket was calming, and Chloe rubbed her nose before going in search of the frozen foods section. She knew she should try cooking properly – it was something she had taught herself at uni – but right now she just couldn't be bothered. One of the perks of living alone, she supposed. Even so, she grabbed some brown bread and some eggs, not wanting to wake up to an empty fridge in the morning. She definitely should have done the shopping on Sunday instead of ordering that overpriced pizza.

She grabbed herself a chicken tikka masala from the freezer and headed towards the alcohol section. That stupid chapel kept coming back to mind, how beautiful she had imagined it looking, her excited discussion with the wedding planner about where to put the food tables and where she wanted to cut the wedding cake. It *annoyed* her that she was this upset. She thought she had moved on.

Was it being here? Had coming back for her parents' house been a mistake after all? It felt like it right now.

She turned down the next aisle and saw someone who did not improve her mood. Who else would be here but Harry, the man from the library. He was wearing a grey woollen jumper beneath his open coat, his hair damp as if he'd just gotten out of the shower. Hoping he hadn't noticed her, she started to back away. He was looking at the beer section.

Just go, she thought to herself. It didn't matter if he noticed her. But she was in no mood to even be near him right now.

He held his basket in his left hand, the one nearest to her. He had picked up a chicken tikka masala frozen meal, identical to hers.

For some reason, that made her only more annoyed. Like he was doing it on purpose.

Scowling, she stomped back to the frozen aisle and deposited the meal back into the freezer. She loitered for a while, but nothing else looked appealing. She ended up leaving without buying anything. She was being childish, but she didn't much care. She was in no mood to put up with Harry's rudeness again.

A cold sleet fell as she trudged miserably from the bright lights of the supermarket. She hadn't realised how lonely she felt until now.

She shook herself. Nothing good would come from feeling sorry for herself. The Pride & Pint would be open, and the curry there would surely be edible.

Her stomach rumbled at the thought. Maybe some wine wouldn't go amiss, either. She drove home, grabbed an extra jumper and an umbrella in case it rained – she wouldn't make *that* mistake again – and walked down to the Pride & Pint. It was getting dark now, the cold weather bringing on an early night, but at least the sleet had been short-lived. The streetlamps had switched on, illuminating the gleaming cobblestones and cottages in warm glows.

The pub was full of people. She stepped into the delicious warmth, the smell of food and beer making her mouth water, and took off her jacket.

'Table for one, is it?' asked a young woman. She glanced around. 'We've just got this one small table by the fruit machines, I'm afraid.'

'Fine.' Chloe was starving by now and she couldn't be bothered finding somewhere else to eat in the cold and dark. The chocolate fudge cake from Hannah's café seemed like centuries ago.

The woman led her to her table, her ponytail swishing side to side. Chloe sat down and picked up a menu. All around them customers talked loudly, laughed and clinked beer glasses. A group of middle-aged men roared at the TV.

'There's someone sitting at that table beside you.' The waitress pointed at the table next to Chloe's. The customer wasn't there at that moment but a satchel and a coat lay on the stool. When they came back, their elbows would practically be touching. 'Is that all right?'

Chloe nodded, deciding she'd be too absorbed in her meal to care. It wasn't until she'd ordered some food and half a pint of cider that a man sat in the place beside her.

'You're kidding me,' she said under her breath.

Not quietly enough. The fair-haired Geordie glanced at her, his eyes widening in surprise. They were brown, contrasting darkly with his light hair, and for a moment, they just stared at each other.

Chloe took a hurried gulp of cider, looking pointedly in the other direction and hoping he wouldn't recognise her. Too late.

'Oh. It's you.'

'Yeah, it's me.' She set down her drink. She felt suddenly defensive. 'All the other tables were full, so they squeezed me in here.'

'You following me?' His deadpan expression meant she couldn't tell whether he was joking or not.

'Oh, yeah. I just can't get enough of you.' Her joke was met with silence, palpable even as a group of men gathered around the pub TV to watch the football. She wished they'd hurry up with that curry.

Chloe sat awkwardly, wondering how the very man she had been trying to avoid had now ended up in the same pub as her. His rudeness at the library sprang back to mind. 'You're welcome,' she said, before she could change her mind.

'Hm?'

'I said you're welcome,' she said with more force. 'For the book. Because at the library, you didn't say "thank you".'

He looked bewildered, and to be honest, she couldn't blame him.

That interaction had played over and over in her mind, but he had probably forgotten all about it before he'd even reached the bottom of the stairs.

It seemed to dawn on him, however, because his eyes suddenly crinkled. *How does he have eyes so dark brown when his hair is so light?* she wondered vaguely. It might be endearing, even charming, if he wasn't such a *bum*.

Chloe shifted in her seat, then brought out her phone. She was still logged into her fake Instagram account. She was only following a few authors, bookish accounts, and of course, her sister Gwen. It was pathetic to stalk her on social media, but it meant she could know what she was up to without having to speak to her.

She hadn't posted anything new in a while. Sighing, Chloe brought out the book she was reading instead.

'Never thought I'd see someone use an old receipt as a bookmark.'

Chloe ignored him. It nettled her when people interrupted someone who was reading.

'It's a sin.' Was that humour in his voice? 'Almost as bad as dog-earing.'

'You're the one who dog-eared the page,' she snapped, closing the book. 'And cracked the spine.'

'I know, I know. A first edition, too. I may as well have ripped out all the pages and thrown them off a cliff.'

'Yup.' She opened her book again, trying to find where she'd left off. 'I bet you dog-ear all your books. And leave the toilet seat up.'

'And get stuck over which meal to buy in the frozen foods section,' he said smoothly.

He smirked when she looked back at him. 'You were watching me?'

'No. I *saw* you. There's a difference.'

'Well, *you* got a frozen meal, too.'

'Oh-ho.' He set down his drink, grinning now. 'Now who was watching whom?'

Chloe let out an accidental growl and buried her face into her book.

They ignored each other until the food arrived. 'Here you are, guys. Sorry for the wait,' said a flustered young woman, setting down their dishes. Steam rose from Chloe's curry, and her stomach rumbled in anticipation until she saw something in the sauce.

'Oh.' She paused. 'Are there peanuts in this?'

But the waitress was already gone, weaving through the crowds to the bar, picking up glasses. Chloe remained quiet. She didn't think when she'd ordered a curry in a pub that it would contain peanuts. But those were unmistakably nuts in the curry. She pushed away her plate, shocked to feel tears welling up in her eyes. It was silly to cry, but she was starving, stressed and it had already been a long nightmarish day, and one bite would make her lips swell up like—

'Peanuts no good?'

Harry was looking at her, fork already in hand, his plate of chicken breast and chips steaming in front of him.

Chloe sniffled, hoping it wasn't obvious that her eyes were glassy. 'I just . . . yeah, I'm allergic.'

She could go up to the bar to complain and have them replace it, but the place was so noisy and busy it would likely take too much time. As though following her train of thought, Harry said, 'We can swap if you want to. I haven't touched this.'

She looked at him. His chicken did look good. But . . . 'No, no. I'm fine.'

'Well, you can't eat that or we'll have to ring an ambulance,' grunted Harry. 'And I can't have you sitting here looking all sad while I stuff my face, can I?'

She wiped her eyes. 'Are you sure?'

'Aye, I'm sure. Your curry looks better, anyway.'

Harry took up the curry and put his plate of chicken in front of her. She tasted some and groaned with delight. 'Thanks.'

'It's fine . . .' He paused.

'Chloe,' she supplied.

Chloe checked her phone as she ate, chuckling at a meme Hannah had sent to her. Harry answered a work call and slid off his stool to step outside. Chloe had almost finished her meal when he came back saying, 'Aye, I know. We'll need to meet up when you come over. Just need a good place to have a meeting.'

Chloe hesitated, then when he'd put the phone down, said, 'The Brew House is a nice café. Quiet. Good caramel lattes.' Hannah had mentioned she needed more customers.

'The Brew House, eh?' was all he said before he shovelled the rest of the curry into his mouth.

She almost asked what he did for a living before reminding herself she didn't care to keep talking to him. Hannah had sent her a text, complaining about something that had happened at her daughter's pre-school. Chloe was enjoying how they had quickly fallen into a rhythm reminiscent of what good friends they were in school; she had missed her. Then Chloe's phone was buzzing in her hand, and she felt joy mingled with relief as she answered the phone. 'Hi, Hannah.'

'Hi. You won't believe what happened at pre-school today.' Hannah sounded exhausted. She went on a rant about a girl Lily had gotten into an argument with in the playground. What should have been a slight altercation between two toddlers ended up blown out of proportion. 'Now we've got to have a meeting about it.' Hannah made a noise that sounded like she was blowing air on her forehead. 'What are you up to?'

Chloe told her. 'There's a match on, so I'm up to my neck in it. Just kill me, right?'

Hannah laughed. 'I can hear how noisy it is. I could use a drink myself. Maybe I'll open a cheeky bottle of wine.'

'Wish I could join you, but I've got work tomorrow.'

They chatted a little more, Chloe sometimes having to stick her finger in her ear when a group of men roared at the pub's television. She ended up telling Hannah about her disastrous date with Dean, and she found herself reluctantly grinning when Hannah snorted with laughter.

'I'm sorry, Chloe, I shouldn't laugh. But we've both had such bad luck with men. No chance of a second date?'

'None at all. I'd honestly rather die.' Her laughter joined Hannah's. Already, some of the tension was loosening from her shoulders. She finished off the last chip, feeling warm and full. 'It's too noisy in here. Can I ring you tomorrow?'

The smile stayed on her face as she put away her phone. Then she caught Harry staring at her.

Not staring. *Glaring.*

'What?' she asked, unnerved.

'Don't you have any consideration?' His voice was like thunder.

'Excuse me?'

'Some of us are trying to eat. They don't want to hear you gossiping right beside them.'

Chloe was appalled. This pub was incredibly crowded and noisy. Harry had had to say that loudly so she could hear. Every few minutes, the football fans roared with joy or outrage at the game playing on the TV. 'I'm not being louder than anyone else.'

'It's just obnoxious.' Harry took a long swig of his drink. 'Totally disrespectful.'

'Disrespectful?' Anger flared in Chloe, dispelling the good vibes Hannah had brought. 'What are you talking about? It's already bedlam in here.' He was singling her out, she knew it. What was his *problem*?

Why would he change plates with her to be kind and then scold her a few minutes later?

Whatever. She didn't have to put up with this.

She snatched up her bag and coat and marched to the bar to pay her bill, not looking back. She still fumed. *Obnoxious? Disrespectful?*

She stormed back to where Harry was sitting. 'You know, you weren't polite at the library, either, but I didn't say anything,' she said to him. 'And it's not fair to tell *me* off when there's that lot.' She jerked her head at the football fans. 'I'm not putting up with this.'

'Not asking you to,' snapped Harry. 'Off you go, then.'

She let out a huff of anger and turned on her heel. She wouldn't waste one more moment arguing with Harry.

Just as I thought. A total bum.

As Chloe approached the house, she thought she saw a movement near her home, and she stopped walking, a frown creasing her brow. A person was standing there, their arms crossed over their chest, looking at the window from the front gate. Chloe froze, not sure what to do, when the person turned around and spotted her.

It was a woman, slim with long hair, and Chloe's reservation petered out in favour of surprise.

'There you are!' the woman exclaimed, marching right up to her. She was wearing a jacket that was much too thin for this cold weather, her blonde hair longer than when Chloe had last seen her. Her polished fingernails were clutched around her slender arms as she gave a cross sigh. 'Where have you been? I've been waiting here for ages.'

Chloe recovered from her shock, and a profound sense of weariness washed over her as she pulled out her house keys from her bag. 'Hello to you too, Gwen.'

CHAPTER TEN

THE KETTLE WAS taking forever to boil.

Chloe watched it as it steadily rattled louder as her younger sister pulled off her jacket. Gwen shivered. 'It's freezing in here. Is the central heating on?'

She didn't wait for a response but switched it on herself then settled onto one of the dining room chairs, blowing air up to her forehead. Chloe tore her gaze away from the world's slowest kettle to look at her. It was awkward, avoiding the topic of why they hadn't seen each other in years, but Chloe was too shocked to want to bring it up already.

'How's it going with, erm . . .' Gwen squinted at the ceiling. 'That guy you were seeing? Simon?'

The guy from Sheffield? 'We actually broke up over a year ago.'

'Oh, right. I'm sorry.' Gwen looked pained, and Chloe almost felt sorry for her. Almost.

'Er . . . what are you doing here?' she asked her. Last she'd heard, Gwen had been sipping margaritas somewhere in Europe. Or maybe it was the Caribbean.

'Hm, what?' Gwen wrung her hands. 'Oh, yeah. Well, I heard you'd come back to move into this place.' She looked around, and at least had the decency to look wistful. 'I, um, wanted to see it for myself.'

'Did you?' Chloe didn't believe it. 'Who did you hear that from?'

'Auntie Paula.'

'Right, right.' Chloe nodded. She supposed word of their parents' house and who it was going to must have reached the relatives. Initially, it was supposed to go to both of them but since Gwen hadn't shown up for any of the meetings or responded to solicitors' calls, only Chloe currently had a key. 'And you came all the way from where? Spain? To see the house you grew up in?'

'All right, look. I'm broke,' said Gwen, looking annoyed. 'My boyfriend broke up with me and my money's run out. He . . . He did it on the plane ride back and then left me on my own at Heathrow Airport. I could barely afford the train ride over here.'

The kettle finished boiling. Chloe poured them both tea, glad to have something to do with her hands. 'And you need somewhere to stay,' Chloe finished the sentence for her. She supposed she should feel sorry for her sister, but Gwen didn't tend to stay with the same man for long. She looked more annoyed about it than heartbroken.

'Well, yes. I mean, it's my house too,' said Gwen stiffly. 'Thanks,' she added when Chloe set down the tea in front of her. Milky with one sugar, she remembered.

Mum and Dad hadn't written an official will, as they had only been in their fifties when they'd died. But only Chloe had responded to enquiries about it, and been here to clean it up and eventually move in. Gwen hadn't come to the house with Auntie Paula to help pack away Mum and Dad's things, a painful process. A prickle of annoyance ran through Chloe at her sister's audacity. 'How long will you be staying?' she asked carefully, fighting to keep her voice even. She noted Gwen hadn't actually asked if she could stay, but that was typical of her sister.

Gwen wrapped her hands around her mug, and Chloe noticed the varnish on her nails was chipped, the skin around them nibbled and raw. 'Well, I don't know. As long as I need to, until I find somewhere else to go.' She sighed. 'I suppose I should find a job.'

Chloe didn't really want her sister here. There was a painful awkwardness between them, in the way Gwen's eyes didn't quite meet her own. But Chloe felt pity as she beheld her little sister. She couldn't throw her out when she had no money. There was plenty of space here for them both.

'Stay as long as you want,' she said with a sigh.

'Yay! Thank you.' Gwen beamed at her and jumped from her chair to give her a hug. Chloe forced a smile as her sister's slender arms wrapped around her. 'You're a lifesaver. You were always the more mature sister, Chloe.'

Chloe wasn't in the mood for Gwen's compliments. She could be sweet when she got what she wanted, then cold the next moment. 'I have work tomorrow,' she said after she'd gulped down her scalding tea. 'You sleep in your old room, all right? I haven't moved anything in there.'

'Where is everything?' Gwen asked as Chloe was straightening up the living room. Her sister glanced around. 'There used to be a big bookcase here, and some framed photos. Right?'

Chloe straightened. She'd never had much of a filter when it came to her sister, and her shock was wearing off in place of annoyance. 'If you had bothered to come to the house after the funeral, Gwen, you'd know that we spent hours – days – sorting out all the old stuff.' It had been a slow, bitter few days, where Chloe had had to endure obscure relatives swapping memories about her parents, reminiscing about Chloe's antics when she was a child, and remarking on the fact that Gwen hadn't joined them. Packing stuff into boxes, nodding along when aunties and uncles and distant cousins lamented that they didn't spend enough time together, then locking herself in the bathroom to cry when the pressure had become too much.

Gwen's eyes narrowed. 'I was stuck in Fiji,' she said. 'I couldn't get a flight out in time, and *someone* wouldn't push the funeral back to wait.'

'Funerals aren't something you can just *push back*.'

'You didn't even try. It takes over a day to travel back from there. And I didn't even hear about the accident until they were . . . and I was ... in shock.' Gwen blinked rapidly, her lips pressed hard together. Chloe looked away, not wanting to broach the subject of the car crash. Not yet.

'And when I did get back to England, I ... I couldn't face it,' Gwen added, folding her arms.

Couldn't face me, Chloe didn't say. She rubbed her face, tired. It had been a long day, and she was in no mood to argue with her sister now. Half an hour ago, she hadn't even known she was in the country. 'Well, all their stuff is in boxes upstairs in the attic, if you ever feel like digging it out.' She turned and headed up the stairs. She was getting ready for bed when she heard Gwen climbing the stairs behind her. She only had one small suitcase, and it banged on every step she ascended. Chloe listened to her sighs and mutters, rubbing her forehead and hoping Gwen found another boyfriend to mooch off of soon.

Chloe's shift at the library the next day started at ten o'clock. At eight thirty she was up, sipping coffee with a plate of toast at the coffee table. Dad had made the table when she was just a child. It didn't match anything else in the living room, but nobody had minded. Even after twenty years, it was sturdy and reliable.

'Morning.' Gwen yawned as she joined Chloe in the living room, her hair somehow still gorgeous in a messy, stylish sort of way. She plopped down on the other end of the couch, wrapping her golden locks into a messy bun.

Chloe grunted in response, staring down at the coffee in her mug. She didn't bring up their conversation from the previous night, and neither did her sister, who sat looking at her phone. When the tension between them was too thick to bear, Chloe rose with her empty plate. 'I'm going to work.'

'What do you do?' Gwen asked. 'Still in marketing?'

Chloe was shocked that her sister actually knew what she did back before Mum and Dad died. 'No. There's not much demand for that here.'

The kitchen and the living room were separated by an archway rather than a door, and Chloe washed her plate as she told her sister she was working at the Wellbridge Library. 'It's just a temporary thing,' she said, drying her hands. 'Until I've saved up enough money to start again somewhere new.'

Gwen giggled, and Chloe stepped into the living room to shoot her a questioning look. Gwen was wearing tiny pyjamas, short shorts that rode almost over the tops of her thighs and a tank top that looked too cold for this chilly late autumn morning, not that Gwen had switched off the central heating last night before bed. Even when she had just rolled out of her blankets and hadn't put on any make-up, her little sister still looked stunning. She was practically a supermodel next to Chloe, who had opted for her comfortable tartan skirt and blouse-cardigan combo, her chestnut hair scooped up into a sensible, boring ponytail.

'What's funny?' Chloe asked Gwen, who still smiled, shaking her head.

'Just you.' Gwen was examining her painted toenails now. 'Chloe, working at the library. It's so . . . you. Being all bookish and boring.'

'Thanks,' Chloe said stiffly. She made to leave.

'Aw, come on. I didn't mean it like that.' Gwen slid off the couch and came to wrap her arms around Chloe from behind, squeezing her tight. Chloe stiffened at first – this was the most physical contact they'd had in years bar their hug last night – but she sighed and relaxed into the hug, reluctantly patting Gwen's hand.

'Thanks for letting me stay,' Gwen mumbled in her ear.

'Yeah, well, don't get used to it,' Chloe grumbled back. 'This is just temporary. For both of us.' This may be Gwen's house too, but surely she didn't see herself living here permanently. She hadn't been able to wait until she could leave when they were kids.

Gwen's slender arms fell from her as she went to open the bread bin on the counter. It was one of the things they hadn't thought to pack away.

'Aw, remember when we got this?' Gwen asked, looking sadly at the little wooden container. She opened it, revealing the half loaf of brown bread Chloe had bought.

'Yeah,' said Chloe softly. Mum had been delighted to find it in a charity shop, exclaiming how posh they were for owning a bread bin. The sisters exchanged small smiles before Chloe glanced away.

'We're buying white bread, by the way.' Gwen slid closed the lid.

'Buy whatever bread you want.' If it kept Gwen from pinching her food, all the better. When they were kids, they had always been at war about what kind of bread they wanted Mum and Dad to buy.

'What are you getting up to today, then?' asked Chloe. She didn't want their time together to be spent in awkward silence. It was easier to go for uncomplicated, everyday topics.

Gwen tilted her head. 'I'm not sure.'

'Maybe start looking for a job,' Chloe suggested. 'Just in case you're here for a while.'

'Like you?' Gwen asked slyly.

'I've only been here a few months. And I don't know how long I'm staying, either. Not much longer. I'm saving up.' Even if they had no mortgage or rent to pay, there were things like bills and *central heating* to pay for. Admittedly, it was great not having a chunk of rent money coming out of her small income from the library. What was the point in paying rent for a flat when the house was here for free? At least until she figured out where she wanted to go next.

'I'm going to be late,' Chloe added, checking her phone. 'See you later.'

On her way to the library, she texted Hannah, telling her everything. Hannah was one of the few people who knew why things were so strained between her and her sister.

She is SO UNGRATEFUL! Want me to come and slap her?

Chloe snorted as she crossed the road.

Nah, best not. Though it'd be funny to see.

Stay strong. She's probably finding another sugar daddy on Tinder as we speak.

Chloe agreed. Gwen liked travel and adventure and Chloe had heard she'd travelled all over the place. She had a gift for finding men to spoil her. Chloe felt a pang of envy, not for the first time. Hannah was right – Gwen would soon get bored of this little town and latch herself on to a new guy to take her away.

Far away, Chloe hoped.

She kept herself busy at the library. There were several bookshelves in the downstairs non-fiction section that had been disorganised for months, and now with the event for the children possibly coming up, everything needed to be just right. So Mrs Cook said.

Gwen's appearance had left her reeling, though there was something strangely comforting about knowing at least one member of her family was around. Even if it was one she had fallen out with. They still hadn't had the talk – the part where you sit down long after an argument and talk it out. She wasn't willing to face that yet. If they were both going to leave soon, they might not have to have the talk after all.

Chloe knelt on the carpeted floor between some large shelves, the children's section behind her. Piles of encyclopaedias and textbooks surrounded her, ready to be put on the correct shelves. She glanced around, wondering if she would see one of them glowing, whether it would work for non-fiction. With everything going on, she just wasn't ready to face the weirdest development of them all. Talking to fictional characters like they were real people – that was something else she hadn't quite worked out in her mind yet. Should she tell Mrs Cook about the strange power she had discovered? Maybe it wasn't a good idea to tell her boss something impossible like that. But she couldn't help feeling that the kindly old woman would believe her.

Still, she needed to see if she could do it again, to prove her powers. But it didn't seem like she could choose which books to use. The first had been an accident. The library chose, nudging her towards glowing books. Or maybe it was the books themselves, the characters wanting to emerge for a little while to give her titbits of wisdom.

First impressions. Believing the impossible. Chloe wasn't sure what the library would come up with next. She wasn't sure whether she was looking forward to it or dreading it.

'Chloe,' called Mrs Cook. Chloe rose, then nudged the piles of books against the shelves so they'd look a bit neater.

She went to the reception to find Mandy Jordan, the headteacher of the primary school, waiting for her. She beamed at Chloe and held out her hand to shake hers, her beady necklace clacking around her neck.

'I forgot just how lovely this place is,' said Mandy fondly, glancing around at the library walls and arched windows.

The three of them swapped ideas for the children's event, and a warm, fuzzy feeling blossomed in Chloe's chest. Mrs Cook's wrinkled face creased with delight as they talked about bringing a class, perhaps two, to the library for a bake sale, to borrow some books and study them in school, and maybe even getting a local children's author to come in for a reading.

'They could design their own library cards,' Chloe suggested. 'Get them around one of the small tables. They might appreciate them more if they designed them themselves.'

'What a lovely idea, Chloe. Have you worked with children before?'

The question made her frown. 'Erm, no. Just the odd babysitting job.'

Clementine arrived just then, perhaps curious about their visitor. He hopped onto the reception desk and gently butted Mandy's arm with his fuzzy orange head.

'Look at that. He likes you,' said Mrs Cook.

'Oh, cats are adorable. Does he live here?' Mandy petted Clementine's ears. 'This library really is something.'

Planning the event reminded Chloe of the Scholastic Book Fair. She sighed in contentment, her worries outside the library momentarily forgotten. Those days in school were the best. If they could create a similar environment, get the children excited about the library and about books, they might make a real difference here. Not only to the library's . . . *happiness*, but for the kids as well.

By the time Miss Jordan left, waving and with a huge smile on her face, Mrs Cook was practically dancing. 'Chloe, this was such a good idea. It's been too long since we had any big events.'

The lights in the library flickered, so slightly that Chloe wondered if she'd imagined it. But she saw on Mrs Cook's face the slight reservation, the fixedness of her smile, and realised that she had noticed it, too.

'Trouble with the lights?' Chloe asked, her heart sinking. It wouldn't do for there to be an electricity problem just as things were going well.

'No, no, it's not that.' Mrs Cook's mouth upturned in a coy smile as she turned to organise some files. 'I think the library is pleased with our plans, as well.'

Chloe hesitated. 'Um, when you say the library is happy, or pleased . . .'

'Yes?'

'Do you mean it metaphorically, or . . .?' She realised how daft that sounded and she backtracked. 'Never mind. That was a silly question.'

'Was it a silly question because the answer is yes or no?' asked the librarian, and wandered off before Chloe could formulate a response.

CHAPTER ELEVEN

MRS COOK ASKED Chloe to go upstairs to find some materials. 'There's a walk-in closet at the back, near the thrillers section,' she said. 'I don't know if you've been in there before. There should be some things in there we can use for the event. Posters, coloured paper, banners, things like that. I'm sure Eric will be happy to help next time he's in. If there's anything else you think we need, start a list and I can order things in.'

Chloe liked the idea of decorating the library for the children coming for the event. She ascended the spiral staircase to the upper floor, where it felt deliciously warm and cosy. Was that chestnuts and chocolate she could smell in the air instead of books and ink? She inhaled, smiling, wondering *how* . . .

Were the curtains more vibrant than before? The shelves gleaming as though freshly polished? Where had Mrs Cook found the time to spruce up this part of the library?

A sense of contentment stole over Chloe as her shoes clacked on the floor. She passed the shelves towards the back closet, more ideas formulating in her mind. It was as though, by discussing things with Mandy and Mrs Cook, the ideas had snowballed. Maybe they could attach banners all across the tops of the shelves in the children's books section. They could have one table full of books facing upward, another table for snacks and baked goods . . .

A glow caught Chloe's eye, and she took a step back, peering down the shelf. Her heart thumped.

A book was glowing.

It was happening again.

For a moment, Chloe loitered. If ever there was a chance for her to explain what was happening to Mrs Cook, this was it. But what if the book stopped glowing while she was gone? She imagined the elderly librarian, panting as she hurried to ascend the staircase with Chloe in hysterics, only for the book to be back to normal.

That would be embarrassing. She supposed she could take the book down to show Mrs Cook, but there was the risk that a visitor would overhear. A glowing book would be difficult to explain.

She considered ignoring it, but the urge to pick up the book was strong. She had already spoken to two men – two larger-than-life, attractive men who had only previously existed in a talented writer's mind.

Who would emerge this time?

Before she could stop herself, Chloe moved to the book. No, it wasn't a book, but a comic. It was on the bottom shelf, though it remained free of dust. She tugged it out and straightened, inhaling sharply as she flipped open the pages, her fingers already trembling.

Brightly coloured, vintage-style art stared back at her, the comic's story told in a dynamic, action-packed way. For a moment Chloe admired the art, having never found much time for it before.

'Chloe?' Mrs Cook called from downstairs.

Chloe swallowed her disappointment. 'Yes?'

'Are you busy, love?'

Chloe's honest answer was yes, but there was no way for her to explain it. She tucked the comic book inside her cardigan and half-ran down the stairs to see what Mrs Cook wanted.

'I quite fancy one of those coffees you brought us that time,' said the librarian, squinting at the computer screen.

'From the Brew House?' Chloe perked up. If word was spreading about Hannah and her uncle's café, that was great. 'Would you like me to go and get you one? The caramel ones are lovely.'

'I suppose I can't lose my teeth twice in a lifetime.' Mrs Cook flashed her a grin. Chloe gave a guilty chuckle; she'd had no idea the librarian's teeth were fake. 'Treat yourself, too, love. Here's a tenner.' She plucked a ten-pound note from her purse.

Chloe ran to get her bag, neatly sliding the glowing comic book into it. She would deal with that later.

Soon she was on her way to the Brew House. To her delight, Hannah was there.

'Want to upgrade to large size for fifty pence extra?' Hannah chirped.

'Best not,' said Chloe, looking longingly at the large cups. 'Mrs Cook's paying.'

Hannah had gone rigid, her face slack with shock.

'Don't move,' said a voice behind Chloe.

Chloe froze, cold fear flooding her. In her peripheral vision, the flash of a knife appeared by her side. Her insides turned to jelly, her brain numbing.

'All right, I want all the money out of the till.' The stranger's voice sounded young. A teenager, maybe younger than Eric. He also held the tremor of . . . fear? 'I've got a knife. I'll . . . I'll use it.'

Hannah still wasn't moving, her mouth opened slightly with shock. 'I . . . what?' she croaked.

'I mean it!' the boy said. 'Seriously. Give me all the money in the till, now!'

Hannah recovered, her hands trembling as she opened the till. It took her two attempts. She whimpered as she fumbled with the cash.

Chloe's bag felt warm. The comic book . . .

The boy, who was shorter than Chloe and had the hood of his jacket pulled up over his head, leaned over the counter, the knife shaking in his hand. Chloe dared take a step back, her heart breaking to see Hannah trembling, hastily dropping five-pound notes on the table.

Chloe reached into her bag, her pulse racing, her palms sweaty. She slowly slid out the comic book and opened it. She whispered a random line, praying this would work.

It was instantaneous. One moment, Hannah was fumbling with the money in the till, tears slipping down her cheeks. The next moment, a broad-shouldered man in a crisp suit and glasses was holding the teenager off the floor by the scruff of his neck, the young man yelping and kicking in fright.

'Didn't have time to change,' said the superhero. 'You are under arrest, my friend.'

'Help!' the boy yelled, flailing uselessly in the superhero's arms while Hannah gaped.

'Call the police,' Chloe mouthed to her. Coming to her senses, Hannah backed into the backroom, pulling her phone from her pocket.

'Thank you,' said Chloe in relief. The knife had clattered to the floor. It chilled her blood to look at it. 'You came just in time.'

'Truth and justice for mankind,' said the man grimly. 'Do you have any handcuffs?'

'No,' said Chloe. 'But I saw some zip ties.'

Hoping Hannah wouldn't mind her borrowing them, Chloe found the zip ties behind the counter. The superhero plonked the boy down onto a chair and, quick as a flash, had his hands tied behind his back. The boy seemed to have given up; he slumped miserably in the chair as Hannah's frantic cries to the police reached them from the backroom.

Chloe marvelled at the tall, chisel-jawed man who had come to them in their time of need. He adjusted his glasses. 'That boy won't be giving you any more trouble.'

Chloe nodded as a siren wailed in the distance. 'I was so scared.'

Looking at the boy now, he didn't look much older than a child. All of the pluckiness seemed to have left him. If she hadn't witnessed it herself, Chloe wouldn't have thought the boy capable of even trying something like that.

She still trembled, though. The sight of the knife, Hannah's sobs.

'Hannah,' said Chloe softly. The shock on her brain was wearing off. Her friend would question how the hero got here so fast. Chloe turned to the superhero. 'I need to send you back home.'

'Right. But first, I need to have a talk with the boy.' The hero took a seat opposite the slumped teenager. 'What were you thinking, son?'

The boy didn't respond. The siren was getting louder.

'Just needed the money,' the boy mumbled.

'Was it worth frightening these ladies for?' asked the man.

The boy looked away. 'No.'

'It's always best to do the right thing, even when you don't want to. It's never as bad as it seems.'

'What would you know?' the boy grunted.

A police car pulled up outside. 'It's time for you to go.' Chloe was still holding the glowing comic book. She heard movement from the backroom; Hannah was on her way back. 'Thanks again, sir.'

'Truth and justice.' He rose and came to stand before her, behind the boy.

Chloe found the last line in the comic book and read it aloud. Hannah stepped into the room just as Chloe was tucking the comic back into her bag. Hannah's eyes widened in shock at the boy sitting at the table, his wrists tied behind him, her eyes travelling from him to Chloe.

The bell above the door jangled and a police officer wandered inside. 'We got an emergency call. Is everything all right?'

There was a blur of a stammered report, questions, the knife being zipped into a bag and the shamed and slightly confused teenager being led outside by the police. Hannah rubbed her face, letting out a low breath as she collapsed onto the chair the young man had just vacated. 'That was . . .'

'Horrible,' Chloe conceded, thinking about the superhero. It was like the library had *known* what would happen, knew they would need him. She shuddered to think what might have happened if she hadn't had the comic with her. Not that the teenager seemed capable of actually hurting them, but you never knew what would happen.

'Who was that guy?' Hannah asked when she'd recovered a bit. 'He helped us.'

'Don't know,' said Chloe vaguely. Hannah didn't need to know about the library's magic. She'd had enough of a shock for one day.

'Chloe, I'm sorry, but I need to go home.'

'It's all right,' she reassured her.

Chloe shook out her trembling hands as she walked back to the library. A few people had stopped and stared while the boy was being taken away by the police, but now the street was quiet again. When Chloe pushed open the door of the library, Mrs Cook said cheerfully, 'I didn't know it took so long to make a latte.'

Chloe explained what had happened. She didn't know how to tell her about the superhero coming to their rescue, so she adjusted the story slightly to make it sound like the police showed up in time to stop him.

Mrs Cook's jovial smile turned to slack shock. 'Oh no, you poor things. How horrible. That's so unusual for this town as well.'

She gave Chloe a hug, one she hadn't realised she needed. She melted into the librarian's short yet surprisingly strong frame, shock keeping her numb as the superhero's words echoed in her mind. *It's always best to do the right thing, even when you don't want to.*

It made her think of Gwen. Chloe was the older sister. Of course, her dilemma wasn't comparable to deciding whether to rob someone, but the hero's words had resonated with her. She had to be the bigger person and do the right thing, even if it seemed difficult.

'Would you like to go home?' Mrs Cook asked.

'I think I'm all right.' Chloe felt safe here at the library, anyway. 'Only an hour until the end of my shift.'

She thanked the librarian and went to put back the comic book, which of course wasn't glowing any more. She thanked the superhero inside the pages as she carefully slid it back into place. She looked around the library's rafters, the weak sunlight shining through the gothic windows. A warm, safe feeling enveloped her. The library was taking care of her.

Chloe got a text from Gwen the next morning on the way to work.

Can we hang out tonight? I feel bad just showing up at your door.

Chloe wondered who this person was and what she had done with her sister.

Sure. I don't have any plans.

Thanks.

A pause, and Chloe watched the little grey bubble as Gwen typed.

I've missed you.

Chloe didn't know how to respond honestly, so she left her sister on read. She hadn't even seen Gwen the previous evening, both women ignoring each other and spending time in separate parts of the house.

Chloe fully expected Hannah to close up shop for the next few days, but on her way to work, the scent of coffee filled the street and there were the usual few customers inside. Supposing she'd better spend the money Mrs Cook had given her for its intended purpose, she went inside to order the caramel lattes.

'Hi, Chloe.' Hannah looked tired but managed a smile. 'I'm just serving this customer, one second.'

The man in front of her accepted the two lattes she gave him, then he turned and nearly crashed into Chloe.

'Oh good,' said Harry, sounding only a little sarcastic. 'You're here.'

'Oh. Hey.' Chloe wasn't in the mood to see Harry right now, but there was no sense in being rude. 'Wait, why is it good that I'm here?'

He held up one of the coffees. 'I had a business meeting in here the other day, and you're right, the coffee here is delicious.'

Hannah looked thrilled.

'I'm glad I bumped into you here. Saves me a trip to the library. I made the deal I was after, so take this as a thank-you.' He held out the coffee.

It took a moment to process what he had said. 'Oh. Hm. Are you sure?'

Last time they'd seen each other, they'd had an argument. *An olive branch?*

'Don't be making me drink two coffees, Chloe. I'll be buzzing all day.'

He raised his eyebrows and she huffed a reluctant laugh, taking the coffee. 'Well, thanks.' She remembered Mrs Cook. 'But I need two.'

'Jeez.' Harry rolled his eyes, handing her the other cup. 'You'll drink me out of house and home at this rate.'

Chloe spluttered, coffee in both hands now. 'Don't be daft.'

'Oh, let him buy them,' said Hannah, a look of delight on her face. 'He tips well,' she mouthed over his shoulder.

Thoroughly confused, Chloe left the café with two coffees she hadn't paid for.

Chloe was working on the computer, going through the customers' accounts. Mrs Cook had asked her to check if there were any books that hadn't been returned. It would be up to Chloe to contact them and remind them the book was due.

A list sat in front of her now. All the members had their names, and some had their phone numbers, email addresses, and mail addresses, depending on what details they had provided when they'd signed up. There was also a history of the books they had checked out.

She couldn't resist taking a peek at Alice Cook's data after quickly checking that the lobby was empty. Only Clementine hung around, wandering over the lobby desk and sniffing at the papers and stationery there.

Mrs Cook had checked out several books over the years, but only one at a time and separated by several months each. *Witching for Beginners*. *English Herbs and Their Natural Healing Properties*. And . . .

'Oh,' said Chloe softly.

The most recent book Mrs Cook had checked out of the library, just before Chloe had started working here, was *Finding Love in Your Senior Years*.

A noise startled her, but it was only Clementine knocking a pencil off the desk. Chloe clicked off the page of data and watched the cat in amusement. His amber eyes fixed on her in defiance as he pushed another pencil, letting it roll off the desk and bounce off the carpet.

Moments later, Mrs Cook walked in, giving them both a motherly smile.

Good kitty, thought Chloe and petted him.

CHAPTER TWELVE

CHLOE WAS ALREADY nervous about spending time with Gwen. Her sister was still new to town, and the thought of her sitting at home alone was strangely sad. Gwen was used to sunshine and yacht rides, not cold little English towns.

Music was playing when Chloe stepped into the house. The heating was on far too high, and she scowled, shrugging off her jacket. 'Gwen?' she called, turning down the radiator.

Gwen was in the kitchen, the music too loud for her to hear Chloe coming in. Chloe swallowed the gasp of horror that crawled up her throat. The kitchen counters were a mess. A dirty cutting board was covered with carrot and potato peel, and the counters held broken eggshells, dirty bowls and measuring cups and spoons. Free parts of the counters were covered in splashes of liquid, the sink somehow full, and even the dining table was a mess. Gwen was in the middle of it all, standing at the hob over a steaming pot, tutting to herself as pop music blasted from her phone.

'Hi,' said Chloe, and Gwen jumped.

'Oh, Chloe! I didn't even hear you come in.'

'Probably because of the . . . music.' She just stopped herself from saying 'noise'. 'Erm, what are you making?'

The contents of the pot, the largest one in the house, were a bubbling brown mess with what she supposed must be carrot and potatoes inside.

'Well, it's supposed to be stew.' Gwen stirred it with the wooden spoon. She lifted it and several thick splodges sluiced off. 'Mr Richardson gave me some potatoes he's grown in his garden. Isn't he cute? I can't believe he's still alive.'

'He wants us to call him Joe now,' said Chloe, silently apologising to Joe for the sad fate of his homegrown potatoes. 'The hob's on too high,' she added and reached to turn it down.

'Oh crap, it's burnt!' Gwen howled and started scraping the bottom of the pan. It didn't smell great, not that Chloe said anything.

The living room was reasonable, though there was a bottle of skin cream, some mascara, Gwen's phone charger, and a dirty mug on the table. The paperback Chloe was reading was on there too, half hanging off the side. She straightened it all up and then went to get changed, more than a little anxious at what Gwen had planned for the evening. Chloe felt a bit better when she had tugged off her work clothes and pulled on a cosy pair of sweatpants.

She slowly went back downstairs, thankful that Gwen had at least switched off her music. Gwen brought her a steaming bowl of . . . whatever she had made. Chloe tried to smile as she said thanks, though it probably looked like she had a toothache.

The dinner didn't taste great. Gwen put a movie on as Chloe ate in silence, wondering if Gwen had dropped the salt into the stew. And the sugar. Would it be better to gulp it down as quickly as she could, or would she succumb to poison if she did that? After choking down half, she subtly placed it on the table beside her book.

At least Gwen had brought wine. She got her glass from the table beside its bottle. Chloe wished Gwen had kept the thought of dinner to herself. She couldn't bring herself to feel grateful. The movie

Gwen had put on was her own favourite, one Chloe didn't care much for. She swirled the wine in her mouth. At least it was better than the so-called stew. Gwen sat with her knees up, her glass in her lap, engrossed in the movie.

Chloe tried watching the film, but her focus slipped as her thoughts wandered to Harry. She hoped his dinner tonight was better than this, though perhaps he had opted for a frozen tikka masala this time.

He had remembered the little detail she had told him at the pub that day. He had remembered she liked caramel lattes, had made the effort to go to the Brew House to buy her one. Maybe he wasn't all bad after all. She wondered what would have happened if he had been there during the robbery instead of her comic-book hero.

Why am I thinking about Harry?

She shifted to get more comfortable, thoughts drifting to the library again. Her special powers. The strangest mystery of all.

Who would she pull out next? Did Chloe *want* to use the power again? It had certainly come in useful at the café. She amused herself for a moment, thinking of all the book boyfriends she had encountered over the years. Or maybe she'd pull out a villain, a scary one who would attack the library, and Chloe would be the hero who . . .

'Chloe.'

She glanced over at where Gwen was sprawled on the couch. She looked annoyed. 'I just said your name twice.'

'Oh, right. I didn't hear you.' Chloe straightened. 'What's up?'

'What's up with *you*? You're all distracted.'

Chloe didn't want to tell Gwen anything. 'I'm not.'

'You are.'

'I'm not.'

'You are.'

It was like they were bickering children again. In this very living room, they had had arguments like this. Imitating each other, engaging in meaningless back and forth fights.

'You're staring off into space,' said Gwen, pausing the movie so Chloe was forced to look at her. 'What's the matter?'

Chloe sighed. 'I'm thinking about that terrific mess you made in the kitchen.'

Gwen's cheeks reddened. 'I was just trying to do something nice for you.'

Chloe didn't have the heart to tell her that Gwen had made a bowl of mud, so she said nothing, sighing as she took the remote from the couch and played the movie, crossing her arms as she looked back at the TV screen. It wasn't fair. She could be doing literally anything else right now.

'All right, tell me. What's up with you?' Gwen snatched up the remote and switched off the movie. She tossed the remote onto the coffee table, where it landed next to Chloe's book.

The noise startled Chloe. 'What?'

'You're fidgeting and thinking about something weird, I can tell.' Gwen put down her glass on the coffee table. Then she stared at Chloe with her elbows on her knees. 'What are you sulking about? Is it me? Being here in *your* house?' Gwen demanded.

Chloe laughed harshly. 'Sure, yeah, Gwen. Everything is about you.'

Her sister scowled at her. 'Out with it. What is with you today?'

'It's nothing to do with you,' Chloe fired back. 'Apart from the fact that you've used up all my food, made a huge mess in the kitchen that I'm guessing *I* will have to clean up, since you cooked.' She sneered at the sad bowl of food she had deposited on the coffee table earlier. 'If you can call that cooking.'

'I tried my best,' Gwen said.

'No, you didn't,' said Chloe. 'I know you can cook. You took food tech lessons at school, then you made Dad that lasagne, remember?'

The women glared at each other.

'If you must know,' Chloe said when the silence stretched on too long, 'I don't know why you're bothering to do all this. You never bothered to reach out before or make any effort.'

Gwen let out a loud sigh. 'That's what this is all about? You know, *you* never reached out to me, either. You're supposed to be the big sister.'

Chloe scoffed. There was only a year between them.

'I never heard anything from you all these years, Chloe. At least I'm trying. I want to know about you, or anyone you might be seeing.'

'Uh-huh. Right.' Chloe nodded mutely, snatching up her wine and taking a sip. Another awkward silence rang between them, and Chloe considered at least the background noise of the film would make this less painful. 'Switch the movie back on, if you want. I don't care.'

Gwen leaned forward to reach for the remote again, but in her anger, or clumsiness, her hand knocked her wine glass. It toppled over, spilling wine all over Chloe's book.

She let out a cry as Gwen gasped, snatching up her glass as Chloe dived for the soaked paperback. Dark red stained most of the front cover, seeping into the pages. She held it up, wine dripping onto the table.

'I'm sorry, Chloe. My hand – the wine,' Gwen babbled.

Chloe grimaced, holding the book between her forefinger and thumb as she half-ran to the kitchen for paper towels. 'Why would I want to talk to you about anyone I might be interested in?' she snarled over her shoulder. 'After last time?'

Gwen made a noise like an angry cat, and a bang from the living room sounded like she had thrown the remote control at the wall. Chloe cleaned up the book as best she could, but the damage was done; the wine had soaked into most of the pages, covering over half of it in a red stain that smelt strongly of berries.

Gwen must have stormed out of the house because she wasn't anywhere when Chloe went back into the living room. Sighing, she gathered the half-eaten mush and the wine glasses. As she grabbed a bin bag for the food waste, Chloe wondered if Gwen really had done all this to be spiteful, or if it was just a clumsy, failed attempt at peace. At an apology.

As Chloe cleaned the kitchen, marvelling at how a stew could have taken so many pots and pans, anger gave way to a prodding sense of guilt. It had been cruel for Chloe to mock her cooking, and to bring up something that had happened so many years ago. Even if it still hurt. Even if Gwen still hadn't said she was sorry.

CHAPTER THIRTEEN

CHLOE WOKE UP late the next day, her short snippets of sleep plagued by strange dreams of endless, polished corridors and of Clementine, his feline head as big as a horse's. She rolled onto her back, looking at the white ceiling where some plastic glow-in-the-dark stars were still stuck from when she was a kid. Birds chirped and an occasional car passed.

She couldn't hear any noise in the house, none of Gwen's music or her moving around in the other rooms. She must still be asleep.

Chloe had managed to live alone for just a few short weeks before her sister had barged back into her life. She had no doubt Gwen had chosen this place because she knew there was no rent to pay. She probably assumed Chloe would pay the bills, too. After all, she had been mooching off people her whole life.

At least Chloe had cleaned the kitchen before going to bed, though she had missed the edges of a counter, the weird food her sister had made now hard and crusting. Chloe wiped it up then put the kettle on, a dull pounding in her head warning her of a coming migraine. She rubbed the bridge of her nose, wondering if she should wake Gwen up and try to patch things up before she went to work.

No, she knew from experience that prodding Gwen awake wouldn't be the prelude to a calm, productive interaction.

As she left the house fifteen minutes before her shift at the library was to begin, Chloe still felt annoyed. She had wasted the evening arguing with Gwen when her night could have been so much better. What would be waiting for her at home that evening? Would half the house be gone, blown up by a plumbing malfunction or something?

'Cheer up, Chloe! It might never happen!' called Joe from his front garden.

Chloe forced a laugh and waved to him before she thrust her hands into her pockets as brown leaves blew past her ankles. It was a dreary, grey day, matching her mood. Maybe Gwen had packed up her meagre belongings and left in the night, not that she had anywhere to go. *Good*, she thought. *Good riddance.*

At that thought, something pricked in her, though. She was glad to enter the doors of the library, and tried to leave her annoyance behind. It had just started to rain, and her hair was beaded with droplets as she slipped inside.

Eric was working today. 'Hi, Chloe!' He waved so enthusiastically he almost toppled off his stool. 'How are you? Would you like some coffee?'

'I would actually, Eric,' she said, taking off her jacket. 'Thanks.'

When Eric had dashed into the kitchen area, Chloe asked Mrs Cook, 'How is the library so warm? I haven't seen any radiators.' No fireplaces, either, though a real functioning one might be risky for the books. 'I could feel the temperature change when I came in.'

Mrs Cook made a 'hmm' sound. 'I think the library is in a good mood today. Just last night it smelt of cinnamon in here. Cinnamon!' She chuckled, and Chloe giggled back nervously, unsure whether Mrs Cook was pulling her leg. Surely the library hadn't conjured heat and scents on its own. But hadn't Chloe smelt something delicious the other day up on the fiction floor? She had assumed it was a nearby bakery, but maybe not. And had she not also experienced a strange kind of . . . well, Chloe didn't believe in magic. Not until recently, anyway.

'Is there something you're thinking about, love?' Mrs Cook looked amused as she tilted her head, her warm green eyes crinkling. 'You've got a far-off look in your eyes. It's the look my son has when he's come up with a new story idea.'

'Your son is a writer?' Chloe asked in surprise, snapping out of her strange thoughts.

'He dabbles, here and there. His stories are quite good, though he's never tried to publish them.'

Eric came back with coffees for them all, and they sipped companionably until a customer came in, a middle-aged woman who offered them all a slightly surprised smile, maybe astonished to see so many people behind the counter at once.

'Good morning,' Mrs Cook greeted her warmly. 'Are you looking for anything in particular, or are you just browsing?'

'Hm? Oh, I actually . . .' The woman blushed furiously. 'I was just coming in to escape the rain while I waited for the bus, to be honest.' She looked around. 'But I'll definitely have a look around. I'll just . . .' She trailed off, then headed in what Chloe was sure was a random direction.

Chloe thought she felt something. Something like a ripple in the air. A sigh, almost.

'I know, I know,' said Mrs Cook reassuringly. 'I can't wait for this event with the children. It's going to be so good for us.'

Is she talking to me? wondered Chloe, taking another sip of the coffee Eric had made for her. He hadn't added enough milk for her liking, but she didn't mind. *Or is she talking to the library?*

The visitor quickly left for her bus without borrowing any books. When she had finished her usual tasks and found herself free, Chloe drifted upstairs to do some dusting. Just past the spiral staircase, above a shelf of mystery books, she spotted water dripping from the ceiling. She stepped forward and saw that there was a leak.

'Mrs Cook!' she called. 'There's a leak in the roof.'

The increasing rain outside meant the dripping was quickly turning into a steady stream. A few minutes later, Eric stood with his hands on his hips, squinting up at the ceiling. The rain drummed on the roof and the arched windows, and the water spilled onto a book-case. 'That's unfortunate,' he remarked.

'I hadn't noticed that leak before.' Mrs Cook looked up. 'My eyes aren't very good.'

'I hadn't noticed it until now, either,' Chloe assured her. 'Maybe it only happened last night.'

'Eric, could you fetch a bucket from the staff room?' the librarian asked.

Eric arrived with a steel bucket. He was tall enough to just about reach the top of the bookcase, and he placed it under the leak. Then he let out a disappointed groan. 'It's ruined some of the books.'

They rushed over to see. Almost the entire top shelf and most of the second shelf had suffered water damage. Emotion welled up in Chloe's chest and she sniffled. She knew it was silly to be upset over damaged books, but she couldn't help feeling that she should have acted sooner.

'Help me shift the shelf, please, Eric,' said Mrs Cook.

Even with their combined efforts, the large bookshelf proved too heavy to move on its own, and so they began the painstaking task of removing all the books. Eric said Mrs Cook should wait in the reception area for customers while they separated the damaged books from the unharmed ones. Clementine appeared, meowing softly at them and sitting with his tail wrapped around his paws, regarding them with large eyes.

Chloe wanted to cry as she deposited the soggy books into a black bin bag. There were some wonderful classics here that would never be read again. It made her think of her own paperback book, the only one she currently owned, ruined with wine. It wasn't a good week for books. All the while, the steel bucket plinked with the leak. It rained hard outside, and soon Eric had to put a mug underneath while he rushed to the bathroom to empty the bucket.

Chloe talked to Eric as they worked, feeling a little silly for get-ting emotional over a bunch of books. She learned that he loved football, and he read a lot in his spare time. 'What about you, Chloe?' he asked. 'Do you, er, have any pets?'

She wondered if Mrs Cook had filled him in on Chloe losing her parents and that was why he hadn't asked about her family. She silently thanked her and said, 'I wouldn't mind a cat.' Clementine walked by, his tail curling briefly around Eric's arm as he passed. 'But I don't know how long I'm staying here. It seems pointless to get a pet when I might be moving soon.' To where, she still didn't know. But she had to start making plans. Sometimes the opportunity to do the things you wanted to do slipped away from you if you didn't seize the day and make them happen.

Even if a small part of her protested at the thought of leaving the library behind.

'I hope you don't go,' said Eric in a small voice, making Chloe smile.

'I'll take over for a bit, if you like, Eric,' said Mrs Cook, appearing at the top of the stairs. 'You keep putting books into the system for me. I can't make sense of that screen.'

Chloe waved goodbye to Eric as Mrs Cook settled at her side. They worked in silence for a few moments.

Before she could think too deeply about it, Chloe said to Mrs Cook, 'So this library, it's quite special, isn't it?'

'Oh yes, I like to think so.' Mrs Cook inspected a book, opening it and letting the pages flip between her fingers, checking no water had seeped into them. 'It's definitely one of the most beautiful in England.'

'It is.' Chloe felt an urge, a pressing nudge, to tell Mrs Cook what she had experienced here. 'What did you mean when you said the library is happy? That it makes its own scents and heats the room?'

'Exactly as it sounded,' said the older woman. 'This library, Chloe. It's like you said. It's *special*. I knew when I met you that your love for books and reading would make you a good match for this place. And I was right, wasn't I?'

'I found something. In a book,' Chloe blurted. She felt so alone right now, and she wanted to tell someone. To have somebody here at the library she could share her secret with. She had the feeling the librarian wouldn't laugh at her, even if she didn't believe what she was about to say. Chloe turned to face Mrs Cook, shifting on her knees. 'Not long after I started working here, I picked up a book. It was, um, glowing. I read a line out loud and . . .' She told Mrs Cook everything, even about the dratted date that had led her to seek refuge in the library late at night; pulling a nineteenth-century nobleman from a book, having a conversation with him, talking about first impressions. Doing it two more times, both times with a book character she knew and loved, brought to life and sent home when she read out their final line.

The librarian's expression was unreadable the whole time, and Chloe was worried that she had overstepped, that Mrs Cook would just be left confused or angry. Then the elderly woman chuckled. She laughed louder, hugging the book she was holding to her chest. Her chortles were full of such delight that Chloe just stared at her.

'Oh, Chloe, thank goodness. You finally worked it out.'

CHAPTER FOURTEEN

'WHAT?' CHLOE'S JAW dropped open in surprise.

Mrs Cook let out another chuckle that became a delighted giggle that made her seem suddenly years younger. She gestured around them. 'The library and its magic. Being able to meet characters from the books. I'm so pleased you can do it, too, and that you've finally realised it's not all in your head. It took the last woman who worked here six months to tell me.'

Chloe was stunned. 'You mean . . . it's not only . . .?' She flushed, not wanting to give voice to the words. She had assumed it was only her who could do it, that she had some kind of powers that had manifested on their own. 'Anyone here can pull out characters?'

'Well, it's different for everybody.' The librarian shifted towards her, setting the book she was holding fondly on the pile of undamaged tomes. The rain was letting up outside now, though the roof still dripped. 'And it doesn't work for everyone. The library chooses, Chloe – it knows how much you love books, how much you care for the stories all around us.'

Chloe thought back to the box of tissues when she sneezed, the occasional sigh of warmth she felt or the scent of chocolate and cinnamon. 'It's a magical library,' she said, feeling a rush of excitement.

It felt like a secret between her and Mrs Cook. A wonderful, delicious secret. Some of the tension, the part of her that she had kept to herself until now, loosened in her shoulders.

'Who have you met?' asked Mrs Cook with enthusiasm. 'Who came out to visit you?'

Chloe told her of the three men she had pulled out, one by accident in the middle of the night, one on purpose, and the third who had helped them at the café. 'Oh! But that day in the café, when that boy tried to rob it. Um, the reason nothing bad happened is because I pulled out someone who helped.' She told Mrs Cook about the superhero dispatching the would-be robber before things could get out of hand, and about sending him back without anyone noticing. 'I don't think Hannah – that's the café's manager – knows. She was in the backroom when I sent him home.' Chloe fidgeted. 'Is that a problem?'

'It sounds like the right book was with you at the perfect time, Chloe. I wouldn't call that a problem.'

Nearby, the curtains fluttered as though in agreement.

'So it only works for some people?' Chloe asked. 'I suppose the library would be quite famous if it happened to everyone who came here.'

'As far as I know, it's only for people who love books enough to work here,' said Mrs Cook. 'And even then, it hasn't worked for everybody. Only a few employees like you have confessed it to me, and it doesn't seem to have worked for Eric.'

'What hasn't worked?' The younger boy reappeared behind them, carrying a tray of tea and custard creams.

'Oh, you are a star.' Mrs Cook plucked a biscuit from the plate. Chloe copied her. 'We were talking about the magic in the library, and Chloe meeting some characters.'

Chloe almost choked on her biscuit. 'Eric knows, too?'

'He was there when I was on a stepladder, trying to get a book on a higher shelf. The library pushed the book closer to my hand so I could grab it. It was either tell him the truth or try to convince him he had hallucinated. And that would have been mean.'

'I haven't seen a book glow,' said Eric sadly. 'Nor pulled out any characters. I wish it would happen for me. I'm glad it's happened for you, though, Chloe.' Eric perked up. 'Mrs Cook asked me not to say anything to you. She said you had to experience it for yourself.'

'If you could pull a character out of any book, who would it be?' Chloe asked him. She didn't know if Eric actually liked to read books or he simply worked here for the money, though earlier he had said he liked reading. Eric seemed to think hard about it, nibbling at the corner of his biscuit like a child. 'Maybe I'd like to meet Arwen or Galadriel from *The Lord of the Rings*. Or Storm.'

'Storm?' asked Mrs Cook.

'You know, from the Marvel *X-Men* comics.'

'So, good-looking female characters.' Chloe laughed, and the tips of Eric's ears turned red.

'Well, how about you?' he asked. 'What's your type?'

Chloe dodged the question by asking, 'Tell me more about yourself, Eric. What do you want to do after sixth form?'

She already knew he was finishing his A-Levels and came to work here on his days off, mostly Saturdays and the occasional morning or afternoon he didn't have lessons. 'I'd love to go to university and study English literature, though my dad thinks it's a waste of time. He'd rather I went straight into a trade, like plumbing or electrical work. Says there's no point in university these days, and most degrees are useless anyway.' He held up a book, inspecting it. Satisfied it hadn't been damaged, he placed it carefully on the pile of undamaged books, which was admittedly much larger than the collection of wet ones. 'Though I'd like to experience university life, too. The degree is just a bonus, really.'

'Speaking of trade work,' Chloe murmured, glancing at the leak. 'We should probably ring someone to come and fix the roof.'

Her heart felt lighter now she had shared her secret with the others, and relieved that they knew about it as well. With Mrs Cook's agreement, Chloe googled the nearest construction companies and found one called Ashcroft Construction.

A crisp female voice answered, and Chloe explained the library roof needed fixing as soon as possible. The woman promised to send someone over that afternoon. Relieved, they finished separating the damaged books and decided to check the bookshelf wood tomorrow to see if there was any permanent damage. At least the rain had stopped, and now the worrying flow had reduced to a dribble.

As Chloe worked, her thoughts strayed to her sister. She wondered if she should call to check up on her, but Chloe, aside from being a bit harsh, hadn't really done anything wrong. Gwen's clumsy attempt at making dinner had only ended in them fighting. Gwen should be the one to apologise first for disturbing her evening, destroying her kitchen and ruining her book.

Chloe snorted. Like *that* would ever happen.

'Bless you,' said Mrs Cook.

The doors opened later, and Chloe called over her shoulder, 'Sorry, the top floor is closed today, but you're welcome to explore the ground floor.'

'Chloe.'

She turned in surprise to see Harry. He held up a toolbox. 'Someone told me you have a leaky roof?'

She stared at him. 'You're a construction worker?'

'Aye, the last time I checked.'

'No.' She shook her head. 'I rang Ashcroft Construction.'

'Yes, that's me. Harry Ashcroft.'

Chloe felt her face was on fire. She'd had no idea that Harry owned Ashcroft Construction. 'Through here.' She tried not to look too agitated as she left Eric in the reception lobby and led Harry upstairs. Clementine was on top of the bookshelf, trying to drink from the bucket. Chloe pointed. 'The leak is up there.'

'Right. I'll need to inspect it,' said Harry. 'Could you give me some time?'

All too happy to escape, Chloe nodded and retrieved the cat. Clementine meowed in annoyance, displeased, but she took him downstairs and gave him some fresh water in his bowl. What were the chances it was Harry's company she had rung this morning? She dearly hoped he didn't think that was intentional.

When she stepped out, she saw a woman and a little girl heading for the children's section. She gasped in delight and rushed to them. It wouldn't do to shout in the library, after all.

'Hi, Hannah,' she said, poking her friend gently in her back.

'Chloe!' said Hannah happily. 'I'm so glad you're working today, I hoped I'd be able to see you. This is my daughter, Lily.'

The three-year-old had her mother's hazel eyes and a curtain of dark brown hair. She waved shyly at Chloe, half-hiding behind her mum's leg. 'Hi, Lily.' Chloe knelt, seeing so much of her best friend in her daughter. 'Nice to meet you. Do you like books?'

Lily glanced at her mother, then gave a non-committal shrug.

'Of course you do.' Hannah looked a little embarrassed. 'She's just a bit shy, Chloe.'

Clementine wandered in just then, licking his chops. He meowed softly.

'Oh, a cat!' exclaimed Lily, pointing. Clementine ignored her, trotting off.

Chloe laughed. 'He's a grumpy boy, but he's lovely once you get to know him. Would you like me to find you some books about cats?'

Lily nodded and took her hand, and they played in the soft play area for a while. Books about cats seemed abundant on the children's bookshelf all of a sudden, and Chloe glanced upwards at the rafters and the arched windows, silently wondering if the library was giving them what they needed.

'And you can take some of these home with you, if you like. It's free,' said Chloe, after they had finished reading some of them. Hannah wasn't wrong, Lily was a shy girl, but she managed to coax a few words from her and even a peal of laughter when they read a funny story about a naughty kitten.

'This was fun,' said Hannah later. 'It's so nice to have somewhere to bring her that's, um,' she lowered her voice as though embarrassed, 'free. And dry when it rains. Plus, I needed a break from the café, you know.' She raised her eyebrows and Chloe gave a sage nod.

'This is exactly what a library is for,' said Chloe sincerely.

'Can we come again sometime?' Lily asked.

Chloe put her hand on her chest. 'Oh my gosh, she is just adorable.'

'Of course we can,' Hannah promised. 'Now, which of these books would you like to take home?'

Chloe was glad to be distracted by Hannah and her daughter. She was trying not to think about Harry up on the second floor, in *her* space, and the fact she had no one to blame for that but herself.

She wasn't sure why she was getting so rattled. She imagined Gwen laughing at her, teasing her for thinking about a guy she was supposed to despise.

Gwen. She still hadn't heard from her sister. She wasn't even sure Gwen had come home after storming out last night, and it had been raining most of the day. Should she text her?

Chloe was heading towards her bag to grab her phone when she stopped herself. Even if Gwen had been out all night, Wellbridge wasn't a dangerous town. She was likely sulking at home. Hopefully she wouldn't take her aggro out on the kitchen again.

A knock sounded on the kitchen door and Harry appeared. 'Hi, Chloe. Well, I'll need to bring in a couple of guys to fix the roof. I've roped off the area, though I've made sure there's still a path to the fiction section for people who need it. We can come by first thing in the morning, if that's okay?'

'Erm. Yeah, that's fine.' She wondered why he was telling her and not Mrs Cook. 'Shall we let the librarian know?'

'Actually, Chloe, now I've got you on your own, I'd like to tell you something.'

'Oh. All right.' She closed the staff room door. Now they were alone with the humming fridge. She leaned against the wall, folding her arms. 'What is it?'

Harry looked suddenly sheepish. He deposited his toolbox on the table. 'We got off on the wrong foot,' he said. 'When we first met, I was short with you. I know I've annoyed you a couple of times, and that time in the pub . . . I wanted to apologise.'

Chloe shifted, not trusting herself to speak.

He fidgeted. 'It's not really an excuse, but I'm a widower. My wife passed away two years ago, and I suppose I've been a bit of a nightmare to be around ever since.'

Chloe's feet felt cemented to the floor. 'Oh. That's . . . I'm so sorry,' she said finally.

His grumpiness made some sense to her now. Hadn't she been grouchy with Gwen, the grief sometimes rising to terrorise her at moments she didn't expect?

'Sorry,' he said. 'My wife and I used to visit that pub all the time, and last time she sat where you were sitting. You weren't to know, but some of the words you said to your friend upset me, I suppose, and I kicked off.'

Chloe's chest felt cold as she recalled laughing with Hannah. *Just kill me . . . I'd rather die . . .*

'I'm so sorry, I had no idea.' Chloe held her face, feeling her cheeks burn.

'Please don't be embarrassed. You weren't to know.' He offered her a small smile. 'I wasn't too delightful the first time I visited the library, either. I recall I insulted a book you liked?'

Despite herself, Chloe smirked. 'Yeah, you said the writing was juvenile. That's okay, it's not everybody's cup of tea.' Her smile faded. What an awful thing, to lose your wife so young, to be surrounded by memories of her. Chloe couldn't imagine. The thought of the man's grief mirroring her own grief for her parents came unbidden, and she found her throat was suddenly tight. 'I'm sorry, too,' she said, when the silence stretched too far for her liking. 'The chicken and chips were delicious.'

He laughed. It was the first time she'd heard him laugh. 'Well, Chloe, thanks for accepting my apology. I haven't always been a grumpy old sod, I promise. And I'll try not to be, from now on.'

She felt a loosening in her chest. Harry seemed smaller, somehow. It couldn't have been easy to say sorry, to tell her something so personal. 'Come on,' she said. 'Let's go and let Mrs Cook know about the roof.'

They went together. Harry gave her a smile on his way out, and something warm blossomed in her stomach.

Now the roof situation was under control, Chloe thought about her sister. She still hadn't heard from her. But then again, why did she care so much? It wasn't like she was going to be staying in Wellbridge for long. Another few months until she'd saved up to move near a city, and that was it. The pay here wasn't all that great, even if she did enjoy working here. Even if the library was one of a kind, and had welcomed her as one of its own by showing her its magic.

Was it her imagination, or did the library seem a little subdued now that Harry had left? She couldn't see it so much as feel it, like how the atmosphere felt different between a party and a church.

As she found herself alone in the lobby, she thought about him. How annoying he had been, how grumpy and standoffish. But hadn't Chloe herself been unpleasant to be around soon after losing her parents? They were both grieving. Both dealing with it in different ways.

She thought back to their interactions. He and his wife had gone to that pub together, and Chloe had unknowingly stirred up some painful memories. Also, if she was being completely honest, she hadn't exactly been the best company, either.

'Looks like we both made a bad first impression.' She wasn't sure why she'd said that aloud, but it all made sense to her at once. She was talking to the library, of course.

Something rippled in the air. *First impressions.*

Chloe and Eric inspected the upper floor. Harry had indeed roped off the leaky area, though now the water was only coming in the occasional drip. 'I'll have to empty the bucket right before I go home,' Chloe said. 'And hope it doesn't rain in the night.'

'I checked the weather forecast earlier,' Eric assured her. 'It's going to be a dry night.'

They put down some tarp, just in case, and agreed that was the best they could do until tomorrow. Tomorrow, when she would see Harry again.

She wasn't sure why, but the thought was a pleasant one.

'Hey, Chloe?'

Chloe stopped at the top of the stairs, glancing back to where Eric stood, his hands in his pockets as he looked sheepish. 'Yeah?'

'I . . .' Eric cleared his throat, his Adam's apple bobbing. 'Nothing, never mind.'

'If you're sure.' She returned his smile and headed down the spiral staircase. The stairs were so familiar to her now, it was like going down the stairs in her own house. She knew the third one creaked, that the polished banister had a slight chip in it right before the bottom. She wanted to know every corner and shadow of this library, to see what else this amazing building could do.

But that would take years. Time she didn't have.

Oh, well. She would have to enjoy herself while she was here, until she sailed towards her next horizon.

Mrs Cook asked Chloe to close the library for the evening, and Eric left at four o'clock. Chloe put out food for the cat and switched off the upstairs lights. She emptied the bucket and placed it back under the leak, watching as the occasional drip plinked into the metal container. She couldn't resist scanning the shelves in the fiction section, secretly hoping that she'd find a glowing book . . . but they all sat there, innocently dim and unremarkable.

She replayed Harry's confession in her mind. Him looking abashed as he apologised. The way his large chest moved as he'd laughed. How dark his eyes were in contrast to his light hair.

How the library seemed to miss him.

She recalled Mrs Cook talking to herself. At first she had assumed it was because she was elderly, but maybe she hadn't been muttering alone. Perhaps she had been talking to the library.

Feeling a bit silly, Chloe cleared her throat and said, 'Hi, um, library. I'm sorry your roof is leaking. It's going to get fixed tomorrow. By people who work for Harry. You like him, don't you?'

Nearby, the curtains fluttered in response, making a grin slowly spread on Chloe's face. The windows were closed, so there was no breeze to cause the curtains to move, but it didn't scare her. It made her feel reassured. She wandered up the corridor back towards the leak, where she watched the water drip down. Every ten seconds or so, a fat droplet would drip into the bucket with a soft plink.

'We have to keep you in top shape,' she said. 'We've got an event coming up soon. Lots of kids reading children's books, like Lily did.'

The library seemed to shiver with delight, a rush of warmth washing over Chloe. It ruffled her hair, making her laugh. 'I'm looking forward to it, too.'

She double-checked the reception desk was clean and tidy, and spotted something on the desk. A folded piece of paper.

Huffing, Chloe picked it up. It was identical to the note she had found before, a torn page of notebook paper folded in half. She opened it.

I like you.

Chloe read it again, the three simple words written on the page in thin, elegant writing.

She had brushed them off as forgotten rubbish before, but . . . was someone leaving her notes?

How childish, she thought. She slipped it into her pocket, wondering if it was Harry who was leaving the notes, if it was some kind of joke.

After switching off all the lights, giving Clementine one last scratch behind his ears and locking up the library, Chloe remembered she didn't have anything to read tonight. Not unless she was going to try to decipher the text among the wine stains in her book.

There weren't any books in her parents' house. She had an e-reader, but it wasn't the same as holding a paperback. She would have to rectify that.

No. What was the point in starting a collection if she was leaving soon? She had to stop thinking of this arrangement, her staying at Mum and Dad's, like it was permanent. She should sell the house and use the money to get a nice place by a city where she could start a new career. There wasn't anything to keep her in this town.

Not even a job that she was starting to love.

CHAPTER FIFTEEN

CHLOE LOOKED UP at the stars in the sky, only a few clouds drifting by. It indeed looked like it was going to be a dry night. She picked up a frozen meal from the supermarket, hesitated, then bought one for Gwen as well. It seemed mean to ignore her.

When she entered her home, the scent of cinnamon hit her. 'Gwen?' she called, hearing music. Her stomach dropped. If her sister had destroyed the kitchen again . . .

'In here,' Gwen called. Chloe stepped into the kitchen.

It was clean, only a glass mixing bowl and spoon in the sink. 'I made cinnamon rolls,' said Gwen, pulling off some oven mitts. 'I didn't know what time you'd be back, but I think I timed it quite well.'

'Ah. Did they . . . uh, turn out okay?' Chloe pulled off her jacket and draped it over the chair at the dining room table. A tray sat on it, covered with a clean tea towel.

'I think they did.' Gwen was wearing a simple dress, her blonde hair straightened. It glimmered in the kitchen light.

'I bought dinner.' Chloe held up her shopping bag. 'Though maybe you've eaten already?'

Gwen hadn't, so they ate together. Though they were being polite to each other, there was still a strained silence between them. Chloe tried to think of something to say. With people like Hannah, topics came up with ease and you could chat for hours. But with Gwen, who daintily ate her steaming food while staring at the wall, Chloe struggled to find *anything* to talk about.

She supposed years of bitterness couldn't be cured with cinnamon rolls and frozen lasagne.

'This is so much better than the Brown Slop of Doom I made yesterday,' Gwen remarked, holding up a forkful of instant lasagne.

Chloe smirked. 'I wasn't going to say anything.'

It was almost annoying how beautiful the cinnamon rolls had turned out. 'Where did you learn to bake these?' Chloe asked around a huge mouthful. The dough was perfectly set, the result light and fluffy with a hint of sweetness. She and Hannah could compare notes.

She supposed her sister would say she'd learnt to bake in France or Austria or something, but Gwen held up her phone. 'Good old Google.'

They washed up together as well, Chloe washing and Gwen drying, like when they were teenagers. Some days they would laugh and chatter. But those felt like centuries ago. The evenings that stood out most in Chloe's mind right now were the ones when they'd bickered. Chloe would purposely put soapy dishes on the rack to annoy Gwen. Gwen would declare that she would wait until they were dry and make herself a cup of tea while Chloe glared at her, elbow deep in soapy water.

Soon the dishes were dried and put away, the remaining cinnamon rolls in a Tupperware box in the fridge. 'Chloe . . .' said Gwen, fidgeting. 'I got you something.'

She ran to her room, soon returning with a box tied with ribbon. Her brow furrowing, Chloe took the box, which felt heavy in her hands, and opened it while Gwen leaned against the kitchen counter, watching. Inside was a book. Chloe took it out, her throat feeling suddenly tight.

'It's the one I spilled wine over,' Gwen said softly as Chloe turned it over in her hands. It was the same edition, except it was new and unblemished, the lettering on the front cover reflecting in gold, its spine unbroken and the cream pages free of wine stains.

She was . . . touched. This wasn't like Gwen at all. Something warm and uncomfortable spread in Chloe's chest. 'Aw, Gwen.' She was shocked to feel tears well up. 'This is . . . Thank you.'

'Another cinnamon roll?' asked Gwen.

Chloe gave a reluctant grin. 'Go on then.'

They ended up polishing off the lot, and Chloe was uncomfortably full by the time they collapsed on the sofa in the living room.

'Those were delicious. You may have found your calling.'

'Thanks.'

Both of them leaned back on the couch. Chloe turned her head to look at her sister, to really look at her. Unfiltered, natural. Up close, she could see the stress lines in her sister's make-up-free face, the dark shadows beneath her eyes.

Then something occurred to her. 'Gwen, how did you pay for this book? And all the baking ingredients? You said you were broke.'

Gwen winced, then gave a sheepish laugh. 'Ah, yeah. I was hoping it wouldn't come up this early.' She pulled a plastic card from her pocket and handed it to Chloe. 'I kind of took your debit card out of your wallet while you were asleep. But I'll pay you back!' she shouted when Chloe opened her mouth. 'I promise. Once I get a job. And I made sure you had cash to pay for stuff before I took it.'

Maybe if it had been a lone occurrence, this wouldn't have bothered her. But the stress of the day, this house, *her sister*, made rage build inside her.

Chloe held the plastic between her fingers. 'You stole this from me?'

'Borrowed,' Gwen quickly said. 'To do something nice for you, you know. I promise to pay you back once I have an income.'

'Are you *kidding* me?'

It took Chloe a moment to realise she had shouted. Gwen flinched from her, her blue eyes narrowing. 'What is the big deal?'

'You can't just take people's stuff, people's money, and expect them not to be angry about it!' Chloe sighed, massaging the bridge of her nose. More anger tingled on her skin, threatening to burst out of her. Instead, she rose from the couch. 'I'm going to bed.'

'Please don't be annoyed.' Gwen almost sounded pleading. 'That's all I bought.'

'It doesn't matter. It's disrespectful. You don't just help yourself to what's mine.'

Gwen's face hardened. 'I see.'

'Good.' Chloe slammed the living room door behind her.

The cinnamon rolls churned in her stomach.

Clementine relaxed on the windowsill cushion in the upper archives, one of his favourite spots. His tail twitched left and right as he watched humans walk around outside. They all had their little tasks and quirky behaviours he didn't quite understand. He knew what a smile meant, knew that salty drops of water came from their eyes when they were sad. He had found a book left open once, one for children about emotions, and he had studied it intensely to better understand people. They had better appreciate his efforts. Clementine was a busy cat, with cat responsibilities, and he had put them aside to study this fascinating species.

He stretched, kneading the soft material of the cushion, and watched a woman walk her dog until she disappeared around a corner. Then he leaped from his windowsill to begin his nightly patrol of the library. What this place would do without him, he didn't know.

His bell jangled as he went down the spiral staircase, his paws silent on the wood. He thought he heard something creak as he went, and he glanced at the silent bookshelves around him. All was well here.

Maybe Mrs Cook had left a treat for him before she'd left. She did that sometimes. Clementine's paws pattered on the lobby carpet as he headed towards the kitchen.

He stopped in his tracks.

A cat was already there, licking her paw as she glanced up at him. Clementine sat, enraptured. She was a chubby thing, with grey and black tabby stripes. Her eyes, brown and yellow, looked at him as she stood on all four of her paws, her tail straight up.

She was the most beautiful creature he had ever seen. Clementine found himself stiffen, any question of who she was and how she had gotten here somehow fleeing his mind.

Come now, Clementine, he chastised himself. He was not an adolescent kitten laying eyes on a female for the first time. Clementine straightened, showing off his long, orange-furred legs, regarding her with quiet interest.

She trotted past him, past the main doors and towards the west wing. Clementine huffed. She had not even greeted him. In his own house, by God.

He followed the tabby cat, watching her enchanting tail swish left and right. Her feet were all white, matching the snowy fur on her chest. Clementine's bell jangled as he sped up, surprised at how fast she could go.

He found her standing in the middle of the children's section, licking her paws. He stopped and leaped on top of the kids' bookshelf, regarding her with curiosity. This was the first time he had ever seen another cat in here.

She looked at him again and his heart melted. Why, she was enchanting. Truly.

Clementine groomed himself, conscious of the tuft of orange hair that always stuck up on his back. He ran through possible behaviours: he could get the ball from the kitchen, or chase her around, or simply straighten himself and let her take in the beauty of his fiery coat.

He opted for the latter, jumping onto the soft play area before her. The female watched with interest as he stretched, taking up as much space as he could with his legs and tail. Then he ignored her, grooming himself again.

The female stepped towards him with a soft meow. Her eyes were like lamps, reflecting the bookshelves around them and sparkling like a thousand stars. Clementine watched her, his little heart racing. He stuck his behind in the air, tail swishing, inviting her to play.

With a delighted meow, the tabby female raced off. Clementine streaked after her, his bell jangling, pleasure washing through him.

He chased her around the library, across beams and the tops of bookshelves. When he caught her, they rolled around, their elated meows echoing around the archives. Then she chased him, following his jangling bell. Sometimes the female would sit, vacantly staring at the wall as though she had forgotten what they were doing. But Clementine would sneak up behind her and playfully tap her back.

What an angel, Clementine thought. He couldn't remember ever being this happy. Not with another cat, anyway. Memories of his time before he came to this library were a blur, but he was certain it wasn't a good place. Where he was and who he was with now, though, this was happiness.

They played for hours, long after the sun had risen, and Clementine was happily licking her neck, ensuring her lovely tabby fur was clean, when a book fell open in front of him.

Clementine approached it, curious. The female followed him, sitting on her large behind as she watched, probably wondering why he had stopped cleaning her.

The book had cartoonish pictures of a cat, one of her staring at an empty bowl, another with her leg in the air, staring vacantly into the distance. There was no doubt about it; it was the same cat that sat next to him, tilting her head as she watched him with interest.

Clementine should have known such a beautiful female, a queen of the felines, would be from a story. As he watched, the page turned. The scent of something washed over Clementine. Not a scent he knew, but one that doubtlessly belonged to humans.

'Meow,' said the female.

Clementine looked at her, reluctant. She couldn't go back. Hadn't they had such a wonderful time together tonight? Wasn't she going to stay?

He butted his head against her white chest, purring against her fur. He would convince her to stay. It was nice having another cat around. He still needed to show her the garden, the upper archives, show her how to walk along the beams upstairs so they could watch the humans together.

The female's white paws softly touched the book. It was on the last page now, the paper version of the cat staring up at him. Clementine shifted on his paws, his tail thumping the floor. It wasn't fair. He had not asked for this.

The tabby licked his cheek, her whiskers tickling his nose. Clementine backed away and leaped back up onto the bookshelf. Well, if she was ready to leave him, he wouldn't stop her. A true gentleman let their woman be happy, even if it meant not getting what he wanted.

He settled onto the shelf, not looking at her, and rested his head on his paws. He wondered if salty water would come from his eyes, too.

A warm sigh ruffled his fur. The book had closed, and it was no longer glowing.

Clementine went back to his cushion on the windowsill, tired as he watched the moon shining through the clouds. He kneaded the squashy cushion, comforted by the thick curtains hiding his presence. He hoped none of the humans would come and disturb him up here. At least not for a while.

CHAPTER SIXTEEN

WORKERS ARRIVED AT the library the next morning, as Harry had promised, to start working on the leaky roof on the second floor. Men with tools and hard hats climbed the spiral staircase, sharing banter and laughter that echoed around the upper archives. Clementine had hissed and streaked away as soon as the tools had come out, disappearing downstairs with a flash of his bushy orange tail.

'I think I remember picking up a book here not too long ago,' Harry remarked to Chloe. 'It was a non-fiction book about my trade. It was' – he pointed – 'from that shelf over there, I think. Did the non-fiction used to be up here? Not sure I remember.'

'Non-fiction used to be over in the upper east wing, yes,' said Mrs Cook. 'The library must remember you, Mr Ashcroft.'

She caught Chloe's eye, and they both smirked at Harry's confused nod.

They all stood at the top of the stairs as the men with tool belts shifted the bookcase and the metal bucket that had been collecting water, so they could start work, all expertise and professionalism. They worked well under Harry, and he led them with instructions that told them he was in charge without being bossy or condescending.

Chloe found herself getting a bit flustered, hovering between the downstairs area and thinking of finding excuses to go talk to him. She wanted to mention getting dinner, reclaiming the wasted night at the pub, but surely now wasn't the right time. He was working.

'Did you grab that stepladder, Tony?' called one of the workers over his shoulder.

The man called Tony made an angry noise. 'Oh no, I forgot. I'll go and get it.'

'No need.' Mrs Cook pointed, and they all looked towards the far wall, half hidden in shadow. A stepladder stood there, shiny and new.

'Was that there before?' asked Harry, folding his arms.

'Probably not.' Chloe and Mrs Cook exchanged another amused look.

They went downstairs, Chloe recalling that Harry had asked for the rest of the fantasy books. At the time she'd gotten distracted and hadn't ordered them. Mrs Cook explained to her that if the books weren't registered on the system, she would have to order them in. After rifling through the files and finding they only had the first two, Chloe picked up the phone.

Then something caught her eye on the desk.

Books, arranged in a neat pile. Chloe picked up the top one; it was the third volume in the series. And underneath it were the rest, all with attractive matching covers.

'Now you're just showing off,' she murmured aloud to the library, putting down the phone. 'But thank you.'

Chloe worked at the computer, checking the wage slips. It was another small job Mrs Cook had assigned to her. With only the three of them as employees, it didn't take too long. Chloe decided to check Harry's borrowing history. She glanced over her shoulder, then went into the list of library members and their records. She hesitated before she clicked on *Harry Ashcroft*. This wasn't an invasion of privacy, was it? What books you read was hardly private business. Before she could talk herself out of it, she clicked on the link.

The Meaning and Symbolism of Flowers, checked out last week at 2:45pm. Why was he checking out a book like that?

'It's none of your business, Chloe,' she sang quietly to herself, clicking off the tab. She didn't like flowers. They reminded her of bad times.

After much hammering and called orders, Harry appeared in the reception area with his workers trailing behind him, carrying their tools. 'The roof's all fixed,' he said. 'Though your cat doesn't seem too happy about it.'

'Clementine had claimed that little spot for himself,' said Mrs Cook fondly. The ginger cat sulked in her arms, looking even grouchier than usual as his tail swayed back and forth.

'Well, maybe we can make that little area for him,' suggested Chloe. 'Shift the bookcases and make a cat play area. Then anyone who goes upstairs to the fiction section can see him.'

As Mrs Cook settled the bill with Tony, Chloe found herself alone with Harry. 'I . . . um, got your books,' she said, showing him the pile on the desk. 'Would you like to check them all out?'

Harry picked up the third book in the series, turning it over. 'It's like new. I've almost finished with the second one, so this is canny timing. Thank you, Chloe.'

'Don't thank me. Thank . . .' She was going to say the library, but didn't know how that would sound. *Ah, screw it.* 'Thank the library. Mrs Cook is right, it likes you.'

'Er, right.' Harry looked amused as Chloe put the books into a bag for him. He thanked her and turned to go.

'Listen,' Chloe blurted as he headed for the door. Harry turned. 'Let's . . . Let's start over. Go to the pub, or somewhere. For dinner. Again. Properly, I mean. If you'd like to.' Heat rose to her cheeks. 'I owe you, for the curry and for the coffees. So if you'd like to do something . . . er, sometime?' *Stop babbling*, she thought. 'I don't have your phone number,' she added meekly.

Harry opened his mouth just as the library's front door opened, a cold breeze flowing into the room. A young blonde woman came in, her long hair flowing behind her.

Chloe's eyebrows rose. It was Gwen.

Her beauty lit up the room, from the elegant way she moved to her soft smile as she glanced around. Had she put on make-up? Harry's co-workers stared for a little longer than necessary before slipping through the door behind her.

Chloe's stomach dropped at the sight of her sister.

'Hi, Chloe,' Gwen sang, dancing over to her. 'So this is where you work.' She glanced around. 'Wow, it's lovely.'

'Yeah, it's the only library in the town,' said Chloe, not quite able to keep the edge from her voice. 'Um, this is Mrs Cook.' The librarian smiled at her, still holding Clementine in her arms. 'This is my sister, Gwen.'

Harry was still there, head tilted in expectation. Feeling it would be rude to exclude him, Chloe reluctantly said, 'And this is Harry.'

'Hi, Harry.' Gwen waved at him. Was it Chloe's imagination, or did their gazes linger a heartbeat longer than necessary?

And why did she care?

Chloe busied herself with rearranging papers on the desk, suddenly feeling very annoyed with everyone.

'Do you need anything, dear?' Mrs Cook asked Gwen as Harry came over to Chloe. 'Are you looking for a book? Eric just came in for his shift. He can probably help you out.'

'Would next Friday work?' said Harry, standing in front of the lobby desk. It didn't seem that anyone else could hear them.

Chloe looked up to meet his gaze. Her mind was suddenly blank. 'Er . . . Friday?'

'For dinner.' Amusement danced in his eyes. 'Let me make it up to you properly.'

Was Chloe hearing this right?

'Hmm.' She turned from him to put a file on the back shelf so he wouldn't see her smile. 'Oh, go on then.'

They exchanged phone numbers. *Ashcroft*, she thought with amusement. What were the chances?

'I'll text you.' He waved goodbye to the others, and Chloe watched him as he left. She wasn't sure why he had been secretive about it, but she was also relieved.

'Who was that?' Gwen asked with interest.

'I told you. Harry. He came to fix the roof,' said Chloe, not meeting her gaze.

'Yeah, but he talked to you.' Gwen came to the spot where Harry had stood a moment earlier, then prodded Chloe on her shoulder. 'Who is he?'

'No one, Gwen.' Chloe swallowed a sigh. 'Do you need something? I've got a lot of work to do.'

Eric emerged from the kitchen area just then, and his eyes widening at the sight of Gwen. She had curled her hair today and wore a dress and leggings, a belt accentuating her slim waist.

'Ah, Eric.' Mrs Cook passed him. 'Would you help the customer, please?'

The teenage boy gaped at Gwen. 'I . . . I . . . Can we help you?'

Despite her discomfort, Chloe couldn't help meeting Mrs Cook's eye right before the older woman slipped into the kitchen, coughing into her elbow to hide a giggle. It was just like Eric to be left speechless by a pretty woman.

Gwen leaned her elbow against the desk as though she'd spent her life in this place. 'I came over because I wanted to see where Chloe works. And I was hoping I could find some job listings here. Libraries are good for that, aren't they?'

'I can help,' Eric said, and he almost tripped over a stool as he hurried to where Gwen stood.

'Hopeless romantic, that one,' said Chloe to the library, shaking her head.

Chloe pretended to be busy on the ground floor archives, shelving random books as she watched her sister. She couldn't shake the feeling that Gwen had an ulterior motive for showing up at Chloe's workplace. Gwen, of all people, would know that the internet was a much better place to look at job listings. It felt like an excuse.

Eric asked questions about what Gwen wanted to do and where she wanted to work, as though he were an expert on the subject.

Despite her tension, Chloe couldn't help mirroring Mrs Cook's grins as Eric, in order to show Gwen a newspaper he had plucked from the rack, leaned so far over the edge of the desk that it surely was digging into his stomach.

'Newspapers are good because you know the jobs listed there are legit. There are a lot of scams online, you know,' the teenager babbled. 'There's loads here. Retail, if you like fashion. And here you have bar work, if you'd like that sort of thing.'

'Are you even old enough to work in a bar yet?' Gwen asked with interest.

Eric huffed. 'I turned eighteen last May.'

Still a baby, thought Chloe.

'How are you doing?' asked Mrs Cook, appearing quietly at Chloe's side. Chloe supposed it was quite obvious that she wasn't doing any real work and was simply listening in to Gwen and Eric's conversation.

Chloe gave a noncommittal shrug. 'I'm fine.'

She hadn't asked, but she wondered if Gwen had ever had a job in her life, or if she had survived this long by flitting between rich men. For a moment, Chloe allowed herself to fantasise about being flown first class in private jets to Paris, Milan, New York, Singapore, being lavished with gifts and sipping champagne and relaxing on sun-soaked yachts. Now she lived in rainy old Derbyshire with her sister.

Did Gwen miss that life? Was she really looking for a job so she could start paying her own way, or would she jet off with the next guy who asked?

'Eric seems to like her,' Chloe remarked to Mrs Cook, who chuckled.

'That's just Eric being Eric. Teenage boys,' she said, like that explained everything. It wasn't likely Eric was Gwen's type.

Chloe watched as Eric went to sit down, only the stool was several feet back from where it had been a moment ago. Eric's eyes widened and he yelped as he fell to the floor on his bottom, disappearing behind the lobby desk. Mrs Cook and Chloe clutched each other in silent laughter.

Chloe could have sworn she felt a ripple of amusement from the library, too. They had both managed to straighten their faces and look busy by the time Eric emerged from behind the desk, grumbling and rubbing his behind.

'Thanks for the help, Derek,' Gwen called cheerfully over her shoulder fifteen minutes later, a notepad page of job listings and phone numbers tucked into her wallet.

'You're welcome. And it's Eric,' Eric called back, but Gwen had already left, the heavy oak doors closing behind her.

Chloe couldn't deny that Gwen *looking* for a job was a positive thing. At least she wasn't planning on mooching off of Chloe for ever. Whether she did indeed pay her back for the kitchen supplies and the book remained to be seen, but Chloe was willing to choose her battles.

CHAPTER SEVENTEEN

CHLOE FOUND SHE could hardly wait for Friday. Harry seemed to be invading her thoughts.

She told herself it was just the change of pace of the weekend that she was looking forward to. Even if the memory of Harry's laughter brought a reluctant smile to her face, or the way the corners of his brown eyes creased when he was pleased about something. No, this was just an opportunity to spend time with a guy who didn't forget his wallet so she'd pay, or call his mum in the middle of the date.

It's not a date, she reminded herself. Just two . . . friends hanging out. No, Harry was barely a friend. Two *people* hanging out for the sake of peace. And nothing else.

Harry texted her and asked her to meet him at an Italian restaurant in town the coming Friday. She hadn't been there before, and a big stupid grin spread on her face as she tucked her phone away. Mrs Cook gave a knowing smile but said nothing.

She had seen no more glowing books so far this week, and Gwen proved to be almost pleasant company. Chloe made spaghetti Bolognaise and asked Gwen to join her. After all, it was strange for them to eat separately when they were both in the same house.

'So, um.' Chloe hoped she wouldn't regret this. Gwen sat opposite her, in Dad's old chair, adding parmesan to her meal. 'How's the job hunt going?'

Gwen told her about the jobs she had applied for. Cafés, restaurants, retail. 'Though I don't think anyone's going to want me when I don't have any job history,' she said, twirling spaghetti with her fork. 'Maybe I need to work on my CV.'

Chloe ate steadily, knowing what was coming. She counted to three in her head before Gwen perked up and said, 'Hey, Chloe, maybe you could help me out.'

She chewed slowly, watching as Gwen pouted, staring at her with expectation. She wriggled on her seat like a child. 'Please, Chloe! I'm rubbish with computers and writing and stuff.'

Chloe finally swallowed. 'All right, all right, I'll help you.' The stronger her CV was, the better chance Gwen had of finding a job.

After dinner, Chloe dug out her old laptop. She hadn't used it in a while, but it booted up with little trouble. Gwen loitered behind Chloe, hovering annoyingly until Chloe told her to get a chair. It scraped over the kitchen tiles.

'Show me your CV so far,' said Chloe, and Gwen got it up on her email.

It was a bit of a mess, different fonts, and missing important information like her date of birth and current address. Chloe's organised side, the part that loved arranging books in alphabetical order at the library, got unreasonably irritated and chose the 'select all' function.

'Wow, you're really good at this,' said Gwen with a guilty giggle as Chloe straightened out her CV.

'All right. Remind me what A-Levels you got.'

Their conversation became uncomfortable as they referenced their teenage years. Their sentences became shorter, the silence between Chloe's questions broken only by the sound of typing.

'I didn't know you got a B in biology,' said Chloe with interest. Gwen shrugged.

After getting her A-Levels, Gwen had met a guy during a trip to a nearby city. He'd been rich and taken a liking to her. He had asked her to join him on a trip around the world.

Mum and Dad, of course, had been completely against it.

'You're only eighteen, Gwen,' Mum had said, in this very room, pacing and shaking her head while Dad sat in grim silence. He had still been smoking back then, and though Mum insisted he stand at the back door whenever he had a cigarette, the air still held the stale fug of tobacco. 'This guy is a stranger. You can't go jetting off with some random man.'

'I'm an adult,' Gwen had argued. Chloe had been listening from the doorway, but she hadn't wanted anyone to know she was there. Chloe herself was preparing to go off to university. It was typical of Gwen to try and steal her thunder. Did she really want to go off with some guy she'd just met or was she just looking for attention?

'Besides, he's rich,' said Gwen, and Chloe saw her take a seat at the table, crossing one perfect leg over the other. 'He let me ride in his car, *and* he took me to a fancy hotel . . . I mean, uh, a restaurant. He wants to take me on his private yacht.'

'But he's a stranger, Gwen. It doesn't matter how much money he's got,' Dad said, looking up. He had the same blue eyes as his youngest daughter, and Gwen swallowed as he looked at her. Out of their parents, she had always been closer to Dad. 'This is ridiculous. You're not going.'

'The only ridiculous thing is you both expecting me to stay in this boring town for ever,' Gwen snapped, gaining her feet in a flurry of movement. 'I don't want to go to university.'

'You don't have to,' said Mum in earnest, stepping forward to take her daughter's hand. Gwen snatched it away, stepping back. 'You can get a job and think about what you want to do. There's still plenty of time. Just don't throw your life away for someone you barely know.'

'He could be a weirdo, Gwen,' added Dad. 'He could already be married. Terrible things happen to girls who go off with strangers.'

'He's not a stranger!' Gwen cried. 'I've known him for months, if you must know. We're in love. I'm going, and you can't stop me.'

Gwen strode out of the dining room, so fast Chloe wasn't prepared. She almost ran into her, and they both glared at each other.

'Were you listening to our conversation?' Gwen sneered.

'Maybe. You'd know plenty about sneaking around,' Chloe snapped back.

Gwen just scoffed at her and stomped up the stairs. She was gone the next day.

'Chloe?'

Chloe started, realising she had been staring unseeing at the laptop screen while the memory surfaced. She cleared her throat and said, 'Could we work on this tomorrow? I'm a bit tired.'

She thought her sister would argue, or at least press her for more, but she nodded and stepped back as Chloe rose from the chair, painfully aware that the memory that had flooded her mind had happened in this very room.

She splashed cold water on her face in the bathroom. Coming back to Wellbridge, to her parents' home, had been hard enough. She didn't know if she could handle it at all if Gwen was here.

Who was she kidding? A batch of cinnamon rolls and a new book – paid for with Chloe's stolen card – wasn't enough to erase what had happened between them seven years ago.

Clementine watched Chloe come into the library that Wednesday. She smiled at him, but he could see dark things under her eyes, like shadows. He meowed and rubbed himself against her leg anyway, curling his tail around her calf.

'Lovely boy.' She knelt to pet him properly. He found he didn't mind, and purred softly as her gentle hands found his favourite spots. She looked happier when she straightened. Clementine was rather pleased with himself.

He watched the humans work, unsure whether he preferred the library when it was just him or when there were people around. People he liked and trusted. The skinny boy, Eric, was here. Clementine couldn't gauge his age, but he looked like a kitten.

Clementine watched the day go by from the top of the shelf behind the lobby counter. He liked how people looked at him when they came into the library and saw him lying there. Like he was doing something funny and cute, even if he was just watching them.

He watched Chloe now, thinking how her brown hair was the exact same colour as the chestnuts that sometimes fell in the garden. When she went to the non-fiction section, he followed her, the bell on his neck ringing. He sometimes wondered if he would see the stunning female tabby cat again, but the children's section was empty, all the books piled neatly on the shelf.

Clementine passed Chloe, then glanced behind him to see a piece of lined paper sitting on the nearby soft area. He picked it up in his mouth then meowed softly at Chloe.

'What have you got there, Clem?' Chloe reached out and he dropped it into her hand. She opened the paper and her eyebrows came together. She made a strange noise, like she was exhaling a lot of air at once.

'This again.'

Curious, Clementine followed Chloe into the lobby.

'What's up, Chloe?' Eric asked, turning from the computer on the stool, his elbows resting on the desk.

'It's so silly.' Chloe held up the paper. 'I keep finding these notes everywhere. First an inked heart, then a message saying "*I like you*".' She held up this one. Clementine couldn't read the odd squiggles on the paper, but then Chloe said, '*Coffee sometime?* Are these being left by . . .' She stopped herself, her cheeks going pink.

Clementine sat between Eric and Chloe, watching them with interest.

Eric had gone quiet. Then he said, 'I didn't think you were finding them.'

'What?'

Eric slid off the stool, nervously scratching the back of his head. 'I thought someone was throwing them away or something. I tried to put them close to you, so you'd see them first . . .'

'It was you?' Chloe looked down at the paper in her hand. 'Why?'

Oh no, thought Clementine.

'I thought it was obvious.' Eric stepped towards her, fiddling nervously with his shirt.

Stand up straight, boy, Clementine admonished. Or he would have, if he could talk. *Like this.*

He rose up like he had to attract a female, walking with straight legs and his tail up and confident. Eric didn't notice him, looking at Chloe with earnest eyes.

'I really like you, Chloe.' Eric's voice held a tremor now. 'I have since I first met you. You're so beautiful, and you're always nice to me. I'd like to go out with you.'

Clementine risked a glance at Chloe. He didn't understand all of the emotions that flickered across her face, but he understood pretty well when she took a step back.

'Oh, Eric.' She put a hand on her chest. 'I . . . I'm so sorry. I don't think of you that way.'

'What?' Eric's face crumpled up. That's the only way Clementine knew how to describe it. Like he was in pain.

'You're a nice kid, but I see you more like a little brother.' Chloe rushed behind the desk and picked up her bag. 'Erm. My shift ends in half an hour, but I'm going to go now. I'll adjust the shift schedule tomorrow, okay?'

'I'm sorry. I thought you liked me, too,' said Eric, looking stunned. 'I mean, those conversations we had. The time we've spent together here. I love you, Chloe.' He winced as soon as he said it, as though aware he was blurting things out in his panic.

She let out a groan, clutching her bag to her shoulder. 'I'm really sorry.'

She slipped outside, leaving Eric standing on his own.

Clementine pawed at his leg, meowing softly. He knew heartbreak when he saw it. He had felt it, too.

Eric sniffled and ran from the room, leaving the lobby empty. Clementine followed him, chasing the boy's retreating skinny legs until Eric sank into an armchair in the lower archives. Clementine watched from a dark corner, tilting his head.

There they were. The leaking eyes, smelling of salt. They ran down Eric's cheeks as he sniffled, wiping at his face.

Clementine understood. He ran back through the lobby, his bell jangling, and back to the children's section, looking at all the books on the shelves. He searched until he found it – the large book about the tabby cat, the darling female snatched from him all too quickly. Using his paws and cursing the feline gods for not giving him opposable thumbs, Clementine managed to tug the book out enough for him to clamp his jaws around it. He scurried back to Eric, the book in his mouth.

Eric had his face buried in his hands when he found him, his shoulders shaking. Clementine deposited the book on the ground and mewed until Eric glanced up.

Clementine put his paw on the book, willing him to understand. Sometimes you liked someone, but they left anyway. It didn't mean you were worth less.

'You like that book, boy?' Eric wiped his face and picked up the book. He patted his lap and Clementine leaped up. He sat on the armchair, tail swishing, then sniffed at Eric's face. Still very salty. This boy was in a bad way.

He did what he knew made humans happy. He gently butted his head against Eric's skinny shoulder, purring. Eric pulled him onto his lap and stroked a hand down his back. He wasn't as gentle nor as attentive as Mrs Cook or Chloe, but Clementine put up with it. He wanted Eric to feel better.

He licked Eric's cheek, tasting his sadness. He gently meowed. He didn't fully understand what all of this meant, but what Clementine did know was that one of the kind humans who looked after him was upset. He purred on Eric's lap until he could feel the human's heart rate starting to go down.

'You're such a good friend, Clem.' Eric cuddled him close. 'Thanks. I think I'm okay now.'

❖

Chloe welcomed the sting of the cold air on her cheeks. It was cool against the flush of embarrassment.

What the heck had just happened? Chloe had thought – assumed, foolishly – that it had been Harry leaving the notes all over the place. After all, they often showed up shortly after he did. She'd had no idea Eric liked her. He was a kid, still in school. Eighteen, but still far too young for her. She had always assumed his chatter was friendly. Just two colleagues making conversation.

She groaned, walking as fast as she could, as though to flee the problem she had left behind. She had not handled this well. It had been brave of him to confess his feelings like that, and she had dashed away from him.

She brought out her phone and found Mrs Cook's number. Then she hesitated. Would it be wise to involve their boss in all this? She wouldn't want to embarrass Eric further. Clutching her phone, Chloe was unsure what to do, and reached home without messaging anyone.

When she'd deposited her bag in her room and flopped onto the couch with a cup of tea, she felt a bit calmer. Hopefully Eric wasn't having too bad a time. He was an adult, after all, even though barely.

She held her phone in her hand, still unsure what to do. Text Hannah and ask her for advice? Message Eric, saying . . . what? That she was sorry? She hadn't done anything wrong.

She decided to sleep on it, but by the next morning she was feeling sick. Whether it was nerves or she had caught something, she was unsure. But she rang Mrs Cook and told her she couldn't come in today.

'I just don't want to give you what I've got,' she mumbled. 'I'm sorry. Will things be all right without me there?'

'Oh dear, are you all right? Have a rest today. Eric and I can hold the fort until you're back. If you need to take tomorrow off as well, let me know.'

'Thanks. See you tomorrow, hopefully.'

Chloe hid under the covers for most of the day, downloading the Kindle app on her phone and rereading some books she had loved when she was a preteen. They were easy to devour now – it had taken her days or even weeks to read them when she was a child, but now she finished some old favourites in an hour or two, fondly revisiting the stories. Thinking about her childhood made her feel worse, though, and eventually she fell asleep in the early afternoon, only waking up in the evening when she heard Gwen clattering around downstairs before leaving the house.

It was late at night when Chloe woke up. She was starving. It was a rainless night, and the moon shone in through her window. She felt gross as she climbed out of bed. She didn't feel sick any more, but maybe that was because her stomach was empty.

Hoping they had something in the house to eat, Chloe went downstairs, switching on all the lights. She was making herself some toast when she heard Gwen come home.

Her sister cleared her throat and wandered into the living room, setting down her keys.

'Hi,' called Chloe, not wanting to scare Gwen.

'Hey, Chloe,' Gwen called back. Was it her imagination, or was Gwen slurring?

She found her sister in the living room, rubbing her temples. Even from here, Chloe could smell the alcohol on her. She took a big bite of buttery toast, waiting until her back was to her before wrinkling her nose. So she had been out drinking, maybe on a date. She probably got men to buy her drinks all night.

Typical Gwen.

'Night,' Gwen called after her. Chloe pretended not to hear.

CHAPTER EIGHTEEN

CHLOE FELT RESTED by Friday morning and woke up early to take a long shower. The embarrassment with Eric was still there, but she felt much more ready to face it now. And besides, she had to be in top shape for her date with Harry tonight. There was no way she was going to miss it.

Not a date, she reminded herself.

It was a quiet day at the library, and after finishing her usual tasks, Chloe decided to check if anybody had borrowed a book yesterday during her sick day. It turned out a few had, as well as people bringing books back. The girl who said she'd seen the romance recommended on TikTok had returned the book she'd taken out. Chloe hoped she'd liked it.

The shift at the library passed quickly, and when she got home, Chloe locked herself in her room to get ready, thoroughly glad she had not confronted Harry about Eric's notes. He had asked her to meet him at the Italian restaurant later. She was determined to look good this time. It had nothing to do with him meeting her much more attractive sister. None at all.

She felt like a child doing something mischievous when she stuck her head out of the bedroom door, listening out for music or the buzz of the TV. If Gwen saw her all dressed up, she would ask too many questions, and Chloe wasn't ready to talk about Harry yet. When she heard the shower running, Chloe stepped into the hallway and hurried out of the house.

Glad for her warm coat, Chloe walked into Wellbridge and to the restaurant address Harry had texted her. He was already there, waiting for her outside, his broad back to her as he examined the delicate cursive writing on the restaurant's windows. He was wearing his trench coat, lights from the restaurant's interior making his hair shine gold.

'Hi,' she said, walking over to him. 'Have you been waiting long?'

'Only a couple of minutes.' He held a small bag in his hand. He held it out to her. 'Are you okay? The librarian said you were ill and didn't go to work yesterday.'

She was touched. 'Much better, thanks.' Inside the bag was a small box of chocolates, coffee flavoured. 'Oh, Harry. Thank you.'

'You're welcome,' he said gruffly. 'There's no nuts in them, I checked. There isn't really anywhere inside to put flowers,' he added, looking a bit shy as he put his hands into his pockets.

'I prefer chocolates anyway,' said Chloe happily. 'To tell you the truth, I don't really like flowers.'

'Me neither,' admitted Harry. 'They remind me—'

'Of funerals,' they said at the same time. They exchanged sad smiles.

He doesn't like flowers. She wondered again why he was studying the symbolism of flowers, but it wasn't her place to ask.

'Well, let's get inside. It's cold.' Harry opened the door for Chloe. The interior was deliciously warm and carrying the scent of tomatoes and basil.

They eased into conversation, thanking a staff member when they brought a bottle of wine. 'I've been to the Brew House about six times since you recommended it,' Harry said. 'Their baking is terrific. Pretty sure I've already put on a couple of pounds.' He patted his stomach, which Chloe thought looked fine. 'Worth it, though. I can't bake, myself. Can you? I imagine it's easier, with your nut allergy.'

'I don't really bake. My sister makes good cinnamon rolls, though.'

She winced inwardly, not wanting the conversation to be steered towards Gwen. Too late now.

'I couldn't help noticing a certain . . . tension between you two,' said Harry carefully. He poured red wine into Chloe's glass. 'It's none of my business, but . . .'

Chloe fiddled with a corner of the white tablecloth. She suddenly wanted to tell him, to share it with him. After all, he'd told her about his wife. 'Things have been bad between us for a long time,' she said. 'I was actually supposed to get married here in Wellbridge. Forever ago.'

'Oh?'

She nodded. 'We were young. We'd been together all through school and thought we were ready. But . . .' Even after all these years, the memory made her throat tight. She had to say it aloud, give it a voice. 'Gwen got a bit drunk, and I caught them kissing.' She ignored Harry's sharp intake of breath. 'I called off the wedding. Gwen said I was being dramatic, that she was only messing around and it didn't mean anything. But we didn't talk again. Only briefly, before our parents' funeral.'

The thought still made her sick. She and Liam had been together for years, all through school, and at eighteen, she had thought she was ready to marry him. They had planned the wedding, invited the guests, and bought the dress. Gwen, naturally, had been the maid of honour. But when Chloe had caught her seventeen-year-old little sister kissing Liam, her entire world had shattered.

Harry's hand moved across the table and took hers. It was large and warm and covered her cold fingers in a reassuring grip. 'I'm so sorry.'

Chloe looked up to meet Harry's eyes. In this lighting, she could see flecks of green in them. 'About your parents and about what happened with Gwen. Losing one parent is awful, but both, and at the same time. They . . . Did they die together?'

Chloe's chest felt like it was full of rocks, but she took in a long breath, focusing on the warmth of Harry's fingers around hers, and on the ordinary sounds of clinking glasses and low talking. 'They were involved in an accident. Someone was driving down the wrong side of the road and hit them.' She sniffled and Harry handed her his napkin. She couldn't believe she was crying in the middle of a nice restaurant. 'I'm sorry. I shouldn't have brought it up.'

'Chloe, you don't ever need to be sorry for talking about your past.' He squeezed her hand, giving her a gentle smile. 'I understand why you feel awkward around Gwen. It can't be easy, even if it was a long time ago.'

'We haven't talked about it.' She sniffled. 'She left after that, shortly before I went to university.'

'Left?'

'Yeah, she went off with some guy. A millionaire traveller. Our parents were furious.' She dabbed at the corner of her eye with a napkin, hoping her mascara wasn't running. 'It didn't last long. She ended up in Singapore, and the next thing I knew, she'd found someone else.' She stopped talking. No matter how angry she was with Gwen, this wasn't her business to tell Harry. 'Oh no, this is so silly. Can we talk about something else?'

'If you like,' he said, with a tone that told her they could return to the topic of her family whenever she was ready.

'Have you been in construction for long?' she asked, thinking of his company she had unwittingly rung.

'Quite a few years now. I'm from Newcastle originally, but started my company here and have been in Derbyshire ever since. I mainly work in site management. I organise the projects, and sometimes visit them myself if they're local, to assess and give quotes, things like that. Though I used to have more of a hands-on role before . . .' He trailed off, then took a sip of his wine. 'What got you into working at the library?'

Chloe smiled at the thought of the large library with its gothic windows and mahogany shelves and of the cat bringing her out of her dark cloud of despair. The library felt like a haven, one of the few places left in Wellbridge not tainted with bad memories and regret. 'I just love books,' she said. 'My mum would take me to bookshops and libraries all the time when I was a child. And if we read a book about a real place, we'd visit. Sometimes all of us, sometimes just me and Mum.' Gwen had been closer to their dad. She'd had him wrapped around her little finger since she was a kid.

'Working in the library suits you, you know,' Harry said.

'My sister said the same thing,' Chloe grumbled, wondering if Harry also meant she was bookish and boring.

'I don't even think I know anyone who has worked there, aside from you,' said Harry. 'I mean, I've maybe made small talk with the librarian once, but I certainly haven't hung out with anyone who worked there. I remember visiting the library a few times when I first moved here, then when I started my business, I went looking for a book about construction. Ah, here's our food.' The delicious savoury aromas filled the space between them as they picked up their knives and forks. 'Then . . . well, to tell you the truth, I hadn't visited since before Julie died.'

Chloe cut her tortellini slowly, not sure whether to move past the subject of his wife or ask more about her. Still, she had just opened up about her parents and her sister. 'How long has it been since she passed away?' she asked, her voice soft.

'Two years and five months.' Harry twirled his tagliatelle with his fork.

'I'm sorry,' she said quietly. She couldn't imagine finding the love of her life, marrying them and being happy with them, only to lose them so young.

Chloe thought the date had become a bit gloomy. She was glad he had told her about his wife, though. It was a sign of trust. Besides, even though she hadn't lost a spouse, she could somewhat understand his grief. She missed Mum and Dad so much it hurt.

There was a strange sense of relief in knowing they were both grieving, that the library had provided a place of solace and comfort for them.

'So that was the first time you'd been to the library in over two years?' she asked. She ate as she listened, and now the painful moment had passed, she found she was enjoying her lasagne immensely.

'I know there are bookshops all over the place, but I know I'll actually read a book if I borrow it from the library. The one you suggested was great, by the way. To your recommendation.' He toasted to her, and she giggled. 'I'm getting through the rest of them. They're fantastic.'

'They are good,' she said. 'There are loads more in the same vein you'd probably love.'

It was nice to talk about books. It was a safe, easy topic she knew a lot about. It turned out they were both fantasy fans, though where Chloe's tastes moved towards romance and the classics, Harry tended to like high fantasy and historical fiction. They reconnected on thrillers, though, and were eagerly swapping their favourite authors and twists when their dishes were suddenly clean and a smiling member of the serving staff was handing them the dessert menu.

'Did you know that restaurants found that if they ask customers directly if they would like the dessert menu, it's less likely they'll order something?' asked Chloe as she flipped it open. 'Whereas if they just bring you the menu without asking, you're much more likely to order a dessert. Maybe because you see what's available and get tempted.'

'Smart move,' said Harry. 'I heard if you're selling something, it's a good idea to make sure the customer holds it in their hands. Then they're more likely to buy it.'

'I'll have to remember that if I ever end up back in marketing.' Chloe smiled. 'I'm not planning on working at the library for ever, you know.'

'Is that right?' asked Harry. He looked so surprised she almost laughed.

'Well, I might be the type to work in the library, but I just came back to look after my parents' house. And now Gwen is here . . .' She didn't want to say it aloud, but she didn't want to be Gwen's housemate for ever. Especially if the elephant in the room reared its ginormous head every time they were in the same space. She sighed. 'I'm not entirely sure why she came to the library the other day. Google will have more information on jobs than we do. It was funny, though.' She told Harry about Eric's eagerness to help Gwen out and how he'd missed his chair, falling on his bottom. Harry's big shoulders shook as he laughed, and Chloe found herself grinning back. She found she liked making him laugh. The corners of his eyes crinkled in this charming way, delight shining from his eyes as well as his smile.

They ended up choosing the tiramisu. 'Can you double-check there are no nuts in it? She's allergic,' Harry asked the waiting staff.

'Thanks,' said Chloe.

She felt full and happy after the delicious, nut-free dessert. Harry asked a staff member to bring the bill.

'We can go halves,' she offered. They had drunk an entire bottle of wine between them, and she had seen the prices on the menu; it was a fancy place.

Harry shifted in his seat, pulling a leather wallet from his pocket. 'You get the next one, all right? Think of it as a welcome home present.'

Home . . . was Wellbridge her home? Chloe wasn't sure, but she pulled her coat on and they left the restaurant together. She gasped as a strong wind rippled over them. Winter was definitely on its way.

Harry walked her home. She flexed her cold fingers, wishing she had thought to bring a pair of gloves. She glanced at Harry, who walked confidently beside her, his strides long but walking slowly enough for her to keep up. If she moved just a little bit closer, their fingers would brush together. Something had shifted in her tonight. He didn't seem quite so frightful. She wondered if he wanted to hold her hand.

She opened her mouth to ask if he did when Harry said, 'Actually, Chloe, I have a favour I want to ask you.'

'Sure.'

They had entered her neighbourhood now, the quiet town already empty and the streetlights casting golden light on the pavements. A few stars winked above their heads. Harry stopped before her. 'I'd prefer it if you didn't tell anyone that we . . . well, that we've been out together,' said Harry, looking at her. 'I mean, you can tell your sister. But I don't really want anyone to know, yet.'

'Oh,' she said. 'Yeah, sure.'

There was nothing to tell anyway, she reminded herself. Just two friends out for a meal.

'It's just that I haven't been out with anyone since Julie . . . you know. I'm still not sure what I want. Or what this was,' he added. 'I just don't want people getting the wrong idea.'

She found herself almost withdrawing into her coat, like a turtle. She wanted to say she hadn't been on a decent date in a while, either, but it would sound silly after him mentioning his late wife. 'All right, no problem.' After all, this hadn't really been a date. He'd given her a comforting pat on her hand when she'd mentioned Mum and Dad, but she didn't even know if she liked him.

Well, maybe she did a bit. The thought surprised her.

They walked in companiable silence until they reached Chloe's house. 'This is me,' she said, noticing the living room light was on. The faint sound of the TV came from inside. Canned laughter reached them, sounding artificial and strange in the cold evening.

'Thanks for coming out with me, Chloe.' Harry stepped forward and tucked a strand of hair around Chloe's ear. Her breath caught, but Harry simply pecked her on the cheek and drew back. 'Let's do it again sometime.'

'Yeah,' she said, her breath escaping all at once as Harry walked down the path. 'Goodnight.'

'Night!' He waved to her and was soon swallowed by the darkness.

CHAPTER NINETEEN

CHLOE HOPED GWEN had somehow gone to bed and forgotten to switch off the TV, but as luck would have it, her sister was lying sprawled on the couch. Her sitcom had ended, and she had changed to a film.

'Hi,' she called after Chloe. Chloe didn't respond, but quickly slipped up the stairs to scrub off her make-up and change into her pyjamas and dressing gown. She was still reliving the evening in her mind, and she had a smile on her face when she sat in the armchair, the new book from Gwen tucked under her arm.

'Hmm?' Gwen gave her a knowing smile as Chloe flicked on the lamp by her chair.

'Hmm?' Chloe echoed. It was something they'd done as children, mockingly repeating what the other had said.

Instead of becoming annoyed, though, Gwen leaned forward. 'I saw a *boy* outside. Have you been seeing a *boy*?'

Chloe's good mood couldn't even be dampened, not even by Gwen's nosiness, and she burst into laughter. 'Boy? We're thirty soon, Gwen.'

Gwen looked offended. 'You're nearly thirty. I'm sitting pretty at twenty-five, thanks. Don't change the subject. Was that the guy from the library? He was, wasn't he?'

'You're such a busybody. What, were you peeking through the curtains?'

'Of course.'

Chloe snorted. 'Yes, I was with the *boy* from the library.'

'On a date?'

The word 'date' gave her pause. Was her dinner with Harry a date?

She stayed quiet for too long. Gwen squealed, startling Chloe.

'Calm down, Gwen. Nothing happened. He only kissed my cheek and said goodnight.' *A true gentleman*, she thought but didn't say.

'That's it?' Gwen leaned back into the couch as though she was already uninterested. 'He sounds boring, to be honest.'

Chloe's neck prickled. She didn't feel comfortable with Gwen knowing anyone she was seeing, romantically or otherwise. She knew, partly, that it was silly. The kiss with Liam had been such a long time ago, but . . .

Gwen still hadn't acknowledged it. She just sat watching *Bridget Jones* like it had never happened.

'I have a date tomorrow, too,' Gwen said, making Chloe stare at her. Some of the tension in her shoulders loosened.

'You do? That's great.' She privately wondered if the date's name was Dean, the awful mechanic she had had the terrible first date with, the evening that had sent her into the waiting arms of the library. No, it was likely a millionaire who owned a big mansion somewhere in Derbyshire. She hid her smirk and started to read.

It made her feel better that Gwen had a date.

Chloe went to see Hannah and her daughter Lily at the weekend, and they spent a cold, sunny Sunday morning feeding the ducks. To Chloe's surprise, Hannah reported that the boy who had tried to rob the café had come in with his mother in tow.

'She made him apologise.' Hannah sounded amused as she

handed some frozen peas to her daughter. Lily threw them with gusto, jumping with excitement as the ducks raced to peck at the vegetables. 'She said he had fallen in with a bad crowd and it wouldn't be happening again.'

'Well, that's good.' Chloe still recalled how the superhero had picked him up with no effort, putting him in his place quite well. 'Hopefully it won't.'

Hannah nodded grimly. 'Just glad Lily wasn't there.'

It was a pleasant morning with her friend, and Chloe was relieved that the boy had apologised. It made him seem much less threatening, somehow.

Her thoughts wandered to her sister. She wondered if Gwen was in. Her little sister hadn't come back last night by the time Chloe had gone to bed, so Chloe had finished reading her book, wondering if the date was going well. She supposed it must have. Maybe she wouldn't see her sister again now until a post on Instagram popped up telling Chloe her sister had sailed to the Bahamas or the Mediterranean on the arm of some middle-aged tycoon.

A small part of Chloe thought it sounded rather fun, dangers aside. Gwen hadn't run into any trouble so far.

Still, though.

She said goodbye to Hannah and Lily, then pulled out her phone to text her sister. She hesitated, wondering if 'How are you?' was too vague and 'Where are you?' would be too possessive. She finally settled on, *I'm on my way home from town. Do you need anything?*

She walked clutching her phone in her hand, trying and failing to resist the urge to glance at it every couple of seconds. That morning, she had been in a hurry to meet with Hannah and Lily before Hannah had to take her daughter to see her dad, and Chloe hadn't paid attention to whether Gwen's coat or her bag were in the house. She wished she had checked now. It seemed irresponsible, as the older sister, not to know where Gwen was. Gwen's words of Chloe never reaching out echoed in her mind. Maybe she was right. Chloe *was* the older sibling, and she had never spoken to

Gwen aside from the short conversation about the funeral. Not since that night seven years ago.

She hadn't heard any sounds from her sister's bedroom in the night or the morning. What if Gwen had ended up meeting someone unsafe? She wasn't the most cautious of people. Chloe hadn't even asked her date's name, hadn't bothered to find out where she was meeting him.

Finally, the speech bubble popped up on the screen to indicate Gwen was typing, and Chloe almost laughed with relief.

Mint ice cream. Please.

Chloe stopped off at the corner shop and bought every mint ice cream she could find.

She thought Gwen might be in bed, nursing a hangover, but she was wearing sweatpants, the TV on in the background while she straightened her hair.

'Hi,' said Chloe. 'Did you have a good date?'

'What?' Gwen turned to her, her eyes glazed over for a second. 'Oh! Yeah, it was fine. Good, actually.'

They exchanged small smiles. Gwen didn't offer any more information, and Chloe didn't ask, not when she was so reluctant to tell her sister anything herself. For the rest of the day, the sisters stayed out of each other's way. Gwen didn't even ask Chloe for her help with her CV again.

Chloe was nervous about going back to work, to facing Eric. She still hadn't got round to messaging him – what on earth would she say? – because she hated bringing things up. Maybe it would be more comfortable to ignore it and continue as normal.

It wasn't as terrible as she anticipated, though. Still studying for his A-Levels, Eric wasn't a full-time worker, and through the week they only bumped into each other twice. He did look a little embarrassed, but she caught relief on his face that she wasn't going to mention what had happened. That was fine by her.

The library roof was patched up, the space used as a fenced-off play area for Clementine. Chloe used some of the library's budget to invest in a kitty's play area and a brand-new bed. She even managed to find a three-tier cat tree from a charity shop.

'Mr Ashcroft gave us a discount for the roof repair, you know,' remarked Mrs Cook with a knowing smile, while Eric played with the cat, waving a plastic stick with a fluffy, tail-like toy at the end of it for him to chase. Chloe had never seen Clementine so interested in a game before. He made for the toy with his paws, then when Eric pulled it out of his way, Clementine straightened, a look of dignified disapproval on his face that made them all laugh.

CHAPTER TWENTY

IT WASN'T LONG until the big event for the school. The days had slipped by so quickly, Chloe could hardly believe that it was already upon them, and though she, Eric and Mrs Cook had planned and prepared for everything they could think of, Chloe still felt strangely unprepared and terribly nervous.

She and Eric arrived early to make sure everything was prepared, from the book-themed streamers Chloe had printed from the internet, hanging from the bookshelves on the bottom floor, to the long tables with jugs of juice and water, plates ready for the baked goods, and enough coins to provide change for purchases.

The children's corner, a soft play area with bookcases and bean bags, was ready. This entire area would be enough for a dozen or so people.

'Good morning,' said Hannah brightly from the doorway. As promised, she held several boxes in her free hand, the delicious scent of chocolate and cinnamon following her inside. 'Don't worry, this is just the first batch,' she added, lowering the boxes onto the nearest table. 'I've got regular, vegan, gluten-free, and no-nuts versions, Chloe. Hi,' she added, seeing Eric.

Chloe introduced them, Eric giving a nervous wave and then

helping to unpack the boxes. 'Wow, Hannah, this is amazing,' Chloe said. Inside the first box were wrapped croissants. Squares of millionaire's shortbread took up the second. In the third were slices of chocolate cake, and in the fourth and fifth, when Hannah brought them in from her car, were cheesecake and Bakewell tarts.

'This is enough to feed an army,' Eric laughed as they arranged them on trays. With the juice and sweets all arranged, and the books ready, Chloe started to feel excited.

They had decided to only use the ground floor, the event easily visible from the lobby area in case any other visitors came inside. The upstairs fiction area was empty, and there weren't enough decorations to prepare the entire place, but Mrs Cook reminded them that people were welcome to explore if they wished to.

The idea was to get everyone interested in the library again, not only the children. If they could get people to make library cards and check some books out today, Chloe would count it as a success.

The library, too, quivered with anticipation, or so it felt to Chloe. The dark corners and shelves of the building filled the air with scents of flowers and herbs. She could almost feel its delight pouring from the walls, reflecting her own anticipation.

'Take it easy,' Chloe whispered out of the corner of her mouth as she pulled some kids' books off the shelves to lay out on the tables. An almost intoxicating scent of jasmine washed over her. 'These scents are lovely, but we can't explain them to the teachers and parents.'

The air filled with the scent of paper and coffee, and Chloe inhaled slowly. 'Oh, yeah. That's better.'

Mrs Cook arrived, exclaiming her appreciation for the treats available. She hugged Hannah around her middle, squeezing her close like she was her own daughter, not someone she'd just met. Hannah laughed, patting her on the back.

'It's my pleasure,' said the young baker. 'And not entirely selfless.' She held up some business cards.

'We're all here to help each other,' said Mrs Cook, beaming. She checked her watch. 'Just twenty minutes until they're here.'

The headteacher, Miss Jordan, arrived at the library at the stroke of ten o'clock, accompanied by the chattering voices of the children. Chloe couldn't hide her smile as a gaggle of small kids followed Mrs Jordan inside like a row of ducklings, looking around the lobby area with wide eyes. They were around six or seven years old, and they were too adorable in their school uniforms.

Mrs Cook greeted them with enthusiasm and soon the event was underway. 'Hi, everyone.' Chloe waved at the kids as they approached the children's corner, leaving their shoes to step into the soft play area, glancing hungrily or exclaiming aloud at the baked treats on the tables.

Some parents had joined in, smiling politely, and Chloe was relieved to see there was an adult for every four children, leaving little opportunity for things to get out of hand. Chloe liked kids, but she didn't have much experience with them. So she stuck to what she knew best and talked about books.

They started by having a question-and-answer session, and some children told them what books they liked. Then Chloe and Eric spread out some and said they could go and look at them. Some children went to choose a sweet treat. Hannah leaped up from her seat with experienced enthusiasm, and soon coins clinked in the collection box they had prepared.

Chloe found a little girl looking at old adventure books, a woman kneeling beside her. Their identical straight, black hair and high cheekbones told Chloe they were mother and daughter.

'This was one of my favourites when I was your age,' she said, holding up a copy. 'It's about a magic tree that has different worlds at the top, and they're always changing. There's one that has all kinds of ice cream flavours, whatever you want. Chocolate, mint, strawberry, or if you're feeling crazy, you can ask for anything. Like salmon or steak. Do you think you'd like salmon ice cream?'

The girl giggled and took the book, looking at the pictures inside. Happiness filled Chloe as she watched her. There was something wonderful about seeing a child with a book.

'What ice cream flavour do you think you would ask for?' the little girl's mum asked.

'Hmm.' The girl looked so cute and thoughtful it took all of Chloe's willpower not to squeal and hug her. 'Hamburger flavour.'

Chloe burst into laughter. 'That sounds . . . interesting.'

Some of the boys took interest in a huge copy of the *Guinness Book of World Records*, crowding around it and giggling at the outrageous statistics. Another boy was reading a book about trucks with a teacher. A parent went to help Hannah with organising selling the baked goods. Many children sat eating, using paper plates Hannah had brought, as a teacher showed them a large picture book about a mischievous dog. Chloe found herself listening, entranced by the story.

Later, Eric read from a book in the soft play area, sitting in a bean bag chair. Most of the kids were cross-legged on the floor in front of him, listening. Eric did all sorts of funny voices and gesticulated to make the little ones laugh. Chloe walked around, checking that everyone was busy, and returning the adults' warm smiles. She couldn't help noticing that the jugs of juice never seemed to run dry, the cakes and treats refilling themselves on the plates.

Somebody came into the library, attracted by the noise. Chloe glanced up and realised with a jolt that Harry Ashcroft had just wandered in. His brown eyes sought hers, and he smiled openly and raised his eyebrows when he saw her.

'Hi!' she said, winding through the children to approach him.

'Hey, Chloe,' he said, offering her a bag. 'I heard there was an event . . .' He trailed off, looking around at the kids, some of whom were still listening to Eric, others who were having second helpings of cake. 'Oops. I didn't realise this was for children only.'

Chloe chuckled. 'Thank you.' She took the bag of donuts from his hands. Mrs Cook materialised from nowhere, taking the bag and jerking her head in an indication for Chloe to go with Harry.

'You're welcome to stay, if you like.'

'Oh, go on then.' His eyes crinkled, and Chloe tried to ignore the flutter in her stomach.

They wandered through the event, talking to the children, recommending books, and helping Hannah with the money. Chloe was secretly delighted that Harry had agreed to stay and help. The earnings would go towards getting more kid-friendly things for the library, once Hannah got her share for the café. 'Maybe we could do another event around Christmas-time,' Chloe suggested. 'Presents and books and a Christmas tree.' It was a lovely image, and she amused herself for a moment by imagining Clementine, curled up beside an imaginary fire with stockings hanging above it, a little Santa hat on his head.

'The library truly is your calling,' Harry remarked. 'If you want it to be.'

Chloe couldn't deny she felt happy at work, a luxury not many people had. The pay may have been low, but here, she wasn't paying rent. For a moment, Chloe allowed herself to imagine living in Wellbridge long-term. Maybe even permanently. It was true that the thought of putting her childhood home on the market was a sad one. Not all memories here were bad. And she was quickly making new memories. Happy ones.

Did she really want to move to a city and get a regular job, paying high rent and starting over?

Harry's hand brushed hers, as though he could sense the thoughts bouncing around her head. Chloe cleared her throat and looked around. 'Looks like Eric is in his element too.'

The young man did indeed seem to be enjoying himself. A pile of books he had already read were beside him, his socked feet lightly bouncing as he sat in the beanbag chair. He held a large book, a story about a naughty monkey, gesturing with his free arm, making some of the children laugh. Chloe's brow furrowed. There was something off about the book. She examined it as Eric held it against his side. Then her heart leaped in alarm.

The book was glowing.

Something thumped upstairs.

Several parents and kids glanced upwards, questioning each other with strange looks. Eric, oblivious, carried on reading.

Mrs Cook caught Chloe's eye from across the room, and soon Chloe and Harry had reached her. 'Did he just . . .?'

'I think he just did.' The librarian's eyes widened. Clementine appeared from the doorway leading to the foyer, streaking past them in an orange blur. Several children exclaimed in delight at the sight of the cat. Chloe was halfway to the door when there was another rumble, louder than the first.

'Um, should we be worried?' asked Harry.

Chloe looked helplessly at him. 'I have to tell you something about the library.'

'Who wants to try making their very own library card?' called Mrs Cook. She nodded to a teacher, who pulled out a box of pencils and coloured paper and glue sticks seemingly from nowhere. Mrs Cook threw Chloe a look over her shoulder, raising grey eyebrows. 'Go,' she mouthed. 'Eric! Why don't you help Chloe, dear.'

It finally seemed to dawn on Eric what had happened as the children ran towards a little table prepared and ready for a build-your-own-library card event.

Clutching the book, Eric ran over to Chloe and Harry, and they ran into the lobby area.

'Did I do it?' Eric asked as Chloe snatched the book from him. She flicked through it, taking in the pictures of elephants and tigers and the bright purple monkey.

'Do what?' Harry asked.

The sound of books dropping loudly on the floor upstairs made them all jump. Faint echoes of chattering reached them and Chloe exhaled. 'Well, let's hope it isn't the tiger.'

'The tiger?' Harry's confused look would've made Chloe laugh if she hadn't been so worried.

They stopped at the top of the staircase, panting. Clementine's play area was a mess, his food bowl upturned, his toys scattered everywhere. Books were all over the floor, and sitting at the top of one of the shelves . . .

'Whoa,' said Harry.

A purple monkey, comically cartoonish, crouched on top of the bookcase. It stared at them all with big brown eyes, its tail swishing.

'Er,' said Chloe. This was really happening. Seeing a human

character emerge from a story was one thing, but this monkey looked laughably unreal, as cartoonish and weirdly proportioned as it did in the book in her hands.

'Chloe, tell me I'm not hallucinating,' said Harry slowly, backing away and nearly knocking Eric down the stairs. 'Tell me you're both seeing a purple monkey on the shelf.'

'Yeah,' said Chloe. 'I'll explain later. He came out of the book Eric was reading.'

'How do we put it back?' said Eric. 'Oh my goodness. So I *can* do it.' He sounded torn between worried and gleeful, while Harry looked like he was having an existential crisis.

'We have to read his last line from the book to get him back in. Whatever line the monkey says last will send him back.' Chloe opened the book, but fast as lightning, the monkey tore towards them. It ran across the top of the bookshelf and landed on the carpet in front of them. In one quick motion, it had run past and snatched the book from Chloe's hands. It tore off with it, giving high-pitched chattering squeaks.

'Hey!' she yelled as the monkey chattered, the book in its paw as it bounded away. It disappeared around the thrillers section.

Eric stood with his hands on his cheeks, his mouth open in a big O. 'Oh no, oh no. We have to get the book back.'

'You think?' Chloe asked, recovering. She was appalled at the monkey's cheek and furious with herself for letting the book go so easily. 'All right, let's not worry. It's only a monkey. Eric, you go that way.' She pointed to where the monkey had scampered off. 'Harry, are you all right?'

Harry looked startled, but nodded. 'Let me help.'

'All right. You go that way. We can trap it. Hopefully.'

There was no telling what the parents or kids would say if they saw the mischievous purple monkey from the story having suddenly come to life, destroying the fiction section. They would probably panic. Eric and Harry, who appeared to have shaken off his shock, obeyed Chloe, running for the shelves. Monkey chatter and the sound of pages tearing reached her.

Chloe screamed. 'Don't rip the books, you little monster!'

The monkey appeared on top of a nearby bookshelf, the book still in its paw. It bounded across the shelves, hooting with excitement. Eric and Harry reappeared, panting.

Chloe ran after the monkey. Sometimes it disappeared, only small hoots and chatters betraying its whereabouts. For a terrifying few seconds they couldn't see or hear it at all, and Chloe was worried it had gotten downstairs until they saw it swinging from its tail from a nearby curtain rail, the book open in its hands as though reading it.

'We need something to catch it in,' she said. 'A net, or something. Help us!' she asked the library, desperate now. They had been up here for ages already. It would only take a curious teacher or a child sneaking up here, then it would all be over.

Eric appeared beside her. 'What if he rips up the book? If we destroy it, will that make him disappear?'

'Destroy a *book*?' Chloe gave him such a stare that Eric wilted.

Harry had blanched. 'It doesn't need to come to that. You just have to read the final line of a page, right?' He shook his head. 'This is unreal.'

'We need to read the monkey's last line,' she corrected him. 'Let's get the book back. Quick.'

A long net, like one for catching bugs or fish, appeared beside Clementine's area. One moment the area was empty, and the next, the net had materialised there. It was several feet long. Chloe snatched it up, sweat on her brow now. 'Eric, you go that way. Harry, over there.' She nodded towards their respective corners. 'If you go for it from the sides, hopefully it'll come down onto the floor.'

'What if it goes on top of the shelves again?'

'Hopefully the net is long enough. We just need to tire it out.' She was already panting herself, the thick wool cardigan and trousers not ideal for running around the library. She hoped Mrs Cook and the teachers were keeping the kids occupied well enough. She risked a glance downstairs, but the bottom floor of the archives looked to be empty for now. They should have thought to barricade the door.

The purple monkey chittered above them in the rafters, almost mocking. It bounded back to the curtains and swung from the rail by its hand, watching them all.

'All right. Go!' she cried, and Harry and Eric ran to the monkey from each side. Eric grabbed the curtains and shook them, and the purple monkey gave a scared cry and leaped from the rack, still clutching the book as though it knew they needed it.

It soared right over Chloe's head. She turned and smacked down the net with full force. She missed the creature by inches and it sprinted off. Its happy little squeaks sounded almost like it was laughing.

Chloe cursed, wiping her damp brow. 'When I catch him . . .' She mimed strangling.

Harry chuckled. 'We only need to get the book,' he reminded her. 'Maybe we can knock it out of its hands.'

'Can I try?' Eric extended his hand and Chloe begrudgingly handed him the net. Eric didn't have much more luck, though it was admittedly quite funny watching him trying to catch the monkey. The little purple cartoonish creature would stop, looking at the book upside down, tail swishing. Eric would sneak up to it in silence, then the character would leap out of the way right as he swung the net.

'This is hard,' he whined after the fourth attempt.

'I think we're tiring him out,' Harry encouraged them. 'Just a bit more. Come on, let's corner him over there.'

The library, aside from producing the net, didn't seem to want to help them any more. Chloe almost felt its eyes, watching them in amusement as they chased one of its characters.

The other side of the upper floor held the general and contemporary fiction section. 'I wonder if we can get another character out to help us,' said Eric, eyes scanning the shelves for more glowing books.

'Another character?' spluttered Harry.

'Sometimes the books glow and a character comes out,' Chloe explained. 'That could work, Eric, but it could also make things worse. Besides, I don't see any lights in the shelves.' She made an annoyed noise. There were three of them here already. She refused to be bested by a cartoon primate that wasn't even *real*. 'Monkey, where are you?' she called. A small chatter answered her.

It was almost cute. Almost.

Eric still gripped the net in his hands, but Chloe saw in the corner what looked like a laundry basket. She snatched it up, examining it. Something random Mrs Cook had left up here, or more help from the library? She spun it in her hands. It was the perfect size. 'I don't know about you two, but I've *had* it with this monkey.'

They spotted the purple creature in a corner, clutching his book to him. 'Maybe we need a different approach,' said Harry, laying a gentle hand on her elbow. 'We're just frightening him off. Maybe . . .' He lowered his voice as though worried the mischievous monkey could understand them. 'Maybe we should draw him close, then catch him.' He looked at the basket in her hands. 'Would you like to do it? Or shall I try?'

Chloe almost handed the basket over, but she smiled at him. 'Thanks, but I feel like this is my responsibility.' She wasn't entirely sure why. 'But be ready to grab him if I miss, all right?'

Harry stepped back with his arms out, reminding her of a football goalkeeper. She swallowed a giggle and turned back to where the monkey waited for them, still staring with its annoyingly adorable eyes.

'You like the book?' Chloe asked, her voice gentle as she stepped forward. 'Look, it's got you in it.'

The monkey's little chest rose and fell rapidly, its big cartoon eyes looking at the ripped page. Chloe felt a glimmer of compassion for the little creature. If it hadn't just spent the last half-hour giving them the runaround, she'd feel a bit sorry for it.

'That's right, read the story,' she sang, spotting Eric creeping up in the corner of her eye. 'You're a great character in that story. All the kids loved reading about you. You're a cheeky little monkey, aren't you? Why don't you drop the book in this basket for me.' She held it out.

She didn't think it would work, but she didn't expect the monkey to blow a raspberry at her. A full-on, eyes closed, tongue out, loud raspberry that left her mouth hanging open. Harry's laugh echoed behind her.

Eric leaped forward, swinging the net in a wild arc. The monkey shrieked and made to streak past Chloe . . .

'Gotcha!' She dived on the monkey, covering it with the laundry basket. The monkey screamed and panicked inside, thrashing as she held it down. She sat on the basket as the monkey screeched. She grinned up at the others, blowing air up her warm forehead. 'Now, that wasn't so bad, was it?'

CHAPTER TWENTY-ONE

HARRY KNELT TO slide the book out from inside the basket. The monkey clutched on, but Harry was stronger. 'C'mon, now, don't be silly,' he said, and with a sharp tug, the book was free.

'Oh, quick, quick. The whole of Derbyshire can probably hear that racket,' said Chloe as the basket moved beneath her. 'You have to do it,' she said to Eric. She wasn't sure how she knew, but something told her the same person who brought the character out had to put them back. Harry laid a hand on the basket, helping her keep it down, as he handed over the book to Eric. 'The last page, read out his last line. Hurry!'

His hands shaking, his face bright red from running around, Eric opened the book. He read aloud, ' *"You were right, Crocodile," cried the purple monkey. "There were enough bananas for everybody."* '

At the last word, the thrashing and noise under the laundry basket vanished in an instant, and the basket stopped moving. Breathing hard, Chloe rose and checked inside. The purple monkey was gone.

They all breathed great sighs of relief as Chloe picked up the laundry basket. Eric lay the net against the wall. 'I . . . That was an interesting way to find out I could do that, too.'

'And by "that", you mean . . .?' Harry was staring between them. 'What? Pulling characters out of books?'

'Exactly,' said Chloe. 'This library is magical.'

The word rang between them. Eric gave an enthusiastic nod beside her. 'She's right, Harry. Mrs Cook can do it, too. And the library makes its own scents, and some things move on their own, and . . .'

'Let's not overwhelm him,' Chloe laughed as Harry rubbed his temples.

The upper floors seemed so quiet now that the chattering little monkey was safely back in his book. 'I might not have to say this,' said Chloe, rearranging her lopsided cardigan, 'but Eric, please check whether a book is glowing before you read it. You never know who might come out next time.'

They headed downstairs, Chloe trying to think of a plausible reason why the three of them had needed to be up here for so long and wondering if they'd be in trouble with Mrs Cook. Chloe glanced around the library, trying to gauge its reaction. She felt a faint sense of . . . amusement from the wooden rafters and arched windows. Like that had all been a great joke.

'Do that again, and we won't invite anyone else,' she muttered as she pushed open the door that led to reception.

Well, she tried to. The door wouldn't budge. She pushed hard, but it refused to move.

'Did it lock by accident?' asked Harry beside her.

'That door doesn't lock.' Eric came up beside her and pushed it. Chloe was about to huff at him that he wasn't any stronger than she was, but the door opened easily at his touch.

She glanced upwards again, knowing the library had locked the door for her on purpose. 'Ha, ha, very funny.'

'Who are you talking to, Chloe?' Harry asked beside her.

Her cheeks burned. 'The library, of course. Do you think it can't hear me?'

'After seeing cartoon animals running around?' He glanced up at the rafters above them. 'I'm ready to believe anything.'

Chloe tensed when they rejoined the event in the children's section, but it didn't appear anyone had noticed anything. Chloe, Harry and Eric blended back into the group, and Chloe noted that almost all of the cakes and treats were gone – the library had stopped refilling them, then. She supposed Hannah would have noticed something was up eventually. Eric bounded over to the soft play area, slipping off his shoes and asking what book he should read next. He scrutinised with squinting eyes the book the children had chosen, as though checking for a glow, making Chloe and Harry exchange amused grins.

Mrs Cook gave her a warm smile as Chloe came up to her. 'Everything's sorted out,' said Chloe. 'But the book got damaged in the process.' She handed Mrs Cook the children's book Eric had passed to her. The monkey had torn a page nearly in half.

'I didn't doubt you for a second.' The librarian took the book, looking under her glasses at the ripped page. 'This is nothing some tape won't fix. Well done, Chloe.'

'It was a team effort. And, um, Harry Ashcroft knows about the library's magic, too.'

'How's he taking it?' she asked with interest, glancing over at him. He had picked up a piece of chocolate cake and was leaning against the far wall on his own.

Chloe wasn't sure.

The kids chattered noisily, and no doubt Mrs Cook had encouraged the noise to mask the racket upstairs. Almost all of them were holding books, parents smiled on the sidelines, some of the teachers were helping put used paper plates and plastic forks into bin bags, and to Chloe's delight, several children ran with enthusiasm to listen to Eric's new story.

The children all went home with a book each, and with shiny new library cards, many of them with elaborate, colourful patterns and pictures they had designed themselves. The parents promised to visit again soon, the teachers were all smiles and enthusiastic handshakes, and later they found they had raised over a hundred pounds for the library's funds.

'Thank you so much for your help, Hannah,' said Chloe when the last teacher had slipped out of the door. 'Your treats are truly amazing.'

'I have some left. It's weird, I don't remember making this many. Often it seemed like the cakes . . . There were more of them than I thought, you know?'

Harry, Chloe and Mrs Cook all shared knowing looks.

'Anyway, I've got a bunch left. No one's got a gluten allergy, have they? Anyone vegan? These ones don't have nuts, either.'

When they confirmed that they could eat her treats, Hannah happily handed them the spares. Eric dived for the cheesecake with boyish enthusiasm. 'Thanks, Hannah.'

'My uncle is going to be so pleased,' said Hannah happily. Bags and empty boxes in hand, she waved to Chloe. 'This was so fun. Let's do it again.'

'Bring Lily next time, okay?' Chloe called after her as Hannah stepped outside. The doors closed behind her.

They all exhaled. Chloe was acutely aware that Harry was still beside her. His presence was warm and comforting, and somehow, the event had felt even more enjoyable with him here.

'That was fun,' said Eric, stretching his arms above his head.

'It's good to let loose and *monkey* around sometimes.' Harry's eyes crinkled as Chloe snorted with laughter.

'That joke was awful.'

Harry stayed to help clear up, even when Chloe said he didn't have to. 'What else am I going to do on my day off? Sit around watching Netflix?' He smiled at her as they cleared up the books the monkey had spilled upstairs. Eric had filled in Mrs Cook on what exactly had happened, now they were out of earshot of the parents and kids. He made himself look more heroic than he had been, hinting that he had been the one to trap the monkey with the basket.

'Then I read his last line from the book, and he disappeared like *that*,' Eric boasted, clicking his fingers. 'Didn't I, Chloe?'

'Yes, Eric. You were fantastic,' she agreed. He beamed at her, and she felt something between them. A small nudge of reassurance that they were okay.

'The whole day was a success,' said Mrs Cook happily. 'Although I wonder why the library allowed *that* particular book to glow when Eric was reading it?'

Chloe had wondered the same thing. 'Maybe the library thought it would be funny.'

The lanterns glowed brighter, a happy scent of cinnamon rolling over them all. Chloe laughed as Harry gasped in shock.

'You're really having a conversation with this place?' he asked, looking around in awe. 'And here I thought the cartoon monkey coming to life was the strangest thing.'

Clementine, having hidden throughout most of the event and the entire chase with the monkey, reappeared with quiet dignity, meowing softly.

'You could have helped us catch the visitor,' said Chloe with affection, kneeling to scoop up the cat. He let her, purring softly when she petted his head in the spot she knew he liked it. 'You could have grabbed his tail or something.'

'This is the most fun I've had in a while,' said Harry. When his large hand reached out to pet Clementine, the orange cat let him, meowing softly into his palm. 'Monkey and all.'

Chloe beamed at him, feeling suddenly very fond of all the people around her.

The books were cleared up, the earnings locked safely away, and the tables and chairs back to their original positions. Harry had been strangely zen about everything that had transpired. 'You're not freaked out by all this?' Chloe asked him when they were alone.

'A bit,' he admitted. 'But I take it as it comes.'

Chloe nodded, feeling like she understood. Unbelievable things could happen at times, but you'd give yourself a headache if you tried to deny it when it was right in front of your face. Even if it came in the form of a purple cartoon monkey.

'Do you have any plans for Bonfire Night?' he asked.

'None,' she said. In truth, she had been so preoccupied with the library event and with everything else going on that she hadn't spared a thought for 5 November. She had hardly noticed the turn of the month, only the colder, longer nights reminding her of the upcoming winter.

'There's an event on at Thornbridge Hall.' Harry scratched the back of his head. 'I've never been before, but I've heard good things. If you'd like to go? With me?'

Something happy danced in Chloe's chest. 'Harry, you helped us catch the purple monkey. How could I say no?'

'A purple monkey? That's not some sort of euphemism, is it?' said Mrs Cook, entering the kitchen and coming up beside them with a plate of leftover cakes in her hands. Eric giggled from the next room.

'No, it's not!' Chloe's cheeks burned. 'Harry was . . .' She remembered what he'd said about wanting to keep their outings private, swallowed, and said, 'getting ready to leave. I'll text you,' she mouthed to him over Mrs Cook's shoulder.

'Take some of the baked goods home, too, Harry. I shall pop if I eat all these,' said Mrs Cook, packing a Tupperware box into Harry's hands. 'There you go, love. It's the least we can do for all your help.'

'Thanks.' He waved to them. 'Goodnight. I have to be getting through the rest of those books I borrowed.'

Chloe found herself smiling as she watched him go, the light reflecting in his hair. He stepped outside and glanced back, giving her a wink before the door closed behind him.

When Chloe turned, she saw Mrs Cook watching her, a knowing smile on her lips.

'What?' Chloe asked, half amused.

'Nothing at all, my love. I just wish I could give you some glass slippers and a carriage for your date at Thornbridge Hall.'

Chloe's cheeks blazed.

She happily marked 5 November in her phone. Though it bothered her a tiny bit that Harry wanted to keep their outings a secret, it also really wasn't her co-workers' business. Even if Mrs Cook had worked it out in five seconds. Chloe had a feeling you wouldn't be able to hide anything from the librarian.

CHAPTER TWENTY-TWO

CHLOE CHECKED UP on the customers' late returns. Last time she had closed the window without finishing going through the list. She saw that there were three books that hadn't been returned to the library yet.

'The first step is to send a letter to their address,' Mrs Cook explained. 'Then if they don't bring the book back or respond after seven business days, ring them.'

It sounded simple enough. Chloe dug out the template for the warning letter, changing only the names and addresses, and printed them off to be sent. The library fees for the late returns weren't super expensive, but Chloe hoped that the people would get their letters and remember to return the books to where they belonged.

The third book on the list was overdue by several months, longer than Chloe had been working here, and the letter had gone ignored. 'Oh dear,' said Mrs Cook. 'I haven't been keeping on top of this, have I?'

'It's all right,' Chloe reassured her. 'I'll give them a call.'

She had the phone number and address in front of her in the

database. It was a home phone number, and nobody answered it. She supposed they must be at work.

'She lives nearby,' said Mrs Cook. 'H. Campbell.'

'Hm?' Chloe clicked on the record to see the full name. 'Oh! It's Hannah.'

She didn't even know her friend had come to the library before the event. Reassuring Mrs Cook that she had Hannah's private number, she sent her a text message.

Hannah soon responded with an apology, saying she must have forgotten.

Could you come and pick up the book at my house this weekend? And I'll pay you the fee. If that's okay? We could have a cheeky cup of tea as well?

Chloe didn't mind and said as much back. She hadn't visited Hannah's home yet, and it would be nice to see where she was living now.

I'll see you on Saturday.

'It's sorted, Mrs Cook. I'll get the book back on Saturday,' she reported to the librarian. Chloe went out to post the other late notice letters, briefly wondering if the books they had borrowed had started glowing. She amused herself for a moment by imagining a character escaping from a book while someone was reading it, ready to cause havoc around their home.

The thought was funny at first, but then she was alarmed. That would never really happen, would it?

She brought it up with Mrs Cook, who tapped her chin in thought. 'I shouldn't think so, Chloe. I think the library's magic is confined to these walls, and it seems only certain people are allowed to see it at work.'

'The superhero came out at the café,' Chloe argued.

'That's true, but the comic book only started glowing when it was inside the library, right?' Mrs Cook glanced at the beams above their heads. Clementine was on one of them, sitting with his tail hanging off the side, regarding them with a haughty look. 'Hey, library? Books are not magic when they're outside these walls, right?'

The building creaked its response, and Mrs Cook gave a satisfied nod. 'Nothing to worry about, love.'

That Saturday, Chloe entered the address she had saved from the library account's information into her GPS. Hannah's house wasn't too far from here, and anticipating a cup of tea and a good hour of gossip, she drove to the Hazel Lane neighbourhood. Today was sunny and cold, and Chloe couldn't help admiring the picturesque landscape as her car trundled over the country road. The hills, traditional cottages, and fields dotted with sheep were cute and cosy, more comforting than a city skyline.

Feeling cheerful, she pulled up to number seventeen, parking her car next to the black Saab in front of the house. It was a terraced home, maybe two-bedroom, with stuffed animals on the windowsill that made Chloe smile. They had to be Lily's.

The fee for the late library book wasn't too bad, but Chloe still made up her mind to buy a few cakes at the café this week to soften the blow. Hannah was a busy mother, and no doubt the library book was tucked away on a shelf somewhere, an honest mistake. She knocked on her friend's door and it opened a minute later.

Lily stood in the doorway, her long brown hair a mess like Hannah had been trying to put it up for her while Lily was wriggling around. The little girl rubbed her eyes.

'Hi, Lily.' Chloe crouched, recalling that children prefer for adults to be at their eye level. 'I'm here to pick up a book for the library. Is your mum coming to the door?'

'My mum?' Lily looked confused. 'No, this is my dad's house.'

'Sorry?' Confusion swept through Chloe as heavy footsteps approached the door.

'Who's there, Lily?' said a man's voice and the door opened fully.

Before her, balder and with a beer gut, stood Chloe's ex-fiancé, Liam.

For a moment they stared at each other, Chloe's eyebrows rising in shock. The blue eyes were the same, though his brown hair had thinned. There were food stains on his old shirt.

'Wow. Chloe, is that you?' Liam's face lit up. 'You look good.'

'Uh,' said Chloe, thoroughly confused. 'Y-you're Lily's dad?'

Liam and Hannah. Liam, Lily's dad. The idiot who only saw her on weekends.

'This is your house,' she said finally, her brain slowly catching up.

'Chloe, want to see my Hot Wheels?' Lily asked, taking her hand.

'I heard you were back in town, Chloe. How've you been?' Liam asked, like the last time they saw each other hadn't been her yelling at him for kissing her sister. In a daze, Chloe let Lily pull her to the living room, where toys and books were scattered across the floorboards and a cartoon was playing on the TV.

'I'll make you a brew,' said Liam, halfway out the door. 'Milky with no sugar, right?'

It sickened her that he remembered, but she gave a weak nod. 'Uh, yeah. I'm just going to run to the toilet . . . Lily, I'll have a look at your cars in a sec, okay?'

'Okay.' Lily was already eating some crisps, entranced with her show.

Chloe locked the door to the bathroom and rang Hannah, her heart thumping a hundred miles an hour. She felt like a criminal, sitting on the closed toilet seat and leaning forward, as though that would make her voice quieter. Her migraine was coming back.

'Hi, Chloe. Are you nearly here? Did you get lost?'

'Hannah!' Chloe hissed. 'What the hell? I'm at Liam's house!'

There was silence on the other end of the line. Then, 'What?'

'The address on your library card must have been wrong. It sent me here to Liam's. Lily is here. Lily's dad is Liam?'

'Oh, no. I'm so sorry. I'll be right there. I must have gotten the library card when I lived there and . . . just wait there, okay? I'm sorry. I'll be over in five minutes.'

Chloe held her cup of tea in her hands, feeling so awkward that she almost wished she was facing Eric and talking about her rejection instead. It would be less painful than this.

Lily was their saving grace, happily assuming Chloe was her dad's friend, chattering on about her different Hot Wheels cars while Chloe watched Liam out of the corner of her eye. It was surreal, seeing him here. She had always remembered him at eighteen, perfect in her eyes until he'd betrayed her. But this guy was . . . older. Imperfect. Balding. *Normal.*

'This is the fastest one, watch.' Lily pulled back her car and let it go. It raced across the floor and hit Chloe in the foot.

'Oh!' she said, even though it didn't hurt. 'Wow, um, Lily's talking is really good for her age.'

'Yeah, she's my little genius,' said Liam proudly.

She sipped her tea, glad that at least she had that to do while waiting for Hannah. Damn him, but the tea was made perfectly.

Hannah burst in five minutes later, which felt more like five hours. Her face had blanched and her cardigan was done up lopsidedly, the buttons fastened one too high. She looked between Liam and Chloe.

'Mummy!' cried Lily, jumping up from her toys and going to hug Hannah around the waist.

'Hi, Hannah.' Liam rose, wiping his hands on his jeans. Maybe he had the decency to feel uncomfortable, too. 'Cuppa?'

'No, thanks, Liam. I'm just here to pick up Chloe.' Hannah was breathless, like she had run all the way here. Chloe set down her cup and said bye to Lily, who seemed a bit upset her mum wasn't staying.

'It's all right, Lily. Hey, want to watch *Paw Patrol*?' asked Liam, and Lily waved goodbye.

'I still need that book,' Chloe reminded Hannah.

Hannah slapped her forehead. 'Right.'

It took some time, but Liam finally dug out the library book from one of Lily's toy boxes. Chloe could guess why Liam hadn't been back to the library to return it if he knew Chloe was working there.

Nausea squirmed in her guts. Liam, Lily's father. She still couldn't believe it.

She couldn't breathe properly until she stepped outside and the cold air hit her face. 'Chloe, I'm so, so sorry,' said Hannah quickly. 'Let me explain.'

They walked up and down the street, leaving their cars in Liam's front drive. 'How did that even happen?' Chloe found herself asking. It just seemed so unlikely.

'Oh, it's so stupid.' Hannah sighed. 'Everyone else had gone, you know? To university or whatever. I asked my cousin to set me up on a blind date, if you can believe that, and it turned out to be Liam.'

'And he got you pregnant.' Chloe raised an eyebrow.

'It was dumb. I laughed at first, thinking it was a joke, but my cousin worked with him and didn't know about . . . everything. About you. And you had already left by then. We got to talking, one thing led to another . . . We weren't even going out. I didn't even like him that much, and when I decided to keep the baby, we tried living together for a bit.' She gestured towards Liam's home, rolling her eyes. 'I suppose I must have made my library account when my address was registered there. I'd forgotten all about it.' She rubbed her hands over her face. 'I'm sorry. There never seemed to be a good time to tell you. Either Lily was there, or we were talking about other things . . .' Chloe knew she meant Mum and Dad's deaths. She guessed she could understand that. Who would want to drop a fresh bombshell on a grieving friend?

'This is just so weird,' Chloe said. Her ex-fiancé had slept with her friend, and they had a child together.

'He's one of the few people, apart from me, who didn't leave this town after school,' said Hannah. 'We were reminiscing, you know? And I suppose I was lonely and a bit desperate. Too many tequilas, and next thing you know, I was knocked up. But I really wanted to keep the baby, and I've been doing just fine by myself.' Sorrow filled her gaze as she gently took Chloe's wrist. 'Do you hate me?'

Chloe walked alongside her. 'Of course I don't hate you,' she said finally. Something strange had happened. Seeing Liam as he was now had shifted something in her. And despite her continued awkwardness with Gwen, she just couldn't bring herself to feel anger at Hannah. As she'd said, Chloe had long left by then. Things had been over between her and Liam for years. If anything, she felt bad for Hannah that she was now tied to Liam for ever in their joint parenthood.

'Good, because I was going to tell you, eventually.' Hannah blushed. 'You've been so great, with the café and everything, and I just feel like I've been a terrible friend. I didn't expect to see you walk in that day . . .' She was rambling now, and Chloe half listened, trying to process her feelings.

'I need to take this library book back,' she said eventually, even though she wasn't working at the library today.

'The fee, right?' Hannah looked anxious. 'Just let me know how much it is, and I'll come in and pay during my break or something.'

She still looked so upset that Chloe took her shoulders. 'Hey, listen. I'm not angry at you. A bit surprised, but that's all. Liam and I had long since broken up.' She smiled at her. 'I got over Liam a long, long time ago. You haven't done anything wrong.'

'Oh, Chloe.' Hannah sounded tearful as she hugged her. 'You're amazing, you know that?'

They talked about normal things as they reached their cars. *Paw Patrol* was on the television so loud they could hear the cheery theme song through the living room window. It was still wild that the little girl in there was not only Hannah's, but Liam's, too. Chloe still wasn't sure how it made her feel. It was weird. And kind of funny.

Chloe hugged Hannah goodbye, reassuring her again that she wasn't upset with her, and drove back to the library to return the book. A few more days wouldn't make much of a difference to the fee, but she might as well.

She supposed everyone did make mistakes. And any bad feelings she might have about the fact had been diminished by Hannah being so apologetic and embarrassed about it. At least it meant she hadn't lusted after Liam while Chloe was with him. And if Liam and Chloe had gotten married, it was doubtful he and Hannah would have gotten together.

It wasn't until she drove home and took a hot bath that Chloe realised why it didn't bother her as much as it perhaps should. She had gotten over Liam a long time ago. Maybe she had still been upset about everything that had transpired, but she had felt nothing at seeing him except shock. There was no old flame rekindling, no heartache or pining for what they had lost.

No, when Chloe closed her eyes and let someone she liked wander into her mind, it was a brown-eyed construction worker who made her heart flutter and a smile tug on her lips. She wasn't sure when it had happened, when Harry had gone from annoying stranger to a friend. Maybe more.

She dunked her head under the surface of the bathwater, the heat heavenly on her scalp.

CHAPTER TWENTY-THREE

THE EVENING OF the fifth proved cold but dry, and a little windy.
It was the perfect condition for fireworks. Harry picked her up in his
car, parking down the street so that Gwen wouldn't see him and
bother her with questions. Chloe rushed from the house before her
sister could ask her where she was going, and sighed in relief at the
warm interior of Harry's car. She kept glancing at Harry as they
drove, his large hands on the steering wheel, shifting gears now and
then as they talked about books and films and music.

She felt strangely calm around Harry. And something else, too. A
sense of excitement.

She looked out of the window at the passing houses, reminding
herself not to lose her head. She and Harry were barely friends. A
chaste peck on the cheek didn't change that. Maybe she was looking
at this too deeply.

Still, she couldn't help sensing that there was a certain energy
between them. She wondered if he felt it too. She couldn't tell as
she laughed at his jokes. All she knew was that she felt calm and well
in his presence. That things didn't matter so much.

The car park at Thornbridge Hall was full, and after circling
around for ten minutes, Harry sighed.

'Sorry, Chloe. Didn't think this through.'

'It's all right,' she reassured him.

They ended up parking somewhere else. The walk soon warmed them up, though, and as they approached the venue, the air smelled of smoke and crackled with excitement. People with children wrapped up in thick coats and gloves wandered around the hall grounds. There were dogs on leads, their owners' breaths fogging in front of their lips as they talked and laughed.

'I hope the poor doggies aren't scared of the fireworks,' said Chloe as a toy poodle trotted past on a lead.

'You like dogs?' said Harry, sounding delighted.

'Yeah, I don't know which I like more, dogs or cats.' She thought of Clementine. 'Cats are more aloof and make you work harder for their affection. Makes it more worth it when they let you pet them.'

'So you like having to do some chasing?' Harry asked slyly.

She burst out laughing. 'Maybe.'

'Noted.' Harry looked around. There were several small fires going already. 'I used to be scared of loud noises when I was a kid,' he said. 'When I was about five, I'd jump and start crying at the slightest thing. My mam brought me to a fireworks festival to cure me of it.'

'Wow,' said Chloe, not sure how to feel. 'That seems, um, harsh?'

'Maybe, but it worked,' he assured her. 'Though she told me I screamed the whole time and buried my face in her jacket. Then right at the end, I looked up and exclaimed, "Wow, it's so pretty." Then it was over.'

'Your mum sounds strict,' said Chloe as they climbed a grassy hill, people chattering all around them, the air smelling of smoke and cooking food.

'She's great. I'll introduce you sometime.'

Harry casually mentioning Chloe meeting his mother brought on a swooping sensation in her stomach, but they were distracted by a young woman who looked half frozen asking to see their tickets. Harry produced them and they were told they could get a free jacket potato at a nearby stall.

'Not bad,' Chloe remarked later, holding her box of chilli baked potato smothered in salty butter in her hands. People were lining up for hot chocolate and marshmallows, and the air held a heavenly mix of savoury and sweet food. Chloe huddled next to Harry, his warmth a relief in the cold night. The fireworks display would start in fifteen minutes.

Some children played with sparklers, laughing as they waved them around to spell their names or make shapes. They went to see the fire pit, which Chloe thought was quite small, but its warmth was delicious. Harry bought Chloe a hot chocolate and she happily sipped. It was gloriously creamy.

'It's starting,' said Harry, flinching only ever so slightly as the first of the fireworks screeched and popped into the sky. People oohed and aahed at the bright display. Chloe glanced around to see the people watching with delight. A few dogs cowered between their owners' legs; others looked unbothered. A man wrapped an arm around his boyfriend's shoulders, cuddling him close as they looked skyward. It was a beautiful moment, everyone stopping what they were doing to stand together and watch the fireworks.

Harry had a smile on his face, the lights reflecting in his eyes. Maybe it was the atmosphere or the fireworks, but Chloe thought he had never looked so handsome. His lips were parted in wonder, a look of innocent joy on his face.

A loud bang of a new firework caught her attention. It fizzed and crackled into hundreds of silver lights that faded into smoke. Harry's hand took her free one and squeezed tight.

The crowd watched in awe as the display hit its climax, colours exploding high above them in an orchestra of squeaks and pops and crackles. When the lights faded and all that was left was the sharp scent of lingering smoke, Harry turned to look at her, pleasure on his face. It made his eyes crinkle in a charming way.

'Fireworks,' he said, tucking a strand of her hair behind her ear. 'They never get old.'

He leaned down towards her, and Chloe felt a wave of joy, almost giddy with happiness. She nodded slightly and wrapped her arm around his neck, pulling him towards her. Their lips met. His were soft, the scent of his aftershave filling her nose, and his mouth parted eagerly to taste her, sending a shiver of desire to her core.

People talked and laughed around them, but Chloe didn't mind. Harry's strong arms wrapped around her waist as he kissed her, his touch full of promise. No one had kissed her like this in ages, and heat rushed to Chloe's cheeks, a contrast to the cold air. When he pulled back, he was grinning and she was breathless.

'You've no idea how long I've wanted to do that,' he said, taking her hand. 'I like you, Chloe.'

His words made her laugh. Chloe spent the rest of the evening on cloud nine. He held her hand for the rest of the night, his large thumb often running over the back of her hand. She was still walking on clouds when Harry dropped her off at home later. After he'd turned off the engine, he cupped her face in his hand and kissed her slowly, deeply, seducing a groan from her throat. Now they were alone, he lingered, planting soft, gentle kisses along her lips and her cheek. She sat in her seat, low music playing, pleasure tingling across her skin as she craved more.

Did he want her to invite him inside? Chloe wanted to, whether Gwen was in there or not. Her fingers found the top of his jacket and clung to his collar. She was about to ask him when Harry's lips reached her ear. His breath warm on her earlobe, he whispered, 'Goodnight, Chloe.'

She closed her eyes, reminding herself to breathe. Right. He wasn't ready. And that was okay.

'I had an amazing time,' she said, opening the car door. 'See you again.'

'Soon,' he promised, and she felt his eyes lingering on her as she climbed out of his car. He waited until she was at her door, and she waved at him, watching until his car had disappeared around the corner, the rumble of the engine fading away.

She still saw fireworks when she blinked, the taste of the hot chocolate and the masculine, comforting scent of Harry still on her lips as she went inside the house, sighing happily like a teenager on her first date. What was happening? She felt scared of these new feelings blossoming for Harry, but at the same time, she wanted to embrace them. She pressed her fingers gently against her lips, wishing she could keep the sense of him on her for longer.

Gwen wasn't here, the house empty. The thought was strangely lonely; she had gotten used to her sister greeting her and badgering her with questions when she returned. Oh well. This was peaceful. Now she could soak in the glorious aftermath of her date with Harry with no distractions.

When Chloe flicked the lights on, she noted that Gwen had managed to clean up after herself – the living room was neat, the cushions in their proper places and Dad's coffee table free of curled-up receipts or forgotten plates. The kitchen, too, sat unblemished, only a few things in the drying rack. Chloe put them away, wondering if Gwen was on a date of her own again. Maybe with the same guy as before. Chloe made a mental note to ask her sister how it'd gone.

The house was quiet, though fireworks occasionally popped and banged outside, people still celebrating. It almost felt like it had at the beginning after Chloe had come back, the first night she had spent here alone after the funeral. The aunts and distant relatives had gone home, some with boxes of clothes and other bits not precious enough to keep hold of that they promised to pass on to charity shops. With the last box in the attic and Mum and Dad's room door closed, Chloe had sat here and cried for hours.

After that, she'd gone back to Sheffield and her marketing job, and for several months she'd tried and failed to find some normalcy with this dark hole in her life where her parents used to be. Then when a solicitor had contacted her to sort out the legality of the property, she had taken it as a sign to finally admit defeat and leave her office job and tiny flat and move out here. Soon after, she had found the ad for the job at the library.

The library had been a solace. She didn't know what she would have done without Mrs Cook, Clementine, the library, and even Eric. Now she allowed herself to think about Harry, to enjoy a harmless fantasy of going on more dates with him, holding his hand, talking about anything.

But that was only a distraction. Gwen's presence could be annoying, but at least it was noise. Noise that distracted her from old memories.

Chloe wandered through the house and paused at the bottom of the staircase, where the moonlight shone through the arch-shaped frosted glass of the front door window. She couldn't keep looking for distractions.

She let the memories of her childhood wash over her.

Dad coming home from work, coughing from smoking too much as he closed the door to announce he was home. Chloe playing with Gwen as a child, then fighting over something silly, then making up. Playing a board game with their parents. The memories were painful, but Chloe let herself feel them. That was the way to get over the past – by facing it, feeling the agony, then letting it fade on its own.

Pushing it down or running away from it only made it fester in the deepest, darkest corners of your mind. Then it would come back at the worst possible moment, in the form of tears or anger or worse.

Chloe let her tears fall now, sinking onto the bottom stair. She missed her mum and dad more than she could bear. She wished that she had made more of an effort to spend time with them. A Facetime call every few weeks and the occasional text had not been enough. They had been so young that she had assumed, foolishly, that they would live for decades yet, that they would grow old together, sitting in rocking chairs with grandchildren on their laps. Mum's hair, blonde like Gwen's, would turn grey, her pretty face wrinkled. Dad, who shared Chloe's chestnut brown curls, might have gone bald eventually, or he would have proudly sported thick hair of salt and pepper.

If they had been on that road only a few minutes before or after, they would have been fine. Would have maybe heard of an accident with another car, an anecdote before they carried on with their lives. At least they had died together, on the same day. Horrible for

Chloe, but perhaps a comfort for them. Mum and Dad had been soulmates, everyone could see that.

For a long time, Chloe had felt angry with the old man who had driven down the wrong side of the road and crashed into them. Of all the terrible people in the world who could have died that day, why her parents? They had been good people. Normal, nice, had worked hard and loved their daughters. But the old man had been having a mental breakdown, or so Chloe had heard. He'd been confused and panicking.

It didn't make the loss any easier to bear.

She buried her face in her palms, sobbing, her heart in splinters. It was on this very step that she had opened her GCSE results, Mum and Dad sitting either side of her, congratulating her on getting an A in English. She sniffled, wiping her dripping nose. This wasn't how she was supposed to feel after such a great date.

Could she possibly stay in Wellbridge, with all the memories here? Running away and staying in the city hadn't helped much. And what about Gwen? Would she be abandoning her if she moved away? And what about the library? Harry?

Chloe hugged herself, and then texted Hannah, asking for funny pictures and memes to cheer her up. Within minutes, Hannah had sent a picture of her daughter Lily, covered head to toe in bubbles from her bubble bath, only her face visible. Chloe snorted and went to grab a tissue. She felt a bit better after crying. It had been a real ugly cry, too. She hadn't bothered to be quiet or tried to muffle the noise.

Along with the pain came guilt. Guilt for not spending more time with Mum and Dad. She had been so eager to escape this place, to leave Wellbridge and its memories of Liam and the botched wedding behind and finally go to university, that her contact with her parents hadn't been much more than the occasional phone call. She had spent so much time running away, but it hadn't really helped.

She let out a rattling sigh, laying a hand on her chest as Mum and Dad's smiling faces filled her mind's eye. Then Gwen's. If she was going to leave Wellbridge behind again, she would do so with better memories. There was no point in feeling guilty. Mum and Dad had known she had loved them.

Even with this mantra echoing in her head, Chloe went to bed with a heavy heart. She curled up under the blanket and said goodnight to Hannah.

Text me anytime you're feeling low messaged her best friend, perhaps sensing that Chloe was missing her parents.

I'm always here. I love you, Chloe.

Thank you, I love you too she texted back, sniffling. She closed her burning eyes, thinking instead of the fireworks display and her first kiss with Harry. She considered whether to tell Hannah, and couldn't help smiling to herself, feeling like a teenager and her first kiss. That had been with Liam. How different he had been from Harry.

She had gotten over Liam a long time ago, and wondered how different things would be now if she had married him after all. Maybe she would be Lily's mum. But would she be happy? She hadn't felt anything when she'd seen him.

She punched her pillow and snuggled into it, telling herself that now wasn't the time to dive into *that* rabbit hole. Her nose still blocked, Chloe managed to fall asleep, and didn't hear when Gwen came home later that night.

CHAPTER TWENTY-FOUR

CLEMENTINE WATCHED A streetlamp flicker outside, dearly hoping that tonight would be uneventful. It had been a busy week, humans walking all over the place, some reaching to pet him, many of them making a terrible mess of the books. He sat in his secret spot on a ceiling beam in the upper archives, his tail swishing this way and that. The streets were empty, and now and then the wind would blow, hooting against the stained glass.

He landed softly on the floorboards and moved in silence through the shelves. Maybe the automatic feeder would have left more food for him. His bell tinkled as he ran down the stairs, his stomach rumbling in anticipation.

The door to the lobby opened on its own as he approached it. Clementine stuck his nose in the air, pleased, and slunk through towards the kitchen.

A thump and a playful giggle from the lower archives stopped Clementine in his tracks.

He examined the dark front lobby, wondering if he had only been hearing the wind. He hesitated, then decided to check anyway. He was the library's night guardian, after all. When the humans weren't here, Clementine was in charge.

He trotted past the lobby desk and across where light from the streetlamp outside bled in through the gothic windows, casting its beam on the carpet. He reached the children's section and looked around. Everything looked normal. The soft play area, the shelves of children's books, the pictures of human kittens and the sun and animals.

Then Clementine glanced up.

Sitting on the top shelf was a cat.

Not the elegant, tabby female Clementine had met and lost. No, this was a huge cat, long and proportioned like a human, with black fur and wearing a ridiculous hat of red and white stripes. His tail, thick as a human's arm, swished too as he looked down at Clementine with interest.

Clementine's orange fur stood on end. He meowed.

The cat swung down to land noisily on the carpet. He had a thin neck with an enormous red bowtie wrapped around it. His face wasn't really feline, but cartoonish, with a small nose and a wide, smiling mouth.

'I know it is dark and the humans are gone, but we can play games and have lots of fun!' sang the Cat.

Yes, I'd rather not, thought Clementine. He turned to walk away, then yelped in horror when the giant Cat snatched him up with two gloved hands.

'Another cat, hip-hip, hooray! I know lots of good games we can pl—'

Clementine squirmed until he was free, furious. His paws hit the carpet and he ran, streaking past several non-fiction bookcases until he found one with a space. He leaped onto it and lay low, offended. Who did that hideous feline think he was?

Clementine trembled as he listened to crashes and singing all around the library. He caught sight of the Cat running past, giant feet thumping on the carpet. He was balancing books on his arms and strange things were coming out of his hat. An umbrella, a fishbowl, and all manner of items Clementine didn't know the names of.

No, this thing was not a human and not really a cat, either.

Clementine waited until the Cat had gone quiet, perhaps going to explore other parts of the library, then sneaked slowly down from the shelf, keeping as silent as he could. If he moved too quickly, his treacherous bell jangled, so he walked slowly, ears perked up for sounds of his enemy.

He reached the children's bookshelf. There it was, near the bottom of a pile of books. A glowing book.

Clementine tried to get it out, but it was weighed down by more books. A shriek of delight and a great crash sounded from the lobby. He didn't have much time.

Clementine pulled off each book with his paws, sliding them along until they fell. They lay scattered around the play area, but there wasn't much he could do about that now.

'Little cat, where are you? Orange ball of fun! Big Cat wants to play, so don't hide or run!'

Clementine yanked out a book that had a cartoon picture of the exact character terrorising the library. Clementine kicked it open. He had watched Chloe do this. Didn't she go to the back of the book?

He flipped through, looking at the pictures as he batted at each page to turn them. The Cat made a terrific mess in this story, too, though it looked like he cleaned up after himself in the end.

Clementine realised with dismay he couldn't send the Cat back to where he had come from. Clementine couldn't read. How had the tabby cat sent herself back?

He sat on his haunches, tired from all the batting and pulling, and frustrated with this furry nuisance. The Cat could not be here when Mrs Cook arrived tomorrow. The librarian was small and old, and might not be able to avoid the hideous creature long enough to read the character's last line and make the magic work.

He glanced around the library. It was always quiet at night. Clementine let out a soft 'meow'. The library didn't respond.

He understood now. It was up to him to make things right and defend his home.

Clementine's claws came out, just for a moment. The other cat may be bigger and stronger, but no one had the cunning and stealth skills of Clementine.

He trotted back to the archway that separated the children's and non-fiction from the lobby. The big Cat had found the light switch, and the lobby was now flooded with light, stark and bright. The Cat was flying a kite, somehow without any wind, laughing.

'Oh, this library is fun, this library is cool, I'll invite my friends, they'll love it, too!'

Not your friends, thought Clementine with a groan. His time was running out. Papers had fallen from the shelves, pens and other bits of stationery all over the carpet. The shelf behind the lobby desk was a fright, files and papers scattered all over the floor and desk.

Clementine ran to get the book, clamping it in his jaws. This was the only thing that might work.

He meowed as loud as he could, the book still in his mouth. He dropped it onto the floor as the huge Cat came over. Clementine trembled, but he refused to move.

'A book! Oh, look! What a handsome Cat,' said the Cat, snatching it up. 'And he looks just like me, fancy that, fancy that.'

Clementine was getting tired of the silly rhyming, but he walked over to the Cat, meowing his encouragement.

As he hoped, the giant Cat read aloud the story, taking pleasure in his own mischievous tale. All the while, Clementine looked around.

'Oh, look, see here, it's all about me! Why, I'm as handsome as handsome can be.' The Cat looked pleased. 'That's right, I clean up after myself. I'll dust and tidy all the floors and the shelf!'

Clementine took refuge on the shelf behind the lobby desk, watching as the Cat reappeared with a strange machine that cleaned up the mess he had made. Soon the books and papers were back in their places, the computer back on the desk and shining, good as new, and the Cat leaped off it, giving a grin that looked almost feline. But not quite.

Clementine rested his head on his paws. At least the nuisance had cleaned up after himself.

'Now, let's finish this book, it is quite a read. How thrilling I could come here in your hour of need!'

Hour of need? Clementine stood on his four paws, highly offended. But the Cat continued reading his story aloud, and then finally, he reached his own last line.

'Oh!' he said in shock as he faded. 'Oh my.'

Then he was gone.

Clementine leaped down from the shelf, looking around. He picked up the book, no longer glowing, in his mouth and carried it back to the children's section.

What a frightful evening, he thought as he tried to slide it back onto the shelf. He didn't do a very good job, but he hoped the humans wouldn't mind too much. Then, exhausted, he collapsed where he was and slept until the rising sun warmed his fur.

Chloe didn't remember falling asleep, but suddenly her alarm was going off and she woke up half off the bed, drool on her pillow. Today was Thursday, and Chloe listened out for sounds of Gwen as she readied for work. She didn't hear her downstairs, but she thought she could hear a low voice talking when she walked past Gwen's door.

'Oh,' she murmured, realising her sister might not be alone. She hurried and finished getting ready, eating the last of one of Hannah's delicious nut-free croissants before exiting into the icy autumn air.

She found Clementine in the lobby, lethargic with his tail swishing. 'Are you all right, Clem?' she asked, hurrying to him. He let her pick him up, and purred as she held him close. Chloe felt alarmed. He wasn't sick, was he?

But Clem perked up at her presence, licking her arm as she petted him between his soft ears. He didn't look sick, just tired. 'Busy night?' she asked softly, and Clementine gave a soft meow.

They had a few customers today, news of the successful school event travelling around fast. Hannah had left a pile of business cards for the Brew House on the lobby desk, and Chloe made sure everyone who came to visit the library got one. Chloe kept busy, chatting with the friendlier visitors, recommending books, and even making two new library cards and registering their membership.

'Lots of companies prefer to start using apps now, don't they?' said a middle-aged woman as Chloe inputted her details into the computer. 'I prefer physical cards. I kind of miss them taking up space in my purse. And what if your phone runs out of battery and you can't use the app? Then you'd be stuck, wouldn't you?' She held up the copy of the historical romance set in Scotland that had glowed all those weeks ago. Chloe had inspected it thoroughly before letting the visitor check it out, ensuring that there was no burning hue illuminating the pages. 'That's why I prefer physical books, and cards, too,' said the woman. 'You don't have to worry about batteries and chargers for those.'

Chloe nodded politely, letting the woman chatter. She smiled broadly when she accepted the little purple library card with her name printed on it.

'That's lovely,' she said, bringing out her purse. 'Thank you, duck.'

It had been raining heavily that morning, and Chloe had driven to work. Now it was the end of her shift and the rain had stopped, the ground dark and damp, a taste of rain still in the air. Chloe played music, the window down, enjoying the cold breeze. As she waited in traffic, she glanced over a stone wall to the graveyard.

She still hadn't visited Mum and Dad's graves since she'd been here. She could tell herself she had been busy, that she was waiting to go with Gwen, but the truth was she was nervous. Scared, even. The funeral was a sad blur, and being in their house was difficult enough, let alone visiting their resting places. She had only just started to accept the memories the house conjured. Seeing their gravestones would be like peeling back the layers of clumsy healing on a wound and letting it bleed again.

She was about to turn from the window to change the song

when she spotted a man walking along the graveyard, a bouquet of flowers in his hand.

She would recognise him anywhere. It was Harry.

He hadn't noticed her in the line of afternoon traffic. He walked with his usual confident stride, though there was something slumped in his posture. Chloe could spot the flowers in his bouquet: pink chrysanthemums and lavender freesias. Chloe squinted, sure she could also see several daisies in the wrapped paper.

Daisies in a bouquet? she thought with curiosity. He must be visiting his wife Julie's grave. She felt a prickle of worry. Was he regretting their date at the fireworks display? Did he feel bad about their kiss?

A sudden loud honk behind her made her jump nearly out of her skin. The car behind had beeped. She hadn't realised the traffic in front had moved on.

She quickly waved an apology and sped off down the road, hoping the noise hadn't drawn Harry's attention.

CHAPTER TWENTY-FIVE

THE NEXT MORNING, a man Chloe didn't know came into the library. He looked around the lobby at the rafters above, the medieval arched windows, the rows and rows of bookshelves, his thick eyebrows raised. Chloe watched from the corner of her eye, recalling her own first time entering the library. Her reaction had been much the same.

'Hello,' she said warmly when the man had had his fill of staring around the lobby area. He looked at her, not smiling back. There was something about the firm, hard line of his mouth and the coldness in his eyes that made her uneasy.

'Hi.' He strode towards her. Chloe was aware of the desk between them, but his approach still made her nervous. Perhaps noticing this, the man stopped, loitering in place and shifting his weight from one foot to the other. 'Um, can I ask you something? Were you at the fireworks display the other night?'

Chloe didn't see the point in lying. 'Um. Yes.'

'And that was Harry Ashcroft you were with, right? At Thornbridge Hall?'

Chloe relaxed a little. Obviously, the man knew Harry. 'Yes,' she said, carefully now. 'Sorry, who are you?'

'I'm someone who knows him.' The man fidgeted, looking sulky as he thrust his hands into his pockets. 'Look, it's best you stay away from him, all right?'

'What?' she said in surprise. 'From Harry? Why?'

'He's bad news,' the man grumbled. 'He's trouble. Stay away from him if you know what's good for you.'

Curiosity and a hint of indignation ran through her. 'What do you mean?'

'Just trust me.'

'I don't trust you. I don't even know you.' Chloe was becoming truly annoyed now, and she crossed her arms over her chest. 'Stop being cryptic. You came to my workplace for this?'

'Yeah, I heard you talking about the library at the event. I'm not a stalker or anything,' he added.

Chloe wished Mrs Cook or Eric would show up, but they were busy with other customers in the library. This man was making her feel more and more uncomfortable.

He must have seen it on her face, because the stranger headed towards the exit. 'I'm leaving.' When his hand was on the door, he said over his shoulder, 'Just ask Harry whose fault it is that his wife died.'

The door closed with a dull thud behind him, leaving Chloe alone and confused.

'What was that?' she asked aloud. The library's lights flashed brightly for a moment and a sigh that smelled like lavender washed over her.

Mrs Cook had been in a great mood ever since the event with the schoolchildren. Hannah's café was enjoying some more publicity too, according to her excited messages and photos of the little eatery being full to bursting. *We keep running out of cheesecake* she texted Chloe. *This is amazing. We HAVE to do this again.*

'Maybe we should plan something for Christmas, now it's coming up,' said Mrs Cook happily, as she cleaned up the lobby desk.

Clementine had perked up and was back to his usual self, watching them from his spot on top of the shelf after eating from his feeder. 'We could get some tinsel, gather some of the books with a Christmas theme, and have a reading. Ooh, I think there's a local author living in Kendall, I should check. Hannah could make mince pies. Could you ask her when you see her, Chloe?'

Chloe responded with as much enthusiasm as she could muster, half thinking about what the strange man had said before leaving so abruptly that there hadn't been time to process his words and ask more questions. No doubt he knew Harry and held some kind of grudge against him. What had he meant by whose *fault* it was?

Chloe hadn't asked how Harry's wife, Julie, had died. She had assumed, since she must have been young, that it had been an accident like Chloe's parents. She swallowed, her throat suddenly tight as fear curdled in her stomach.

'Chloe, are you all right?' Mrs Cook looked alarmed. 'You don't look well. Are you feeling poorly?'

'I . . .' Despair filled Chloe. When she had first met Harry, she hadn't liked him. Found him annoying and rude. What if he had used his charms to attract her and made her like him, but he wasn't really a very nice person at all? What if he was dangerous? She had gotten into his car, let him kiss her . . .

'I am feeling a bit sick, yes,' she said faintly.

Mrs Cook made a sympathetic noise. 'You can take the rest of the day off, if you need to.' She was so kind it made tears spring to Chloe's eyes. She turned to quickly brush them away before the librarian could see.

The thought of going home and being alone with her thoughts was worse than staying and trying to keep herself busy. Chloe knew what she needed right now: somebody to talk to. Someone who didn't know Harry and who wouldn't judge her. 'No, I think I'm okay, actually.' She sniffled. 'I'm going to go upstairs for a bit and, uh . . .' She couldn't think of a task that would take her to the fiction archives.

'You go, dear.' Mrs Cook nodded knowingly. 'Sometimes we do

need some time alone in the *fiction* section, hmm?' Her warm green eyes turned towards the ceiling. 'Give her a couple of choices, won't you?'

Something rippled in the library. Like a confirmation.

'Thanks,' said Chloe, grateful. 'I won't be long. And if you need me . . .'

'I'll call you.' Mrs Cook was already sitting at the computer. 'I hope you find what you're looking for, Chloe.'

Chloe hurried to the spiral staircase in the next room that led up to the fiction section. Clementine followed her, his bell jangling. Nobody was here now, almost as if the library had ensured the place would be empty for this moment. Chloe strode past Clementine's corner, and the cat jumped onto his bed, watching as Chloe wandered the shelves.

Mrs Cook's request had been heard in the library. Many of the books glowed, golden rectangles among the romance, fantasy, and even mystery sections. Curious, she picked up a large hardback in the latter section, giving a small smile. Ah, yes. A genius detective from London should be able to help. She needed objective advice and logic right now.

She read out the first line from the book, picturing firmly in her mind the character she needed. Then felt the familiar breath of magic wash over her and a new presence nearby.

'Oh.' A shuffle. 'Oh dear.'

There he was. 'Sir?' she asked, stepping into the next aisle.

He was taller than she had expected, his thin physique making him look even more so. A deerstalker cap sat atop a head of dark hair. Alert eyes fixed on her over a hawk-like nose.

'Hello, detective,' she said politely. She still held the book in her hands. She tucked it beneath her arm. 'I was wondering if you could help me with something.'

'Well, I suppose I'm not doing much else at the moment.' He straightened, fixing her with an analysing look. 'How can I help?'

They went to sit on the armchairs by the window. Well, Chloe sat, while the London detective examined the curtains and floors with a thoughtful look. Chloe didn't see the point in meandering around the subject. She told him all about Harry, her growing feelings for him, Julie, and what the strange man had said to her this morning.

'So the question is, how do I approach this to get the truth?' she asked the detective. 'Do I risk it, or should I stop talking to him?' Despite the fears the stranger's words had inspired in her, the thought of cutting Harry off made her chest squeeze with misery.

'If you ask him yourself, he could lie,' observed the detective. 'Hmm. Maybe you need to catch him off guard. Don't ask him any specific questions. Did the man say who he was? Perhaps he is the one lying.'

Chloe knew all this, but somehow it was nice to hear it come from someone else's mouth. 'I suppose he could be a competitor, but it seems like a lot of trouble to go to just to spoil a new relationship.' A relationship Harry didn't want people to know about. Was there a reason for that, other than him not being ready for people to know he was moving on from his late wife?

'Well, one thing is for certain. You must ask him. Gauge his reaction and hear his explanation.' The detective rummaged in his jacket pocket, then his face fell in dismay. 'I don't have my pipe with me.'

'Sorry about that. Smoking isn't allowed in this library.' Chloe rose to her feet. 'It's all right. I'm sending you back now. Thank you for your help.'

'Another important case solved,' the detective said drily. He tipped his hat as she smiled at him, flipping to the back of the book.

The detective had said what Chloe needed to hear. She wasn't going to be a cliché like in a bad romance novel, avoiding the topic and breaking her own heart by simply not talking to Harry and asking him his side of the story outright. Miscommunication tropes were so out. Chloe whipped out her phone to text him, and then hesitated.

Would asking Harry outright be a good idea, or would he lie? She should at least ask him in person so she could see the look on his face, work out whether he was lying. So instead of asking him over text, she asked, *Can we talk?*

It took a while for him to text her back, and Chloe was taking care of the accounting sheets when her phone buzzed in her pocket.

Sounds ominous. What about?

'Your wife' wasn't something Chloe wanted to write in a text, so instead she wrote *Nothing bad, but can you meet me tonight? My shift ends at 6.*

I'll wait for you outside. Car or no car?

No car.

Chloe was antsy for the rest of her shift. She apologised to Mrs Cook and asked her to double-check the sheet. The last thing she needed was to make a mistake because she was stressing over a man.

The first man she had had feelings for in years. That was what made all this so much worse. She wasn't ready to be hurt again. Harry was one of the few good things about Wellbridge. If something bad happened between them, she wasn't sure she could face continuing living in Wellbridge. She didn't need more pain for her slowly healing heart.

Which was why she should just ask him what that strange man had meant. It would bother her no end if she didn't.

Clementine crouched beside a shelf, keeping himself as close to the floorboards as he could. There was something in here. A creature, running around on tiny paws in a place where it should not have been.

Mrs Cook was in the lobby, doing some last-minute tasks before she closed the library. Animals almost never made it into the library, but there was something here. And Clementine meant to catch it.

Little feet scurried past the children's section. Clementine moved in silence, careful not to let his bell jangle. Excitement ran across his fur. He was hardly ever able to hunt, but surely Mrs Cook wouldn't mind if he caught something inside the library? He had never seen another non-human in here before. Not one from outside. It smelt different. He could hear a tiny heartbeat, the fast breathing of an animal much smaller than himself.

There! It was a little mouse. Its nose twitched, its ears moving this way and that as it looked around with black, beady eyes. Clementine examined the mouse with interest. He had never seen an animal wearing clothes before.

No matter. Clementine jumped after the mouse, meaning to pin it to the floor like he had with the frog.

But the mouse scurried off just in time, its tail swishing as it took refuge beneath a nearby bookcase. Clementine howled his annoyance, crouching to swipe at the little mouse underneath the shelf. There was only a tiny gap between it and the carpet, far too small for Clementine to even fit his paw through.

The mouse was wiping his face with a handkerchief, a tiny one barely bigger than one of Clementine's claws. 'That was a close one,' the mouse remarked. 'Nice try, kitty, but you have to be faster than that to catch me.'

Clementine stood straight. Had he been a human, he might have gasped. The mouse was speaking the human language. And using a handkerchief. He was like a little boy in a mouse's body.

'Clem?' called Mrs Cook, coming in from the lobby and looking around for him. 'What is it? What are you meowing at?'

Clementine didn't take his eyes off the little creature, but the mouse didn't seem to want to move, knowing that if it – he? – ran off, Clementine would follow. The cat meowed for her attention, and he waited until Mrs Cook was crouching beside him, her line of sight following his.

'Oh, thank goodness. A person,' said the mouse. 'Please tell your cat I mean no harm. I think I came here by mistake.'

Mrs Cook's eyebrows rose and her mouth opened in a little O. Then she shook her head and smiled, saying, 'My goodness, you gave me a fright.' She picked up Clementine with her gentle hands. 'Out you come, little one. Clementine won't hurt you, I promise.'

Clementine huffed, reluctantly withdrawing his claws. The

mouse wore a white hat and a red jumper, and he cautiously crawled out from beneath the shelf and dusted himself off. He took off his hat. 'It sure is nice to meet you, ma'am.'

'Oh, you too,' said Mrs Cook fondly, petting Clementine.

The librarian seemed to have taken charge of the situation. The cat lay in Mrs Cook's arms and let the elderly woman take them to the children's section, all the while talking with the mouse about cities and families and all kinds of things Clementine didn't care to understand. He hadn't been allowed to catch the mouse, though truly, he was already getting quite bored of the little creature.

Clementine wriggled out of Mrs Cook's arms and hopped onto a bookcase, sulking as he watched her pluck a glowing book from a nearby shelf. 'This should send you back home to your parents,' she promised.

'Thanks,' said the mouse, sounding grateful.

After flipping to the back, Mrs Cook read out a passage. The mouse took off his hat and bowed to her before vanishing.

'Clemmy, aren't you such a good boy.' Mrs Cook petted Clementine, stroking his face and around his ears until his bad mood evaporated and he mewed his approval. 'You didn't try to hurt him, did you?' She drew back, looking around the library. 'But that's so strange. Who brought him out?'

Clementine hadn't seen anybody here during his patrol. He lay his head on his paws, tail slowly swishing as he watched Mrs Cook fold her arms, frowning with her eyes closed as though she was thinking deeply about something.

'Hmm. Well, never mind.' She gave Clementine one last pet and kissed his head. 'I have to be getting home. See you tomorrow, Clem.'

CHAPTER TWENTY-SIX

TRUE TO HIS word, Harry was waiting for Chloe outside, a scarf around his neck that matched his brown eyes. Despite her anxiety, warmth flooded Chloe at the sight of him. How was it that some people made the world around them brighter when they showed up? There was something calming about his presence even as nerves danced in her chest like erratic fireflies.

'Hi, Chloe,' he said. 'There's a café down the road that's still open. Shall we talk there?'

It was dinnertime, but Chloe didn't know if she'd be able to eat anything, her stomach was so tied up in knots. She ordered a bacon sandwich and a decaf coffee anyway at the little corner café.

'I've never been here before,' she remarked, taking off her jacket. She almost felt bad for going to a place that was surely competing with Hannah's café, but she wouldn't be able to talk privately with Harry with her best friend there.

They chose a corner table by the window for privacy. Chloe glanced outside, half expecting to see the weird guy watching them, loitering on the pavement. But the cobblestone street was quiet, save one woman walking her dog.

Chloe watched them for a moment, wishing she were the dog

and her worst problem right now was not being allowed to chase pigeons.

'Chloe, is everything all right?'

She whipped her head around to face Harry. He had taken off his scarf and jacket and was wearing a green knitted jumper underneath that reminded her of cosy nights in and Christmas-time. 'Yes.' She perched on the seat, wondering how to broach the subject. Now that they were here, she almost wanted to leave it alone.

They made small talk about work and the weather for a while, but the unsaid topic ballooned between them. Like avoiding talking about Mum or Dad or Liam when she was with Gwen, except a hundred times louder. Even when their coffees came, it buzzed around her like a bothersome fly, filling her with frantic energy.

'Okay. I'll just ask.' She set down her cup. It clinked in its saucer.

Harry was good at looking nonchalant, but he straightened slightly at her words, as though he was privately battling the same anticipation and dread.

Chloe told him about the man who had seen them at the fireworks festival and his ominous words in the library that morning. 'He said . . . to ask you whose fault it was. About Julie.' She winced, hating to bring it up but also knowing she couldn't avoid the subject if this thing between them was to go on.

She expected Harry to fervently shake his head, to say he had no idea who that man was, and what a ridiculous thing to say. She thought he might insist Julie's death had been a horrible accident and the stranger was trying to cause trouble for no reason. What she didn't expect was for Harry to let out a bitter laugh and rub the bridge of his nose. His eyes were closed when he said, 'Right. Jason.'

'So you know him, then.'

'I do.' Harry looked at her. 'You see . . . Jason is my wife's brother.'

'Oh.' She took a sip of coffee, letting the creamy, rich warmth run across her tongue. 'All right. Go on.'

Something flitted across Harry's face. Pain. 'After the funeral,

Jason said it was my fault. He's . . . not entirely wrong, either, if I have to be honest.'

'What happened to her?' Chloe's heart thumped. 'Please, just tell me.' Harry had no idea of the number of terrible possibilities that were tumbling through her mind right now.

He leaned back, his large chest rising and slowly falling. 'We had just bought our house in Wellbridge. The bills were high, and the purchase had left us broke. My business was taking off but I was still paying off my course. I wanted to wait, you know, before having children. I thought in a couple of years, I'd have saved up enough and been in a better place financially.' He took another sip of coffee. Part of Chloe wanted to urge him on, to rip off the Band-Aid, but she understood that he was perhaps mulling over the words, choosing and shaping them to say it right. She shifted in her seat and mirrored him, sipping with caution as she burned with curiosity and dread.

'When things were better for us and I'd paid off some bills, we started trying for a baby,' said Harry. 'But then they found the cancer in her ovaries.' Harry grimaced in pain. Or guilt. 'Maybe if we had seen a doctor sooner, if we had tried to get pregnant just a couple of months earlier, they would have found it before it was too late.'

Chloe was silent. The café around them kept going; people talked, spoons clinked against mugs, a coffee machine hissed in the next room. Harry breathed deeply, as though trying to contain his emotion, and Chloe wished they had found a more private place to talk. She rummaged in her bag and brought out a packet of tissues, sliding them along the table towards him.

Harry took one, holding it in his fist. 'Jason blames me. Says it's my fault I made her wait. And he isn't wrong, is he?' His jaw was set, and Chloe could tell he was trying not to cry.

'It's not your fault,' she said softly as her heart broke for him.

'It is,' he said, staring down at the tissue. 'If I had said, "sod it, we'll manage," they would have found the cancer sooner. She could have had better treatment. She was only twenty-seven.' Chloe was horrified to see tears slip free of Harry's eyes, and he reached up to wipe them away. The whites of his eyes had gone red and he looked out of the window, perhaps trying to distract himself.

'I'm sorry,' she said. She wanted to take it back. Poking her nose in. How could she have thought Harry was capable of hurting his wife? 'It isn't your fault. You couldn't have known what was going to happen.'

'Yeah.' Chloe supposed Harry had gone through all this by himself, battled with the guilt and the truth. 'But I still have to live with it every day and wonder *what if.*' He rubbed his face again. 'Ugh. Jason probably doesn't like to see me moving on. When she . . . died, he wanted to fight me. He tried to start something right after her funeral. He's blamed me ever since.'

'He needs to move on,' said Chloe firmly. 'You didn't cause Julie's illness. Nobody would have wished it on her, especially you.' And though it hurt to say it, she added, 'I can tell. You loved her very much.'

Harry seemed to calm himself. 'I did, but there comes a time when you have to look to the future.'

Chloe wondered if Harry felt uncomfortable here with her. She had her own memories of Wellbridge to do with her ex-fiancé Liam, her sister Gwen, and her parents. The chapel, certain streets, even shops. How many of the restaurants and cafés around town reminded Harry of Julie? The streets, the events? Chloe couldn't bring herself to feel jealous of a woman who had passed away, but she felt like she was intruding.

It had been only two years, but all that time, Harry had been on his own. She understood the guilt about being ready to start moving on. 'Sometimes, when I'm feeling happy,' she said, her voice quiet, 'I want to stop myself. I don't think I deserve to feel happiness when Mum and Dad died so recently. Like I'm insulting their memory by smiling when I should be grieving them every moment of the day.'

Harry turned his gaze to her.

'But they wouldn't want that.' Chloe swallowed, her own grief creeping up to form as tears. 'I know it's different, but in some ways it's the same. You feel responsible. And Jason thinks you are, too. But I think if I were Julie, I would want the man I loved to be able to find happiness. And deciding when the time is right for that would be his choice, no one else's.'

Harry took Chloe's cold hand and brought it to his lips. He held it there, clasped before his mouth, warming it with his large hands. She kept her hand there, feeling the soft warmth of his breath against her knuckles, and he hung on to it like a life raft.

'We can go as slow as you want,' she whispered.

The sandwiches arrived, though the mood between them was now sombre. Chloe wished Julie's brother, Jason, had been more forthright instead of giving her an ominous message. Maybe Gwen was right. She read too many books. She had read the situation all wrong. Guilt squirmed in her for thinking badly of Harry and letting the situation escalate, but at least now she knew the truth.

They ate in silence, Chloe trying to think of something to say to break the tension. If she mentioned doing something for Christmas in the library, would it just drag up memories of Christmases with Julie? But also, why should she skirt around the subject?

Skirting around subjects was . . . a speciality of Chloe's, arguably.

'That was nice,' said Harry, finishing off his coffee. He lowered his voice. 'But I think Hannah does it better.'

She giggled. 'I owe you, remember?' she said when Harry took out his wallet to pay. 'Don't think I've forgotten.'

He met her eyes, and she saw the ghost of a smile. 'Aw, I thought you had.'

They ended up agreeing to pay half each, and left the warmth of the café to step into the chilly early winter air.

'It's snowing,' said Chloe in delight. White flakes fell all around them. With the mystery of Jason's words settled and her stomach full of bacon, Chloe's mood lifted. She looked up at Harry, who returned her smile and took her hand.

The streets fell quiet with the snowfall, and already the roofs looked sprinkled with sugar. They walked to her place in comfortable silence, Chloe pondering everything. They were both grieving and vulnerable, but she felt she was ready to date. Harry seemed so, too, even if he wanted to take things slowly. Their entwined fingers were a testament to that.

'So is this why you don't want anyone to know that we're going out?' she asked Harry as they strolled up the street towards her house. 'Because of Jason?'

'Not only because of him,' said Harry. 'I was worried, I suppose. Of what people might think of me seeing someone new. Of what *I* might think. Part of me felt I was betraying her. I know that's silly.'

'It's not.' They had stopped walking now. Here between the houses, the wind was gentle. Snow fell silently all around them, settling in Harry's hair and melting on his pink cheeks. 'I can't understand it fully, but I can try. Like I said, I sometimes feel guilty when I'm not grieving my parents. When I start to enjoy being in their old house without crying for them. Even though they would want me to be happy.'

'Julie said that to me, as well,' Harry said. 'When she was . . . near the end. She told me to find happiness.'

'Then let yourself find it.' Chloe cupped his face, feeling the stubble beneath her palm. She remembered seeing him at the graveyard, the book about flowers he had borrowed, how he had added daisies and freesias to the bouquet.

A snowflake fluttered between them to land cold on her nose. 'Let yourself be happy. With me, or with whoever else. When you're ready. Jason is angry now, but he won't be for ever.'

'I didn't smile for a long time after her funeral.' Harry covered the hand on his face with his own. His warm brown eyes roamed over her face. 'And as you know, I was grumpy all the time.'

A reluctant laugh escaped her. 'Yup.'

'But that first time, meeting you in the library that day. The way you shouted "You're welcome" after me when I was . . . less than polite.'

She groaned. 'You heard me say that?'

'I did. So did Mrs Cook.' His eyes crinkled. 'You made me smile again.' He leaned towards her, his warmth draping over her, until their faces were nearly touching. 'I smiled all day after that. People so often treat me like I'm fragile, awkward, they don't know what to say, like I'll fracture at the wrong word. But you only ever treated me normally. And ever since that day, you've only interested me more. Even when we argued at the pub. I was fascinated by you.'

He inclined his head to kiss her, tasting of peppermint. Chloe closed her eyes, savouring him as the snow fell in a flourish around them. His heat was delicious, and she leaned into his strength as his tongue slid along hers, full of hunger and promise.

When he broke the kiss, Chloe said, 'I'm okay with taking things slowly for now. We'll tell people when you're ready to.' She still hadn't told Gwen about Harry, after all. All her sister knew was what she had worked out for herself.

The drama with Jason made Chloe think of her ex-boyfriend. Not Liam, her ex-fiancé who had kissed Gwen, but the guy she had been seeing in Sheffield. She told Harry about him as they covered the last few paces to Chloe's house. 'I was seeing this guy, but it wasn't anything serious.' She glanced skyward, briefly hoping the snow wouldn't stick. 'When I got the news about my parents' accident, I came straight to Derbyshire to see them in the hospital. I was supposed to be meeting him that day, but I switched off my phone and forgot to tell him I couldn't make it. I'd forgotten all about it.' She sighed, recalling the nail-biting anxiety as she had driven as fast as she'd dared to the Royal Derby Hospital, everything related to Sheffield and the people in it completely gone from her mind.

Harry squeezed her hand. 'That's understandable. Who wouldn't forget?'

'You'd think so, wouldn't you?' Chloe said. 'I went to visit them. I was at the hospital for hours.' She didn't want to go into all the terrible details about her parents' injuries. 'I finally remembered to switch my phone back on sometime later that night. Simon had blown up my phone. So many missed calls and text messages. I told him what had happened, hoping for some sympathy.' She could still smell the garish antiseptic scent of the bright hospital hallway, taste the cheap coffee, hear the clack of her shoes as she'd stepped outside, trying to find enough phone signal to call him back. The angry tears she'd shed. 'He just gave me a hard time over it, saying I should have let him know and that I was selfish for keeping him waiting.'

'Selfish?' asked Harry, appalled.

'Right?' Chloe nodded. 'He went on and on about the plans he'd made, as if I hadn't just told him my mum and dad were . . .' The word 'dying' caught in her throat.

'Some people have no empathy.' Harry looked satisfyingly irked on her behalf. 'What a jerk.'

'Yeah.' It still annoyed her when she thought about it for too long. She had ended things shortly afterwards and blocked him on everything. After that, Chloe had been truly alone. Until she had come to Wellbridge. 'What I'm trying to say is that people can be insensitive. They can't see past their own needs.'

They had reached Chloe's front door. The cold was starting to seep into her toes, and she couldn't wait to get warm. Chloe turned to face him. 'Sorry,' she said quietly. 'You don't have your car with you, do you?'

'I'll manage.' He smiled and kissed her on the lips. It was a slow, seductive kiss that promised so much more, and Chloe found herself breathless and hot as he held her face, his fingers firm but gentle. His thumb slid along her jawbone, settling delicately on the hollow of her throat.

The question rose to her lips. *Do you want to come inside for a bit?* But maybe – clearly – he wasn't ready for that. She wanted to move things along when they were both ready. He wanted to take things slowly, and that's what she would do. Surely she could control herself.

Even if she could see the spark of desire in his brown eyes as they roamed over her face as though trying to commit it to memory.

'Goodnight, Harry, I'll text you tomorrow, thanks for walking me home,' she said all in one breath. She gave him one last peck on the lips and went inside. His absence felt like she was stepping into a cold room rather than a heated home. She glanced through the frosted window to see his vague shape leaving, hands thrust into his pockets as he took long strides down the street. She watched until he had disappeared around the corner.

CHAPTER TWENTY-SEVEN

GWEN WAS IN and awake, wearing some fluffy pyjamas. There was no music playing and the TV was switched off. To Chloe's shock, her sister was reading a book.

'Are you feeling ill?' she asked as she set down her bag on the nearby armchair. She rushed to her sister's side and laid a hand against her forehead. 'Are you unwell? Should I call an ambulance?'

'Ha, ha,' remarked her sister, glancing up as Chloe smirked. She was reading the book she had bought as a replacement for Chloe's. Which wasn't surprising, considering they didn't own any others. 'I wanted to see what all the fuss was about this book. That library of yours, it's . . .' She searched for the right word. 'It's actually really beautiful.'

Chloe flushed with pleasure. Even though it wasn't her library, she still felt a rush of pride. 'I love it, too. What do you think of the book?' Gwen wasn't very far through it. Twenty pages at best.

Gwen pursed her lips. 'It's going slowly. I haven't read a book since, what, Year Ten? *Of Mice and Men*.'

'GCSE English. I remember,' said Chloe fondly. 'Did you actually read that one, or did you just google the synopsis?'

Gwen threw a cushion at her. 'What's wrong with wanting to get back into reading?'

'Wrong? Gwen, it's the best thing ever.' Chloe felt a surge of happiness. 'I've got so many books to introduce you to.' Already, several titles came to mind. What would Gwen be most likely to enjoy? Fantasy? Romance? Thriller? Maybe smut?

'All right, calm down,' Gwen said, as though she could see the shelves flicking through Chloe's mind. 'I'm not sure if I even *like* reading yet.' She gave her sister a knowing look. 'Besides, I saw a certain *someone* outside.'

'We really need to get darker curtains,' sighed Chloe. 'I'm allowed to have friends, you know.' She slid off the couch and busied herself with her handbag, though she wasn't entirely sure what she was looking for.

Gwen snorted. 'Most people don't kiss their friends.'

'Gross, you were spying?'

'Of course.'

Gwen grinned, and Chloe couldn't stop her reluctant smile either. 'I got a job,' said Gwen, and Chloe's mouth fell open in shock. Gwen looked at her over the book, a glint in her eye. 'Remember, I was out the other night? And a few nights since then?'

'On a date, you said the first time,' said Chloe. 'And I heard you talking the other morning.'

'I was on the phone, you muppet.' Gwen rolled her eyes. 'The first evening was a job interview, and I've been working shifts there. It's the bar on High Street, the Pride & Pint. You really helped me with my CV, Chloe. I wrote all about mixing drinks that time I was in Barcelona, and they loved it.'

It took a moment for the words to sink in. Gwen hadn't been out on dates. She'd found a job. All by herself. No wonder she had smelt of alcohol that night. Chloe had assumed she'd been out drinking. But she had been serving it.

'Gwen, that's amazing. Congratulations!' Chloe threw her arms around Gwen's shoulders and hugged her hard. It was the first time they'd hugged like this in . . . Chloe couldn't even remember how long. Too long. She squeezed her sister tight, loving the feel of her embrace. She kissed her cheek, which smelled of her make-up. A comforting, feminine scent. 'That is amazing. I'm so proud of you.'

'It's just a bar. Nothing special,' said Gwen begrudgingly, though her cheeks pinked a bit. 'Anyway, I can start paying towards the bills and stuff. It's the least I can do. Considering I live here.' She shifted. 'As soon as I get my first wage, I'm paying you back for the ingredients and the book and stuff. And we can start splitting the bills.'

'If you were going to an interview, why did you say you had a date the other night?' Chloe asked. She hadn't seen a reason to question Gwen's explanation for being out. Gwen was stunningly gorgeous, always had been, and could go out with whoever she wanted. Chloe hadn't doubted that she'd find plenty of matches on whatever dating app she might use. Had it been because she didn't want to jinx the interview, or was it to protect Chloe's feelings? Instead of avoiding the topic, she asked her outright. 'Was it because of my . . . friend?'

Gwen nodded, drumming her polished fingernails on the book. 'Well, I knew you were uncomfortable with me knowing about him. The time I walked into the library and saw you both. I didn't want you to think I was interested in him. That I might . . .' Gwen looked down, a curtain of blonde hair hiding her face. Chloe stood frozen, suddenly hoping she'd say it and also hoping she wouldn't. She felt like her stomach had tied itself into a knot. Like she stood at the edge of a cliff and a single word would throw her off.

She opened her mouth to stop her, but Gwen looked up at her. Her blue eyes, so like Dad's, were glassy. 'Chloe, I'm so, so sorry.'

Chloe dropped to her knees in front of the couch, a breath loosing from her chest.

'I've been avoiding saying it for too long. You and Liam were so sickeningly adorable.' Gwen sniffled and wiped her nose on her sleeve. 'I was jealous. You were getting married and I wasn't. I wasn't even seeing anyone. I didn't even *like* him. I was just young and sad and stupid.'

The carpet pressed into Chloe's knees, but she couldn't move. That had been the strangest part about finding Gwen and Liam together. She had never acknowledged him with more than a grunt when he entered the room, had never showed any interest in him.

'I betrayed you.' The words seemed like an effort, like Gwen was fighting an inner battle. 'Then I . . . I tried to brush it off like it was nothing.' Gwen took Chloe's shoulders, her delicate thumbs stroking over her collarbones. 'I was such a *bitch*.'

A small laugh burst from Chloe. It sounded more like a sob.

'Then I ran away and didn't talk to you because it was easier than facing it,' Gwen whispered. 'Jetting off with a rich guy was easier than talking to you about it. And then . . . then missing the funeral . . .' Gwen dissolved into sobs, and Chloe joined her, breaking down to see her sister crying. These weren't the self-pitying crocodile tears she had seen Gwen use before. All the pain in the world lay in them. 'I couldn't even face you. Chloe, I'm so sorry. I've been the world's worst sister. And you've been looking after me, and I've been so stupid, and I . . .'

Chloe hugged her sister close. Something broke between them – a wall built from awkwardness and grudges and jealousy. They cried in each other's arms, riding the wave of misery and sorrow and forgiveness together. Chloe rocked Gwen in her arms, no longer feeling anger or frustration. Only empathy and gratitude.

'I'm so sorry,' Gwen whispered. 'I ruined your wedding, then pretended I'd done nothing wrong. For years. I barely spoke to Mum and Dad, didn't join any family events, just so I could avoid you. And now they're gone, and I've wasted all this time, and it's taken me all these years to even acknowledge it.'

'It's okay,' Chloe whispered, stroking Gwen's silk-soft hair. 'It's all right. You're here now. Besides, it all worked out in the end.' She let out a long breath, closing her eyes. 'Who knows if it would have even worked out with Liam anyway. If he hadn't kissed *you*, it would probably have been someone else.' Life would have been very different if she had married Liam. Hannah's daughter, Lily, wouldn't have been born. Chloe wouldn't have gone to university. She wouldn't have met Harry. 'Besides, you saved us a lot of money on the wedding. I got student debt instead of wedding debt.'

Gwen gave a watery chuckle. 'You're the worst.'

'No, you are,' she mumbled against Gwen's shoulder. They parted, and Chloe noticed how the tension was gone from Gwen's face, nothing but honesty and sorrow laid bare. It was a marvel to behold, oddly beautiful. Things felt more relaxed between them now. Chloe wiped away a tear, black from mascara, from Gwen's cheek. 'You're getting my book all wet.'

Gwen laid it down carefully on the couch arm. 'I wouldn't want to have to replace it again. Books are expensive.'

They exchanged sad smiles. 'Let's go to Mum and Dad's graves this weekend,' said Chloe. She still hadn't gotten around to it, avoiding it like Gwen had avoided this topic. 'We owe it to them. We'll get some flowers and go and show them that we've made up.'

Gwen sniffled. 'Yeah, Chloe. I'd like that.'

Clementine slinked among the non-fiction shelves when it was quiet and everybody had left. He liked it down here. Upstairs had sunlight, and during the day the ground floor always had more people. Clementine liked people, for the most part. They petted him and sometimes the little ones fed him, even though Mrs Cook asked them not to. Now, however, the library was closed and Clementine was happily alone with his feline thoughts. There wasn't a cat in sight, not a female tabby nor one in a hat and a bowtie.

But like so many nights these days, Clementine found he wasn't alone for long. He turned a corner to find a child, her legs tucked up to her chest. Clementine rather liked her hair; it was orange, like his, and hung from her ears. She had her face buried in her arms and her shoulders were shaking.

Clementine padded towards her, his tail swishing through the air. She wasn't holding a book.

The girl looked up, startled by Clementine. He sat, curling his tail around his feet, and looked at her. The girl's grey eyes widened. The whites of them were pink, those salty drops of sadness drying on her freckled face. Clementine felt alarmed. This girl was sad.

'Hello,' said the girl, reaching for him. Clementine hesitated, flinching from her fingers. He didn't usually let strangers touch him. He had memories of being a baby, of rough human hands and shouting, though it was all a far-off memory. The girl drew back, looking disappointed. Clementine knew that water on a human's face meant something bad was happening. He didn't like to see that. Slowly, he approached her and pushed his head into her waiting palm.

The girl sniffled, stroking his back. Ah yes, he liked that. A purr rang from him, and she giggled with amusement.

Her lap looked comfortable. Humans were warm. Without waiting for an invitation, Clementine crawled onto the girl's lap. As he expected, she gave a sound of delight and continued petting him.

'Where am I, little guy?' she said, sniffling again.

Clementine thought that was a strange question. People who came here came for books. He had watched Mrs Cook carefully. And the kitten boy-human, and the girl-human who called herself Chloe. They all seemed to know what they were doing. Visitors, too, though Clementine made himself invisible to unknown humans when he could, when he wasn't watching from the shelf behind the reception desk.

He looked up at her face. 'I'm lost,' she said, still stroking his back. Clementine supposed he should leave, but her soft hands felt so nice against his fur. 'I ran into the barn. The children were teasing me. They always call me Carrots, because of my hair. But the colour sure looks beautiful on you.'

Clementine meowed. He hadn't yet mastered the way of humans speaking, but he hoped he managed to get across that he understood. He was the most handsome cat he knew, and he had met many. Well, seen pictures of them.

'There sure are a lot of books here.' The little girl glanced around. 'Oh, gee, now I can't move.'

Clementine remembered the cats who had visited his library, how they had eventually returned to their books. This girl was the same, then. Clementine continued his purr, the noise increasing when the carrot-haired girl ran her hand down his back again.

'You know, I always feel better when I talk to animals. I love cats.' To Clementine's horror, she hugged him close. This was too much, and he leaped off her lap.

'Sorry.' She giggled. 'Oh boy, I sure feel better. You're the best.'

There would be no other humans here until tomorrow, and the little girl was lost. He could tell by the way she glanced around, worry now entering her eyes. She was tall and skinny, and she looked fearful. 'Where are the lights?' she said.

Clementine forgot humans couldn't see well in the dark. He supposed he should try to get the girl back. She wasn't crying any more, but she didn't seem to want to stay. Clementine ran towards the children's section.

'Hey, kitty! Where're you going? I need you to help me find a way out of here! Hey!' The girl ran after him, her hair streaming behind her. Clementine found the kids' section and looked around at all the books. Surely one of them was the right one. It would be glowing.

He was startled when the key turned in the lock in the lobby. The girl gasped as Mrs Cook's sweet, flowery scent entered the library.

Clementine trotted to the lobby, his jingling bell announcing his arrival. Mrs Cook would know what to do.

'Hello, sweet boy.' The librarian knelt to pet him. Clementine meowed at her, loud and purposeful, then trotted back to the children's section. As he thought, the girl was still there, standing meekly and half hidden in shadow.

'Another one, hmm?' Mrs Cook sounded amused. 'Come on, now, dearie, let's get you home.'

'You can get me back?' The girl sounded so relieved. Clementine felt a little sorry for her. He rubbed himself against her bare leg until she giggled.

'All you need to do is tell me your name, and we'll get you back in no time,' said Mrs Cook, laying down her bag. 'It's a good thing I forgot my purse, isn't it, Clementine?'

'What a sweet name.' The girl petted Clementine again, smiling. The cat knew what human happiness looked like, or at least the simple version. He thought she looked happy now, and Mrs Cook seemed to have things under control.

'Have you been crying?' Mrs Cook asked the girl as she rifled through shelves. 'Are you all right, love?'

The girl nodded. 'I was lost. The kids were giving me a hard time. I was in the depths of despair, so I ran to the barn, but I woke up here. With your cat. I sure feel better now, though. What an adventure.'

'Ah, here it is.' Mrs Cook rose, an old book in her hand. 'We'll have you back in no time. Say goodbye to Clementine, dear.'

'Bye, Clementine! This sure was fun.' The girl beamed. When Mrs Cook had finished reading her line aloud, the waving girl was gone.

Thank goodness, thought the cat. There had been a few too many newcomers in the library lately for his liking.

Tail in the air, he left the human to it and went in search of the bowl of water Mrs Cook had likely left out for him. He found it in the kitchen.

'You know, I could have sworn I put my purse in my bag before I left earlier.' Mrs Cook cocked her head, looking down at Clementine. He stopped in front of her, mirroring her head tilt. That always made her laugh.

Her wrinkled face creased. 'Well, hopefully it's not a sign of dementia,' she said cheerfully, then switched off the lights. 'Goodnight, Clementine, love.'

CHAPTER TWENTY-EIGHT

CHLOE WAS AT Aldi, pushing along a heavy trolley full of shopping. She had decided she was going to be more proactive about making sure they always had a full fridge and freezer and they planned their meals. Now Gwen was working too, they could start sharing the food expenses.

She was comparing brands of washing powder when she sensed someone watching her. Unnerved, Chloe glanced up to see a man walking towards her down the aisle. She recognised him at once. It was Jason, Julie's brother.

Having no desire to speak to him, Chloe threw a random box of washing powder into her trolley and made to wheel it away.

'Excuse me.'

Chloe knew he was talking to her; there was no one else on this aisle.

'Excuse me,' he said more loudly, following her with heavy steps.

Chloe sighed and turned around, using the trolley as a barrier between them. 'Yes, Jason? Can I help you?'

Jason looked taken aback, clearly surprised that Chloe knew his name. 'I was just wondering if you'd thought any more about what I said. About Harry.'

Chloe glared at him. Up close, Jason wasn't really that intimidating, but she still didn't want to be alone with him. Not even in the bright artificial lights of a supermarket aisle. Had he just seen her here by coincidence and decided to chat, or had he followed her here?

'Are you going to stay away from him?' Jason pressed.

'It's none of your business,' Chloe snapped back. She considered abandoning the trolley and making a run for it, but instead she said, 'Can't you just try and move on?'

Jason scowled. 'Harry gets to live on, while my sister . . .' He let out a shuddering breath, and Chloe almost felt sorry for him. 'Why should he get to be happy?'

Chloe didn't have the time nor the energy for this. She turned with her trolley and walked off, hoping Jason would give up. She found more shoppers, feeling safer around other people, but still Jason pestered her, his trainers squeaking on the floor as he followed her trolley.

'Just promise me you'll stay away from him,' he said. 'He only looks out for himself.'

'I don't have to promise you anything.' Sweat poured down her back now; there was a long line of people waiting in the check out queue. Finally, she half-jogged down an aisle of cereal brands, where a male member of staff was coming along with a pallet of goods to put on shelves, and headed for the toilets.

Jason was loitering at the other end of the aisle, probably aware of how uncomfortable he was making her but still not going away. Chloe felt breathless and anxious; she didn't want him near her. Would the staff member take her seriously if she said anything?

The staff member passed her, not noticing anything was amiss. Sighing, Chloe put her trolley beside a nearby shelf and went into the bathroom.

She wondered if it would be melodramatic to call the police. Jason hadn't touched her, just followed her. But you could never be too careful.

She pulled out her phone, but instead of ringing the police, she found herself calling Harry. She double-checked that the toilet door was locked and leaned against it, her breathing heavy and fast as she wondered if Jason was still out there, waiting for her. Didn't he know it was rude and intimidating to do that to someone? How long had he been following her? He could be harmless, but she didn't want to take that chance.

Harry picked up the phone. 'Hello? Chloe?'

'Hi, Harry.' She might sound paranoid, but she said it anyway. 'Um, Jason is here. I think he followed me into Aldi.'

A pause. 'What?'

'Jason. You know, Julie's brother.' Her pulse raced as she felt guilty for disturbing Harry when he was probably at work. 'I don't know what to do. Should I call the police, or . . .?'

'Has he touched you? Hurt you?' She had never heard Harry's voice go dark and dangerous like this before.

'N-no. He just kept asking me if I was going to break things off with you. I tried walking away, but he followed me. I'm in the bathroom.'

'Right. In Aldi, you said?' There was a rustling noise on the phone. 'I'm on my way. Do you think you can alert a member of staff? I don't know if the police will do anything. Absolutely call them, though, if things get worse.'

Chloe opened the toilet door, holding the phone to her ear. If Jason came near her, she decided, she would scream. But she couldn't see him anywhere. 'I think he's gone.'

'Well, stay near the tills anyway. I'll be there in ten minutes, all right? Are you okay?'

'I'm okay. See you.'

When she put the phone down, Chloe retrieved her trolley – it was where she had left it, and nothing appeared to be missing. A few more shoppers were milling around now. A woman with a toddler, a man and his daughter, a couple. Her heartbeat slowing, Chloe felt almost silly for her racing heart and sweating palms, but she hadn't liked Jason coming up to her like that.

She loitered, scrutinising the faces of any man she saw who

was alone. She was finishing up her shopping when Harry arrived, striding towards her. He'd thrown his coat over a knitted jumper and jogging pants. Chloe felt much safer now he was here, and she managed a smile.

'You all right?' he asked, putting a warm hand on her back. He helped her pack her things onto the conveyer belt at the checkout as she told him the rest of what had happened.

'Jason's harmless, as far as I know, but . . .' Harry's face was grim. 'Shall I take you home?'

She reassured him she had come by car, but he walked her to her vehicle anyway, pushing the trolley for her and loading the bags into the boot. 'Would you like me to come home with you?'

'I'll be all right.' She couldn't help glancing around the car park, half expecting to see Jason hanging around in the trolley area or behind a lamppost, but she couldn't see him. 'Thanks for coming out. Were you working?'

'Hm? Oh, no. I was actually taking a nap. Late night at the office.' He gave her a lopsided grin as she looked at him in dismay.

'I woke you up? I'm sorry!'

'Hey, don't be.' He opened his arms and she leaned into him, not realising until now how much she needed a hug. 'I'd have come no matter what I was doing. Even fighting a dragon.'

'That would've been hard to get away from,' Chloe mumbled into his chest.

'I'd have asked the dragon to reschedule while I went to help my girlfriend.'

The word 'girlfriend' gave Chloe a bubbly, happy feeling, and she chuckled as she pulled away from his warmth. 'Thank you for this.' She kissed his cheek.

'I'll follow you home, if you like. Make sure you're safe.'

The thought was appealing, but Gwen might be around.

'I'll be okay.' She waved and turned away before he could protest too much.

At home, Gwen was getting ready to work her shift at the Pride & Pint, but she hung around to help Chloe unpack the shopping.

Chloe told Gwen what had happened, leaving out some personal details.

'That must have been scary,' Gwen said. 'You did the right thing. There are creeps everywhere.'

'You don't think I overreacted?'

'No.' Gwen put away a carton of eggs then gave her sister a serious look. 'There are weird dudes all over the place, and bad stuff can happen if you let your guard down. Even if Harry knows this Jason guy, you don't. And people don't do messed-up stuff, until they do.'

Chloe nodded, raising her eyebrows at Gwen's wisdom. 'Nothing bad ever happened to you, did it? While you were out on your . . . um, excursions.'

'Nothing too terrible,' said Gwen, shaking back her blonde hair. 'That guy doesn't know where we live, does he?'

'Not unless he's followed me home, which I don't think he has.' Chloe peeked out of the curtains just in case, but their street was empty; even Joe wasn't in his garden. It was reassuring that at least Harry knew Jason personally. He didn't have a criminal record or anything like that. Maybe she was being jumpy, but she hated the idea of Jason hanging around outside their house.

'Let me take the evening off work,' said Gwen. Chloe wanted to tell her not to, but Gwen had already picked up her phone to ring the pub. Since they were both home, they spent the evening watching movies from their childhood, ones they *both* liked. Later, they checked and double-checked all the doors were locked before going to bed.

Even with her sister there, Chloe tossed and turned that night, falling into bad dreams about Jason trying to break in. Eventually she knocked on Gwen's door, and her sister answered with her hair in a mess.

'Can I sleep with you?' Chloe asked, her voice small.

Gwen made a sympathetic noise and hugged her. They cuddled up together in Gwen's bed, and Chloe, comforted by her scent and her warmth, soon fell asleep.

The next day was a Sunday, and the library was closed. Chloe decided to visit the Brew House, feeling bad she hadn't seen Hannah since she'd found out about Liam being Lily's father. With everything else going on, Chloe couldn't bring herself to be upset or annoyed about it. The bell jangled above her head and she gave Hannah the brightest smile she could. Hannah's face lit up, and it wasn't long before Chloe was sitting at a table with a caramel latte and a croissant. On the next table was Lily, who waved at Chloe before continuing with her colouring. Chloe noticed with amusement that the picture she was colouring was the purple monkey from the storybook Eric had read that day.

As it was mid-morning on a Sunday, the café was pretty busy. A middle-aged man was working in the café too, occasionally coming in from the back to replenish the sweet treats and help serving customers. Hannah introduced him as her uncle, the owner of the Brew House.

'Ah! You must be Chloe.' Her uncle threw a tea towel over his shoulder to shake her hand. 'I've heard a lot about you.' He stopped to ruffle Lily's hair then disappeared in the back.

Chloe had walked here this morning, not wanting to scare herself more by refusing to leave the house on her day off. Gwen had left, too, deciding to help out at the Pride & Pint during the lunch rush to make up for not going in the previous evening. Chloe had not seen Jason on her way here, thankfully.

She wondered what Harry was up to. Did he work on Sundays? She texted him, asking if he was around and would like a coffee date.

I'm at the Brew House.

I've heard of that place. Good caramel lattes, my girlfriend told me.

Chloe giggled. Lily looked at her, a question in her eyes. Now Chloe knew that Liam was her dad, she couldn't help seeing the resemblance.

Chloe was on her second latte when Harry walked in, the room brightening as he did. He ordered a black coffee and came to sit with Chloe, giving her a smile.

She stared back. 'What happened to your face?'

'Is it bad?' he asked, looking concerned as he touched his cheek. All around his left eye was the purpling of a fresh bruise.

'It looks horrible. Who hit you?' Chloe had a feeling she knew the answer before Harry told her.

'I went to have a chat with Jason about stalking you in the supermarket.' Hannah brought over Harry's coffee just then, and she raised her eyebrows at his black eye. 'He wasn't happy to see me. But he won't be bothering you any more.'

They sipped in silence. She wondered if she should mention how scared she had felt last night, not able to sleep at home in case Jason was lurking outside. In the end she decided it was best she didn't.

CHAPTER TWENTY-NINE

CHLOE HAD BEEN avoiding going to the graveyard since she had moved back to Wellbridge. Moving back into the house was difficult enough, but seeing Mum and Dad's graves, side by side, felt like too much.

One day, she had told herself. *When I'm ready.*

She was glad that her first visit to Lucy and Thomas Keeton's graves was with her sister. On the way there, they sang along to some songs, the few of them they could agree were good when they were teenagers. The car park was empty, and a sense of calm stole over Chloe as they climbed out of the vehicle and into the cold autumn air.

Gwen's long blonde hair rippled down her back like a golden curtain as they walked together. Chloe had opted for a high pony-tail, her chestnut-brown curls just reaching her neck.

'I've always been so jealous of your hair. It's just like Dad's,' Gwen said as they walked through the car park towards the graveyard.

'You like mine?' asked Chloe in surprise. 'I'd never have thought it.'

Gwen took her arm, linking them together as they reached the expanse of green. It was a beautiful stretch of land that held the sense of quiet that always seems to accompany the resting place of the dead. A stone chapel, worn by time, watched over rows and rows of gravestones, many of them in the shapes of crosses. Trees, almost void of their browning leaves, dotted the area. The grass crunched beneath their feet, the frost clinging to the blades, as the sisters walked together in search of their parents.

They held bouquets of flowers in their free hands. Chloe had chosen roses for Mum and Gwen had gotten some orchids for Dad. Though their parents had loved both their children equally, Chloe had always felt closer to Mum. Their trips to libraries and bookshops, the way Mum would braid Chloe's hair and read to her before bed. Gwen liked going swimming and playing chess with Dad. That was until the family had fallen out over Gwen kissing Liam, and Gwen had run off with her older boyfriend.

Chloe was scared to ask how many times Gwen had seen Mum and Dad in person since she had left at eighteen. She was only aware of that one Christmas during Chloe's first year at university. Gwen could probably count all the times she had visited them on one hand. Whatever guilt Chloe was feeling for not contacting them enough, Gwen's must be a hundredfold. She could tell by the way her sister's shoulders had slumped, the way she looked sadly down at the flowers. Chloe couldn't think of any reassuring words; like her, Gwen had likely assumed Mum and Dad would have years left, and there would be time to patch things up. So she just gave her arm a squeeze.

They talked as they walked, sharing memories of them all together, visiting a theme park, going to the theatre in Buxton, and their holiday as kids in Spain.

'Remember how Dad got burned? Mum had warned him to put on sunscreen but he didn't listen.' Laughter rang in Gwen's voice.

'Oh, yeah. He looked like a lobster.' Chloe giggled. 'And Mum was entirely unsympathetic.'

'If you'd just listened to me, Thomas . . .'

Dad had been bright red for the rest of the holiday. 'We'll have to see if we can find the old photos,' Chloe said. 'I'm sure there are ones of Spain in the attic.'

'That'll be tough,' Gwen admitted as they passed some old gravestones, people who had passed away over a hundred years ago. 'Seeing the pictures, I mean. But maybe it'll be . . . I don't know, therapeutic, too.'

'Let's do it when we get home.'

Chloe couldn't remember exactly where the graves were. The memory of the funeral was a blur. They passed a familiar-looking part of the graveyard, and a gravestone caught Chloe's eye.

'Did you find them?' asked Gwen as Chloe slowed to look down at the stone that read,

HERE LIES JULIE ASHCROFT, LOVING DAUGHTER AND WIFE.
22ND APRIL 1996 – 30TH MAY 2023.

A bouquet of flowers sat on the grave, more freesias and daisies like before. Harry had been here.

Chloe moved on. It didn't take them long to spot the twin graves, shinier and newer than most of their counterparts.

'Here they are.'

A lump formed in her chest and crawled up to her throat. Suddenly it was summer last year again, the birds chirping and the sun shining in a brilliant blue sky like there was nothing wrong in the world. Mournful music, some old rock song Dad liked, played as the caskets were lowered, side by side. Auntie Paula's gnarled, firm hand patted Chloe's as she murmured words of comfort Chloe didn't hear.

The stone of the graves glimmered in the weak morning sunlight, the tops sparkling with frost. The letters, gold engravings, shone bright as new.

HERE LIES LUCY KEETON, LOVING WIFE AND MOTHER.
19TH FEBRUARY 1970 – 3RD AUGUST 2024.

Seeing her mother's name engraved in stone broke a dam inside Chloe. She knelt to lay the flowers before the gravestone, sniffling, tears slipping hot and fast down her cheeks. Gwen sighed beside her, laying her orchids on Dad's grave, which read,

HERE LIES THOMAS KEETON LOVING HUSBAND AND FATHER,
16ᵀᴴ JANUARY 1968 − 3ᴿᴰ AUGUST 2024.

'We should come here more often,' said Chloe when they had wiped away their tears.

'Definitely.' Gwen nodded, palming her cheeks. 'We owe it to them. *I* owe it to them,' she added more quietly, and Chloe squeezed her hand. Her fingers were cold.

They cleaned the graves, swapping memories good and sad, from the games they played as kids to trips to the beach. It was funny how grief could blur memories; Chloe could not recall one of the many forgotten arguments, the times their parents scolded them for something or other. It was a marvel how some memories only Chloe remembered, and others Gwen reminded her about. Sometimes Gwen would mention a day and the memory would resurface. They cried as they talked, the sadness broken suddenly by laughter from recalling something funny.

'Chloe, do you remember when Mum wanted to try a tester for that moisturiser?' Gwen's tear-filled giggles had led to hiccups, and her chest jumped every now and then.

'Oh my goodness, I do.' Chloe closed her eyes, remembering their mother, her greying blonde hair in a bun that day.

'She squeezed way too much out.' Gwen rearranged the flowers on Dad's grave. 'And was standing there with a big pile of goo in her hand, not knowing what to do.'

'We were the most moisturised children in Derbyshire,' Chloe said, and they both burst out laughing, clutching each other.

Chloe could feel the rift between her and her sister heal almost like a physical force, a bridge that had broken down slowly slotting back into place, brick by brick, a feat as wondrous as the magic of the library. Years of things left unsaid, of time wasted, of experiences missed. In this moment, surrounded by nature and close to their parents, Chloe wanted to stay in Wellbridge. Stay here with her sister. She wanted to catch up on everything that they had missed out on, spend time together and make new memories. She liked this town. The good memories were becoming more abundant than the bad. She had Gwen, their home, her wonderful job at the library, her friend Hannah and . . .

And Harry.

His dimpled smile materialised in her mind for a moment, bringing on a different sort of ache. His black eye, earned by defending her. She glanced around the graveyard. Harry had been here, too, and the thought was a comfort. He was leaving flowers, flowers he had researched the meanings of, for his late wife.

They left the graveyard behind, and Chloe's heart felt lighter than it had in months. It was as if by shedding the tears and sharing the memories with Gwen, they had healed something between them and in her heart.

The sun rose and peeked out from behind the clouds, warming their skin. This really was a beautiful place. Sad, of course, but with the dried autumn leaves blowing around and the last of the frost glittering on the headstones and in the grass, it felt cold and peaceful. Sad and serene. Two clashing emotions that made her feel both romantic and melancholy.

They had almost reached the car when Chloe's phone started ringing. Brow furrowing, she pulled it out. It took a moment for her to register that someone was calling her from the library phone.

For a moment, she felt alarmed. Today *was* her day off, right?

'Hello?'

'Chloe, is that you?' Eric's panicked voice reached her. There was a strange noise in the background. Banging and ripping and . . . was that a scream? 'Um, where are you?'

'It's my day off. I'm at the graveyard,' she said, then the concern caught up to her. Neither Eric nor Mrs Cook had rung her on her day off before, and those sounds definitely did not belong in the quiet library. 'Eric, what's going on? Are you all right?'

'We . . . Um, there's a problem. I'm really sorry, but we need you here right now.' There was another crash in the background, making Chloe flinch. 'It's the characters. The book characters. A lot of them have escaped their books and we have no idea how. Dozens of them, more than Mrs Cook and I can handle. Please come and help us!'

Gwen watched her, eyebrows raising in expectation. 'Who is it?' she mouthed.

'The characters have escaped their books?' said Chloe, dazed. 'What? How?'

'We don't know. None of them were glowing this morning and no one's been reading them. I don't think so, anyway. No, stop! Put that down!' he screamed. There was a scuffle and his fast breaths rushed down the phone. 'Chloe, please come. This is getting out of control.'

'Right,' Chloe said. 'Hang on. I'll be there as soon as I can.'

'What's going on?' asked her sister.

Chloe hesitated. She hadn't told Gwen anything about the library's magic. Where would she even start? And was Eric right? Were there love interests and purple monkeys causing havoc inside the library right this moment? It certainly sounded like it.

She was about to tell Gwen she'd drop her off at home, but an extra pair of hands might be just what they needed. And she felt a sudden fierce desire to tell Gwen everything.

'I need your help with something. Here.' She thrust her phone into Gwen's hands and clambered into the car. 'Ring Harry and ask him to join us. Then I've got something to tell you about the library.'

CHAPTER THIRTY

DURING GWEN'S URGENT but confused call, Harry promised to get there as soon as he could. And by the time they arrived at the library, his car was already parked next to Mrs Cook's little Ford. Gwen was still firing questions at her as Chloe stopped beside Harry's car and climbed out. From outside, the library looked normal. Quiet, even. That was good.

'But what do you *mean*, characters come out of the books?' Gwen demanded as Chloe strode towards the enormous double doors, her heart pounding. 'Is this some weird book club thing? You aren't making any sense.'

'Trust me, I didn't believe it either at first. But you'll see what I mean in a minute.'

The blinds were drawn in the front windows, the sign in the nearest one reading CLOSED. That made sense. Chloe wondered if the main door had been locked, too, but it opened at her touch.

She pushed open the doors and stepped inside into the lobby area. Usually, it was quiet and welcoming, with not much going on except someone manning the front desk with its shelves of files behind it and the one computer, the children's section to the left and the door to the lower archives to the right.

Now, it was unrecognisable. Bedlam.

Books had been thrown across the floor, a sea of them scattered all over the lobby carpet. An entire bookcase lay on the ground as though a giant had pushed it over. Papers from behind the lobby desk had been pulled out and thrown around, scattered like white leaves.

People ran or walked around in a mixture of clothing – medieval tunics and gowns, battle armour, floral dresses, spacesuits. A red-haired boy dressed in green *flew* over their heads, making Gwen scream and duck, covering her head. Voices, banging, echoes, laughter, animal noises and shouting sounded all over the library. All Chloe could do was watch in awe and rising horror.

She heard Eric shouting something unintelligible from upstairs. Where were Mrs Cook and Clementine? Were they all right?

'What on earth's going on?' Chloe called over the cacophony of noise.

'Chloe? Is that you?' Mrs Cook appeared, breathless and clutching a book to her chest. 'Thank goodness. We need to get these characters returned to their books.'

'Can't you just read their last lines and get them back in?' Chloe shouted as something crashed on the floor above, making the whole floor shake. 'That's what usually works.'

'We've tried, but there are so many books glowing, and the characters need to *hear* the line being read,' said Mrs Cook. 'I'm not sure what's happening. Eric arrived for his shift, and all the books started glowing, and even though we didn't read any of them, they all just started to appear.' She looked around in dismay at the mess of books and papers. Among the fallen books, several of them glowed.

They rushed through the lower archives and up to the fiction section, and Chloe's heart sank as she heard the unmistakable sound of a monkey screeching and chattering. 'It's that purple monkey again.'

'Purple monkey?' demanded Gwen. 'What do you mean?' She kept glancing at the ceiling as though terrified something else would fly over her. Chloe dearly hoped no books about dragons were glowing today.

'Chloe?'

Chloe's heart leaped to her throat as Harry appeared at the top of the winding staircase, panting. 'We have a problem.'

'I guessed that,' Chloe breathed. Somehow she felt calmer with Harry here. The noise subsided somewhat as, despite the chaos around them, he smiled down at her. Her breath caught in her chest as she took in his face, the bruise around his eye. Maybe it was the adrenaline talking, but she thought he'd never looked so handsome.

Eric appeared beside him, his hair ruffled, and the spell was broken. 'Oh! Hi, Chloe. Hi, Gwen. I've counted ten up here,' he said, panting as he pointed. 'Characters, I mean. There's a detective smoking a pipe near the window. I asked him not to.'

'We have bigger problems, Eric,' said Mrs Cook, striding forward.

Something big and bright dived at Chloe and Gwen from the ceiling. They both screamed this time, ducking just in time to avoid the floating man – a ghost? – who'd appeared wearing a bell-covered hat and a bowtie of bright orange. He cackled as he threw a pile of books into the air.

'Watch out!' Chloe pulled Gwen out of the way as the tomes thundered onto the floor, loud as a dozen battle drums.

The poltergeist let out a joyous whoop and disappeared straight through the closed door.

Gwen had paled. 'Was that . . .?'

'If you've read the book, you'll know he's a mischievous one,' said Chloe. She groaned. 'Who else is out?'

The answer was, seemingly, everyone.

Men with wings and tattoos, slender elves with pointed ears, and women with long, flowing hair and dresses had appeared in the library, slipping between the shelves, talking or glancing around. Dogs and monkeys and parrots sat on top of shelves, some of them wearing clothes. Some of the human characters watched the group with interest, others argued and rifled around bookshelves as though trying to find a way home. Others sat calmly. It made Chloe think of an absurd fancy-dress party.

'Oh gee, it's the cat again!' A little girl with red hair in pigtails darted forward and scooped up Clementine. She hugged him close. 'Boy, it's good to see you.' She looked at Mrs Cook with big, grey eyes. 'Ma'am, I sure am sorry. I don't know how I got here again.'

'Welcome back, dear.' Mrs Cook, despite the chaos around them, seemed calm. 'Are those children being nicer to you?'

'Kinda.' The girl let Clementine drop to the floor. He streaked off between some shelves, probably to look for somewhere to hide.

'Well, they will.' Mrs Cook winked at her. 'Trust me.'

'Madam Chloe.' A familiar man in nineteenth-century attire appeared, looking panicked. 'I am awfully sorry to disturb you, but it appears I have landed here again. How do I get back home?'

'Hello,' said Chloe weakly. Despite everything, she felt a rush of affection to see the man she had met that night after her bad date – the first time she had discovered the power of the library. 'We're having some trouble here. We need your help.' An idea struck her and she turned to the others. 'Eric, Harry, Gwen. We need to get the books these characters are from. We have to read the final line they say in the story. That'll get them home. It shouldn't be too difficult, the books are glowing, after all.'

'First thing is that damn monkey,' said Harry. He shrugged off his jacket, and Chloe tried to look anywhere but at his large shoulders as they moved. 'He's ripping up all the books.'

Mrs Cook let out a pained moan. Chloe couldn't blame her.

'Don't you remember his last line?' Chloe swivelled to Eric. 'Maybe we don't need to be holding the book for it to work.'

Eric looked stricken. 'Oh! Right. Erm . . .' His face screwed up. 'Oh, man. It was something about bananas . . .'

'Think on it while you look for the book in the kids' section downstairs,' said Chloe. She wasn't about to waste time chasing that mischievous creature around again. 'Mrs Cook, can you find the book that naughty poltergeist came from? If he's anything like in the story, we can't let him out of here.'

'I can find it.' Mrs Cook nodded and strode towards the kids' section. 'Out of the way, love.' She shooed away a confused-looking pirate.

'Harry, Gwen,' said Chloe. 'Come with me.'

They rushed back downstairs, leaving the chaos behind them for Eric and Mrs Cook to sort out, and searched near the doors and windows. Thankfully, they could still hear the ghost whooping and singing as he swept through the library's lower floors, knocking over bookshelves. It seemed like he couldn't leave the library. Or he simply hadn't decided to, yet. Chloe didn't want to think about what might happen if he escaped. It wouldn't be easy to explain that.

As they made it back to the lobby, something rumbled in the non-fiction section.

'That doesn't sound good,' said Gwen.

In the next room, between some enormous shelves, two young men, perhaps Eric's age, were fighting. One was pale and dark-haired, and when his mouth opened in a snarl, Chloe spotted long canines. His opponent was handsome with russet skin and raven hair. As they watched in shock, he growled as his knees hit the floor. Gwen clapped her hands over her mouth as the young man's limbs lengthened; he grew, clothing tearing around his growing form. Fur sprang from his body and his face elongated into a beast's. His mouth became a muzzle; his hands transformed into sharp claws. The vampire and the wolf clashed together in a series of growls and tearing. Gwen backed up until she was against the shelf, her eyes wide open in terror.

'I think even you know who they are,' Chloe said to Gwen, snorting with laughter to combat her fear. The pair fought, snarling and scratching and snapping at each other, knocking over books and overturning tables. The three backed up, getting out of their way.

'Still think working at a library is boring?' Chloe asked, half dragging her sister away from the mayhem.

They passed bored-looking scientists, strange-looking monsters from kids' books, and skidded to a halt when they saw a woman in a glittering white dress, her hair the colour of moonlight and swept up in an elaborate hairstyle. Pure hatred burned in her eyes as she raised a long, glittering stick.

'Get down!' bellowed a powerful male voice.

The three of them turned and Gwen screamed, cowering and covering her head. An enormous, real-life *lion* stepped onto a nearby upturned bookshelf. He was the size of a car, with a shaggy mane and enormous paws. Golden eyes looked over them all. 'I said get down!' yelled the lion.

The three of them ducked, Harry's arm wrapping around Chloe's shoulders as he shielded her with his body. They fell to the carpeted floor, landing clumsily on fallen books. Magic soared above them, narrowly missing them and making goosebumps spring up on Chloe's arms. The wave of silver hit a window and it shattered. Icy air swept inside the library, glass thundering to the floor as the woman laughed and laughed.

'Was that a lion? This is insane!' Gwen scrambled to her feet and bolted for the main doors of the library. Chloe and Harry jumped up and ran after her. Chloe's mind rushed as they left the lion and the witch to battle each other. They rushed past the children's section, the soft flooring taken up by magical creatures and talking animals who seemed content to sit around and watch the forming battle with interest. Clementine was nowhere to be seen, or perhaps the orange cat had simply blended into the crowd of animal characters.

Could they really get all the characters back into their books before they destroyed the library? Everywhere they looked, there were more. Was the library letting this happen, or had it lost control of the magic?

Bookshelves slid out of their way as they ran for the main doors. 'Gwen, stop!' Chloe shouted. 'We can't leave. We have to get all the characters back into their stories. We have to read out their last lines to them. It's the only way.'

'Are you dreaming? We need to call the police,' Gwen panted, pulling out her phone.

'We just need to get the characters back into their books,' said Harry, raising his hands. 'I'm sure most of them don't want to be here. Right?'

Chloe hadn't realised that several of the characters who weren't fighting had found refuge in the lobby. It was a mishmash of people – a stern, greasy-haired professor dressed in black, a serious teenager dressed in winter furs, a pointy-eared boy in a green tunic talking to what looked like a fairy or pixie in his hand. He was the one who had flown over them earlier. Gwen lowered her phone and scowled at him.

'Library, block that door, please,' Chloe panted. At once, an enormous bookshelf slid over to cover the archway separating the lobby from the west wing. She felt bad for the characters who might get caught in the fighting crossfire, but the quickest way to help them was getting them home.

Gwen paled when the bookcase moved on its own, then she gave Chloe a look that said, *Fine, I'll trust you. Get on with it.*

Chloe approached the group. At least here, no one was fighting. 'Hi, everyone.' Nerves danced in her chest as she stared around at them. So many of them were otherworldly, cartoonish or magical. Some of them had weapons, and she tried hard not to glance at them. 'I'm so sorry you're here. We didn't do it on purpose.'

'Where exactly are we?' asked a young woman in leathers who looked like she had been malnourished then forced to gain muscle very quickly. Her olive-green eyes fixed with suspicion on Chloe.

'You're in . . . well, our world.' Chloe spread her hands helplessly. She hoped Mrs Cook had been able to find the book to subdue the poltergeist, at least. They could still hear the shrieking of the monkey upstairs and she hoped Eric wasn't having too rough a time. 'In our library. A place of books. *Your* books.'

'What do you mean?' asked the boy in the tunic, looking up with interest. The fairy flitted to his shoulder, leaving a golden trail like a shooting star.

'Erm, Chloe,' Gwen whispered. 'Maybe skip the explanation for now? The last thing we need is for them to have an existential crisis.'

'Right,' said Chloe. 'We want to get you back to your own worlds as quickly as we can, but we need your help.' She turned to Harry and Gwen, both of them looking at her with optimistic expectation; they trusted her to fix all this. It was bolstering as well as terrifying. 'We have to collect all the books we can find that are glowing and put them here.' She tapped the lobby desk, then moved some papers out of the way. 'Everyone, please find books in this library that are glowing orange and bring them back here. I don't know what's happening, but I think . . . the library has lost its grip on its magic. Some of it, at least.' She dearly hoped reading the books would send the characters home. It was the only thing she could think of.

The others nodded. The characters were looking at her, some with cool mistrust, others with interest, and others still with eagerness. A little girl with a red cape and hood beamed at her, clutching a basket in her hands.

'Listen, if you help us gather the glowing books, you'll be able to get home a lot faster,' said Chloe.

The red-hooded girl sped off. Others mumbled something or glanced at each other, then everyone was walking in different directions, in search of glowing books. Some squeezed through the gap between the shelf and the doorway to the west wing. Gwen picked her way through scattered papers and tomes, too, and Harry and Chloe were suddenly alone together.

He held out his hand. 'And what's our job?'

She took it, liking the warmth of his hand around hers. 'We've got some reading to do.'

Clementine was getting tired of all the noise.

When he had decided to live here, Mrs Cook had given him food and a place to sleep. The humans were usually kind to him, and he liked the quiet of this place. Now everywhere he ran, there was someone there, whether it was a human or a human-like creature or a mean, chattering animal that tried to grab his tail.

He hissed at a nasty-looking man and squeezed between some books on a shelf, sitting with his paws in front of him. This wasn't ideal, but he would have to wait it out.

He meowed quietly, thinking of Chloe. With her curly hair and flowery scent and her long skirts and the way she scratched between his ears after giving him some extra treats. She would figure all this out, he knew it.

CHAPTER THIRTY-ONE

HARRY AND CHLOE held a book each, the piles of gold-rimmed novels on the desk between them getting steadily higher and more numerous.

'Oh, good. This one is yours,' said Chloe to the girl in leathers. She agreed with Gwen that telling the characters they were from books might lead to some kind of freak-out, but there wasn't really any other way to do it. 'I read you a line, and you'll be home quick as a flash, okay?' She flipped to the end of the book, her finger trailing down the paper until she found the character's very last line. She read it aloud.

She glanced up, but the girl was gone. Chloe looked around, but she wasn't anywhere to be seen. 'Good,' she said happily, closing the book. It was no longer glowing. 'That worked.'

A terrific crash in the next room made her jump. The vampire and the werewolf must still have been fighting, or perhaps it was the witch and the lion. She knew it was imperative to get them all back first, but they just had to work with the books they had.

Gwen arrived, ashen-faced, with three more glowing books in her arms. 'Chloe, what do we do if some of the characters don't want to go back? Or if they're too busy fighting to listen?'

Chloe swallowed. 'One problem at a time, Gwen.'

'And what about the lion?' She pointed a shaking finger towards the west wing.

'He's a good lion, remember? He's busy fighting the witch. Just let them get on with it until we find their book.'

'Special discount if you need me to repair the library again,' whispered Harry, and Chloe snorted a laugh.

'What do you mean, it's *my* book?' demanded a character wearing a complicated Victorian gown. 'I'm not in any book. Let me see it.'

'I will, in a second. Hold on.' Harry quickly flipped to the last page. He read a line out loud so quickly it was almost a babble. The woman's gloved fingers had just reached out to snatch the book from him when she faded into nothing.

It was quick as an eyeblink. Collecting herself, Chloe said, 'Well done, Harry.'

He blew out air from his pursed lips, snapping the book shut. 'I learned from the best.'

Chloe shifted, hiding her smile.

Some characters were resistant. Harry had to chase the boy and his fairy all around the library before finally shouting their last line to them. The mischievous lad said 'Aww,' with disappointment before disappearing, the glow on the book in Harry's hands fading. Mrs Cook and Eric appeared soon after, Gwen having told them of Chloe's plan.

'Isn't he charming?' whispered the librarian as Harry huffed out a breath, placing the book carefully on the pile.

'Who?' said Chloe vaguely, pretending to be going through the remaining pile of glowing books to hide her burning cheeks.

'Is the lion still here?' said Eric, looking nervous.

'Yes. A-ha! And his book is here.' Chloe retrieved the enormous tome – it was a collection of all the volumes in the book universe. She handed it to Eric. 'Would you like to do the honours?'

Eric's Adam's apple bobbed as he swallowed, nervously looking around at them all.

'Aren't you a fan of books?' Gwen asked. 'You know the lion is good, right? It's the witch you have to watch out for. She might turn you to stone.'

Eric let out a yelp, violently shaking his head. 'I can't do this.'

'Yes, you can. Before they destroy the library.' Chloe took Eric's elbow. 'C'mon, Eric. Animals are your strength, remember? No one can send purple monkeys and magical lions back to their worlds like you can.'

Eric's skinny arm trembled in her grip as they both stepped into the non-fiction section. Cold air rushed through the broken window. For an awful moment, Chloe thought the lion and the witch had escaped into town, but then she spotted a glint of the witch's gown around the corner of a nearby bookcase.

'Send her back first,' Chloe whispered. 'She's more dangerous.'

Eric's hands trembled as he opened the huge book, finding her story and her last line. 'I think that's it.' Chloe jabbed the page. 'Nice and loud, now, Eric.'

A terrific crash sounded and the lion roared. All the hairs on Chloe's neck stood on end and primal fear swept through her. She wondered if all of Wellbridge had heard it. 'Hurry up!' she urged.

Eric's voice was loud and clear as he read out the character's last line. He was halfway through when the witch appeared from around a corner, her white hair tumbling around her livid face.

'What is this magic?' she roared, marching towards them with speed. She raised the cruel-looking wand in her hand.

Eric's voice went high-pitched as he read out the final few words. The witch snarled, her wand held high, then she vanished. Warm magic swept over them.

Eric gasped, looking stunned.

'Well done, Eric.' Chloe patted his shoulder.

'I nearly peed my pants,' he wheezed.

Chloe laughed, though she trembled too as she rose. 'Now, where's the king?'

The mighty lion now sat on a fallen bookshelf and Chloe gazed at him in awe. He yawned, showing dozens of sharp teeth, then shook his shaggy mane, calm now the witch no longer posed a threat to the library.

'Your Majesty,' Eric addressed him, and Chloe had to cough into the crook of her elbow to hide her laughter. 'We're going to send you back to your world now. The witch is still around there, so you'll still have to fight her. Sorry.' He swallowed.

'Do not be sorry, son of Adam. You are very brave.'

Eric looked confused. 'My dad's name is Keith.'

'Um, Eric, let's get him back into his story,' said Chloe hastily. 'Goodbye. Thank you for protecting us from the witch.'

The lion bowed his enormous head as Eric read out his line. He faded at once, leaving not a trace of himself behind.

Chloe knuckled her eyes, sighing with relief.

'Chloe, we have a problem.'

Chloe didn't much care for new problems right now. They had spent the past three hours going through the glowing books, sending back the characters, willing or unwilling. She could see the issue without Harry having to voice it to her, though.

They had checked every inch of the library, every shelf, and even asked the library itself to confirm it by moving aside bookshelves. As of right now, there were only Chloe, Gwen, Mrs Cook, Harry, Clementine and Eric left in the library.

'So why are there five books left?' Gwen asked, her hands on her hips. She had rolled up her sleeves to the elbows, her long hair in a messy bun. She had done her part, reading several characters back into their books, and seemed to have embraced the library's magic without any more resistance. Chloe could have hugged her.

Instead, she looked down at the books left on the table. They varied in sizes, some hardbacks, some paperbacks, one of them a ragged old comic. New-looking and worn. Varying genres. The only thing they had in common was that they were all still glowing.

'The broken window.' Chloe dragged her hand down her face. She was exhausted and hungry and was in no mood for this.

'Somewhere out there, the characters are loose. We need to get them back.'

Gwen sank to the floor, massaging her calves. 'How do we even know where to start?'

Eric wrung his hands, looking nervous. Even Mrs Cook had paled. Clementine was nowhere to be seen.

Chloe studied the books on the desks. 'No dragons,' she confirmed, mostly to herself. 'That's good, at least. Actually . . .' She picked one up.

It was as she had thought. Almost all of these books had another thing in common: Chloe had pulled characters out of them before. She had talked to them about love, friendship, jealousy, forgiveness.

'Five books,' she murmured. The detective, the Scottish warrior, the nobleman, and the superhero. The fifth book was a children's one, perhaps one Eric had read at the event. It was a story about a mischievous giant cat that entertained children on a rainy day.

There had to be some meaning to this. She looked around the library, hardly registering the scattered books and papers, the mess the characters had left behind. At least all was quiet now, but . . .

'These characters,' she said, holding up the book, 'they're mostly . . . you know, normal-looking. No elves or witches or lions.' A sudden image of the lion walking down a street in Wellbridge came to mind. She glanced at her sister, who was no doubt thinking the same thing, and they both giggled guiltily. 'They're all humans, except for this cat. So that's something. Hopefully they'll, uh, blend in until we find them, and they'll think the last one is a fancy-dress costume or something.' She grimaced as she said it, knowing how ridiculous she sounded.

'Can you give us a clue?' Mrs Cook asked, glancing to the ceiling. 'Are they in places Chloe has been to before?'

The library's lights flickered once.

'Me?' Chloe asked in surprise.

'Oh yes, dear. I think since these are characters you've met before, they are going to be in significant places.' Mrs Cook leaned against the lobby desk. 'What did you talk to them about?'

Chloe glanced at the historical romance in her hand, recalling talking with a Scottish warrior about putting faith in something even if you don't believe it yet. But where would that lead him?

Chloe's phone rang, making everyone jump. It was Hannah.

'Hi, Hannah,' said Chloe, trying not to sound like she was dealing with a magical library and its escaped characters.

'Chloe, there's a guy here,' said Hannah's hushed voice. 'Um, he keeps mentioning a library. He seems quite lost. Do you know him?'

Chloe nodded to the others. 'Does he have red hair? And is he wearing a kilt, by any chance?'

'Yes!' Hannah sounded excited. 'He's quite cute, too. Though he keeps saying he's trying to find his wife.'

'I'll be right there. Don't let him leave.' Chloe hung up and looked around at her team. 'First stop, the Brew House.' She grabbed the book and stuffed it into her bag.

When they were outside, Mrs Cook locked the library doors; they all agreed it was unlikely the characters would come back on their own, and it would be worse to have a passerby walk in and see the terrific mess. As for the broken window, there wasn't much they could do about that at the moment. Chloe didn't want to think about how long it would take them to clean it all up, but they had bigger problems right now.

'Don't let him leave' had sounded natural at the time, but Chloe wasn't sure how Hannah was going to stop a six-foot-something Scot who probably had a dagger and wouldn't be afraid to use it if he felt threatened. Hopefully it wouldn't come to that.

'We should hurry,' she said. Harry strode beside her as they sped up. It was mid-afternoon now, the sun hiding behind clouds. A weekday. Not many people around. 'Wait.'

They all skidded to a halt.

'We don't all need to go,' she said, looking at them all. 'We need to find the rest of the characters.'

'I've got the other books.' Eric held up his satchel. 'Just got to make sure no one sees them glowing.'

'But what if one of us finds a character but they don't have the right book with them?' asked Gwen.

Chloe groaned. She was right.

'Let's all keep in touch.' Harry brought out his phone. 'Here, I'll make a group chat.' Once they were all added, he said, 'Just message the location if you find someone. Do we all know who we're looking for?'

They discussed it and agreed. 'I'll go with Eric,' said Gwen, raising her eyebrows to Chloe. Eric looked overjoyed at having been chosen. 'Mrs Cook, are you coming?'

'Of course. Good luck with your hero.' The librarian winked at Chloe.

CHAPTER THIRTY-TWO

'LOOKS LIKE IT'S you and me, Harry,' Chloe said.

'I can't think of a better way to spend an afternoon,' said Harry. 'C'mon.'

There were a few people on the street where the Brew House was, and Chloe forced herself to walk at a normal pace, even though her heartbeat thundered. All it would take was a conversation with the Highlander to know he was not of this world. She had her bag tucked under her arm, could feel the warmth of the book as it rested against her side.

The bell above the door jangled as they entered the café. Hannah was upon them in moments, her eyebrows raised as she jerked her head towards the corner.

'Oh, wow,' breathed Harry.

'There he is,' she murmured back.

A middle-aged couple sat nearby, talking to each other. They glanced a few times at the large Scotsman sitting in the corner, looking puzzled as he studied the piece of cake in front of him. He looked as bedraggled as when Chloe had first met him, but at least this time there was no straw in his red hair.

'Hannah, could you close the café? This won't take a minute.'

'Um, I'm not sure, Chloe.' Hannah twisted her apron in her hands, looking uncomfortable. 'Afternoons tend to get busy.'

'I'll reimburse any money you lose,' Harry promised, stepping forward. 'Trust me, you don't want to miss this.'

Hannah glanced between them. 'Right. Sure.' She turned the sign on the window so it said CLOSED and began to usher some of the perplexed customers out.

Chloe glanced at Harry, silently telling him to stay put. Harry busied himself with looking at the menu and asking Hannah all about the specials while Chloe slipped into the chair opposite where the Highlander sat.

He raised his eyes slowly. 'Hello, Chloe.'

'Nice to see you again,' she said, glancing over at the nearby couple. She couldn't make him disappear while they were here; it would be too difficult to explain. 'How did you get here?'

'I don't really remember.' He picked up the spoon Hannah had given him and turned it over in his hand with interest. 'A lot has happened since we last spoke.'

'It has,' she agreed. 'Listen, I can send you back in just a minute, okay?'

'Good.' He nodded. 'I need to get back to my wife.'

'Yes, you do.' Chloe's heart warmed at that. She looked over at where Harry was standing with his arms crossed, tapping his chin as though thinking about what to order. She tilted her chin to the plate in front of him. 'That's cake. Have you had it before?'

'Nothing like this.' He scooped up some of the cream and tasted it. His eyes widened and he clapped a hand over his mouth. He quickly swallowed and said, 'It's so sweet.'

Chloe giggled. After what felt like an age, the couple got up to pay their bill, and Hannah closed the door behind them.

'All right, what's going on that I have to close the café?' Hannah demanded, marching over. 'Who are you?'

'Just watch,' Harry said with a smile, now holding his own plate of chocolate cake.

Chloe brought out the book. 'I'm sending you back again. I'm sure your wife is waiting for you.'

'Aye. Goodbye, Chloe.'

'Hopefully for the last time.' Chloe opened the book at the last few pages and found the line. The red-headed Scot closed his eyes with a smile, and faded away before their eyes.

Hannah gasped, backing away so fast she crashed into the couple's table. A mug wobbled and fell off, and Harry caught it just in time. 'Are you all right?' He set down the mug and helped Hannah into the seat.

'That . . . I wasn't expecting,' Hannah breathed, a hand over her chest. 'He just disappeared!'

'Yeah.' Chloe snapped the book shut. 'And we've got four more characters to send home.'

'Characters?' Hannah asked weakly.

Chloe quickly explained. 'I know it's a lot to take in,' she said. 'But it's true. Eric let out a cartoon monkey during the event for the schoolchildren and we were chasing it all around the library, trying to get it back home.'

'I did think there were way more cakes than I'd made.' Hannah rubbed her temples, looking tired. 'This is a lot to take in, Chloe.' She gave a loud gasp. 'That man who helped during the robbery!'

'Right.' Chloe nodded. 'He was a superhero from a comic book. He appeared right when we needed him.'

'Just roll with it,' said Harry around a mouthful of cake. He jabbed his cake fork at his plate. 'This is delicious.'

He set down far too much money, insisting it was a tip and payment for closing the café. Ignoring Hannah's weak protests, he wished her a pleasant day and Chloe tucked the book back into her bag.

'They've found a character,' said Harry when he pulled out his phone.

'Where?'

'The pub.' Harry glanced around. 'The Pride & Pint.'

The Pride & Pint. It was the pub where Gwen worked. Where Chloe and Harry had swapped dinners that time. Maybe Mrs Cook was right, and the characters were going to places Chloe knew and had experienced significant moments. 'Then let's get there as quickly as we can. They might need our help.'

They soon found Gwen standing outside the pub, looking anxious as she paced. She gestured them over and pointed through the window. She whispered, 'Is that the guy from the comic book?'

'At least he isn't wearing his superhero outfit,' said Chloe as she recognised the broad shoulders and dark hair of the American journalist. He was nursing a Budweiser in his large hand as he looked with fascination at a football rerun on the television. Some women in a booth were eyeing him with interest, giggling among themselves.

'I can't make him disappear in the middle of the pub,' murmured Chloe. Asking the proprietor to close it was out of the question. 'Where are Mrs Cook and Eric? Who has the comic?'

'Eric has it,' said Gwen.

Chloe brought out her phone and messaged them.

Found the comic-book superhero. Can you come to the pub on High Street?

The grey speech bubble appeared at the bottom, and Eric responded, *We've got a situation of our own here. Come to the chapel.*

'The chapel,' Chloe murmured, staring at her phone. 'Surely not *that* chapel?'

But it made sense, didn't it? Another place in Wellbridge that held memories for her.

She quickly texted that they would be there soon. The chapel was on the other side of town, but that only meant a fifteen-minute walk. Ten if they hurried. It didn't look like the superhero was going anywhere anytime soon. Even if Eric texted them the line they needed to say, they couldn't make him vanish while surrounded by forty or so other people.

'Gwen, stay here and text us if he leaves,' said Chloe.

'I'll go inside.' Gwen straightened. 'Maybe I should talk to him or something. I'll see if I can get him to come outside . . .' She trailed off as she marched into the pub, and the sound of loud talking and the scent of beer washed over them for a moment before the door closed behind her. Chloe risked a look, seeing Gwen lean casually against the bar, glancing over to where the superhero sat, still alone for now.

'I hope Gwen reaches him before those women do,' said Chloe, anxious as she noted the almost-empty pitcher between the ladies and the way they kept glancing over at the journalist in disguise. There was certainly no sending him back when he was the centre of attention. 'C'mon, let's see what Eric and Mrs Cook are doing.'

'Doesn't Eric have the books?' Harry asked as they half jogged along the cobblestone street. People hardly glanced at them as they hurried past, probably assuming they were running to catch a bus. 'Why does he need us there?'

Eric hadn't elaborated, but Chloe had a sneaking feeling there was a good reason he needed everybody there.

'Thanks for being here with me,' said Chloe as they passed the post office, slowing as they reached a hill. 'I can't imagine this is what you thought you'd be doing on your day off, running around after book characters . . .'

'Chloe, there's no one else I'd rather be with.'

Chloe's stomach somersaulted, but she was too nervous to do more than give him a grateful grin. Adding to her worries was the fact they were heading to the place where she and Liam had been about to get married. The last time she'd come here, she had started crying.

Then she'd run into Harry.

She inhaled, filling her lungs with sharp, clean air as they found the chapel grounds. It was at the end of a long street overgrown with weeds, brown leaves scattered along the grass. Eric waved at them from near the entrance, calling something as he pointed upwards.

'What's going on?' Chloe asked, breathless now. Somehow, being here wasn't as bad as she'd imagined. Yes, this was where her wedding would have taken place, but it didn't seem so terrible now.

Not with her friends around her and Harry nearby. 'Where's the character? Don't you have their book?'

'Oh, we have their book.' Mrs Cook held up the glowing children's book.

Chloe glimpsed the cover and groaned. 'Are you kidding me?'

'The problem is, every time we try to read him the line, he puts his hands over his ears and refuses to listen.'

Chloe grimaced. 'Well, I'm sure the four of us can overpower him. Where is he?'

Eric pointed upwards. An enormous cat with a red and white stripy hat was clinging to the chapel roof. He had a red bow tie and grinned down at them.

'That's a giant cat,' Harry remarked, as casually as though he were commenting on the weather.

'May I?' Chloe asked, reaching for the book. She flipped to the end, but it was as Eric had said. At the sight of the book, the giant cat screamed, climbing further up the chapel roof. He clamped his hands over his ears and yelled and sang so loudly they feared all of Wellbridge would hear.

'This isn't going to work,' said Chloe with a groan. She quickly read the character's last line in silence, committing it to memory. She was going to need both hands for this. She glanced around the chapel building. There didn't seem to be anywhere they could climb. No ladder or anything.

'What about Gwen?' Harry asked suddenly.

'What about her?' Chloe asked with some irritation. 'She can't climb, either.'

'No, no.' Harry sounded amused. 'I mean the superhero in the pub. If she tells him there's a cat stuck on a roof—'

'He'll come and save him,' Chloe finished his sentence, and a smile grew on her face. 'That just might work.'

'Superhero?' Mrs Cook asked. Harry explained while Chloe pulled out her phone. She texted Gwen, but she wasn't seeing the message.

The cat on the roof started singing, his voice so shrill that he'd surely attract people at any moment.

> *'On the roof, I sit so high,*
> *Watching the humans shout, oh my!*
> *They try to climb, they try to leap,*
> *But catching this cat is no small feat!'*

If anyone came running and saw him, she didn't know how they could explain it. Chloe quickly called Gwen, hoping her sister would hear her phone ring in the noisy pub.

'Chloe?' Gwen answered. The background noise was people laughing and the buzz of the TV.

'Hi, Gwen. Are you still with him?'

'Well, yes. I'm sitting with him, but those girls are here, too.' Chloe heard her sniff in annoyance. 'They seem to think I'm, um . . .' she whispered, 'trying to steal him.'

> *'Wave goodbye and tip your hat,*
> *There's no way you'll catch this cat!'*

Chloe covered her free ear, thoroughly annoyed now. 'Steal him from whom? Look, you need to get him over here,' she said. 'We've got a character stuck on the chapel roof and only he can get him. Can you tell him it's an emergency?'

'You're from *where*?' asked a woman in the background, unnaturally loud and with her words slurring. 'That isn't a real city.' Giggling erupted from behind Gwen.

'Gwen, this is your time to shine,' said Chloe fiercely. 'We're at the chapel. The one where . . . you know, on Baker Street. Tell him someone needs his help – right now!'

'Okay. Yes. I can do this.' An uncomfortable silence rang between them, broken by the sound of shattering glass. Gwen cursed. 'I'll get him there as quickly as I can.'

The phone cut off, and Chloe glanced upwards again. She could see the tip of the naughty cat's hat. Clearly, he was having a good time basking in his mischief and singing with his terrible voice. Unsure whether Gwen would be able to deliver on her promise, Chloe glanced inside the chapel. The door was open but there was nobody there. Loud thumps on the roof told them the cat was on the move.

'Hurry up, Gwen,' Chloe murmured. The inside of the chapel was cobwebby and old. Did anyone even still use it any more, or had it been abandoned to the elements? Wooden benches stood in rows, an aisle leading to a dais. Did it used to get decorated with flowers? Did they hold funerals here once, or celebrate christenings and weddings? It was deserted now.

Harry had followed her inside, his presence like a warm blanket. Chloe glanced around sadly, the memories coming back: discussing colours and flowers with the wedding planner, imagining herself walking down the aisle, picking out the perfect dress. The many awkward phone calls to tell people the wedding was off. The nights of crying herself to sleep, the bitterness when Gwen discarded Liam almost at once, jetting off with her millionaire without a word of apology.

Harry's arms wrapped around her from behind, his chin resting on her shoulder. 'Are you all right?'

There was so much promise in that simple question. 'Yeah. Just, you know, memories. I was supposed to marry Liam here.' She turned to face him. She was painfully aware of the ticking clock, that they still had more characters to find, but with the sun shining through the stained-glass windows, the soft sound of tweeting birds outside and Harry's arms around her waist, it was easy to not care. Just for a moment. 'I want to make new memories here in Wellbridge. With you.'

The words left her mouth of their own accord, but she knew them to be true. Wellbridge felt more like home than the city ever did. 'I love my job. Even with days like these.'

'You don't get much of that in an office.' Harry's brown eyes crinkled as they roamed her face, making her feel like he had peeled back her cover and was reading her every thought. She stood on her tiptoes to kiss him.

It felt right. Like home.

He softly kissed her back, holding her close.

A swooshing sound outside made her jump, and the doors burst open. A silhouette of a man in a superhero suit stood in the doorway, his cape flowing behind him. He held a woman in his arms.

'Gwen!' Chloe said, half shocked, half annoyed. 'You let him carry you here?'

'He insisted.' Gwen was blushing as the superhero gently set her down.

Chloe looked him over and groaned. 'How many people saw you?'

'It isn't my fault,' Gwen insisted. 'I did as you said and told him that someone at the chapel needs his help. Right?' she asked. The superhero, who had discarded his glasses and suit, stood with his fists on his hips, looking around in expectation.

'What's going on here? How can I help? Are there burglars here? Bad guys?' He glanced around.

'Not quite. There's a cat, um, stuck on the roof.'

'Clementine?' asked Gwen, looking stricken.

'A bit bigger than him.' As though to prove her point, sharp thuds on the roof indicated the cat was still running around up there. 'Could you get him down? He might fight back, but . . .'

'Truth and justice.' The superhero rose into the air, his cape flowing behind him. Despite expecting it, Chloe watched in awe. It wasn't every day you saw someone flying. Outside the library, it looked even stranger.

'Oh, well done, Gwen!' Mrs Cook clapped her hands as the superhero floated above to the chapel roof. They all watched each other, listening as the cat screamed, then shot off some mischievous poems about tights and capes. The superhero said something, there was a terrific bang, and suddenly he was flying back down, the cat thrashing in his arms.

'No chance, mate,' Harry remarked as the superhero landed between them all. 'He's much stronger than you are.'

'Eric, hold down this arm. Harry, you hold the other,' said Chloe. 'Um, sir, could you cover his mouth?'

The cat was making a racket, his screeches bouncing off the chapel grounds. It sounded like several cats were being terrorised.

'I do not remember him being this bad in the book,' Chloe grumbled as the three men wrestled him. As soon as they had him trapped, Chloe quickly recited the last character's line in the book, as close as she could get to the cat's pointed ear.

The cat faded and the superhero was suddenly standing alone, looking pleased with himself. 'Another successful mission.'

'Thank you for your help,' said Chloe, grateful. Eric was already handing her the comic book. 'It's time to send you back, too.'

'Even though those girls were *very* interested in you,' said Gwen slyly. She looked the superhero up and down. 'Aw, do we have to put him back right now? He could help us catch the others.'

Chloe gave her a pointed look. 'We have to. I'm sorry,' she added, looking at him. 'You're just too conspicuous. How many people saw you flying here? How are we going to explain that?'

'Maybe they'll think he was a bird or a plane,' said Mrs Cook.

Chloe snorted. 'Thank you for your help, but it's time to get home.' She found the final page of the comic. 'Say goodbye, Gwen.'

Pouting, Gwen waved at the handsome superhero, who saluted back with a grin. Chloe read out the final page of the comic book and he disappeared into nothing, leaving them alone in the chapel grounds.

Chloe released a breath as the comic book's glow faded. 'Three down, two to go.'

CHAPTER THIRTY-THREE

THEY LEFT THE abandoned chapel grounds and took a breather, Chloe checking the skies in case any of the flying characters had made it out. They examined the books they still had left.

'Where else is significant to you in this town, Chloe?' Mrs Cook asked.

Chloe glanced around at them all. 'Home,' she said, counting them on her fingers. 'After that, I don't know. The supermarket?' She met Harry's eyes. *The Italian restaurant where we told each other our secrets?*

'Maybe we should split up again,' Eric suggested.

'What if more characters have come out at the library?' Gwen asked.

'Please don't say that,' said Chloe with a groan. 'All right, look. Let's check the restaurant. And, um, the supermarket as well, just in case.'

'I could go home,' Gwen offered. 'See if anyone is there.'

They split up, though Chloe took Harry's sleeve. 'Stay with me?'

'Shall we check the restaurant?' he asked with a smile.

Eric scurried off to check the supermarket and Mrs Cook headed back to check on the library. They hurried along to the restaurant where they had eaten together, where Chloe and Harry had shared so many of their secrets. The place was open, a delicious savoury scent already wafting onto the street.

Chloe's stomach rumbled. It felt like a lifetime since the omelette she'd eaten with Gwen this morning. A supposedly normal morning where all they had to do was visit the graveyard. 'Do you see anyone?' she asked Harry.

Chloe stepped as close to the restaurant window as she could without touching it, hoping no one would see her looking and think she was weird. The restaurant seemed fairly busy, with waiting staff moving around the tables. Couples and families sat together, none of them looking much like the two remaining characters.

'Look, over there,' whispered Chloe, pointing towards the bathroom.

A man who could only be the illusive detective was striding back from the direction of the restaurant toilets. He looked so painfully Victorian era that Chloe was surprised no one else in the restaurant was craning their necks to look at him. Well, some of them were, eyeing him with interest before going back to their meals. Chloe hoped no one would try to talk to him.

He wore a tweed suit and boots today, and Chloe couldn't miss his height and his hawk-like nose. He regarded everything he saw with a thoughtful frown, as though he had encountered a mystery here and he was trying to solve it.

'That's interesting,' said Harry. 'The characters need to use the toilet like real-life people do?'

'It looks that way,' said Chloe, hoping the detective hadn't been back there looking for clues or something. 'They eat, too. Like at the café, the Scottish warrior had some cake, didn't he?'

They couldn't sit outside all evening, waiting for the detective to leave. Already, he had returned to his table, where he had set down his deerstalker hat. A half-finished meal sat before him. Chloe watched as he tucked a large serviette into his collar to serve as a napkin bib, then tucked into his spaghetti with meatballs, still frowning thoughtfully.

'I should go and talk to him,' said Chloe. 'Who has the book?'

'I think Eric has it.' Harry had already pulled out his phone. 'Look, it's cold. Why don't we go inside?'

That was better than standing out here. They stepped into the delicious warmth and Harry got them a table for two. There wasn't time to eat, so he ordered them both soft drinks. Looking a little irked that they hadn't ordered food, the waiter rushed off while Chloe texted the group chat, asking whoever had the book to write the character's last line as a message.

Eric obliged soon after as the waiter was bringing them glasses of lemonade. Chloe risked a look at the detective. He had nearly finished his meal.

'I'd better go and talk to him.' Chloe took an obligatory sip of her drink then sidled over to the detective. She wished he hadn't chosen such a conspicuous table; he was in the centre of the restaurant, and several people were watching him with amusement.

'Good evening, madam,' said the detective, setting down his cutlery. 'We have met before, haven't we?'

'We have,' she said, glad he remembered. 'It's me, Chloe. You gave me some advice last time we met.'

'Did you bring me here again?' His stare was intense as he put some spaghetti in his mouth, chewing slowly. 'For what purpose? Do you need my advice?' He looked around. 'Or is there something more sinister at work here?'

'I'm afraid it wasn't me who brought you here this time,' said Chloe. 'And it's nothing sinister,' she quickly added. The last thing they needed was for him to inspect every little detail of the restaurant. 'If you're ready, I can send you back to London as soon as possible.'

He nodded, wiping his mouth. 'And the topic of last time?'

'Last time?'

The detective removed his spotless napkin bib, folding it neatly beside his clean plate. 'You had a problem, I recall. A matter of truth and lies and a certain young man.' He must have followed her gaze to where Harry was sitting, his chin resting in his hand while trying, and failing, to not look like he was watching them. A small smile appeared on the detective's face. 'All resolved, I trust?'

'Yes. You said just what I needed to hear.' Chloe smiled back at him. 'I'd say your task is complete.'

'Such a hurry. Fine, I'll settle the bill.'

'Don't do that,' she said in alarm as the detective pulled out a worn-looking wallet.

'What'll it be?' The money he was pulling out looked nothing like what Chloe had seen before. She looked in fascination at the gold-coloured coins with the royal head that could only be Queen Victoria. The detective laid them out on the table.

A waiter was coming towards them. Chloe had to think fast. 'Debit card, please,' she quickly said.

The waiter glanced at the detective. 'Um, sure.'

Chloe raised her eyebrows at Harry, jerking her head towards the door. He was over in seconds.

'Let's go for a walk,' said Harry brightly to the detective, taking him by the elbow. 'You can smoke your pipe outside.'

'You've been in a fight,' said the detective, rising as Harry took him towards the door, looking at Harry's black eye.

'Yeah, you should see the other guy,' said Harry as Chloe quickly paid for the detective's meatball spaghetti. She stepped into the cold to see the detective lighting his pipe, the spark of his match illuminating his large nose.

'Do you think they suspected anything?' Chloe asked. She smacked her forehead. 'Oh no. Our drinks.'

'I'll get them,' said Harry. 'You've got the last line, right? It's better if you do it now. There's no one around.' He dashed back inside to pay for the drinks as the detective regarded Chloe with a questioning look.

'Time for you to go back home,' said Chloe as cheerfully as she could, pulling out her phone.

'This has been a strange night, but the dinner was excellent.' The detective put on his deerstalker hat. 'Goodbye, Chloe.'

Chloe quickly read the line of the book from the group chat, dearly hoping there were no mistakes. The detective gave her a small nod and he faded to nothing. Harry stepped out of the restaurant a moment later, straightening his trench coat.

'It's done,' she said, tucking away her phone. 'Did the staff mind?'

'I gave them a big tip,' said Harry. 'It'll be fine.'

'Thanks. At least it's done.' She returned his relieved grin, wondering how much today had cost him. Chloe's stomach was growling; the detective's pasta had looked amazing and the scents coming from the restaurant were divine. But they still had one more character to find: the nobleman Chloe had first spoken to when she'd discovered the library's power. It felt fitting that he should be the last.

They checked the group chat, but nobody had said anything. It didn't look like he was at the supermarket; there had been enough time already for Eric to check it. Chloe messaged everybody to let them know the detective was safely back in Victorian-times London, and ten minutes later they all met outside the library.

'It looks like all is quiet in there,' Mrs Cook reported. 'I didn't find any more characters wandering around and none of the books are glowing. And Clementine is safe and warm in his bed.'

'That's good news,' said Chloe with relief. She glanced around at the group. 'Where's Gwen?'

Her sister hadn't joined them, even though she had seen the group chat messages. Chloe swallowed, trying not to feel concerned. Gwen was hardly ever without her phone. Was there a reason she couldn't respond?

'I'm sure she's all right,' said Harry, probably seeing the alarm on her face.

'I'll ring her.' Chloe did so as they walked through the library car park and back towards town. The phone rang and rang, but Gwen didn't answer.

'I wonder if she's at home,' said Chloe. 'Let me check with Joe. He can see if the lights are on, at least.' She didn't want to waste time driving back if it would just lead to a dead end.

Their neighbour picked up the phone right away. 'Hello, Chloe? Is that you? How lovely of you to call me!'

'Hi, Joe.' Chloe paused, wondering how to phrase this without it sounding strange. 'Um, I'm wondering if you could do me a favour.'

'For you, love, anything.'

She clambered into Harry's car. Mrs Cook said she would drive Eric there. 'Could you just check my house to see if any of the lights are on? Does it look like anyone is in?'

There had been enough time for Gwen to reach their house on foot, but that didn't explain why she wasn't answering her phone.

There was the sound of shuffling and the grunts and sighs of an old person rising out of a comfortable armchair. 'All right, love, no problem. Is everything okay?'

'Yes. I'll be home myself in a minute.'

She heard Joe moving aside his curtains. 'Oh! Yes, the living room light is on. Looks like the TV is on, too.'

'Really?' said Chloe with interest. She doubted they had forgotten to switch off the TV and lights when they had left this morning. In fact, they definitely hadn't – she and Gwen had gone straight to the graveyard without watching anything. And they hadn't needed the lights on when the sun was up. 'Thanks, Joe. I'll be back soon.'

'Want me to ring you if anyone leaves?' A mischievous, conspiratorial tone entered Joe's voice. 'I've got a good view of your front door from here. I can wait outside if you like, I've got my cane—'

'That won't be necessary,' said Chloe quickly. They had left the car park now, Harry driving, with Mrs Cook and Eric behind them. 'But yes, please keep an eye on the door. There's no need to go outside, though. It's a cold night.'

'Almost there,' said Harry, and they turned into the Moorhall neighbourhood. Chloe tried ringing Gwen again, but the phone rang twice before going to voicemail.

They parked outside the house, gravel crunching beneath the tyres. As Chloe stepped out into the cold air, she spotted Joe shuffling towards them, his cane in his hand.

'No one's come out of there,' he reported, looking pleased with himself. 'What's going on, then? Are you having a party?' When he saw Harry, Joe's mouth fell open and he leaned comically back, his hand over his mouth. 'Harry Ashcroft!'

'You two know each other?' asked Chloe in surprise as the two men shook hands, Harry laughing.

'I helped him with some repairs a couple of years ago,' Harry explained, looking delighted. 'You look well, Mr Richardson.'

'Everyone, *please* call me Joe,' said the old man. 'Oh, I'm so pleased you and Chloe are friends. Isn't she lovely, Harry?'

'Aye,' Harry grinned as Chloe's face burned. 'She's canny.'

'Everyone really does know everyone in small towns,' said Chloe, rubbing the bridge of her nose. It was kind of adorable.

Eric emerged from Mrs Cook's car. 'Do you think he's in there?' He spotted Joe and quickly hid the glowing book behind his back. Chloe silently prayed Joe hadn't noticed.

Mrs Cook appeared, looking concerned. 'So this is where you live, Chloe? What a nice neighbourhood.' She smiled when she saw Joe. 'Hello.'

Joe gazed back. 'Hello.'

Chloe, Harry and Eric glanced at each other, their eyebrows raised as Mrs Cook and Joe stood for a moment, small smiles growing on their faces.

'I'm Alice,' said Mrs Cook as she reached out her hand. Joe took it, bringing her knuckles to his lips. Mrs Cook gave a high-pitched giggle more appropriate for a teenager than a woman in her seventies.

'Erm, I'm going inside,' said Chloe. 'There's something we need to check, remember?'

'Alice is our boss,' Eric piped up. 'She's divorced, too,' he added.

'And, um, Joe is widowed,' said Harry.

'You work at the library?' Joe looked positively charmed. 'Oh, my goodness. And here's me buying books for my Kindle. I need to go over there at some point. Do you have the classics?'

Mrs Cook smiled, more composed now. 'Shelves and shelves of

them.' Was it just the lighting, or had Mrs Cook's cheeks turned pink?

Leaving the bizarre scene behind, Chloe pushed open the front door of her house, light from the corridor bleeding onto the street. Eric and Harry followed her inside.

The TV was blaring, and Chloe was relieved to hear Gwen's voice, sounding relaxed.

'He *is* here!' Eric exclaimed when they reached the living room doorway.

There was Gwen, sitting in her usual spot on the couch. The nobleman from the classic book, the man Chloe had met in the library that rainy night, sat in the armchair, ramrod straight. He jumped to his feet when he saw Chloe and gave a hasty bow.

'It's nice to see you again,' said Chloe.

The dark-haired nobleman was wearing a deep-blue tailcoat and polished shoes, his dark hair curling over his spotless collar. 'It is a pleasure, Miss Chloe.'

Chloe didn't know how to respond to a bow, so she nodded back at him then said to her sister, 'Gwen, I've been trying to ring you.'

Gwen leaped to her feet too, and pulled Chloe into the kitchen. Harry hastily asked the others to sit, making conversation.

'I found him standing outside,' Gwen whispered. 'He's going on about some girl. I didn't know what else to do, so I brought him in. He nearly had a fit when he saw the TV and the speakers. I didn't dare answer my phone.' She gave Chloe an apologetic look. 'Sorry. I shoved it underneath the couch cushion. Didn't want to spook him.'

'And switched on the TV? What are you even watching?' Chloe craned her neck to see.

'Look, there's me again.' The nobleman was pointing at the screen. 'Though they have the gardens all wrong. Mine are at least twice that size.'

Chloe was horrified. 'You're letting him watch the TV show of the book?'

'I thought it might give him some confidence,' Gwen argued.

'I was in the middle of explaining it to him. Look.' She strode past Chloe and plopped herself on the couch, squeezing herself between the nobleman and Eric, who quickly made room for her. 'See how handsome the actor is? You're super popular in this world.'

'He *is* handsome.' He appeared deep in thought. 'And she is lovely,' he said, when the actress appeared on screen. 'Though I'm afraid they cannot do justice to her beautiful eyes.'

'Of course they can't,' said Chloe, her mind racing. How would this affect his character? What if he came across a part in the show that hadn't happened for him yet? The characters remembered her when they came out of the story, that much was clear. What if they took memories back to the story? Would it change the book? This wouldn't do at all.

She reached for the remote to switch off the TV, feeling that was the first problem they could solve.

'Oh, no, don't!' said Gwen. 'This is a good part.'

'You've watched it?' Chloe asked, grumbling as she set the remote back down.

'Of course I've watched it. Just because I haven't read the book.' Gwen tutted then said, 'Look, this part is great. She didn't like him at first. But she does in the end. Enemies to lovers, a classic trope.'

Chloe snorted. What did Gwen know about tropes?

The nobleman, sandwiched between Gwen and the side of the couch, watched the TV in riveted silence. 'Remarkable,' he said finally. 'I remember all this happening. It's like a dream.'

'I think we need to talk,' said Chloe firmly. 'Gwen? How about you make everyone some tea?'

The sisters stared at each other for a moment. 'Fine,' Gwen sighed.

'I'll come,' said Harry, then grabbed Eric's skinny shoulder. 'C'mon, let's help Gwen make tea.'

They all made as much noise as they could in the kitchen, clattering mugs and talking loudly about nothing. The nobleman gave a little groan of disappointment when Chloe finally switched off the TV, but she sensed it would be a bad idea to let him watch any more.

It was irresponsible of Gwen to let him in the first place. Gwen had even less knowledge of the magic of the library than they did.

Eric's hand appeared around the corner of the archway leading to the kitchen, holding the glowing book. Chloe hastily plucked it from his fingers then set it in her lap, taking a seat in the armchair.

She found she didn't want to send him back right away. Instead, she asked, 'This must be very strange. Are you all right?'

The nobleman looked thoughtful. 'Well, this is indeed all very strange. Will it happen again?'

'I don't know. I don't fully understand it myself,' Chloe confessed. She hesitated, then asked, 'And . . . um, what about the lady you mentioned last time we met? Did she see past the first impression?'

His face lit up. It was a marvel to see his brown eyes twinkle with joy at the mention of the woman he loved, a sight that made Chloe's heart warm. 'Oh, yes. It was a torment. I had to learn so much. But I realised the inferiority of her rank, my family's wishes, none of it matters. I'm afraid I blundered it quite horribly. When I try to express my feelings, I end up saying the wrong thing.' He looked both sad and angry at himself. 'This dream, or vision, is quite a relief.' He pointed at the now black TV screen.

Chloe was torn between wanting to send him back to his story and to reassure him things would all turn out all right. The kettle was boiling in the kitchen, Harry and Eric talking about football. Part of Chloe wanted to keep him here for a bit longer; everyone was here, and there were no more characters that needed sending back. But . . .

'I think it's time you went home,' said Chloe finally. 'I can't explain it all, but it's been a busy day, and there were a lot of people like you here.'

'Like me?'

'From other places,' said Chloe.

'Do you have any advice for me? About the woman I love?'

Chloe hesitated. How much could she tell him? 'What happened the last time you talked?' If she could work out exactly where in the story he was . . . 'What were you doing before you found yourself here?'

'We had a disagreement. I was writing her a letter. Her family has acted appallingly, but I haven't behaved much better. Then I found myself here. That lady – Miss Gwen? – found me. And then . . .' He gestured towards the TV.

Chloe brightened, knowing which part of the story he meant. It was the turning point of their relationship, the beginning of the enemies becoming lovers. Chloe couldn't help tensing up, hugging the book to her chest as a giggle burst from her. She was suddenly in her first year of university again, the story a comfort to her after the heartbreak with Liam, knowing that the happily ever after was just around the corner. 'Please don't worry,' she said. 'She will forgive you.'

'You think so?' He didn't look convinced.

'I know so. Just . . . keep doing what you're doing. All I can say is that first impressions don't matter, not that much. So long as you get a second chance.'

'And what about you?' he asked, to her surprise. 'Have things improved for you?'

Chloe glanced to the kitchen, where Harry was laughing about something. 'They have,' she said, her voice soft. 'Tremendously.' She opened the book. 'Let's send you home.'

'Aw, already?' Gwen had appeared in the archway, a cup of tea in each hand. 'Won't you stay for tea?'

'Thank you, Miss Gwen, but I'm needed elsewhere.' The nobleman rose to his feet. 'Miss Chloe, I thank you for your help and your advice.'

Harry and Eric appeared, and they all watched as Chloe confidently read aloud the nobleman's last line in the book. Sure enough, he faded, and the glow on the book did, too.

Gwen sighed slowly, setting down the teacups and collapsing on the couch. 'Looks like we're done.'

'Where's Mrs Cook?' asked Chloe, realising the elderly lady hadn't joined them.

'Still outside.' There was a smile in Eric's voice as he peeked through the curtains. 'Look.'

Mrs Cook was still chatting with Joe, both of them laughing about something. Chloe had never seen Mrs Cook look so flustered. Joe said something that made her giggle, her hands over her mouth.

'Well,' said Harry, joining her at the window. 'Who would have thought it?'

CHAPTER THIRTY-FOUR

CHLOE COULDN'T EXPLAIN it, but now they had finally sent the last character back into their story, the books they carried with them now unremarkable and not glowing, she felt a shift in the air. A sudden absence of something in Wellbridge. It was not a melancholy loss, but more like a noticeable lack of . . . something. Magic, perhaps.

'It's done,' she said to the others. Even if she hadn't known it, she would be able to feel it. 'Do you feel that, too? Like the magic is gone.'

'Gone?' Harry looked stricken.

'Hopefully not gone from the library itself.' Chloe thought it would be awful if the moving bookshelves, glowing books and personality of the library were gone for ever. 'There's only one way to find out, isn't there?'

They fetched Mrs Cook from outside. She seemed surprised that they had sent back the last character already, and Joe gave them a cheerful wave. They went back to the library. It was already evening, but Harry went to the Brew House, open late for dinner, and bought them all lattes and sandwiches. They rested in the library lobby as they sipped and swapped funny stories about their adventure, how they'd narrowly missed being caught.

'Do you think there are videos of you being carried through the air on social media?' Chloe asked, anxious as she pulled out her phone.

'I checked already. There's nothing.' Gwen sounded a little disappointed.

'That's a good thing,' Chloe reminded her sister. 'Though I suppose people would have just dismissed it as fake or AI generated.'

'Maybe no one seeing it was part of the library's magic. Or just a happy coincidence,' Harry remarked, scratching his chin. It was the first time Chloe had heard him say the word 'magic' aloud, and it made her tingle all over.

Chloe took a bite of her egg salad sandwich, trying not to stare at him too much. Their kiss in the chapel still lingered, and now that their task of helping the library was complete, she allowed herself to think about it.

'Chloe, you've got egg on your chin,' said Gwen.

Scowling and wiping away the mess, Chloe glanced around. 'I suppose we should close the library tomorrow so we can get this mess cleaned up.' She sighed as she took in the fallen bookcases and scattered papers. There were hundreds of books on the floor, but at least none of them were glowing any more. It would take hours to get everything tidied up. But the characters were at last all back in their stories, and that was the most important thing. There were no more mischievous poltergeists or enchanted animals or talking lions.

'Who was that guy with the tattoos?' asked Gwen. 'You know, the one who could—' she cleared her throat, 'uh, fly. He was here earlier. He had a huge wingspan, and his eyes were . . .' She trailed off, looking dreamily in the distance.

'Why? Are you going to ask him out?' asked Chloe with a smirk.

Gwen shrugged. 'Maybe he'll want to come out of his book now and again.' She looked confused. 'That is such a weird sentence. Who *was* he, Chloe?'

'Maybe you should read the book and find out,' said Mrs Cook, her eyes twinkling. Eric snickered into his coffee.

'Yeah.' Gwen laughed. 'Maybe I should.'

'I still can't understand how this all happened,' said Mrs Cook. She glanced around the library, a look Chloe now knew meant she was thinking about the library herself, trying to understand it. 'Did your magic . . . break?'

Something fluttered in the library's lights, a rush of cold washing over them. 'Hmm. That means no.' Mrs Cook tapped her chin.

'I think I know.'

Everyone looked at Harry, who set his coffee cup down on the reception table. He looked suddenly nervous, and Chloe couldn't help wondering if there was something he had done. Something he could control here, too.

'You said this library takes a liking to people, right?' he said. 'Well, ever since I met Chloe, I feel like I've been given a second chance. I didn't think I deserved love again after my wife passed away, but . . .' He took Chloe's hand.

She felt Eric, Mrs Cook and Gwen watching them, but she only had eyes for Harry. His closeness was electrifying.

'Maybe I'm reading this all wrong, but I don't mind,' Harry said softly. 'I'm ready.'

He smiled around at the group. 'Chloe and I are going out. She's my girlfriend. And not a secret girlfriend, either,' he added. 'That is, if you'll let me be your boyfriend.'

Gwen whooped, looking delighted. 'I knew it.'

Eric looked comically crestfallen, while Mrs Cook beamed at them both.

'If this is my second chance, I'm taking it with both hands and a whole heart,' said Harry. 'What do you say, Chloe?'

Chloe couldn't help feeling the same. This was her second chance, too, after living a life of fear after her ex, always wanting to escape somewhere new and start again. But right now, this was where she belonged. With this library, with her sister, in the town where she grew up.

With Harry.

'Yes,' she said with a giggle. 'I'll be your girlfriend.'

He hugged her close, and the library lit up with a warm glow. Everyone gasped as the bookshelves righted themselves, rising from the floor to settle onto the carpet with gentle thuds. Books swept from the floor and flew back to their places, covers flapping like wings, and settled on the shelves side by side. Debris that had fallen swept up to the walls and the ceiling, dust collecting into a neat pile and depositing itself in the bin. The whole building creaked as the library straightened up, broken things fixing themselves. In moments, it was good as new. Even the carpet looked cleaner, the wooden walls shining like polished brass and the lanterns glowing happily in their squeaky-clean glass holders.

'The window?' Chloe asked, and they all went to the non-fiction section in time to see the shattered glass rising from the carpet, coming together like shards of a jigsaw puzzle and slotting into place. The cold air blowing from inside halted and the curtains fluttered as though pleased.

'All along,' said Mrs Cook in amusement, her hands on her hips, 'you could keep yourself clean and tidy. Fancy that.'

'The leak in the roof!' Chloe exclaimed. 'You didn't need fixing, did you?'

The lanterns glimmered. A ripple of amusement.

'The library knew I had borrowed that book about construction and knew I would come here to fix the roof,' said Harry.

'So we would meet again,' said Chloe. Her heart felt light. All along, the library had wanted them to find each other.

Harry kissed her, and she laughed against his lips. 'We fixed the magic.'

'I don't think it was broken to begin with,' said Gwen, looking around in awe. 'The library wanted to give you both a new chance at life. At love.' Her eyes went glassy. 'Chloe, I swear I'll never say books or reading are boring again. I am so happy for you both.'

'So am I.' Eric looked between them. 'All right, I know Chloe is *super*-hot, but I'm a bit young for you, I know that now. Plus, you did tell me no.' He held out a hand to Harry, his face solemn. The women glanced at each other then looked away, trying not to laugh. 'Take good care of her, Harry. Thank you for making her happy.'

Harry shook Eric's hand, then gave him a friendly pat on the shoulder. 'And thank you for being her friend.'

Gwen hugged Chloe, and Chloe hugged her back, relishing her sister's warm embrace. She realised she didn't feel worried at all. Harry and Gwen knew each other and that was okay. She trusted them both.

'Well, now that Chloe and Harry have found their happy endings, do you promise not to let any more characters out of their books?' Mrs Cook asked the library. 'Well, not dozens of them at once, anyway. We don't mind if books glow *sometimes*.'

Clementine appeared, meowing as he curled around Eric's leg.

'Clem!' Chloe exclaimed. The cat didn't look any worse for wear, though he seemed relieved that it was quiet and peaceful in the library again.

Eric picked him up, cuddling the purring cat close to his chest. 'Are you all right, little boy? Was it scary and noisy in here?'

The library felt warm and cosy again, and there was no sign of the mayhem that had erupted here today. Mrs Cook held her latte in her hands, her eyes crinkling as she looked between Chloe and Harry. 'All this trouble for a new librarian. The library must love you.'

'I love the library, too.' Chloe hesitated. 'And I've decided to stay. I can't possibly imagine living or working anywhere else.' She knew the words to be wholly true as she squeezed Harry's hand. 'Or . . . being with anyone else.'

'So you're staying? YES!' Eric whooped. Clementine leaped out of his arms, regarding the young man with disdain. His bell jangled as Chloe knelt to pet him. 'Don't tell me the cat is magical, too?' she asked Mrs Cook. 'He always seems to understand everything I say.'

She scooped up the cat, his furry warmth enveloping her. Harry put his arm around her shoulders and said, 'Chloe, I'm so glad you're staying, too.'

'Me too,' said Gwen, nodding.

Mrs Cook simply raised her cup in a toast, her eyes twinkling as the library creaked its satisfaction.

The library was back to normal, and it didn't seem like any more characters would be jumping out of their books anytime soon. One quiet afternoon, when winter rain drummed on the roof, Mrs Cook locked the doors and took Chloe aside.

'There's one more thing you should know about this place,' she said to her. 'Or, more appropriately, about its occupant.'

They both glanced at Clementine, who was stretching, his mouth open in a big yawn. He looked at them both as if to ask what they were staring at, then gave a soft meow.

'About the cat?' asked Chloe.

'It'll be easier to show you.'

Mrs Cook led Chloe to the staff room. Chloe hardly used the room except to deposit her bag as the kitchen area was more comfortable. The cramped room was little more than a sink, some lockers they never used, and a few boxes.

Chloe helped Mrs Cook move aside some of the boxes until they came to a safe in the wall. 'I didn't know this was here,' said Chloe in surprise.

'I don't use it much,' Mrs Cook said. 'But there's something important in here I want you to see.'

Mrs Cook opened the safe. It was an old-fashioned one with a combination lock. The door swung open, and Chloe, curious, peered inside.

There was only one item inside the safe. A book, old and frayed, with only a hundred or so pages. Mrs Cook reached in and carefully pulled it out. In the faint light of the staff room, Chloe could see the book was glowing.

'Is this what I think it is?' Chloe took the proffered book. On the old, worn cover was a cartoonish picture of a cat. A ginger cat with amber eyes and a haughty look.

'Shortly after I started working here, I saw that this book was glowing,' said Mrs Cook, a fond look on her face. 'I suppose your first experience with the library's magic was the same. I read out a line, and suddenly there was a cat before me. Well, I fell in love with him, and . . .' She looked at Chloe. 'I didn't want to put him back.'

Chloe studied the book's title and author. She had never heard of them, and she was entirely sure she had not seen this book in the children's section, either.

'It's an unusual story,' said the librarian. 'But Clementine doesn't have a good time in it. It's a sad story about abuse and abandonment, and . . .' Mrs Cook pulled out a handkerchief and dabbed her eyes. 'Oh, how silly of me, getting in such a state. I read the whole story, and there's a happy ending, but I just couldn't send him back. I've kept that book in the safe for nearly ten years.'

'Ten years?' Chloe echoed in awe. 'Clementine's been here for that long?'

'And you know what? In all that time, he's never gotten sick. Never aged. He eats and he sleeps, but that's it.' Mrs Cook sniffled. 'Do you think I'm a silly old woman, Chloe? Should we send him back to his world, like we sent back the others?'

They were back in the lobby now, Chloe holding Clementine's book carefully in her hands. Clementine, maybe sensing they were talking about him, came up to them, the bell jingling on his neck.

'I think,' said Chloe carefully, 'that the library just wouldn't be the same without Clem.'

Clementine meowed softly as she picked him up. He felt every bit as real and wonderful as any real cat. He *was* real. That was part of the library's magic. 'How about it, Clemmy? Would you want to go home?'

Clementine saw the picture on the book cover, purring as Chloe petted between his ears. Then he turned away from it, his tail swishing.

'I think that Clementine belongs here,' said Chloe. 'And that the book belongs in the safe.'

'I think I just needed to hear it from someone else.' Mrs Cook picked up the book, handling it gently. 'I'll lock this back away and Clementine can stay here. Would you like that, little boy?'

They both cuddled Clementine, feeling his warm fur and his whiskers against their cheeks. It didn't matter that he was from a book's world. This was Clem's home.

Like it was Chloe's.

EPILOGUE

Two years later

'ARE YOU SURE you're going to be okay, Gwen?'

Despite their long conversations, all the house viewings, the paperwork, and the moving truck being parked outside the house for the last two days, Chloe felt suddenly unsure.

'Chloe, I'm a big girl now. I can surely live by myself.'

Joe had hugged Gwen, tears in his eyes as he'd said goodbye to her, despite her only moving a couple of miles away. It had made it really sink in that Gwen was leaving.

The one-bedroom terraced house stood gleaming in the summer sunshine. Gwen had her blonde hair in a ponytail, her hands on her hips. Chloe never would have thought she'd see her baby sister wearing jeans, of all things. They suited her.

'That's the last of the stuff,' said Harry, coming outside and looking delicious with his shirtsleeves rolled up to the elbows. 'I put the box at the top of the stairs. Hello, love.' He kissed Chloe on the cheek. 'Did you come to see Gwen off?'

'I had to see this place for myself, since you've been so secretive about it,' said Chloe, elbowing her sister. 'It's nice. Got a little garden and everything.' She nodded around the small grassy space before the front door.

Harry slid his arm around his fiancée's waist as Gwen stepped into her new home. 'Are you sad she's leaving?' he asked Chloe quietly.

'I'm sure you'll make a less messy housemate.' Chloe kissed Harry on the lips.

'I heard that,' Gwen yelled over her shoulder.

Despite being happy that Gwen was moving into her own place, Chloe did feel a pang of sadness. These past two years had been full of late-night movie watching, trips to the library and bookshops, and hours of cooking together. Some of their dishes had even turned out pretty well. Anything tasted good after the Brown Slop of Doom.

'We're having a summer event at the library, then it's Eric's send-off party tonight,' Chloe reminded her when they had stepped inside, the cool interior a pleasant relief from the summer heat. The open-plan kitchen and dining room was so quaint, so girly and so Gwen. 'Are you coming?'

Gwen straightened from unpacking a brand-new box of plates and bowls. 'Of course. I wouldn't miss it.'

'Mrs Cook will be there, too. She and Joe don't go on their cruise until next week.'

Things had been quiet since the elderly woman had retired from the library, putting Chloe in charge in her place. The responsibilities were greater, but for nearly two years now, Chloe had found the library a sanctuary, from its gothic windows to its cosy armchairs to its shadowy corners full of secrets. She still took out characters from glowing books from time to time, the library always seeming to know who was best for her to talk to or learn from. Since that day Harry and Chloe had announced their relationship, there had never been another incident of the characters coming out on their own. The six of them, including Hannah, had promised to keep the magic of the library a secret – a secret only those who loved books enough to work there were privy to.

In return, Chloe hosted more events in the library. People came in daily now, and with every visitor and borrowed book, the library became happier. Perhaps it was because she was the manager now, but Chloe swore she could sometimes *feel* the library's emotions. Hannah brought Lily in almost every afternoon, and Chloe was becoming very fond of the little girl.

Sometimes, in the dark corners of the library's spaces, she thought she spotted the spark of a cigarette or the forked tail of a dragon, but then she would chase it and find there was nothing there. Maybe the characters could come and go as they pleased, now. And that was okay with her, so long as they didn't all jump out at once or run amok around Wellbridge.

'I'll miss you.' Gwen hugged her close as Chloe laughed.

'We're still in the same town,' she reminded her. 'And we'll meet up all the time.'

'Still.' Gwen straightened and beamed at Harry. 'You look after my big sister, you hear? No leaving dirty dishes in the sink or spilling wine over people's books. That's my job.'

Harry and Chloe stepped outside, leaving Gwen in her new home. Chloe actually felt a flicker of sadness that her sister wouldn't be waiting for her at home any more. But Harry would be moving in with her next month. A big move, one that they had both agreed they were ready for.

'Would you like to have dinner with my parents tomorrow night?' Harry suggested when they climbed into his car. 'I can drive us to Newcastle in the morning.'

Chloe smiled. 'That sounds lovely.'

She had been so nervous the first time she'd met them, but Mr and Mrs Ashcroft had welcomed Chloe warmly into their home. When Harry had proposed, producing a ring one late evening in the library lobby when they were alone together, his mum and dad had been thrilled.

'Welcome to the family, Chloe.' Harry's mum had kissed her cheek and held her so close it'd brought tears to Chloe's eyes.

As they drove home, Chloe twisted her engagement ring on her finger as she marvelled at how much she had fallen back in love with Wellbridge. Everywhere she looked, the good memories outweighed the bad, and now she honestly couldn't imagine living anywhere else. Her childhood home had become a loving house where she was to make new memories with Harry.

The sadness and loneliness she had experienced as a young woman here, now felt like a different lifetime. An old chapter long forgotten. She had learnt a lot about love, friendship, family and forgiveness. Even now, the library of second chances taught her something new every day, and the most important lesson of them all was how to love again.

The End

ACKNOWLEDGEMENTS

There is a certain magic about books, and it was so much fun writing about books that are actually magic! I lived in Derbyshire for a big chunk of my childhood, so it was fun writing a book set there.

I want to thank the wonderful authors who shaped my childhood with their stories, especially those whose characters appear in *The Library of Second Chances*. My childhood favourites include Jacqueline Wilson, Enid Blyton and Darren Shan. It's an honour to be able to write a book about something perhaps many people have wished they could do: pulling out and talking to characters from their favourite stories. I had so much fun with the idea.

I would like to thank Areen Ali and Joe Thomas, who worked closely with me during the writing of *The Library of Second Chances*. A huge thank you as well to my wonderful agent, Edwina de Charnacé, who made all this happen. Thank you too to Rose Cook, the audiobook editor, and the rest of the team at Wildfire. I adore the front cover and appreciate all the hard work you do in getting the book on the shelves and into readers' hands.

Finally, I'd like to thank my close friends, family and partner for their support and encouragement, reading early drafts and giving their feedback and suggestions. Thank you especially to Sara Karwisch, who reads all my early drafts and whose feedback is always insightful and inspiring.

The Library of Second Chances was a joy to write, and I appreciate you, the reader, for picking it up. Never stop dreaming.